HER LAST LIE

J.S. LARK

First published in 2023 by Bloodhound Books.

www.bloodhoundbooks.com

Print ISBN: 978-1-5040-8883-1

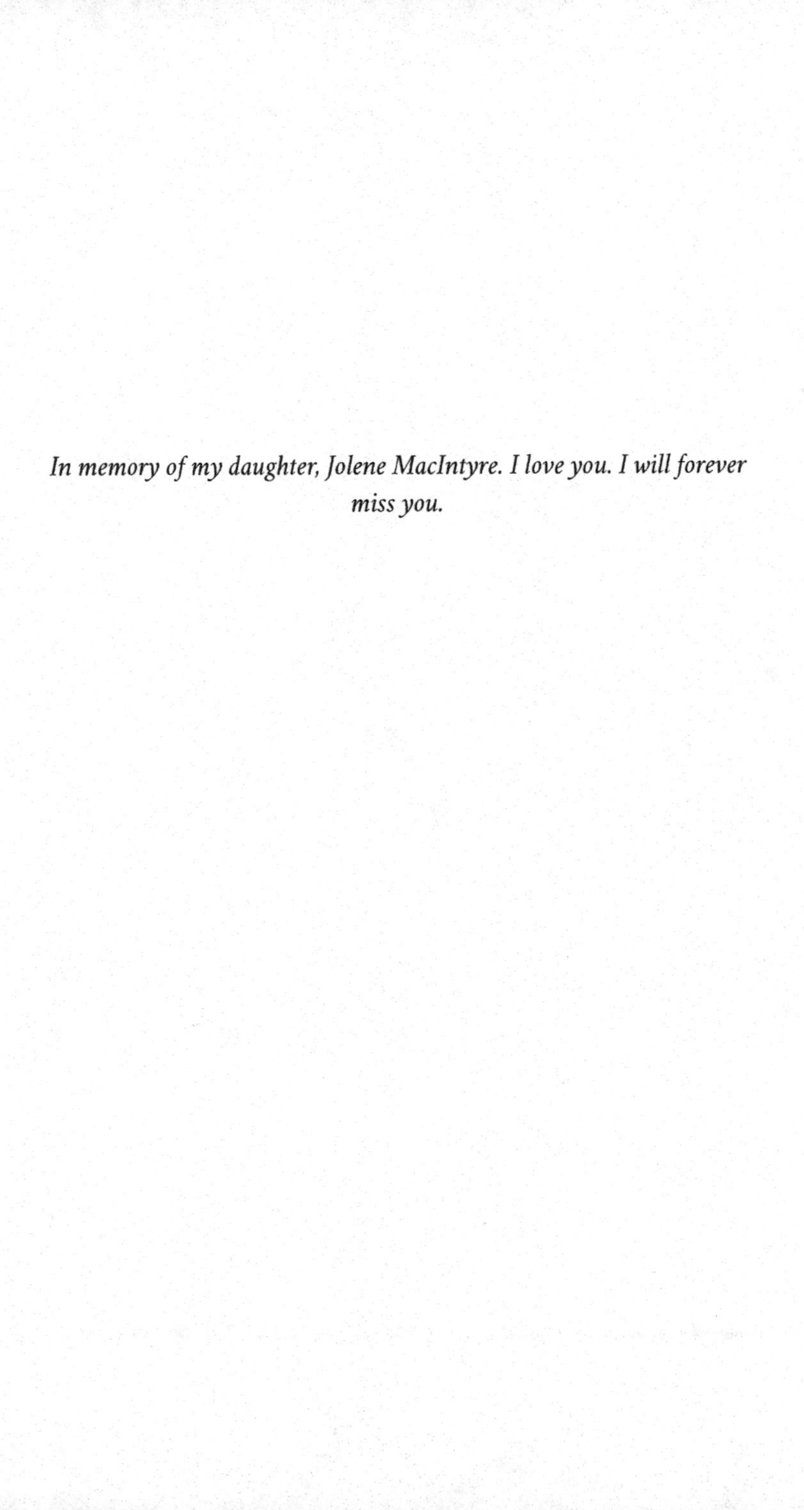

In memory of my daughter, Jolene MacIntyre. I love you. I will forever miss you.

PROLOGUE

Today, I killed two ~~birds~~ men with one stone. Well, one boy and one man. Now that is that...

CHAPTER ONE

Nick's hand braces mine, holding firmly.

'Morning. Are you okay?' His pitch is lower than normal. Sterner. Usually, I'm welcomed with a *good morning* in a warm, jolly tone at the start of my daily commute. Where has the good gone this morning?

I step off the historic grey-stone jetty onto the first wooden stair of the small ferryboat. The fine strawberry-blond hair covering the back of his hand brushes under my thumb.

'Yes. Why?'

The rubber soles of my pumps squeak on the varnished wooden boards of the deck. His hand releases mine.

At full capacity his boat seats fourteen – six on the benches in the covered area of the cabin and eight on the open-air benches. On this first run of the morning the seats are nearly always empty, apart from me.

His smile is usually so wide it forms a dozen thin wrinkles reaching from the corners of his blue eyes and fanning out across his sun-bronzed – nutmeg-like – freckled skin. Today, there's no smile.

He glances along the jetty, looking towards the place where

the stone begins its stretch out into the lake. There are no other passengers. Maybe he's expecting someone? I sit on a bench as he looks the other way, across the expanse of water.

The otherwise empty, calm, mirror-like lake reflects the woods and mountains surrounding the valley, and the cloudless blue sky above them.

Nick's gaze catches on mine, just for a second, before he reaches to untie the rope that's wrapped around an iron bollard rooted in the old jetty. If he expected someone else, he's not waiting.

The half-hitch knot is released and the rope slips free. He does this, tying and untying the rope, a hundred times a day.

'PJ,' I call his dog. A charcoal black Patterdale Terrier.

The dog sits at the bow most of the day, like an old-fashioned figurehead on a sailing boat, quietly watching passengers and wildlife, but when I travel he sits next to me. PJ jumps down from the gunwale, the rim at the edge of the boat, and walks to me. He likes having his ears stroked, he likes the scratch of my manicured nails.

'There are two dozen police officers in the far corner of the lake,' Nick says with his back to me as he wraps the rope around the iron cleat on the boat, in a figure of eight. 'They've enclosed the whole bay in blue-and-white tape. I won't be able to stop at the Southend Jetty today. They're in white coveralls on their knees on the beach at the moment.' He passes PJ and me. His eyes sometimes purple and sometimes blue, like an amethyst jewel changing in different lights, catch hold of my gaze. Today, in the shadow of his baseball cap, his irises are matt indigo. His wide, dilated pupils obscure the richness of the colours that will show when the sun catches his face and he smiles. His hand lifts and lowers the rim of his cap, in an unusually nervous expression as he looks away.

'Have you heard any news? Do you know what's going on?'

'No.' My fingernails comb through PJ's hair.

I look beyond him, drinking in the view. I can't see the south end of the lake from here. I don't want to. This journey is a small dose of mindfulness for the beginning and the end of my working day. I'd rather not see the police activity and let a criminal or an accident defile this beautiful, safe place.

The thump of Nick jumping down onto the deck has every muscle in my body leaping. He turns to the cockpit and leaves the door open, so we can talk. He leaves it open every day, unless it's raining heavily. Then, I sit inside.

The engine whirs into life. The water stirs around the boat, lapping and slapping at the hull as Nick steers away from the jetty, out of the shallower water.

'It must be serious,' he says. 'There's a white tent covering something.'

My gaze is pulled towards the southern end of the long lake, despite my desire to ignore it, even though the high banks around Lowerdale Bay hide it from sight.

I began this commute after Easter when I started teaching in the secondary school, covering maternity leave for the summer, autumn and winter terms. I want this move to be permanent. This place, this life, has been waiting for me to find it. I'm happy for the first time in a long time. Jordan, my youngest son, has settled. I need Eli, my eldest, to be happy too, though. He still claims I ripped him away from the place and the people he liked.

A couple of hundred metres away, the grey stone of Bowick Jetty is visible on the far bank. A ferry has crossed the long narrow lake between Lowerdale village and Bowick town for centuries. The car journey into Bowick would take me forty minutes. Using the ferry is twenty-five minutes.

'Why would I drive?' I once asked Eli.

My eyes are drawn to the first sight of Southend Jetty. Newer wooden jetties stand on stilt-like poles at that end of the lake. Built to connect one of the Lake District's many walking routes.

The jetty on the right-hand side is still hidden by the contours of the lake.

A flash of blue-and-white tape and I begin to see what Nick described – a large area cordoned off and people on their knees crawling across the shingle beach in white coveralls.

'It must be a body.' Nick's voice is grave.

My attention returns to him. His hand lifts off the small wooden steering wheel. He wipes his palm on the stomach of his blush-red T-shirt. 'They must think it's a murder, to be looking at things that intently. I've only seen those white tents on TV.'

'Maybe there was an accident or a suicide.'

He coughs, clearing a dry throat, no longer looking south. His eyes on his destination. 'That's a lot of people searching around the space on their knees for a suicide?'

'Maybe they aren't certain what happened.'

PJ watches the white dots of people crawling around. My fingernails continue combing.

Everyone seems to know everyone in Lowerdale. If it's someone from the village someone will know them. But the boys and I probably won't. We haven't met many people yet and it might be a tourist. Still… Murder… This is such a peaceful place.

Eli will use it as a weapon – a reason to say we shouldn't stay here.

Memories of last night whisper. Glimpses of the hours lost to one too many gin and tonics. Kisses. Touches. The bed creaking as we moved. The ache of internal bruising murmuring about the hours of enjoyable sex – Eli would say any relationship I dare to commence is a reason to leave, too.

My phone chimes. A dulled sound rising from a pocket inside my large handbag that carries everything from keys to my lunchbox. I slide back the zip and dig out my phone.

Jordan. His charming face smiles from the icon. A touch brings the message up.

I'm okay. I've slept okay and I have everything. Don't worry, Mum.

He's made friends the quickest. Earning himself a place on the primary school's girls' and boys' mixed football team with a few good goals. He had a sleepover last night, with a boy who lives on a farm high in the hills outside the village, in a Brontë style, *Wuthering Heights*, setting.

Jordan's absence let me be an adult, not only a mother for a night. I made the most of it.

Good. I'll see you at five-thirty. x

A thumbs-up emoji is my answer.

There is no point in progressing a conversation. When Jordan is with his friends, he has no desire to talk to me. In the life of a ten-year-old boy a mother has to learn her place. Our mother-and-son bond is concealed in private moments.

Teenage boys however – navigating a testosterone-fuelled fifteen-year-old, who is as tall as his father, is very different.

I open Eli's message thread. There's nothing after I was messaged:

I don't want any dinner

At 14:12 yesterday. Although he tried to ring once later in the afternoon.

Eli and I are sailboats that pass one another with enough distance to ensure we don't clash. Tacking continually. Requiring quick decisions. Of course, every decision I make is wrong. I irritate him constantly.

I drop the phone into my bag and look at the reflections playing on the shallow waves the ferry sends running out across the lake.

PJ is still watching the white figures. They'll disappear from view soon, when the ferry is nearer Bowick, obscured by the contours of the lake's edge.

'Do you mind if I put the radio on? I want to know what they say on the news.'

Nick reaches to the radio, not waiting for my answer. But it's his boat. It's his business.

Rick Astley singing 'Together Forever' stretches out from the cabin. A breeze catches the words, sweeps over the water and stirs up more ripples. The reedy smell of the lake water and the heavy scent of pollens travel with it.

Goosebumps rise on my forearm that rests on the gunwale.

The air isn't warm, but it also isn't cold, it's a day that promises warmth. I haven't put my coat on, accepting the promise as true.

Nick tilts his wrist as he holds the small wooden wheel, glancing at his watch. He is due to tie up on the far side at 8am.

Five Lowry style matchstick people stand on the sturdy Cumbrian grey stone of Bowick Jetty, waiting for the ferry's arrival. They're walkers, recognisable from their clothing and rucksacks.

Rick Astley's rich tones fade away. 'Now it's time for Ikbir Shergill with the news.'

I look at Nick. He's looking ahead. The muscles beneath the tanned skin of his arm are taut as he holds the wheel tighter than normal, and the outlines of the tense muscles at the back of his cheek by his ear make me think he's gritting his teeth.

'Good morning. Your news for today. Cumbria Constabulary have advised that the body of a young man was found on the east shore of Lowerdale Lake in the early hours of this morning. It is an area popular for swimming. The police have not said whether his death is considered suspicious...'

The newsreader continues speaking but the subject changes.

Nick reaches out and switches the radio off. 'They're not going to tell us any more than that today then.'

I take one last look at the Southend Jetty before it disappears out of sight. Six figures in white coveralls walk in unison carrying a long black bag away from the tent near the water's edge. A chill creeps through my innards despite the burgeoning warmth in the sunshine. The body in that black bag is someone's son, and perhaps someone's brother, or a husband.

A high wooded promontory in the contour of the bank swallows the sombre image and quickly hides the whole bay.

My gaze follows Nick's to the Bowick Jetty. I watch the people grow in clarity, the engine's hum an ambient sound.

When the ferry nears the jetty, the bottom of the lake becomes visible. Old stone steps descend a metre under the water. There are white paint marks on the stone, marking years when the height of the water was particularly low or years when rainwater flooded down from the mountain tops and gathered in the valley.

As the ferry draws up alongside the jetty, ducks scrabble out of the water and race onto the gravel, hoping someone will throw them seeds to feast on. A mother duck swims past with a dozen fluffy, scraggy ducklings.

Nick switches off the engine and climbs onto the gunwale to secure the ferry with the rope. I wait on the bench, keeping out of his way as he loops the length of rope around the iron bar and ties it off with a half hitch.

The walkers step closer, preparing to board.

'Wait until I'm ready, please,' Nick tells them, not making eye contact as he jumps down onto the deck. He probably says those words a hundred times a day too. It's a rhythmic job. Every day the same. Despite the setting, I'd be bored with the repetition. Tie up, board, take payment, untie, drive, and do it all again.

But today… I'm not sure what to think about the body…

There's a strange atmosphere in the air. Maybe because the passengers waiting to board are feeling concerned and are quieter.

When the boat's secure, I stand up, my fingers sliding free from PJ's hair.

'I hope your day is okay, Jen.' Nick offers his hand to help me balance on the narrow stairs.

'Yours too. Goodbye.' I accept the strong warm grip. 'See you later.' I'm all paid up. I pay in advance into his bank account, so I don't have to faff-around each morning. I step across onto the solid jetty. The stone is smooth from the thousands of people who have made the step before me.

'Goodbye, PJ.' I wave to the dog as though he's human, before I walk away.

'Good morning. Where are you headed?' Nick's voice carries as he welcomes the first of the walkers.

I glance back. PJ is returning to his position at the head of the bow.

A smile lifts my lips as I reach the footpath and walk beneath the canopy of the trees' branches.

The leaves of the beech and ash trees on the far side of a slate drystone wall sieve the sunlight, dappling the shadow on the wide tarmac path. There are picnic tables on the left-hand side, that overlook the bay. Sometimes I eat my lunch here.

In the last few paces, before I leave the waterside, something pulls through me. A strength of feeling, a pressure, like walking through water. The dense friction I'd felt in the air when I'd left the boat. It weighs down my legs and tries to pull me back. Emotions come from nowhere. Sadness. Pain. Fear. I can only assume these strange sensations are because I'm shocked and tired. I didn't sleep much. Yesterday's row with Eli had disturbed me, and the sex was not easily forgotten.

I went to the pub yesterday, to forget the argument Eli left me overthinking.

Like Jordan, Eli has already developed friendships with people at school. But I have no connections here yet and Eli never acknowledges it isn't only his friends we left behind in Oxford. Last night might be the beginning of something for me.

Bowick Academy is a ten-minute uphill walk from the lakeside, tucked into the lower slopes of Keln Rigg Mountain. In the sunshine, the domineering mountain behind the Academy reaches for the blue sky with a glorious promise of spectacular beauty at its rocky peak. On a cloudy day, it looms. A threatening presence glowering over the town.

As I climb the steep pavement, my mind rolls into preparing for the working day, running through lesson plans. The accident or murder or whatever has happened beside the lake will excite the students. They'll be full of tension and chatter.

A glance at my watch tells me Eli won't reach the school for another fifteen minutes.

The school bus takes a twisted route around villages.

I am not his mother in school. He has his father's skin tone, hair and eyes. I am so different in appearance to my sons that Eli can get away with pretending the supply English teacher has nothing to do with him. Soft-toffee-brown-skinned Eli Pelle compared to the pale-skinned Miss Easton is – whiteboard-chalk compared to a delicious smoked cheese. He enjoys how easy it is to fool people and disown me. I haven't challenged it, because what fifteen-year-old boy wants to be in classes taught by his mother – but he's a good boy – a good son. The cracks in our relationship are not his fault.

Oxford has enough schools so I didn't have to work in his. Bowick has one secondary school. We can't avoid each other. Unless I travel miles to work.

The playground is dotted with children and teenagers. The early birds. I walk across the car park to the staff door pulling my pass out of my handbag, swipe the pass and key in my entry code. The door releases.

'Good morning!' I call to the administration staff as I pass the office.

'Good morning!' various voices return in a chorus.

A desire for coffee leads me on to the staff room. It's crowded and noisy. Everyone seems to be speaking about whatever has happened at the lake.

'Good morning, Jen.' Paula Heart, the headteacher, walks over, a mug in hand.

'Good morning.' I continue on my path to the coffee machine. Caffeine is necessary to manage a class of quick-witted teenagers.

'Have you heard what's happened?' she asks as she follows me.

'It was on the radio. Do you know anything more than that?'

'No. None of the parents have called, so I hope none of our families are involved.'

'I told you, it won't be anyone local.' Geography-Geoff's voice rises over every other conversation, joining ours. Geography is a nickname I attributed to him when I first arrived. It's the way I remember names. 'It'll be someone from the city.'

'So only people who live in a city can be murdered.' Every other conversation has ended and now it merges into one, as everyone looks towards Geoff, Paula and me.

I turn my back, pick up a mug and focus on the coffee machine.

'We don't even know it is murder. They didn't say that on the news.'

'It's dreadful, though, isn't it? To think there might be a killer in our town.'

I open the fridge and use the milk.

'The children will be excited. There are news crews in the marketplace.'

A little too much milk sploshes into the coffee.

'Some of them might be concerned too.'

I glance at my watch as I put the milk away. Jordan will be walking across fields to the village primary school with his friend. He is more sensitive than Eli. Jordan will worry when he hears about the body by the lake.

I blow on the surface of the coffee trying to cool it enough to drink it quickly. Ripples flow over the surface as they had over the water earlier. I sip a little.

'The assembly topic this morning is kindness. Quite apt really,' Miss Batty-Beatrice Barron says.

She has very dark hair, and paler skin than mine, milk-white, vampire-ish, hence the Batty.

The only person I've shared my silly names with is Eli. It was a rare moment of shared laughter, and probably wrong of me as these are his teachers. But doing the right things as the single mother of a teenage boy is a daily struggle. We have this game, though, we love to highlight the difference in everyone's colours, their eyes, hair and skin tones. Since he was about five, we've played a game with each other to describe colours with more depth than their simple name. That's why I told him about my silly names for people, because it's like expanding our colour descriptions, a bit of fun. I knew he'd laugh, even though he says he's grown out of the colour game, and I love his laugh.

The conversation flows on around the incident by the lake because things like this happen on the news, in films and books, not where we live.

When Eli's class file into the room after assembly, a stream of noise and commotion travels with them. They are not talking about what's happened, but I can tell from the pulses of adrenaline in their body language they have talked about it and they are thinking about it.

My gaze follows Maddie Cox to her seat. A red-hot warmth rushing up my neck. A blush that must be visible. I am one of those people who blushes from the chest and throat upwards, ugly violent splodges of vivid colour spreading across my skin. She will see it, but I hope she doesn't know that it's because I spent half the night with her mother.

'Take your seats everyone. Settle down.'

Eli is going to be one of the last to come in.

Heavy bags laden with exercise and textbooks thump down on the floor and the metal feet of chairs scrape back on the rubber floor tiles.

The classroom fills until Eli is the only one missing.

I head over to close the door and look along the hallway. He's not out there.

'Has anyone seen Eli Pelle?'

As I shut the door, my gaze runs over the faces and settles on Aiden.

'No, miss, he wasn't on the bus.'

Aiden Whitehead lives in Lowerdale. They wait for the school bus together. If Aiden says Eli didn't come to school. He didn't.

'He wasn't in registration either,' Maddie Cox adds, always needing to get a word in.

I did not check Eli's room this morning. I woke up late, he should have left before I woke. He's good at getting up in the morning. I never chase him. It's a row we don't need to have.

If he's still in bed, I'll kill him. But I can't leave the classroom to do anything about it. If I give this lot a single inch of leeway to misbehave they'll snatch a mile of it. That is the lot of a supply teacher.

I cough to clear a dry throat. 'Take your books out and let's begin.' I sit down and open the laptop to quickly run through the register on the system. Eli is marked as absent. I will shout at him when I see him. His unexplained absence will damage my reputation here. It's obvious I didn't know because I didn't say anything to reception, or to Paula.

The laptop snaps like a crocodile as I shut it too forcefully. 'Has everyone done the homework?'

'I have, miss, can I read mine out first?' Maddie lifts a hand, and before I even have chance to say yes her hand lowers and she folds back the cover of her exercise book.

My nod gives her the cue to carry on.

Her willingness to participate is to my advantage because other children in the class follow her lead. She's a popular strong-willed and self-assured girl. Not unlike her mother.

I'm sure I'm a blotchy-red again. Fortunately, the class are looking at Maddie and Maddie is looking at her book.

While she reads her rewrite of *Macbeth's* witches' scene, her hand rests against the base of her throat. It's a comfort habit she has, telling the secret that beneath that brash, bold character, there is some level of insecurity.

My mind is divided as I teach, my fingers itch to dig the phone out of my pocket and call Eli. The children may not know he is my son but the staff know. They'll know he is *skiving*. What am I going to do? Eli doesn't do things like this. He was upset with me yesterday. Another silly argument spinning up over nothing. No, not nothing, every argument is rooted in the reason we moved here.

A gentle tap strikes on the glass in the classroom's door, interrupting us. Every child looks over. The stainless-steel handle lowers and the door opens.

'Miss Easton.' Paula walks into the room, accompanied by fifty-shades Bethany. 'Would you come with me?' Her voice has a rigid quality. 'Miss Grey will stay with the children.'

Oh no. This has to be about Eli. I leave *Macbeth* lying open on the desk. 'We are discussing the opening witches' scene, Miss Grey, and sharing the opinions they drew in their homework. They are comparing their perspectives with Shakespeare's intended meanings.'

'Thank you, Miss Easton.'

Bethany is also a supply teacher. The school often use her to cover odd lessons and illness. We exchange smiles as we pass.

Paula's expression is grave. There's no colour in her usually glowing olive-oil-coloured skin and her lips are a stiff line.

'Is everything all right?' I ask when I close the classroom door behind me.

'I'm not sure. The police have asked to speak to you.'

The police? Oh Lord? Eli! What have you been up to? I should have checked he was out of bed this morning.

He had a problem with the police before. In Oxford. He'd dropped an empty crisp packet on a pavement, littering at the age of thirteen. He was tall by then and looked older than he was. But there was no justification to shove him against a wall and pat him down looking for drugs or knives. *It was a crisp packet!*

André, my ex-husband, submitted a formal complaint. 'Why assume a ridiculously minor crime might be more?' he'd yelled in the police station. 'Just because of the colour of his skin!'

It took a year to obtain an apology.

Celebrating the colours of human skin began our fun flamboyant descriptions of colour, because white and black are such bland expressions for the myriad of colours we are. I don't like labelling everyone at one end or the other of a spectrum. '*We don't look at people like that,*' I told Eli when he was about six and someone at a birthday party, of all places, labelled him the black kid. '*Look at my skin and tell me what you see. I'm as white as the buttercream icing on the cupcakes, and you look as black as those gingerbread people.*' He'd laughed and run off smiling. Of course, in later years we've had discussions about culture and history and the need to remember and celebrate how he came to be who he is. But who he is, is not *the black kid*. The problem is too many times when he hits institutional systems that is who he becomes.

The soles of my pumps squeaking on the floor tiles is the soundtrack of our long walk through the school hallways. It isn't until we reach the offices, when I see three of the administration staff at their desks, I remember how unusual it is for Paula to fetch me herself.

'This is Miss Easton.' Paula says, stepping back and encouraging me to enter her office ahead of her. Two female police officers are waiting. She closes the door, shutting herself outside and me inside with them.

'Please sit down, Miss Easton,' an older woman with pinned back sun-ripened-wheat-blonde hair says. Deep russet-brown eyes, framed by gold eyeshadow, observe me.

'I'm Marie,' she tells me.

'Do you need me to come to the station?' Is Eli in a cell? What have they arrested him for?

'No, Miss Easton, please sit down.'

I do sit, dropping into one of the comfy seats on the visitors' side of Paula's desk, my legs giving out from under me. Marie sits in another of the chairs. The other officer remains on her feet.

'Can I call you, Jennifer?' Marie asks.

'Yes.' What is this?

'We are sorry to have to inform you that earlier this morning the body of a young man was found in Lowerdale lake by a dog walker…'

I listen but I am underwater. The words are distorted.

'We have reason to believe the body is that of your son, Eli Pelle.'

I sink into dark black water that floods my lungs, stealing the oxygen from my blood.

CHAPTER TWO

'Take a moment, Miss Easton.' Marie's hand touches my shoulder.

I don't know if I passed out, or if I was just lost for a moment, but I am in the chair, my hands covering my face as I shake my head.

'No.' I stand up. My hands falling. There must be something I can do. Anything to prevent those words being said. Hollow legs struggle to hold me up.

'No.'

My legs collapse and I am back in the chair. 'It's not true. It's a mistake. It can't be true.'

'Shall I fetch you something to drink? Water? Tea?' the standing officer offers.

My shaking head rejects anything. Everything.

'We are fairly sure it is Eli,' Marie speaks. 'But we need you to identify the body to be certain.'

'No.' My trembling hands thump into my lap, joining the violent denial – because *no,* it can't be my son. The radio said it was a young man. Marie said man. He's a boy. Just a child… They're mistaken. Nausea presses at the back of my throat, threatening to throw up my breakfast. Every drop of blood drains away from my head in a rush that feels as though someone has thrown a bucketful through my veins and now it's running away, spinning in a whirlpool, like water draining out through a plughole in my heel.

'Let me get you a cup of tea, Jennifer.'

The world is black once more.

'Keep your head between your knees,' Marie tells me. She's squatting beside me. I hadn't heard her move.

They are saying Eli is dead.

I want to hold him. This can't be true. I feel him in my arms, tall and slender, all bone and sinew. I breathe deeply and straighten up. The room comes back into view. They are wrong. 'He must be in bed at home.'

'He's been taken to the hospital,' she answers.

Hope flares. 'He's injur—'

'The body is in the morgue there.'

'Body...' I shake my head. 'I don't believe it. He must have overslept. He'll be at home.'

'Take your time, Jennifer. We'll drive you to the hospital when you're ready.'

It won't be him. When I get home, I'll kill him.

Marie rises from her squat.

A trembling hand reaches to my trouser pocket and pulls out my phone. It recognises my face and flares into life. I touch recent calls to find Eli's number and touch the call icon, raising the phone to my ear. The ring echoes eight times and then...

'Hi. This is Eli. Go away. I'm busy and I probably won't call you back.'

'Tea.'

A mug is held in front of me. I leave the phone on my lap, in case Eli calls back. The tea is sweet. Whoever made it must have put about five teaspoons of sugar in.

'Can we contact anyone for you?'

'No. No one.' I lost my parents long ago. I was born late in their lives. Old age stole them both before I was twenty-six. I had Eli when I was twenty. He's only five years younger than I was when I gave birth to him.

The hand holding the handle of the mug is the colour of mashed potatoes. That was Eli's description when I was suffering with morning sickness while pregnant with Jordan. *'You look like mashed potatoes, Mum.'* He'd held the back of his hand against mine, comparing his beautiful burnt-caramel-brown skin to mine. I shut my eyes. Every muscle in my body quivering.

It can't be him. Why would he have been at the south end of the lake? It's two or three miles away from the village.

They're wrong.

He must be at home in bed.

He's overslept.

They are wrong.

I need to go. The sooner I see this person they want me to look at, the sooner I can ask them to take me home and I'll wake him up.

'He has a younger brother,' I say, putting the barely drunk mug of tea down on Paula's desk.

'Would you like us to send someone to fetch him?'

'No. God no. Let him stay in school.' This isn't true. 'I should tell Paula I won't be able to return to my class.' I stand – too quickly, the room takes a sweeping turn.

Marie's hand wraps around my arm, holding me still for a moment as the other officer bends down and picks up my phone that had slid to the floor and bounced on the carpet.

'My colleague, Lucy, will tell Mrs Heart you need to leave. The school will manage things here.'

The officer passes me my phone. I slide it into my pocket. I need it close, to answer when Eli calls.

My fingertips rub my temple as though I can erase this conversation from my mind.

'Can we go? Can we get it over with?' I pull my arm free from Marie's hold.

'If you are sure you're ready.'

'I need to fetch my handbag from my locker.' I turn to the door. Lucy opens it.

Paula is in the administration office. I don't look at her. I can't think about anyone but Eli.

Marie follows me to the staff room. No one else is in there. She waits as I open my locker and hang my handbag over my shoulder. 'I left my laptop and books in the classroom.'

'Someone else can lock them away for you.'

I close the locker and turn the key, the movements automated. Inhuman.

Eli isn't dead. It's a horrible mistake. When I'm home, I'll run upstairs, push open his bedroom door and he'll be there, lying on the bed in jogging bottoms. I won't kill him, I'll hug the life out of him. I'll tell him how much I love him and whatever happens we will make things work. I'll promise to be more sensible, if he is more tolerant, and I'll never shout at him again.

I step into the back of the police car.

In my mind Eli is tucked under his duvet, the crown of his coal black curly hair visible on the pillow. The smell of his room greets my senses as I mentally stand at the open door. The smell of a boy growing into a man. I imagine myself picking up clothes that need washing, speaking to him as he mumbles replies from beneath the duvet.

Picking up his clothes has driven me mad for the last couple of years. I can't imagine anything I want to do more right now.

Be at home Eli. Be in bed.

'The hospital is in Penrith, it will take us forty minutes or so to reach there,' Marie, who is driving, tells me.

I nod, my gaze meeting her brown eyes in the rear-view mirror. The russet colour is like fading Henna patterns on skin. I look away, my mind full of conversations sharing descriptions of colour with Eli.

'What do you think that green colour is like?'

'Dark seaweed. The one with the bubbles in it.'

Whites, proper whites, not human skin whites, are *'wispy-sunny-sky-clouds'*, or if the white is denser *'coconut-flesh'*.

I stare through the window, seeing but blind. The car travels along roads that wind their way between hills and around lakes, through valleys.

My hand lays on Eli's thigh, as he rides shotgun beside me, in the moment we'd driven into the Lake District. Jordan behind him.

'Look up from the phone's screen for a moment. Look at this,' I told him.

The police are silent in the front seats. My hand lifts and tucks a loose strand of hair behind my ear. The hair falls again, stroking across my cheek.

My heartbeat thuds heavily when the car's indicator ticks to turn right into the hospital car park. In minutes I will know if Eli is here.

'Officer 2213.' Lucy, the policewoman in the front passenger seat, speaks into the communication device attached to her uniform. 'We are here. Please let the hospital staff know we're bringing Miss Easton in.'

If anyone asks me how far the hospital is from the car park, or which way we walk, I couldn't say. One foot just moves in front of another. The world is a fog of colours and sounds. They take me to a small soulless room, with magnolia walls and one medical-style gurney. A white sheet, with the creases of recently opened out pressed folds, covers a prostrate figure.

I know. I know the shape of him when he is asleep beneath his duvet. 'Eli.' I step forward, my heart dropping with the weight of a stone, falling through my chest all the way to the floor.

A man wearing sky-blue scrubs stands beside the gurney,

waiting for the moment he will be asked to move the sheet back. He lifts it. I pull it from his hand. In my head pulling the duvet off Eli's face. I see him sit up and hear his shouts. *'Get out, Mum! Why are you in my room?'*

Eli! My beautiful son… Oh God… It is him. How? Why? 'Eli!' The choked scream erupts and echoes around the room.

My palm presses against his cheek.

He's so cold.

'Best not to do that, Jennifer, in case there's any DNA or fibres on his skin. You don't want to destroy evidence,' Marie tells me.

'Is it Eli?' Lucy asks.

It's a stupid question. Tears are drowning me, spilling over onto my cheeks, rolling down and dripping onto the wipeable black surface of the gurney beside the matted clumps of his cloud of beautiful black curls.

He's such a strange colour, muddy-puddle-water. In recent weeks, his skin darkened in the sunshine, he's spent so much time outside. The boys' skin never darkens to the depth of their father's treacle tones but varies between honey and burnt caramel shades. I use the edible descriptions for my boys. I used to chase Eli when he was small, catch him and pretend to eat him, the foundations of our relationship are fun, it's what everything we have now is built on. Fun. Happiness. Pushing the hardships aside. My scrumptious boy. His giggle – the beautiful wide smile that can part his lips is in my mind's eye. *Not this! Not this…*

Marie pulls my hand away.

'Is it Eli?' Lucy repeats. 'We need you to say so, if it is.'

I whirl around, tepid tears dripping from my chin and anger flaring in a rush. 'Yes of course it's Eli.' *Why would I touch him if it wasn't?*

My blood runs cold when I look back at him. Unbelieving. 'I… How?'

The long black eyelashes which usually define brown eyes

that shine like sard gems, rest on his cheeks. *Open your eyes! Look at me!*

Marie moves my hand away again.

'Mum…' I hear him say, in a voice that tells me he needs me.

'We're not sure what happened,' Marie says. 'He was found in the water at the edge of the lake, naked, with a wound on the back of his head.'

I see now that dry blood has matted and tangled the hair at the back of his head. 'I need to tell his father. They stopped speaking…' And Jordan… How do I tell Jordan?

'We can contact Mr Pelle, if you would prefer us to? Officers will visit him, we won't tell him over the phone.'

'I… He… Yes, that would be easier. But he lives in Oxford. Eli hasn't spoken to him for months.'

'We will contact the local station. That's not a problem.'

'He'll be at work. I have his work address. I don't understand… How?' The word chokes me, wringing more tears from a heart that feels dry. 'I saw a body being carried away from the shore,' I tell the policewomen. 'I didn't know it was Eli. How could I not know?'

Why didn't I check his bed last night when I came home?

Marie's arm wraps around my shoulders. 'We should probably go.'

'I can't leave him!'

'You said you have another son. He needs to be told.'

A strong arm remains around my shoulders, steering me away from Eli, leading me out of the room and the hospital. I walk through the dark storm of a nightmare.

In the back of their car, I stare through the window with eyes that grasp hold of nothing, all I see is Eli's cold, discoloured face. The car slows and reverses, parallel parking against the curb outside the small village primary school.

'Shall I come in with you, Jennifer?' Lucy offers when she opens the car door for me.

'Would you talk to the headteacher? I don't think I can. Then you can leave me here. I—'

'I'm sorry, we can't leave you. Our orders are to stay at the house with you until the family liaison officer arrives. But we will sit in the car while you speak to your son. As soon as you feel up to it the detectives want to talk to you. They need to gather as much detail as they can.'

'Can I walk Jordan home? I don't want to tell him here. I'll meet you at the cottage later.'

'Wouldn't he like a ride in the police car?'

'His brother is dead. I don't think he'll care about your police car.'

When I walk up to the school, my eyes are dry for the first time since I saw Eli. Lucy walks a couple of steps behind me, following in my shadow. I press the intercom button, but my mouth is too dry to speak.

'It's the police,' Lucy calls over my shoulder. 'Please let us in.' She holds her identity card up, showing it to the CCTV camera.

The door's locking mechanism clicks open. I push the door inwards and walk on, leaving Lucy to deliver the news to the administration office.

Children's rucksacks and PE bags hang from waist-height hooks on one wall. Jordan's is there, bulging with clothes from the weekend too. I lift it off the hook and hang it over my shoulder, on top of my handbag.

I tap a knuckle on the glass window in the classroom door.

'Come in,' Miss Azimi calls.

Happy noises reach out from the room, the energetic chatter of young effervescent children. Open seed packets are scattered on Miss Azimi's desk. Groups of children have their fingers in dark compost. The compost is also sprinkled across the tables and floor.

'Miss Easton.' Miss Azimi's dark eyebrows lift to the hem of her hijab, questioning my interruption.

'I'm sorry. I need to take Jordan out of the class. It's urgent.'

'Oh. Of course. Jordan!' she calls, turning to the room. 'Gather up your things, your mum's here to collect you!'

He's in the far corner with his friend Charlie. The boy he's spent the weekend with. His gaze lifts to the teacher then turns to me. There's a tired, I spent most of the night talking not sleeping, expression in the eyes that ask why I'm here.

I beckon, waving a hand saying come to me quickly.

He rubs his hands together showering the floor with compost as he comes. What's left is rubbed off on the side of his dark grey school trousers.

'Mum...'

'Hello, darling.' I ignore the question in his voice. 'Thank you, Miss Azimi.' I lay a hand on his shoulder and lead him out.

'Why are you here, Mum?' he asks as we stand by his peg, while he ties the arms of the navy-blue school sweatshirt around his waist.

Nothing in my life has prepared me for telling my ten-year-old son that his brother is dead. Nothing prepared me to lose Eli.

This is a carefree happy boy who won't exist as soon as I speak.

'I'll tell you on the way home.'

Let his life be normal for a few minutes more. For a little longer, I want to see the wide smile he inherited from his father. The identical smile to Eli's.

I carry the flat rectangular book bag, my hand returning to his shoulder. 'We'll leave via the back gate.'

'Can I have an ice cream?'

Sharon's Ice-cream Parlour is on our route, in the village square, and it's one of Jordan's favourite things about living here – gelato ice cream on the way home. Sharon is not a person I want to face now, but I will face her for Jordan.

'You can have an ice cream.'

The admin clerk in the office sees us in the hall. Lucy is not in the office, she must have returned to the car. I point towards the back door, saying I'll leave that way. I don't want the police to follow. I know eventually they'll realise I've gone but I just want a few minutes more alone with Jordan.

The clerk sends me a heartfelt shallow smile, her eyes glistening. I look away, I can't cry now.

'Come on.' My hand slides from his shoulder. I hold it out for him to take instead. His smaller hand wraps around mine. Eli's larger hand smothers mine.

We'll buy ice cream, sit on the bench outside the church on top of the hill and then I'll tell him.

'Why did you fetch me early, Mum?' he asks again.

'I'll tell you after we've bought the ice creams.'

We walk through the village in silence, hands clasped tensely, as I fight the desire to cry by biting the skin inside my cheek.

An A-frame board stands outside the shop. The amusing anecdotes and cartoons on it regularly change. *Skinny people are easier to kidnap. Add clotted cream and a fudge stick for extra security.* Usually, the silly statement would lift a smile. I think Maddie writes and draws on the board. The cartoons are similar to the doodles on her school books.

Jordan leads the way into the shop, his expression and voice bright.

'Hi. Mum took me out of school.' There's a swagger in the statement. 'Can I have a scoop of raspberry twist and one of caramel crunch in a waffle cone please?'

Eli says Jordan has a way of threading himself through your heart strings until you give him whatever he wants. It's true. His enthusiasm for life charms everyone. His spirit. The non-judging way he likes people.

Sharon doesn't pick up the scoop. Her mouth opens slightly, as though she's about to speak but doesn't know what to say. Shadows ring the cyan-blue eyes looking at me. Shadows that say she didn't sleep after I left last night.

Eyes are my thing. It's always someone's eyes that attract me first.

She smiles.

I can't.

A cherry blossom pink defines her cheekbones and creeps out across her skin, the blush quickly flowing to her ears and becoming cerise.

She wasn't in bed when I woke up, hungover from our afternoon drinking. I'd left her bed and house without a goodbye. I had not even left a note because by the time I woke Maddie must have come home. I crept down the stairs on my toes, holding my shoes in one hand, by the heels, in the dark, through a silent house, not daring to look in any rooms to try to find her, and quietly let myself out the front door.

'Jen.' She acknowledges.

'Sharon.'

I don't know what time Eli died. Potentially I was in her bed when…

'Mum, what are you having?' Jordan prods.

Sharon breaks eye contact, reaching for a cone and the scoop, and leans over the cartons of colourful ice creams.

'Just one scoop of vanilla in a pot with a chocolate flake please.' My voice has a robotic sound. I always order the flake. Eli always eats it. Always. 'No. Not with a flake, just the scoop of vanilla.'

'Your Mum's not being very adventurous today, is she?' Sharon says to Jordan. 'She is usually far more daring than vanilla.'

He grins, his eyes following the scoop as it cuts through the red streaked raspberry twist ice cream, the euphemism skipping over his head.

The colours of a police car passing slowly by on the road catch the corner of my vision. I look down, delving into my handbag for my purse. They've been told we left the school.

They'll be at the cottage when we arrive. I only have a few more minutes for Jordan to be a carefree boy.

The ice creams are both handed to Jordan as my hands are full with his book bag and my purse.

'Thanks,' his voice is eager. He takes his first lick. I pay – not looking Sharon in the eyes.

The day has warmed up so much the ice cream is already melting over Jordan's fingers as we walk out. I take my tub of ice cream with no desire to eat it.

We cross the cobbles in the village square and turn the corner onto a path that climbs the steep slope of the short hill the medieval dark-grey-stone church perches on. Jordan lifts the iron latch and opens the lychgate, letting us into the churchyard that wraps around the church on the slopes of the hill.

We sit on our favourite bench on the east side of the church looking over the rooftops of the picturesque village to the impressive landscape beyond. From the valley to the mountains.

The lichen-covered gravestones standing in front of us have a new meaning. This was the wrong place—

'Jordan.' I put his book bag down on the seat of the bench and the tub of ice cream on the arm.

His tongue reaches out and licks at the edges of the ice cream. In appearance they are their father's boys through and through, but in personality they are more like me. That's partly why Eli and I clash, we are stubborn, opinionated people.

Oh, Eli. How will I live without you?

Tears blur the view. I swallow several times, chasing them away. I have to tell Jordan.

'Jordan, I have to tell you…' I shuffle a little closer on the seat, moving the book bag from between us to the other side of me. His eyes notice my untouched tub of melting ice cream on the arm of the bench.

I rest my arm around his shoulders take a breath and just speak. 'There was an incident by the lake last night.' I swallow back the pain filling up my throat. 'Eli was hurt. He's dead. He died, Jordan.'

His polished agate-brown eyes look at me as they flood with horror yet call me insane. The ice cream cone slips through his fingers, falling, catching on his grey trousers and leaving a smudge. It lands top-down, the ice cream splattering on the path.

The expression in my eyes was probably the same at the school.

'It's true. The police took me to see him. He hit his head somehow. He was found in the water this morning.'

His head shakes. 'No. I saw him yesterday in the park. He said hi.'

'Oh, darling. It must have been after that.'

'How, Mum?' Watery eyes accuse me of lying.

'I don't know. The police don't know. They are meeting us at the cottage. They want to talk to me. They might ask you some questions too.'

'Can I see him?'

'No. You don't want to see him. He isn't Eli anymore.'

The muscles in his throat work, swallowing, fighting emotion. He looks so small in this landscape of extremes, surrounded by towering purple-topped mountains.

'I don't understand.'

'Nor do I, darling.' I bend down trying to scrape up the fallen ice cream with the cone and throw what I can in the waste bin beside the bench, tossing my tub in too. It was a stupid idea to buy ice creams. But I wanted to please Jordan.

My hand braces his shoulder and pulls him close. His tears soak my blouse, and mine drip onto his hair as spasms of grief shake through us both. It's an earthquake that's hit our lives, shaking everything apart. I can't believe it.

CHAPTER THREE

Not one but two police cars stand outside the row of white-painted, slate-roofed, terraced cottages. The one I rent, the place we've called home for these last few weeks, is in the middle of the row.

Jordan and I walk along the road, red-eyed and sniffing; our world, the ground and sky, collapsing around us.

Marie opens the driver's door of the police car as we approach the cottage. Lucy opens the passenger door. They slip their black-and-white caps on their heads.

There's no pedestrian footpath on the cottages' side of the street. The police cars are parked against the front garden walls, either side of the waist-height wrought-iron gate that opens outwards into the street. Our front garden is little more than a metre and a half from the gate to the front door.

A tall police officer climbs out from the second car, his skin is the colour of Marmite – a deep glorious brown. Eli loves the word glorious. He repeats the word excessively sometimes even now. *'It's Glorious, Mum. Glorious! GLORIOUS!'*

'You have a word fetish.' I tease.

'Well, he is the son of an English teacher,' André responds. 'What did you expect?'

'Hello, Jennifer.' Marie calls. 'And you must be Jordan. Hello. I'm Marie and this is Lucy. We've been helping your mum. Has she told you?'

Jordan doesn't reply. The tension in the hand holding mine tightens.

I nod. Telling them he knows.

Marie approaches, walking around the car to meet us. 'The family liaison officer is here.' She glances over her shoulder at the man. 'Jack is an officer from the West Yorkshire Police. We stole him away from a shift on another job. We've borrowed him, he has some experience of supporting families in this situation. Fortunately, in the Cumbria Constabulary we haven't faced many incidents like this. He will explain everything to you and he'll be your main contact from now on.'

'The sergeant has signed off for an officer to remain outside your home,' he says. 'For the time being. To make sure you're not hassled by callers. Don't get me wrong, the press have a purpose, but sometimes press and even public interest can be excessive in the early days. An officer will remain outside to prevent any intimidation or intrusions and keep you safe.'

'Thank you. But right now, we just want to be inside. Excuse us.' I walk between the female officers, drawing Jordan with me. I don't care what experience the male officer has or where he's from. 'Please leave us alone.'

Jordan passes me, releasing my hand to lift the iron latch and open the garden gate. It creaks on its un-oiled rusty hinges.

'Miss Easton, I do need to speak to you as soon as possible,' the male officer says to our backs. 'You may have important information about what happened.'

I lift the front door key from my handbag.

'I'll wait outside, until you're ready,' he continues.

My hand trembles as I slip the key into the lock. I push the door wide for Jordan to walk in first, I follow and close the door behind us. We're surrounded by Eli in the small square living room. On the bookcase. The TV stand. The shelving. I have pictures of my sons everywhere.

Jordan's eyes focus on a photograph of him and Eli on the beach two summers ago, kneeling either side of the super-sized sandcastle they'd built. 'We were going to play football tonight.'

The age gap between them is never a problem. Eli is always kind to his brother.

Anger rushes towards me, storming into me. He's a good boy. He doesn't argue with his friends or anyone other than me and André. Name a teenager who doesn't argue with his parents. But no one else… How has this happened?

I need to talk to the police. I must face this. I need to know what happened.

When I open the front door a few minutes later, it is not only the male liaison officer standing on the steep steps of my short front garden, but two plain-clothed female detectives hold up their badges. Marie's and Lucy's car has gone.

I step back to let them all in.

'I am Detective Inspector Wendy Carter.' One woman reaches out a hand to formally shake mine.

'Detective Constable Arla Saye-Stevens,' the other woman says, offering her hand after I've shaken Wendy's.

I think inspector means Wendy is the more senior detective.

The small cottage is not used to accommodating four adults. The living room is full.

'Jordan, would you make everyone a cup of tea?' I want him to have something to do, something to control.

This is so out of control…

'Little helper,' Eli teases in my mind as Jordan rises from the sofa and heads into the kitchen.

'Do you want milk and sugar?' Jordan asks in a flat tone.

'We all have milk. No sugar,' the male officer answers. 'I'll help you.' He follows Jordan through the wide arch into the kitchen that runs across the back of the cottage.

Jack. I remember the male officer's name. His pitch is deep but warm-hearted.

'Please sit down,' I tell the female officers. 'Use the dining table.' There is one three-seater sofa, facing the TV, and in the opposite corner to the TV a round table with three dining chairs, all the perfect fit for our family of three.

My heart lurches and leaks pain.

Arla turns a dining chair to face the sofa. She sits down when I sit on the sofa.

'We will be as quick as we can,' Wendy tells me, not taking a seat at the table or on the sofa beside me, but planting her bottom on the coffee table facing me at an intimate proximity. 'We don't want to impose too much but we have a job to do and we need your help to proceed…' she carries on explaining some administration things, mentioning that Jack's black knife-proof Kevlar vest contains a camera, and that they'll take recordings and notes. Telling me I need to communicate with the family liaison officer… I really can't take all the words in.

The kettle whistles in the kitchen.

'Tell us what happened yesterday?' There's no warmth in Wendy's voice.

'I don't know. I want to know.'

'So do we, Jennifer, that's why we're asking. You need to tell us all the details which led up to Eli's presence in the bay. Everything. No matter how small or irrelevant it may seem. There is a possibility he could have hit his head accidentally, but it looks unlikely.'

'Let me carry those, lad,' Jack offers in the kitchen. 'I'm sure you're feeling a bit shaky.'

Released from the chore, Jordan rushes back into the room and drops down on the sofa next to me. I raise an arm and he tucks himself underneath it, pressing tight against me in the way he used to when he was much younger.

Jack carries in two mugs, curls of steam rising from the surface of the tea. He leans down and places them on the coffee table beside Marie. 'Would you like another officer to come inside and play with you while we talk to your mum?'

Jordan's head shakes, his chin brushing my breast.

'Okay. You stay right there then.' Jack winks before he returns to the kitchen for the other mugs.

'We can't be certain of anything until the post-mortem is complete,' Wendy says.

Jack places two mugs on the table, one for Arla and him.

My eyes close for a second at the thought of Jordan's body being cut open.

When my eyes open, Jack has turned the chair as Arla had. He sits down facing me. All three of them are facing Jordan and me. It feels like an interrogation.

'We need to ascertain the cause of death, and an autopsy is the only way to do so,' Wendy adds, reading the disgust in my expression. 'What happened yesterday?' she asks again. 'Was it a normal Sunday?'

The other officers withdraw small notebooks from pockets at the same moment.

'Jordan was staying at a friend's house for the weekend. Eli didn't get out of bed until late but that is normal on a Sunday. He came downstairs at about eleven o'clock. I think. We argued because he hadn't put his school uniform in the washing machine, it was on his bedroom floor, and then we argued again because he drank straight from the milk carton while we were arguing about his uniform.'

'And after these rows…' Arla prompts me to progress from her perch on a dining chair.

'He went out.'

'At what time?'

'I don't know exactly, not long after he got up. Quarter to twelve, maybe.'

'To where?'

'He didn't tell me. He rarely tells me. "I don't know yet," is the usual answer.' I hear myself speaking as though he is still here, as though he can still walk out the door and ignore my questions.

'Where might he have gone to? Where did he like to go?'

'The children's playground. The lakeside. The woods. There are so many paths around here, everywhere is accessible and there isn't much to do in the village.'

Jack and Arla write in their notepads.

Wendy's head lifts. 'When did he come back home?'

A hot blush rises from my chest across the skin of my throat. Guilt creeping upwards to swallow me whole.

'I don't know. I went out myself. He sent a message to say he didn't want a Sunday dinner. So I didn't come home until late. When I came home, I thought he was in bed.'

'Did you look in his bedroom?'

'No.' Shame and embarrassment rise in a flood. If I'd tried to find him last night, would he be alive? I will hate myself for the rest of my life for not checking he was here.

'Do you know anything else he did yesterday? Or if he met anyone?'

I face their judgement. 'No.'

'May I see your phone?' Wendy holds out a hand.

It's on the arm of the sofa. I look at it, showing my face for ID and hand it over. Wendy hands it on to Jack, who begins scanning through the contents.

'There's nothing odd in there,' I tell him.

Wendy's gaze sharpens like a pencil point. 'We'll be the judge of that. It's surprising how even the smallest of clues can paint a picture and unearth the truth.'

'Do you think he came home while you were out, then went back out again?' Arla asks.

'Possibly. All I know is his bed wasn't slept in or sat on. I straightened the duvet yesterday morning, after he left, it's as it was when I left.'

'And nothing else in the house has been moved or disturbed?'

'Not that I've noticed, but we were only in here a few minutes before I let you in. I only had time to glance into his room when I used the toilet. What time did he die?'

'I can't say. It's hard to pinpoint exact times of death. The post-mortem may inform us.'

Arla reaches out a hand for the mug of tea on the table beside her. It will be too milky. Jordan always adds too much milk.

In my head, Eli spits a mouthful of tea into the sink. *'You can't make tea for toffee, Jordy. It's disgusting.'* For toffee is another favourite, fetish phrase. Eli learned the phrase from Nanna Fay at the age of three and never let go of it.

'It isn't disgusting, is it, Mum?'

'No, Jordy, it's just fine. You're a good teas-maid.'

I squeeze him tighter against me for a moment.

'I saw him yesterday,' Jordan says, as though my squeeze told him to speak. 'After lunch. In the play-park by the tennis courts.' He slips out from under my arm, straightening up. 'He was with his friends. He was laughing.'

'Nothing looked wrong?' Wendy asks in a gentler voice.

He shakes his head vigorously.

'Who was he with?'

'I only know one of the boys. Aiden.'

'Aiden Whitehead,' I say. 'They are in most of the same classes at school and Eli spends most of his time with him as far as I'm aware.'

'Who are his other friends?'

I list the names of children I've seen him speaking to in school. 'But I don't know who he meets up with outside school, other than Aiden.'

'What else should we know?' Arla's gaze rises from her notepad, her thickly woven auburn plait sliding off her shoulder.

Foxy orange – that's what Eli calls auburn hair.

My shoulders lift and fall in a helpless gesture. 'I don't know. He was a normal teenager. With testosterone-fuelled mood swings, blackheads and acne that made him paranoid about how he looked and what other people thought of him.'

'There's a missed call from Eli here,' Jack looks up from my phone. 'Yesterday afternoon, and not long before this he texted to say he doesn't want dinner.'

'Yes. It was after I received that message I went out. I didn't hear his call. My phone was switched off.'

'You moved here a few weeks ago. At Easter…' Arla prompts.

They have already researched us. 'Yes.'

'Eli's previous school let us know they had some concerns.'

'What concerns?' A frown pulls my forehead. 'There were no concerns that I was made aware of.'

'He was not always well-behaved.'

'Pardon? He's a typical fifteen-year-old not a naughty child. There was one incident. It was a mistake.'

'Might he have been involved with a gang?'

'Are you kidding? Because there was one minor incident or because he is brown-skinned? No.' My head shakes as violently as I speak. 'Cover your ears,' I say to Jordan. I wait until he does it. 'Where has that theory come from? Not every child of colour or mixed race is in a gang! Just as not all paler-skinned children are! My son is not a stereotype! Do not start believing things based on your biases. Eli is a good, kind teenager, not a criminal!' My responses are so loud and adamant Jordan must hear me anyway, despite his palms covering his ears.

'This may be uncomfortable—' Jack starts, using his skin colour to speak out against my torrent.

'Uncomfortable?' I interrupt. 'I found out he died three hours ago! This is hell! But he was not in a gang!'

'Did he take drugs?' Wendy asks, calmly, as though I haven't spoken.

'No. He was fifteen!'

'Fifteen-year-olds take drugs,' Jack unhelpfully punctuates, his eyes not leaving my phone as a thumb moves, scanning through things on the screen. 'And to be fair, Jennifer, you said you have no idea what he was doing while he was out.'

'Are you here to avoid accusations of racism?'

His head lifts, his eyes narrow and he looks directly into my eyes. I've offended him. 'No, Miss Easton, Wendy asked me to be your liaison officer to prevent the risk of unconscious biases on the part of other officers. I agreed, even though it is a bit of a drive over here for me and it will take me away from my family, for the same reason.'

He makes it sound as though I should feel grateful. I don't. That is not one of the emotions in the tornado currently swirling in my stomach. I swallow away the pain and anger from our previous experience with the police. 'Have you looked at his phone? Is there anything suspicious on his phone?'

'We haven't found his phone. It wasn't with… him.' Wendy nearly said his body. I see her mind retract and replace the words before they reach her lips.

'Was he sexually active?' Wendy asks.

'I… I…' I see him smiling in my mind's eye. 'I don't know. He didn't tell me if he was.'

'Can I take my hands off my ears, Mum?' Jordan asks.

I nod and look at Jack as Jordan does. 'He did not take drugs. I know. His uncle, his father's brother, did at one point in his life and had a stroke because of the damage his drug addiction did to his arteries. No one could have persuaded Eli to take drugs, he lived through the consequences suffered by his grandmother and father. His uncle took months to recover from the stroke only to die last year, when he was knocked over by a car while he was drunk.

'Thank you for explaining,' Jack acknowledges in a factual manner, with no judgement.

'Do you think someone took his phone?' I ask.

'It is possible,' Wendy answers. 'The evidence indicates Eli was with someone before, or when, he died.'

'You mean… He wasn't…' *Raped,* I mouth the word silently. 'They said he was naked…'

'We can't say what happened until after the post-mortem.'

Every muscle in my chest solidifies. I can't breathe. I'm gasping for air that can't fill my lungs.

'Mum? Mum!'

'Have a sip of tea.' Jack is on his feet, one hand on my shoulder, leaning over me and holding the mug in front of me. Jordan's hand rests against my back.

I accept the mug and take a few sips, controlling the sense of panic. I must be sane for Jordan. I put the mug down. My fingertips rub my forehead, where a sharp pain is pounding in my skull.

'I have a headache,' I tell the officers. 'I can't tell you any more and as you can't tell me any more either, can we stop?'

Wendy's eyes study my face, looking for something. 'Okay,' she says eventually, rising lithely to stand in front of us. 'But we do need to look around Eli's bedroom before we leave. In case there are any clues that could explain why this happened. Did he have a laptop or any other technology we should be aware of?'

'No. I'm a single parent teacher. The boys use my laptop, we can only afford one, and he did his homework in the living room. There's no space upstairs. So there's nothing personal of his on our laptop.'

'May we look in his room?'

'Yes.' I just want them to go. 'It's the first door on the right at the top of the stairs.'

Arla stands too. Jack slides his notebook into his chest pocket, picks up his mug and drinks down the last of the tea.

'Jordy, set the Xbox up. Let's play with that.' I point at the machine.

I thought it might be a distraction but every game will remind us of Eli's laughter. He teased me over my feeble attempts to compete.

As we play, with the sound turned low, I hear their feet on the creaky old floorboards in Eli's room above, and the sounds of Eli's wardrobe, drawers and cupboards opening and closing. I suppose I should be up there watching them – but I don't have the courage to watch his room being violated by strangers.

When I hear them on the stairs, Wendy leads the way. I get up from my cross-legged position on the floor.

'I'll be outside in the car,' Jack, the last to come downstairs, says. 'If you fancy a game of FIFA, Jordan, give me a shout.' He winks.

Jack opens the front door, not waiting for me to step forward.

Wendy and Arla hover in the living room as though they are uncertain about what to say.

'Goodbye,' I prompt.

'We are very sorry for your loss, Jennifer,' Wendy declares. 'We will find out what happened.'

'Thank you.'

'We'll keep in touch,' Arla adds. 'Goodbye. Goodbye Jordan.' She waves a hand, stepping outside behind Wendy as Jordan looks up from the game.

I close the door, and for a moment my palm lays on the wood as my other hand clings on to the lock, and I let a few tears run free before I swallow them back and return to Jordan.

CHAPTER FOUR

Outside, a police car occupied by a single officer defends my garden gate. Further along the road, on the opposite side, are three cars that are not normally there. They could belong to tourists who are dining in the pubs in the village, or the press. I think they belong to members of the press. Before Jack went home to his wife for the night, he'd stood at the window and said the same.

'Here they are, the vultures come to circle.'

'Who?'

'The press and the nosy parkers. Some of the reporters and photographers are shameless, but worse than them are the glory hunters social media has created. They love to solve a crime and share their theories with the world. It's a money spinner for likes and followers. They think they're Poirot. But don't worry, we'll do our best to keep them all away from you.'

I slide the bedroom curtains across the window with a swish, shutting out the world, turn my back on it and look at Jordan. His head rests on Eli's Chelsea Football Club pillowcase.

We're sharing Eli's narrow single bed tonight, lying among things which smell of him and remind us of him. Jordan is pressed up against the wall. I didn't think Jordan would sleep. I've kept him up until almost midnight. His eyes closed within minutes of lying down. But in the mix of streetlight and moonlight leaking through the thin material of the off-the-shelf supermarket curtains Eli had chosen the day we moved here, I see the tracks of tears on his cheeks.

I lift the duvet, slide into the bed beside him and wrap myself up in the scent of both my boys.

Sleep is a million miles away for me.

The outlines of Eli's belongings piled haphazardly on shelves and strewn across the floor of the small oblong room remind me of the police searching up here. They were looking for evidence they said – for the drugs I know he would never take or the gang I know he wasn't in. My relationship with Eli is tough at times, but I know him.

No. I don't.

I don't know why he was at the far end of the lake that night or who he was with.

I slide the bedroom curtains back with a swish, letting the sunlight in. Two police cars are outside. The driver's door of one of them opens. Jack climbs out, looking up at the bedroom window. He is not wearing a uniform today, instead, he's wearing a white T-shirt and black cotton jeans. I step back, I'm in my nightgown. He walks towards the front gate. I retreat to my bedroom, pull on a pair of black leggings, slide my arms into the straps of a bra and reach behind my back to secure the hooks.

Clunk.

The door knocker strikes on the front door.

I throw a T-shirt over my head, slip my arms into the loose sleeves as I walk downstairs and open the door.

'Hello.' I restrain my uncombed hair in a scrunchie as I speak, tying it up in a ponytail.

Upstairs the toilet flushes. He's woken Jordan.

'May I come in? I was waiting outside until I saw a sign of… you being up.' A shade of maroon, Merlot-red, spreads through Jack's dark skin as he avoids the word *'life'.* Any other day it would have been a careless throw-away phrase.

I swallow against the bitter lump in my throat. 'Sure.' I force the word out through lips that don't want to respond, then cough against my hand, fighting the tears which try to steal the rest of my sentence. 'I was awake. I haven't slept.'

I turn away and cross the living room to the kitchen, wiping tears off my cheeks with the side of my hand.

The letter box rattles as the front door hits the frame with a thump that resonates through my heart. Jack had closed the door with unnecessary force. Eli closes it hard like that too.

How had it felt for Eli? Had he hit his head fighting for his life, trapped underwater, unable to breathe?

I look at the stairs, as though I'll see him walk down.

He won't ever walk downstairs in his boxers, yawning, stretching and smelling of teenage sweat. Hormones. He'll never say, *'Shut up, Mum,'* as he would have done if he'd heard me describe him like that.

'Do you want a drink?' I offer from the kitchen, without looking back.

'I can make it. Jordan showed me where everything is. You'll have to put up with me around here for a little while, I might as well help.'

Autopilot clicks on and I open a cupboard reaching for mugs. He's beside me, leaning past me, the hem of the sleeve of his white T-shirt pulling taut across his bicep. He takes the first mug out of my hand. 'Sit down, Jennifer. I'll make the tea and when we have a drink, I'll talk through what will happen today.'

I turn sharply, almost knocking the mug out of his hand.

'Does anything need to happen?' I can't face things. 'And why are you not in uniform today? Are you a detective too?'

'No. My day job is in serious crime. We don't, fortunately, face many murder investigations, so specialist family liaison officers are rarely needed. I am an officer, not a detective, but I am trained to observe and ask the right questions as much as I am here to support you. The plain clothes today are because I'll be here all day so I don't need a uniform and it's customary to make people feel more at ease and not wear a uniform in these situations.

'But, what you need to know, is time is important. Things need to progress today. We have to build a picture of that day. Of his life. I doubt very much he was at the lakeside alone, at the very least someone left him in the lake and didn't call for help. There'll be a nugget of information in there somewhere to track who was involved and why. We'll find out if there is a worse scenario to consider when they report on the post-mortem.'

My mouth opens, but I don't know what to say.

He puts the mugs down on the work surface and reaches for the teabag container on the side.

'I'll go upstairs and check on Jordan.'

He nods without comment.

I'm running, figuratively. There's no escape.

Jordan steps out of the bathroom as I reach the top of the stairs, wearing the royal-blue pyjamas with little rockets on the trousers that he slept in.

'Shall I do your hair?' I offer. He can manage his own hair, but I want to do it.

'Yeah.'

Even Eli lets me massage conditioner into his hair sometimes, when his curls are in chaos.

'Get dressed first. Jack, the policeman, is downstairs.'

'Am I going to school?'

'Do you want to?' I don't want him to.

He shakes his head.

I touch his shoulder, but the offer of comfort is rejected. He walks on to his room. My fingers slide free.

I return to Eli's room alone and sit on the edge of his bed, to wait while Jordan dresses.

In daylight, the clutter of clothes spread across the carpet irritates me. Instinctively I want to reach out and pick things up. I hate muddle. We have so many arguments about his untidy habits.

Jordan is the opposite. He's a neat freak like me. Everything in his little room has its place. It's used and put back exactly where it came from.

If Eli stood in this room now, I'd be shouting. *'Eli, if you want clean clothes you have to wash them!'* His black school trousers are still on the floor, they never made it to the washing machine on Sunday.

At some point, I'll have to pick up all the clothes he'll never wear again and sort them out, for my mental health I can't leave this mess as it is. I can't do it now, though.

I glance at Eli's alarm clock. I haven't rung the schools to say we won't be in, but no one will expect us to arrive today.

'Mum, I'm ready for you!' Jordan shouts.

We stand in front of the bathroom sink, watching our reflections in the mirror above it. I massage water and then the product through his hair. André cared for Eli's hair from when he was a year old. He taught me how to do it when Eli was three. The memory has the strength of something that happened yesterday. Our mother and son bond grew in those moments, sprouting from a little seed of hope. Later, Nanna Fay taught me how to braid Eli's hair. When he was six, he was really into braids. We spent hours together at the dining table on Sunday afternoons as I unravelled and re-braided growing hair. He loved that, he was impressed by how quickly I learned to plait. He still says he loves the sensation of the tugs on his scalp. That's why he lets me massage the product into his hair sometimes, now he styles his hair in longer natural curls.

My gaze clashes with Jordan's in the mirror, as though we have the same memories in that moment.

I pick up the hair twist sponge from the bathroom shelf and rub it over Jordan's jet-black hair in small circles, shaping the short curls.

'You look perfect.' I smile, unable to look at him anymore as I lay the sponge back on the bathroom shelf. 'You don't have to come downstairs unless you want to.'

'I'm hungry.'

I hadn't thought about breakfast. My stomach is full of emotional turmoil.

Jack is seated in a dining chair, his eyes focused on a smartphone. Two full mugs of tea stand on a dinner mat beside him.

He looks up as we descend, his gaze skips past me and reaches to Jordan behind me. 'What would you like for breakfast, buddy?' Jack rises, sliding his phone into his back pocket.

I step off the bottom stair as Jordan's shoulders lift and drop, shrugging an 'I don't know' answer.

'I'll make you some toast. I saw marmalade in the fridge. Are you a fan of marmalade, Jordan?'

'Can I play with the Xbox, Mum?'

'Yes.' It's not a day for rules on the Xbox hours. 'I'll pour you a glass of milk.'

Jack and I walk through the arch into the kitchen side by side.

'You'll need to make a statement to the press this morning,' he whispers as I reach up to the cupboard for a glass.

He's not going to give me any time to grieve for my son today.

Clunk.

The door knocker thumps on the iron plate of the cottage door. Every muscle in my body spasms in surprise and I nearly drop the glass.

Jordan, Jack and I look at the door in the same moment, as if we'll see through the wood to whoever is standing on the other side.

'Sorry, the officer outside is meant to be managing visitors,' Jack moves first. 'I'll answer it.'

I let him take over, putting down the glass and turning to the fridge.

He opens the front door as I lift out the carton of milk, hiding myself behind the kitchen wall.

'Hello. Can I speak to Jen? Is she home?'

The voice belongs to Nick, the ferryman. I didn't know he knew where I live. But there's a stupid thought. The police cars tell everyone where I live.

'It's okay,' I tell Jack, walking out from the kitchen, the carton of milk left on the work surface. 'He can come in.'

Jack steps back, opening the door wider.

'Jordy, would you pour the milk into the glass.'

'I'll get you some milk, Jordan, you carry on with your game,' Jack declares.

Nick hasn't stepped in. He's on the threshold, PJ sitting beside his boot. His lips attempt a smile as he raises a hand holding a bouquet of chrysanthemums I recognise as one of the bunches sold by the village Co-op.

I cross the room, passing Jack, trading places.

Nick's crude attempt at a smile falls away. It is not a smiling moment. His skin colour lifts to a warm cherry-red that flushes to the roots of his sandy-blond curls. There's no hint of auburn in his hair this morning. There's no sunlight to pick the colour out here. The sun rises on the other side of the cottage, the front garden is in shade.

'I… I'm sorry this happened. I have no idea what to say to you beyond that. But I can't say nothing. I… People are putting flowers down by the shore, but I think the flowers are better given to you. If you need anything, anyone to talk to, or to cry to even, give me a call.'

I nod, a croaky sound that attempts to say thank you leaving my throat. My hand accepts the flowers. They're a blurry jumble of white, yellow and orange through the perspective of tears, like a Monet painting.

'It's okay, you don't have to answer,' he fills my silence. 'I just want you to know I'm here if you need a friend. I know you're on your own, that's all. This…' He pauses, searching for the right words when there are no words. '… shouldn't have happened. I'm sorry,' he says again.

I nod, wiping wet cheeks with my free hand, not attempting to speak this time.

When he turns away, so does the dog.

My gaze catches on the cluster of journalists and photographers on the other side of the road. They're taking pictures, their lenses aimed at us.

I shut the door.

A metallic rattle announces that the slices of bread have popped up in the toaster. I head back to the kitchen. Jordan is engrossed in *Sonic the Hedgehog,* the glass of milk near him on a mat on the coffee table.

'You know the ferryman…' Jack states, his tone making it sound like a question, as he lifts out the toast.

'I use the ferry every day, to cross to Bowick for work.' I slot the rubber plug into the sink and run the cold water, resting the stems of the bouquet of flowers in there.

Jack butters the first round of toast and drops two more slices of bread into the toaster. Then, he reaches into a front pocket of his jeans and withdraws his little black notebook. He slides a short pencil out from the side of it.

'What are you writing?'

'I'll record who calls and what's said.' His voice is kept low, for

Jordan's sake. 'If Eli was killed, the killer is often someone the victim knows.'

'Eli didn't know Nick. He only used the ferry once.'

'Even if the killer didn't know the victim beforehand, sometimes they show up and offer to help because… Well just because they can. I'll keep a record.'

The notebook is slotted back into his pocket, and he twists the lid off the jar of marmalade.

I leave Jack to do whatever he wants, sit at the table, drink the now lukewarm tea, and watch *Sonic* racing on the TV screen, not really seeing.

Clunk.

Another knock strikes on the door at the same time Jack places two plates of toast on the table. The smells of melted butter and sweet orange marmalade rise.

Jordan jumps up, rushing to respond, opening the door wide as though it's a delivery man with a package – as though it's any other day.

'Mum. It's the woman from the ice-cream parlour.' Jordan declares, looking in my direction. Sharon can see in. She sees me. I can't avoid this conversation.

I get up.

'I brought you a tub of your favourite ice cream to put in the freezer, Jordan,' she holds the square container out for him to take, 'and your next cone in the parlour is my gift.'

'Thank you,' he accepts the tub she's holding out.

A bunch of flowers fills her other hand. Red roses.

Her eyes leave Jordan, glance at Jack and then look at me as I walk towards the door.

Jordan passes me, carrying the ice cream in both hands.

She holds out the brown-paper-wrapped bouquet. I accept the roses, a flush of warmth rushing up my neck. I don't want her here. I don't want to remember what I was doing when Eli died.

'That's kind of you, thank you. I'm sorry, though, we're very busy. I can't talk at the moment.'

'Of course. I only wanted to tell you I'm thinking about you and I'm so sorry. What happened... is... terrible. I... I... Can't even imagine...' Her eyes look into mine, searching for a response.

My hand reaches for the edge of the door, preparing to close it.

'Well, I'll say goodbye then. Maddie sends her sympathies too.'

A nod is the only response I am able to give her.

So now Maddie knows he's my son. All the children know Eli Pelle is Miss Easton's son. They know we ignored each other in school and Maddie knows if he saw her in the village streets, he'd walk a metre or two apart from me. He didn't hate me. He was bullied at school before we moved. He didn't want to risk that happening here.

Sharon turns and I close the door before she's even reached the gate.

Behind me, the freezer drawer closes with a crisp, frosty slither, the ice cream shut inside.

Jack is scribbling details in his little black book.

I walk into the kitchen and leave her flowers in the sink with Nick's.

Every muscle I have is tight with panic and pain. I can't eat the toast, my jaw won't function. Jordan eats a slice, though, and returns to *Sonic*.

I sit at the dining table, the heel of my foot tapping aimlessly on the floor, itching for something to do, while knowing if I tried I couldn't concentrate on anything.

Jack's phone rings.

'Excuse me,' he says in the moment before he answers. He opens the back door as he takes the call, 'Hello.' He walks out and pulls the door closed. But the windows are only a single pane, I can still hear him speaking to someone at the police station. He arranges a time for the detectives to return, and then asks, 'Have the kids at the school said anything important?'

They must be interviewing Aiden at the school. If Eli was with anyone, surely it was Aiden.

'And you've found no clues from the phone signals. I suppose the site is so close to Bowick there are a few thousand connections to the mast.'

'What about CCTV? Anything so far?'

Nothing he says gives me a clue to the answers to the questions.

When he ends the call and comes back in, I rise from the chair. 'Someone is interviewing his school friends...' I prompt.

'You heard. Yes, and officers are scanning phone data and CCTV footage from Lowerdale and Bowick.'

'Have they learned anything?'

His answer is a shake of the head.

Wendy and Arla knock on the door not long after midday. Jordan and I are eating bowls of baked beans and cocktail sausages with melted cheese. I forced myself to chew and swallow two mouthfuls, to persuade him to eat too. Those mouthfuls threaten to come back up as Jack opens the door.

Since Sharon's visit, two other villagers and Paula have knocked. Paula told me the school are planning a remembrance service. She said, *'The whole school is in shock,'* her voice trembling and tears shimmering in her eyes. She presented me with a large bouquet of flowers and repeated the offer Nick made, *'If you need someone to call...'*

The flowers are with Nick's and Sharon's, deserted in the sink.

A younger uniformed male officer, his skin a rich cocoa powder colour, walks into the room behind the detectives, crowding the small cottage.

'What's cocoa?' Eli asked the first time I used that analogy.

I smile, even now. *'Powdered pure chocolate.'*

'Hello, Jennifer. This is Samir,' Wendy provides the introduction. 'Samir will stay with Jordan while we talk.'

'Call me Sammy. Everyone calls me Sammy.'

No one usually calls me Jennifer, I introduce myself as Jen, but yesterday I had not been in the headspace to tell them and today I can't be bothered to correct her. What they call me makes no difference to anything.

'I saw you have a courtyard garden at the back,' Wendy continues. 'Could we talk outside?'

It won't be private. It may be surrounded by a six-foot red-brick wall, but it's overlooked on every side as our terraced row backs onto another terrace. There's enough space for us all to sit out there, though. It's a square concrete courtyard containing a single cast-iron table with three matching chairs. Sometimes we eat alfresco here, and I sit and drink wine in the evenings. Around the edges of the yard are raised flowerbeds, built up with more red brick to the right height for seating. The flowerbeds are planted with lavender.

Jack draws the short straw and ends up sitting amongst the lavender. The women join me in the cast-iron chairs at the table. Arla's notebook stays in her pocket. Jack's is withdrawn, and he slips the short pencil free from the side of it.

I lean on the tabletop, the cool iron pressing into my bare elbows as my hands clasp together. The post-mortem was carried out this morning. They know how he died. I'm sure that is what they are here to say.

Wendy takes a deep breath before she speaks. 'Lake water was found in Eli's lungs which means we know he tried to take breaths while under water. That is why he died.'

In my mind I see a scalpel cutting into his skin and the lake water leaking from his body.

'However,' she continues, looking straight into my eyes, 'he was also deliberately struck on the back of the head.'

There is no gentle leading into this.

'The cause of death has been listed as drowning, because we know he was breathing when he either fell into, was thrown into, or was left in the lake. But, the injuries mean we know someone caused his death.

'There are three separate wounds on the back of his head. It is clearly not an accident. Someone struck him from behind. The coroner believes premeditated action was taken to wound him certainly, and potentially to kill him. It may be manslaughter or murder depending on the intent of the perpetrator.'

'So, someone hit him and left him to drown.' I close my eyes and bite my lip hard for a moment, masking my emotional pain by inflicting physical pain on myself. A cold breeze sweeps through the garden in a whirlwind, lifting goosebumps on my forearms despite the warm day. My shoulders shake with a sudden shiver as I open my eyes and look directly at Wendy as though I'll find all the answers in her eyes. 'Why would anyone hurt him?'

'That's what we need to find out,' She answers.

'Did they… was he… touched in any way?' I need to know what he went through.

'There doesn't appear to be a sexual motive. Despite the body being naked there are no signs of rape or sexual abuse. However, the water may have washed away evidence. The coroner has taken swabs and used tape in key areas for analysis. The scientists will look for DNA, fibres and other situational evidence. These have not been examined yet.'

I close my eyes briefly, breathing through the pain in the tight muscles in my throat that want me to scream.

'Officers spoke with all the children he shared classes with in the school, not only those you named,' Wendy continues, ignoring my reaction. 'None of the children were with Jordan at Southend Bay. His closest friends say they separated from him earlier in the evening at Bowick.'

'What time did he die?'

'Late evening to early morning. The coroner has given us a two-hour window between 11 PM and 1 AM. His friends left him around 9 o'clock.'

How did I not know something was wrong? I should have sensed it. My fingertips rub at the pain throbbing in my temple. 'What happens next?'

'We'll reconstruct Eli's day, looking at his message history and social media, alongside the information his friends have told us and any images we find on CCTV and explore any avenues the investigation presents.'

'We want your statement to the press to jog the memories of strangers who may have seen something important,' Jack adds.

'Why did his friends leave him?' I challenge, anger roaring through me and resonating in my voice. 'Did they explain how they expected him to get home?' I wish I'd insisted he told me where he was going. I rub my temple. Why hadn't I? *Because he wasn't ten anymore!*

None of them answer the emotional questions my chaotic mind throws out.

'Can you tell us anything more about the day, Jennifer?' The tone of the question implies there's more I should be able to tell them. Wendy must think I've held something back.

I have, but my afternoon and evening of sex is irrelevant. 'No.'

'You haven't thought of anything else we should know?' She gives me a second chance to come clean.

The only person who might have told them would be Maddie and surely Sharon hasn't told her daughter.

My shoulders lift and drop. Does the movement look as forced as it feels? I hope not. 'No.'

'Officers in Oxford have spoken with Eli's father,' Arla changes the subject.

'Oh.' I can't imagine André's reaction. He hasn't seen Eli for over a year. Eli refused to see or speak to André. He would not accept his father's apology. I should have rung him myself last night. But equally, if he knew, I'm surprised he didn't call Jordan last night.

'He said he'll come here.'

'Did he?' He will be coming to see Jordan then, comfort doesn't reach through a phone. My trembling hand tucks escaped strands of hair behind my ear. I stand up, the iron chair legs scraping on the concrete, my ponytail swaying across my back. 'No doubt he'll call when he arrives. I need a glass of water. I presume you're finished.'

They all follow my lead and stand. Wendy smooths the creases in her suit trousers with a palm. Jack brushes lavender pollen off his black jeans.

I walk indoors ahead of them.

In the living room, Sammy is sitting crossed-legged on the floor beside Jordan, playing on the Xbox. His police hat is on top of Jordan's head.

'Your post came.' Sammy throws a glance towards the colourful array of advertising flyers on the doormat, his thumbs working hard on the controls.

'Where's the newspaper,' I ask, realising it didn't arrive this morning.

'It was intercepted by the officer outside,' Jack says from behind me. 'We thought you'd prefer to avoid the front page.'

'The front page…' I spin around and look at him. 'What's on the front page?'

Jack's eyes open wide, eyebrows lifting, communicating silently – the national newspaper's headline is about Eli.

'I'll decide what I do and do not see.' A tide of anger carries me on a current to the front door.

Click. Click. Click.

The photographers commence capturing my image the second the door is open wide enough.

From the vantage point of the front door at the top of the

short-stepped path, I see my paper on the front passenger seat of a police car. Read and discarded.

Click. Click. Click.

Mother of deceased teenager – the headline I imagine in tomorrow's paper screams. That is all these photographers see.

'Miss Easton!'

'Can you tell me…'

I ignore the voices calling out from the pack, descending the steps, as my eyes lock on the police officer climbing out of the car. Lucy.

'Jennifer! Can you tell me how does it feel to…'

'Miss Easton! Will you look this way a moment?'

No! The answer screams in my head as 'Can I have my paper please?' I hold out a hand, across the garden gate. I won't let anyone dictate my life. I will decide what I do and don't do, what I see and don't see.

Lucy turns back and leans into the car, reaching for it.

Eli's face is printed on the front. A picture taken – stolen – from his social media.

Tomorrow, I'll be on the front page, with my unbrushed hair restrained in an untidy ponytail. Wearing the casual clothes I would never normally be seen in outside.

'There you are.' The newspaper is placed in my open hand.

'Thank you.' I turn my back on the cluster of clicking cameras.

Sammy is standing at the door, he lets me pass, and closes it.

'Oh,' I exclaim, unfolding the paper. Most of the front page is dedicated to our story. Words and phrases jump out. *Troubled past. Broken home. No father. A history of problems at school.*

One brief suspension in his old school when he stood up to the bully!

Further on the article speculates about gangs and drugs, stereotyping my teenage son, judging him by his age and the colour of his skin. For every boy of any skin colour involved with gangs there are millions of boys who are not.

Those who are not, should be the stereotypical assumption!

I look at Wendy, raising the paper. 'Did they get this shit from you?'

'No one has spoken to the press, it's conjecture,' she answers.

'Mum,' Jordan looks up. 'You swore.'

'Sorry, darling.' My anger is snuffed out as fast as a candle's flame dies when the lit wick is starved of oxygen. 'I apologise,' I tell Wendy. 'But there are stupid lies in this article. This isn't right.'

'That's why we want to publish a statement from you,' Jack inserts. 'Then they'll have the truth.'

'We use the press, they can serve a purpose,' Arla interjects. 'When they raise the profile of the case it puts pressure on a guilty mind and jogs the memories of strangers who may have seen something unusual that could be crucial. Press coverage is not a bad thing if we work with them.'

CHAPTER FIVE

When I wake on the third morning after Eli's death, guilt layers itself like bricks building a wall on top of me. Crushing me. How could I sleep? How could I forget Eli for a single moment?

The last time I looked at the clock it was 3.23am, now it's 5.46.

I push the duvet aside and climb out of Eli's bed carefully, leaving Jordan asleep.

Today, I don't open the curtains, so no one outside will know I'm awake. I use the bathroom and dress in my room, pulling on stonewashed blue jeans and a cream T-shirt.

The living room and kitchen are cooler than yesterday, but it's earlier in the day.

I switch the kettle on.

The empty washing basket stands in front of the washing machine, whispering about the muddle upstairs. I carry it up to Eli's room and, working quietly to not wake Jordan, pick up all the dirty clothes from the floor. As I push the clothes Eli will never wear again into the washing machine, in my head I see myself fulfilling the whole of the weekly routine folding clean clothes and sliding them into his drawers. I can't cope with the thought that these clothes no longer need to be put away.

Will I ever be able to throw anything of his away? I can't imagine that.

His England football T-shirt is the last item in the basket. I lift it to my nose and smell the scent of him. I can't lose his smell completely. I'll keep this one thing. I put it on top of the washing machine, close the door with a foot and start a sportswear cycle.

There are no sounds upstairs, no signs that Jordan's awake.

I drink a cup of tea in the garden, leaving the back door wide open so I can hear Jordan if he needs me. The heels of my bare feet lift onto the cool iron chair and I clutch my knees to my chest, waiting for Jordan to wake.

'Mum…' When his voice drifts outside, searching for me, I look at my phone. 06.49.

We leave the curtains closed at the front of the cottage, drink orange juice, eat cornflakes and race each other on the Sonic game until just after eight. Then I chase him upstairs to dress.

Jack will be outside, and we can't pretend to be asleep all day.

When I draw back the curtains and let in the day, Jack is standing with his hand resting on the roof of the nearest police car, dressed in plain clothes again, speaking to the officer in the driver's seat. He must know I left the curtains closed to keep him out.

Further along the street, the cluster of photographers and reporters has doubled in size. I step away from the window as Jack raises a hand, acknowledging me.

He walks to the garden gate. It creaks on its rusty hinges as I open the front door. I keep back, avoiding being seen by the cameras.

'How are you both? I've got your paper.'

I take the paper. He shuts the door.

As I suspected, today my picture, *the mother who doesn't take care of her appearance or her son,* is beside a different social media image of Eli. Anyone who knows me will see the distress I'm in. I don't go out without make-up. I'm a perfectionist when it comes to appearances. I'll put make-up on today.

Aspects of the statement I agreed with the police are in italics at the heart of the article. I drop the newspaper on the coffee table and look at Jack.

'What happens today?'

'We'll be patient and take things as they come. I think Wendy has some news, she said she'll drop by this morning.'

'I don't want to stay here. I need to get out of the cottage for a while.' It's choking me. Eli is everywhere and nowhere, and I don't know what to do. 'Can you help us go out before Wendy arrives? How do we escape the press? Will they follow us?'

'Probably. We can plan some sort of decoy to try to keep them away, though. Where do you want to go?'

'To the lake. To this side of the lake.'

'The officer outside and I will come up with a plan.' He nods. 'And 'I'll come with you.'

'Jordan is dressing. When he's ready can we go? I'll run up and put some make-up on.'

'Okay, I'll organise it now.'

Quarter of an hour later Jack walks out of the cottage ahead of Jordan and me, trying to ruin any pictures by getting in the way. A flurry of clicks and shouts fills the air.

I open my umbrella, on a bright clear-sky day and hold it at an angle to protect Jordan, who walks between us. He's wearing jeans and a T-shirt, it's obvious we're not walking to the school. I hope, though, where we are going is not obvious.

We cross the road, heading for the alley that leads to the tourist car park.

We want the reporters and their photographers to believe we're heading to a car. Even if they do assume that, the hullabaloo follows us. A pride of press on the prowl.

Click. Click. Click.

'Miss Easton!'

'Jennifer!'

'How do you feel?'

'Do you have any news about Eli?'

The front police car engine roars into life as we enter the alley. Sammy is driving. He rolls the car forward and angles it so it blocks the narrow road, the movement saying; *don't follow them.*

As soon as we reach the safety of the alley, the open umbrella falls from my hand and tumbles across the tarmac. Jack can collect it later. 'Come on.' I catch hold of Jordan's hand and pull him into a run, passing Jack. Then almost immediately stop.

A bleached-blonde-haired woman steps out holding a mobile phone in my face. Beyond her a dark-haired dark-skinned woman aims her camera lens at Jordan and me.

Click.

I squeeze the warm hand clasping mine.

'You need permission for that.' Jack is right behind us.

Instinctively I let go of Jordan, reach out and snatch the camera from the dark-haired woman's hand.

'You can't destroy my equipment!' she yells.

'Tell the police.' I flip the camera around, leaving her to face the irony of Jack watching everything.

'I'll sue you.'

'Carry on.'

'I am a police officer.' Jack pulls his wallet from his back pocket, flips it open and flashes a metal badge. 'Turn your phone off and pass it to me,' Jack tells the blonde as the wallet slides back into his pocket. He walks around me, his hand outstretched, as I extract the memory card from the camera.

'You can't take the card,' the photographer is adamant. 'You can't let her take the card,' she tells Jack.

'Write about it to my superior officer,' he answers. 'Now pass your phone over,' he says to the other woman. 'I am going to delete that video.' His palm is stretched out flat and insistently held forward.

'Run, Jordy.' I toss the camera to the photographer. She catches it awkwardly as Jordan and I dodge around her, the memory card trapped in my fist.

'Miss Easton has already made a statement. She's said all she wants to say,' Jack tells them as Jordan and I flee the scene.

This car park is three times the size of a normal village car park, to accommodate camper vans and coaches. At this hour, it's not busy. We run across the middle, as the crow flies. The hardy, hobby-walkers arrive early – they park in the streets and they're on top of the fells by now. The daytime wanderers are eating their full-English breakfasts, reading their papers and discussing where they fancy going in this fine weather.

When we near the edge of the car park, facing the main road, the soles of Jack's shoes strike the pavement behind us. He catches up as we cross the road.

'Will we be in trouble for taking the card and deleting the video?'

'I'll deny it ever happened.' He says, glancing towards me, and passes us a friendly smile as we turn onto the dusty gravel path that leads to the lake. Jordan smiles back.

Jordan needs reasons to smile. He's only a boy. He should not stop smiling and laughing.

As we near the lake, Jack slows, dropping further and further behind us. Allowing us some privacy.

'I want Eli to come back,' Jordan tells me as we leave the path and walk onto the expanse of gravel and pebbles around the dark stone of Lowerdale Jetty.

'So do I, darling.' A spasm, so firm it feels like cramp, grips around my heart.

I swing our joined hands, trying to break loose from the weight of the chains wrapped around us.

The beach-like bays around the jetties are crescents, about

two-dozen metres wide. At the weekends they're often busy, with locals bathing, paddleboarding or canoeing. Today, no one else is here.

The lake laps at the shingle, rising slightly and rolling back, as though it's breathing. Sighing. It sounds like a sigh too.

'Did you hear the police say Daddy will be here soon?'

'Why?' Jordan's eyes remain on the water.

Why now? Why did he not come before? That is his question.

'His heart will be breaking over Eli, and he wants to see you.'

'He wasn't talking to him.' Jordan's reply is blunt.

'I know. He'll be regretting that.'

He sighs just like the lake. 'Will I have to see her?'

'Probably.'

'She won't want to see me.'

'It might be different now. People change, Jordan.'

The expression in his sepia brown eyes implies he doesn't believe me.

Eli would have groaned if he heard me use that colourful word for a colour. He may have grown out of the game, but for me it's a habit that's hard to drop. I don't think I will ever drop the habit now or lose the memories of *our glorious game.*

'Can we skim stones?' The subject of André's girlfriend is quickly dropped.

'Let's. Maybe we can beat Eli's record.' Thirteen skips.

'You'll never do it,' he taunts, already searching for a good stone. 'But I might.'

We stand at the lake's edge, sifting through pebbles, searching out the smoothest and flattest. Then stretch back our arms. 'One. Two. Three,' I call. Angling my stone and spinning it as I throw. The stones kiss the surface of the water as we count the leaps and watch rings ripple out from where they touch.

'Yes,' Jordan pumps a fist when his stone skips eleven times.

The pebble drops beneath the water as the bow of Nick's

ferry peeps around the corner of the southern edge of Lowerdale Bay.

Details of the scenes I watched on Monday morning return to my mind's eye. I see the far end of the lake, even though it isn't actually visible.

The pressure, the tug of emotion in my chest, the heavy, dragging feeling I'd known when I saw the white clothed people carrying that bag pulls through my chest.

Eli's spirit is here. He's in pain. That's what I felt then, and I feel it now.

The ferry progresses around the corner, coming fully into view, steering towards the jetty. Passengers fill the open-air seats, soaking up the sunshine and the views.

Jordan and I stand still, watching. On an island occupied solely by the two of us. Everyone else's lives are the same today as they were yesterday. Ours…

I swallow back tears and whisper on my breath, into a gentle breeze that suddenly sweeps in from the lake. 'I will find who hurt you.'

'Can we watch the ferry dock?' Jordan asks, breaking into motion before I have had the chance to agree.

He runs, leaps onto the end of the stone jetty, ignoring the steps, and races along the metre-and-a-half wide structure.

'Be careful! You'll trip…' *and end up in the water*. I can't say the warning I would normally call. The words stick in my throat.

Nick raises a hand acknowledging us with a visual hello as I step up onto the jetty.

PJ calmly observes us from his position at the bow of the ferry.

I rest a hand on Jordan's shoulder as the side of the boat bumps against the grey stone. There's an impulse to climb aboard and never come back. As though leaving here might mean we can leave the heartbreak behind.

Jordan squats down. Nick hands him the rope to secure. 'Twice around, then I'll tie it off.'

My hand slides into the front pocket of my jeans and rediscovers the photographer's memory card.

As Jordan wraps the rope around the iron bollard, I drop the small piece of plastic and electronics into the water. It dodges slowly from side to side with the motion of the water, gradually sinking.

'Are you okay?' Nick asks. His gaze snags on me as he secures the knot, and his colour rises to a blush beneath his tan and his freckles.

I look towards Lowerdale. Jack is sitting near the entrance to the bay on a fallen tree trunk that was turned into a seat a long time ago with the use of a chain saw. He's watching us, as though he thinks we might climb onboard the boat.

'You have a bodyguard.' Nick pulls my gaze back to him. Behind him, his passengers form a queue. 'Is he a relative?'

'No. He's a police officer. Family liaison.' I answer quietly.

'PJ,' Jordan calls to the dog. He doesn't come.

'PJ,' I call in a light tone as Nick helps people disembark. The dog comes for his daily ear scratch, leaping the gap between the ferry and the jetty.

I squat on my haunches. 'Rub his neck, just like this, just behind his ear.' I show Jordan.

The dog lies with his back on the stone, his mouth open in an expression that resembles a smile. Jordan smiles back.

'How are you?' Nick asks in a low voice.

When I look, there are no passengers left aboard. 'Dreadful,' I whisper as I stand.

He breathes in and sighs out the breath as his hand rubs the back of his neck. 'Would you like me to pop round this evening? Do you want some company?'

'No. I couldn't carry a conversation.'

'I could just sit with you. If that's what you need?' His hand drops to his side.

'No. But thank you for offering. It's kind of you to think about me.'

'It's not really kind. It's nothing. Nothing will make what happened any better.' His gaze travels beyond me to Jordan. 'I'm going to have to go. Come on, PJ. I'm sorry, Jordan, there are passengers waiting at the Bowick Jetty.'

PJ rolls over quickly, rising, turning and jumping onto the boat.

Jordan releases and unravels the rope. He passes it into Nick's waiting hand.

'Thanks, lad.'

My hand rests on Jordan's shoulder as Nick steers the ferry away.

'Do we have to go home?' Jordan looks up at me, his eyes expressing the pain I feel too. At home, there is a gaping Eli-sized hole in our lives. At least outside the lack of him is not faced in a photograph, or a memory, or seen in something he owned, with every turn of our heads. At least here I can pretend he is waiting for us at home.

'No. Let's buy an ice cream and hide in the churchyard. Maybe Jack would like an ice cream too?'

'He's okay. I like him,' Jordan punctuates.

'He is.' If we must have a policeman in our house.

We use a roundabout route to reach the centre of the village – through the bottom of the tourist car park, skirting the edge of the village, entering the square on the opposite side.

Sharon honours her promise of free ice creams, her skin a hot-pink with embarrassment as she fills the first scoop — she, like Nick, awkwardly searching for the right thing to say. I don't think she expected us to come in today. She looks redder still when she asks Jack what he would like.

He pays for his cone of vanilla with strawberry sauce that

matches the colour of Sharon's skin. Then we leave her to greet the next customer and let her blood pressure recover from the unexpected appearance of a one-afternoon stand who became the mother of a murdered teenager that same day.

Jack hangs back again while Jordan and I sit on our normal bench in the churchyard. On the bench we think has the best view. On the bench where I told Jordan Eli was dead. It will always now be the bench where I said those words. We leave the churchyard on the path we used that day. It takes us through the close of modern bungalows, so we return to the cottage from the opposite end of the street to where the police have corralled the press.

They are talking among themselves, not looking out for us.

It takes a minute for them to notice us. In the same moment, I notice a man in the driver's seat of a parked car. The engine is off, but music gently sings out from open windows.

'Dad!' Jordan's hand slips free from mine and he runs.

André's head turns, looking into the rear-view mirror. The music stops. The windows slide up and the car door opens as Jordan hurtles towards the car.

'Dad!'

CHAPTER SIX

'Jordy-boy!' André drops onto one knee, soiling his dark-blue denim jeans on the dusty tarmac road. Fortunately, because he's behind his car, the photographers must miss the shot as Jordan runs full speed into his father's arms. The very personal moment of the pleasure and relief of their reunion is hidden by the car.

Jordan's arms surround André's neck and André's surround him as he rises, picking Jordan up as though he is still five years old.

Click. Click. Click.

The press capture their poignant shot.

Sammy climbs out of the police car. 'No pictures, please! Give these people some privacy!'

I lead the way to the cottage, key in hand. 'Come in. Quickly!' I call back as I open the garden gate.

My nervous heartbeat pulses all the way to my fingertips as I open the door.

Jack's hand hovers behind André, ushering him in.

André puts Jordan down, but Jordan reattaches himself. A limpet on André's side, his head pressing against André's chest.

Jack closes the door.

'Do you want something to drink?' I offer André.

'A coffee would be good.'

'I'll make the drinks,' Jack says, walking past me. 'You guys will want to talk. I'll let the station know you're here, Mr Pelle.'

'Jack is our family liaison officer,' I tell André.

'What happened?' André asks the question of me, his palm settling on Jordan's head. 'I've not been told any details.'

'The police don't know. Someone hit him repeatedly with something and he drowned.'

His Adam's apple shifts as he swallows, and his glistening tempered-chocolate-brown eyes look at me expecting me to give him answers.

There are no answers. No explanations. No reasons for this.

'I miss Eli,' Jordan says, drawing André's attention wholly back to him.

'I'm sure you do Jordy-boy, so do I.' André rubs his hand over Jordan's hair.

'Let's talk in the garden,' I suggest.

'You're going to have to release me so I can walk, Jordy.'

In the garden, Jordan climbs onto André's lap and André's arms surround Jordan's middle. On any other day I would think my son disloyal – today, I am only glad their bond is being repaired.

'How is Camille? Has she come with you?' I open.

'She's upset, but she didn't come. She needs to be in Oxford for work.'

Jordan rests his head against André's shoulder at the news that Camille is nowhere nearby. The wicked stepmother. Although she is not officially his stepmother, they aren't married.

'I can't believe he's gone,' André's voice loses its strength. 'Have you seen him?'

'Yes. I identified him.'

'I'm sorry you had to do that alone.'

I could be mean. I could choose to remain angry because he hurt Eli, and he didn't try hard enough to make amends. But I'm sure he regrets everything. He must be dying with guilt. I won't add to the weight of that. I know how it feels.

I blink several times, clearing tears from my eyes, and wipe them from my cheeks with the heel of my hand.

Tears mark his dark cheeks and drip from the strong line of his jaw onto Jordan's hair. He sniffs and wipes the tears away with his wrist.

'I wish we hadn't fallen out.'

'He'd never have said it aloud, but Eli missed you,' I tell him.

If André had been here with us would Eli have been out in the bay that night? If I had not left André, Eli would never have been here in Lowerdale.

If... If... If... There are a hundred ifs that would put Eli in a different place at that time.

At least I don't have to regret putting another person before my children—

The thought stalls. Losing steam. Because that is why Eli and I argued too. He thought I'd done that too.

He loved me, though. Despite his poor opinion of me. I know he loved me, he'd just hit that teenage point in life when boys don't like to say it.

'You're the lesser of the crap mothers,' he'd told me once in an argument. I don't think he meant it. I hope he didn't mean it.

'I messaged him a few times, you know,' André says. 'He didn't reply.'

I could say, *what did you expect after you shoved your fourteen-year-old son up against a wall just for speaking back to Camille*. I don't. Now is not the time for grudges. 'I know.'

André has a temper. That day is the only time I've known him to be remotely violent, though. It was the day of his brother's funeral. Mylan had stepped out in front of a car after a massive week-long binge of drinking, and that was how André's alcoholic brother died. André helped Mylan break free from his addictions twice, but some people don't want to be saved. His internal organs were already beginning to fail him, he would have died young one way or another. But I know how much it hurt André to lose Mylan, even though Mylan brought it on himself.

André's outburst that day terrified both boys, though. They never went back to his house. He didn't put enough effort into convincing them it would never happen again. Eli gave up on the relationship in the end and so did André. Maybe he thought one day Eli would give in and contact him.

His hand strokes Jordan's hair then rests on his shoulder. 'It feels good to have you in my arms, buddy.'

'Can we play football, Dad? There's a park up the road. I'm on the team here.'

'Later. Your Mum and I need to talk first. But I'm staying for a while, we'll play.'

'How does Camille feel about you staying?'

'She feels how she feels. Eli's been murdered.'

'Murdered...' Jordan sits upright and looks at me. I don't think anyone has used that word around him yet, and if he has overheard things he clearly has not added the twos together in his mind and reached the possibility of four.

'They don't know what happened yet, Jordan. It may have been deliberate.'

'Someone killed him?'

'Yes.'

Jordan's eyes gleam, tears in full flood. I reach out and hold his hand. He slides off his father's lap and comes to sit on mine. It's something he hasn't done for years. His long legs nearly reach the floor, and his damp cheek presses against mine.

A tap hits the glass in the upper half of the open back door. Jack. 'The DI is here. Do you want your drinks outside?'

'Yes please.'

'Are they outside?' Wendy's assertive tone erupts from the kitchen, smashing apart the solace of the quiet garden.

'What is the copper, Jordy-boy?' André leans around the table and taps Jordan's knee, distracting him from the tears. '... a waiter, serving us cups of coffee?' He smiles for Jordan's sake, trying to make him laugh.

'Hush.' I press a finger against my lips. 'Jack's being kind.'

'Hello, Mr Pelle.' I look over my shoulder as Wendy joins us. She has a laptop tucked under one arm. 'Jennifer.'

André's eyebrows lift. He knows I hate it when people call me Jennifer.

'This is Detective Inspector Wendy Carter, André,' I complete the introduction.

He stands up to his full overbearing height and holds out his right hand. 'Hello.'

'Hello.' She shakes his hand, as if this is some sort of business meeting. 'May Jack and I join you out here? There's no Arla today.'

'Okay,' I agree.

Jack walks out with a mug in each hand. He puts one down in front of André and one in front of me.

'I have some news,' Wendy says, taking the third chair at the table as Jack goes back indoors.

Instinctively I rock Jordan in my arms as I used to when he was small.

He pulls away, breaking free and sliding off my lap. 'Can I play in Eli's room?'

'Yes.'

André's gaze follows Jordan as he walks inside, his expression declaring he notices how much Jordan's grown. Physically Eli had become a man since André last saw him.

Wendy opens the laptop as Jack puts a mug down in front of her. He sits on the brick wall, releasing the sweet perfume from the lavender plants either side of him, leans down to put his mug on the floor and then reaches into his pocket for his notebook and pencil.

'An officer found CCTV footage of who we think is Eli.' She pushes the laptop into the middle of the table, so André and I can see the screen, and taps the touchpad to play the paused footage.

'These boys...' Wendy points at four figures who walk into view. They are various shades of grey in the black and white film. '... walked into Bowick from the lakeshore at 18.08. Is this Eli?' She points at one of the boys.

All I see is the back of his head and his shoulders, but I know his head and shoulders. He walks further into view. I know the way he walks. I nod agreement.

'Do you know what he was wearing when he left home?'

'No. I was in the kitchen when he left, I didn't look. But that is him.'

She touches the laptop, pausing the video and leans back in the chair. 'Jennifer, and if I may call you André...'

He nods, agreeing.

'There is something I have not yet mentioned; we always hold some information back. It helps when we are interviewing a suspect if the suspect doesn't know everything we know. Otherwise, they have time to prepare false reasons for evidence. As I've said, there appears to be no sexual motive for the attack on Eli, but...'

I swallow fighting a rush of tears, terrified of the words that might be coming next.

'As you know, he was naked when he drowned. A pile of folded clothes was left on the shore in the bay not far from the body. From this visual, it looks like he is wearing the clothing we found. We need to verify that the clothing is his so we can be certain of the meaning of any forensic evidence on the garments. I have photographs.'

'Do you think someone forced him to undress?'

'We don't yet know why he was naked.'

'Wait.' André points at the screen. 'Would you play the video from the beginning again?'

Eli walks like him, but I doubt André can see that. He rubs his jaw. Eli hadn't only grown taller, his shoulders are broader. The glimmer is back in André's eyes. His Adam's apple shifts as he swallows, trying to control his emotions.

'Do you know the other boys?' Wendy looks at me.

They all have sweatshirts on, two are wearing baseball caps and all I can see are the backs of their heads. But Aiden has longer, wavy hair. 'This is Aiden Whitehead. The others… I'm not sure. Maybe Jason Parker and John Wood. We haven't lived here for long. Aiden took Eli into his friendship group at school. I didn't know he saw anyone other than Aiden outside school.'

André looks at me. 'Why didn't you know who he was with? That is parenting boys rule number one.'

'Where were you?'

He breathes out quickly, restraining a reaction.

In the first place it is my fault André wasn't here. I can see he wants to say that. I broke up our happy family before Camille arrived on the scene. That is why Eli and I had a broken relationship too, because ultimately his father may have done something wrong, but Eli knew it would not have happened if I hadn't ended my relationship with his father.

'We have a lot more footage for officers to explore.' Wendy continues, disregarding our spat. 'Aiden said he saw Eli but didn't accompany him to Southend Bay. He claims Eli did not say he intended going anywhere other than home. Aiden chose to walk back, and Eli chose to call a taxi.'

'Can I see the clothes?' I ask.

She clicks on an icon at the bottom of the screen. The image opens. The grass-green hoody, his favourite, is discarded, in the way it would be on his bedroom floor, thrown on top of his bleached blue-denim jeans with the fraying holes in the knees. *'They look like a tramp's jeans,'* I said when he bought them. I glimpse the scarlet red T-shirt at the bottom of the pile, that was bought a month ago. A sock is peeping from the white trainer it's been stuffed inside, bright blue and sunflower yellow. Those silly too short socks he wouldn't stop wearing. My mind's eye sees them stuffed into the trainers left under the coat hooks by the front door at home, just as he's left them in the picture on the screen.

'They are Eli's clothes,' I confirm. 'He undressed himself,' I say. 'He shoves his socks into his trainers like that.' They look as though he is coming back to collect them and slip them back onto his feet.

As my eyes lift from the laptop's screen, my gaze catches on André's and I see the guilt I feel reflected. We both played a part in why Eli was there on that day but blaming each other won't bring him back.

Then I notice Wendy watching us with an unnerving interest. I look at her.

'Where were you on the evening Eli went missing, Jennifer?'

'No one calls her Jennifer,' André declares. 'It's Jen.'

'Oh. I'm sorry, you should have said.'

'It's okay,' I answer, and swallow, because I can't, won't, say where I was. It's too late to admit the omission now. They'll think I was hiding something and it makes no difference. 'I went to the pub. To The Greyhound.'

'You went to the pub… While he was out there doing who knows what?' André gives me a hard look.

'He's fifteen, and a foot taller than me. If you ha…' I lower the tempo of my voice, reminding myself there is no point in arguing and that he's only lashing out at me to ease his own feelings of guilt. 'Telling him what to do never worked.'

'You should have rung me. I would have tried.'

Maybe he's right. Maybe if I'd tried to facilitate a reconciliation, things would be different. *If. If! IF!*

'Is there anyone who can confirm you were at The Greyhound?' Wendy asks.

'I... A few people. Gary who owns the pub. Nick Mason who runs the ferry.' And Sharon, who I definitely don't want them to talk to. If they can hold back nuggets of important information from us, I can withhold irrelevant embarrassing information from them. 'Why do you need to check?'

'Just tying up loose ends. We've been told Eli argued quite a bit with his mother, although he didn't tell people you were his mother, did he? The children said he treated you like any other teacher in classes.'

'I *was* his teacher in classes. And yes, we argued. He's fifteen. You know what kids are like. He pushes boundaries all the time. Testing me and hating me for saying no. I wish I had said no more often. I wish I'd said don't go out that day. He didn't like moving here and leaving his friends. Contrary to what you were told, he liked his last school. He was bullied for a period of time and that came to a climax in a fist fight, which is why he was suspended, briefly. He wasn't taking a chance on becoming known as the supply teacher's son here because he did not want to stand out. But we love each other.' If I say it enough times I will convince myself that is true. *He loved me. He did love me.*

She nods, but her expression doesn't say she believes me. It's impassive.

'Am I a suspect?'

'At the current time, everyone is a suspect,' she answers cryptically and then moves the conversation on. 'Why would someone hit him?'

'I...' I'm not sure what to say, my innards have been scooped out like a Halloween pumpkin.

'We don't have any idea of a motive yet?' Jack says from his position balanced on the wall of the flowerbed. The lavender heads around him tremble, releasing their sweet perfume every time he writes something in his little book.

'Eli didn't fight with people.' André's announces. 'He could be impatient, but he had a cool temper. It took a lot to kick him off, and even then, he may have shouted but he was never usually physical. Apart from that one time, I've never known him hit out.'

Wendy is still looking at me not André, as though she is studying me, looking for something specific.

'Please tell me you don't think I hit my son?'

'Maybe it wasn't deliberate. Maybe it was an accident in an argument.'

'I would never hit my sons, no matter how frustrated I am!' *Is she serious?*

She swallows and smiles, ignoring my anger. She'd be a great poker player. 'You did argue the morning before he died, though, didn't you?'

'We argued most days. As I've said, he was a typical teenager, brim-full of hormones.'

'What did you argue about that day?' Wendy pushes for more.

I breathe in. I've told her already. Is she testing me? 'He hadn't washed his school clothes. I have told you this.'

She doesn't respond.

'You should have rung me and told me you needed help,' André says quietly.

'What would you have done?' I snap. 'Thrown him up against a wall and shouted at him?'

A blush rises through his skin, a subtle rouge in his dark colouring. *'You look like a ripe blackberry, Dad.'* I hear Eli describe the tone of his father's blushes.

Wendy's attention turns to him. 'André, would you elaborate?'

'It was a one-off incident. I didn't hit him. I didn't hurt him. Apart from embarrassing both of us and giving him a shock. It caused a rift between us. He stopped speaking to me.'

'You scared both the boys so much they haven't been near your house for more than a year,' I finish.

André swallows, a muscle flickering in his cheek, near his

right ear. 'I'm not proud of it. I was grieving for my brother. It would never have happened again and I'm sorry I didn't convince him of that. But it has nothing to do with this.'

'Why did Aiden say he left Eli to come home alone?' I ask Wendy.

'I'm sorry, I can't tell you.'

'Why?'

'Because we are building up the picture of that day and we need to be sure different aspects of it are correctly remembered and not drawn from anyone else's evidence,' Jack responds. 'Even when people believe they are telling us the truth, if we tell one person what another said, it can change what they remember or encourage people to miss important details.'

'And as I said,' Wendy adds. 'When we identify a culprit there is a better chance of conviction if we have not told everyone everything we know. However, Aiden did say,' Wendy progresses. 'That he and Eli saw you that afternoon, before they walked over to Bowick.'

They are feeding me information in the style of a jumbled-up jigsaw puzzle, handing over snippets of knowledge that don't connect. Here, have a corner, now an un-connecting edge, now a centre piece…

'Where?'

'In the village square, near the ice-cream parlour. He said Eli wasn't happy after he saw you. He was in a grumpy mood for a while after that.'

'I didn't see them. I didn't see Eli.' My hand lifts and my fingers rub at the pain that throbs through my temple. 'I need to take some paracetamol,' I say, standing.

Abandoning them without saying more, I head off in search of paracetamol in the kitchen. I didn't know he saw me, but I know what he must have seen, and I know what he would have thought.

He left the village after that.

I pour a glass of water from the tap, pop the tablets out of the foil, swallow them and wash them down. Then I go back outside. I can't hide from this.

André is leaning forward, looking at the footage they have of Eli again.

'Did Aiden say whose idea it was to walk over to Bowick?' I ask. 'I presume they walked.' The nonchalance in my voice sounds as forced as it feels.

'It was Eli's,' Wendy confirms my guess.

My arms fold over my chest.

It was solely my fault he was there that night. My actions that afternoon directly led to his death.

CHAPTER SEVEN

At 5pm exactly, André closes the front door behind Jack and looks across the room to me, a hand sliding into one front pocket of his jeans. 'Shall I order something in for dinner, to eat with you here?' His hand withdraws his phone.

'We live in the middle of the Cumbrian countryside, Deliveroo don't cover the village.'

'Then I'll go somewhere and pick something up?' The phone returns to his pocket.

'There's a fish and chip shop up the road, Dad.' Jordan looks up from the TV screen.

'I'll walk along there and get something.'

'I'll come with you.' Jordan rises from his cross-legged position on the floor, the Xbox controller discarded on the TV stand.

'Jordan will be photographed by the press.'

'Put a hooded top on, Jordy. He'll keep the hood up, Jen. Any pictures won't be worth publishing.'

'What about you? They'll want pictures of you too. You'll have to wear one of Eli's tops.'

'Will it fit me?' He sounds surprised.

'Yes.'

His head shakes, his expression shifting to reflect thoughts of self-disgust. 'I didn't know him at all anymore. His tops would not have fit me the last time I saw him.'

I don't answer. It's true.

After they've left, I climb the stairs and carefully position myself in Eli's room, half hidden by the curtain. I watch them walk along the road. Hoods up. The press-pack follow, moving as one, trying to capture their next headline image.

It won't be a good picture, but to me their image is precious – tall André and shorter Jordan beside him.

Pain grasps at my heart, clutching tight and so hard I can't breathe for a moment, because he and Eli looked like this only a few years ago.

The police officer climbs out of the single car that remains as our guard, holding up a hand towards the camera lenses.

My eyes, my gaze, lifts to the rooftops, the chimneys, and reaches beyond them to the woodland climbing the slopes of Keln Rigg Mountain. I can't see the lake, but I know from the pattern of the trees where it is.

Eli told me he thought he'd seen an Osprey from his bedroom window the morning after we moved in. He probably did. There is a nest in the woods on the far side of the lake.

My head rests against the wall. I feel like bumping my head repeatedly to make myself suffer physically. Perhaps that pain could silence the agony inside.

Why? Why him? If only I... If. IF!

What did he think when he saw me in the village, kissing Sharon? I'm an idiot.

My phone chimes in my back pocket. I slip it out to look at the message.

Jack: *Is it okay to call?*

Yes, I type back.

A millisecond later the phone rings, vibrating with the

rhythm. My thumb brushes the answer icon. 'Hello. I thought you'd stopped working.'

'I'm a police officer, I never really stop working. It's a vocation not a job. I wanted to let you know we have Eli's phone. Someone tried to sell it in town.'

'In Bowick?'

'Yes. The man has no obvious connection to Eli. He said he found it in the wood around the south end of the lake. He didn't know it belonged to Eli. Forensics have it now and they are searching that area. They may have some more information tomorrow. We'll speak then.'

'Okay. Thank you for letting me know.'

'Finding evidence can take time, Jen, but the information is building.'

I nod as though he can see. 'Thanks.'

'Are you okay with Mr Pelle? I mean on your own together. There are no problems?'

'We're okay.'

'See you in the morning, then.'

'Thanks, Jack.'

'You're welcome. Goodnight.'

'I… Bye.' I can't answer goodnight. Nothing is good now.

He ends the call.

I have no idea what they'll find on his phone. I never checked to see if he watched porn. I didn't want to know. He was only fifteen, I didn't want to think of my son exploring sex at that age. But he was naked when he died, and his clothes had looked as though he'd chosen to undress. If he was swimming naked, I can't imagine him doing so alone.

I sit on Eli's bed, my thoughts stunned into silence, I don't know what to think or do. There is nothing I can do to bring him back.

When the front door knocker strikes, announcing Jordan's

and André's return, I race downstairs. I was supposed to be watching, to be ready to open the door.

We sit around the dining table to eat, the smell of salt and vinegar rising from full plates of gloriously golden battered cod and chips. They are tasteless.

'Where are you staying tonight?' I ask André, avoiding taking another mouthful.

'I have a room at The Greyhound Inn. In the village square. I'll ring Mum after dinner. Jordy would you like to speak to Nanna?' His empty fork is left to rest on the edge of the plate. He isn't eating either.

Jordan nods, his mouth full. He swallows. 'I haven't seen Nanna Fay for ages.'

'I know, and she'd love to see you. You'll see her soon.'

After dinner, I scrape nearly all the food André bought into the bin, while they speak to Fay on a video call in the garden. I load the dishwasher and set it running, playing the game of real life as I live in a parallel universe that doesn't contain Eli.

Afterwards, André and Jordan play on the Xbox. I stare at a magazine, trying to read but not reading a word.

There's a sudden sense of déjà vu, yet the boy I remember is Eli beside André.

At eight, it's still light, but I tell Jordan, 'You need to get ready for bed, sweetheart. You should have a bath.'

'Do I have to?' He looks over his shoulder, not moving from his position, his knee touching André's.

'Yes.'

'Don't worry, Jordy-boy, I'll hang around and tuck you into bed.'

He doesn't want to be tucked into bed anymore, he's not three—

'Thanks, Dad. Will you read to me?' Jordan rises from the floor.

I can't remember the last time Jordan wanted me to read to him.

'Switch your game off and put things away,' I say, before he can run off.

'Don't worry I'll do it,' André responds. 'You go and run your bath.'

I drift into a daydream as André tidies up. I never thought he would be here. I hope Eli sees him. I hope he knows we are all together, that we are missing him together.

André straightens up and turns. His gaze catching on mine. 'I should have pushed it more, made him listen to me,' he says. 'I wish I'd visited. I should have come up here. I could have given him some sense of reassurance it wouldn't happen again. Meeting away from my house might have helped.'

'It wasn't the house that was the problem, was it? It was you standing up for her over him and doing it so violently. But, anyway, we can't change the things that happened.'

He sits at the other end of the sofa, his long legs stretching out and filling up the floor space like Eli's used to.

'Mum offered to look after Jordy for a couple of weeks. He shouldn't have to be here with the police and press outside.'

I like Fay. She's kept in contact with the boys. They've spoken at least once a month since André and I separated, but… 'I can't let him go.'

'You've got to do what's right for Jordy and being stuck in here with the press out there, it's not right. He needs to get out. He saw a friend in the chip shop, he asked if he was going to play football after school tomorrow. He wants to.'

But how can life continue as normal. It isn't normal. It shouldn't be normal without Eli. If it becomes normal it will be as though I don't care. I rise, turning my back on André and the conversation. I can't deal with it.

'Would you like a beer? I have some in the fridge,' I offer.

'No thanks, and don't avoid the conversation. That was

always what was wrong with us, you avoiding telling me the truth.'

'I told you the truth,' I call back without a single pause in my step, as I fetch a bottle from the fridge for me.

'Eventually. When you stopped pretending you were someone you weren't.'

'I never pretended. I just… It doesn't matter. It's all history now.' I close the conversation and pop the cap off the bottle, using the bottle opener on the wall.

Upstairs the bathroom door hits the side of the bath as it often does when the boys open the door too quickly and footsteps jolt the old floorboards, creaking through the ceiling. Jordan's left the water running into the bath while he fetches his pyjamas.

I walk back into the living room.

André sits forward, his hands resting on his knees. 'I want to see Eli tomorrow. Say goodbye. The police said it's going to be weeks before they'll release the body. Will you come with me?' His eyes plead. 'I don't want to go on my own.'

'What about Jordan?'

'That's exactly why I think he should go to Mum. Or she could come here. There will be times we can't be with him. But tomorrow, we can take him to play football then go to the morgue.'

'I'm not sure. I wouldn't want to leave Jordan.' And I don't want to see Eli's body again.

'We'll make sure Jordan's okay, and that he's with a parent he trusts.'

'Eli isn't… I mean… He doesn't look like Eli anymore.'

André nods, understanding what I'm saying. But his expression doesn't change. 'Will you come with me? I have to go, Jen.'

'Okay.' I wouldn't want to see Eli's body on my own either.

Later, I watch André seated on Eli's bed beside Jordan reading a few chapters of Harry Potter as Jordan's head rests against his arm. I lean against the doorframe, with arms defensively folded. Not defending myself from André but from the battling emotions twisting through my insides. In my head I feel Eli behind me looking over my shoulder. Then I feel the weight of his chin resting there, as though he's about to say something sarcastic.

I turn as though I'll see him.

Of course, he isn't here.

Who killed you? Why? Why?!

CHAPTER EIGHT

Immediately After I close the door on André, I head upstairs to bed, exhausted by grief. Jordan is fast asleep in Eli's bed, so I don't disturb him. I leave him there and sleep in my own bed. But my bed feels odd, because nothing is the same as it was the last time I'd lain here, and it's my fault. Tears creep from the corners of my closed eyes and roll onto the pillowcase, dampening the soft cotton.

At 6.18am, Jordan pushes open the bedroom door. When he sees I'm awake he runs in and hurls himself on top of the bed beside me. 'I want to go to school today.'

'Do you?'

His head rests on my shoulder. 'There's a football match after school.'

I wrap my arms around him.

'Can I go?'

'If you want to go, you can.'

'Will you come and watch me play football after school, with Dad? It's a proper match. Against Westbrook Primary School.'

That explains the desire to be there – it's a team event, he wouldn't want to let the team down. 'Yes. I'm not going to work.'

'I just want a normal day, Mum. Can Dad walk to school with us?'

I stroke his shoulder. 'Yes, darling.'

We are dressed and almost ready to go when the door knocker wraps down with a hard strike just after 8am.

Wendy stands beside Jack. Her gaze immediately drops, taking in Jordan's grey trousers and navy T-shirt with the school logo on the chest.

'Jordan is going to school,' I say before she comments.

Wendy nods as she steps in.

'Have you had breakfast?' Jack asks closing the door behind them. Stirring up a crushing feeling in my chest as the room fills up and feels too small suddenly.

Jordan nods. He's busy putting what he needs into his book bag, and I'm about to start packing his lunch.

'I have questions to ask, but we'll talk when you come back,' Wendy says. 'Would you like a ride to school in a police car, Jordan?'

'No,' I answer quickly. 'He wants a normal day.' And I want you to go away. 'Would you wait outside, please?'

Wendy and Jack look doubtfully at me. But this is my home. My sons' home.

'Okay.' Wendy turns back to the door. 'We'll wait in the cars.'

I leave them to let themselves out and carry-on. 'What do you want in your lunch box, Jordan?'

André arrives ten minutes later, with perfect timing, at the precise moment we're ready to go. I messaged him to say Jordan was going to school. It will free us up to visit the morgue.

When Jordan opens the door, André says, 'You look smart.'

He isn't a bad father. It's my fault things changed, and he was under a lot of pressure the day he lost his temper.

Small droplets of water glimmer on the shoulders of his waist-length black coat. I look at the window. There are drops on the pane. It's raining. Never mind. It's an excuse to hold an umbrella and pull up our coat hoods as we walk.

We keep Jordan between us, ignoring the reporters and photographers who call out. Jack joins the uniformed police officer standing in front of the press, his posture saying, *leave this family alone*.

We use the direct route, it's not far. The school entrance is just beyond the other side of the square. The ice-cream parlour isn't open yet. The cafés are. People, mostly tourists, fill the inside tables and cluster under patio umbrellas outside. The smell of frying bacon drifts from open doors. My stomach rumbles, reminding me I'd forgotten to eat breakfast and barely ate any dinner.

Today's newspapers are in a Perspex display outside the Co-op. My newspaper didn't arrive this morning. I'll collect one on the way back.

In the final metres to the school's gate, parents' and children's eyes turn to look at us but no one speaks. The heat of a blush crawls up my neck as we enter the playground. Safe inside the boundaries of the school, within seconds Jordan's friends surround us, saying hello to the friend they must have been thinking a lot about.

Thank heavens primary school age children can cut through social fears and awkwardness with uninhibited ease.

I leave André outside with Jordan, walk on to the reception door and press the call button on the intercom.

'Hello.'

'Hi. This is Miss Easton, Jordan Pelle's mother, may I speak to the headteacher please?'

'Of course. I'll press the door release. Come in.'

The headteacher's eyebrows rise when she sees me walking into her office. I doubt she expects Jordan to attend today. I wouldn't. The expression is quickly mastered.

'Hello, Miss Easton. How are you? How is Jordan?'

I don't answer. No words feel appropriate. 'Jordan is attending school today.' I dive in to rush out everything I think I should say. 'Please be mindful of the reporters and photographers trying to gain access to him. Other than that, though, can you try to structure his day as normally as possible. That's what he'd like.'

'Of course. Of course.' She doesn't know what to say any more than I do.

'Thank you. Call me if there are any problems.'

In the same moment I leave the office, André walks out of Jordan's classroom. He's brought him inside before the other children.

'He wanted to show me his classroom,' he says as we walk along the corridor side by side. 'He seems okay. He's settled with his teacher.'

'Good.' My voice cracks, breaking with the weight of sadness in what is meant to be a happy word.

André reaches past me and presses the stainless-steel release button for the door. His hand touches my waist, encouraging me to exit first.

Outside, his arm lays around my shoulders. It's a familiar feeling, the weight of his arm hanging across my shoulders, like an old, well-worn coat I've found hidden in the attic and remembered that I loved. Even though it's been years since we last walked side by side like this the comfort of his familiarity is overwhelming. For a second it feels like an expression of love. It isn't that, but it is comfort I desperately need today.

I lean against him slightly as we walk away from the school, as I used to do. 'My newspaper didn't come this morning. I want to collect one.'

'Okay. Where from?'

'The Co-op.'

His arm slides off my shoulders when we approach the shop.

The images on the front pages of the papers in the Perspex newsstand are identical. Someone stole a picture of me and

Jordan at the lake. Perhaps the women Jack and I stood up to acquired their picture after all. I lift the Perspex lid and take out a paper, wondering if I'm torturing myself reading the fiction written between the facts the police have released.

'Why would you want to read that?' André asks, clearly thinking the same thing.

'Because I'd rather know what's being said about us. You know, if he was a girl there would be hundreds of people travelling miles to hold candlelight vigils at the lakeside and the papers would be raging about making the country a safer place not accusing him of taking drugs and joining gangs. Don't boys count as much? It should be safer for boys too. You should be safe to live your life no matter who you are or where you go.'

The automatic doors slide back, welcoming me into the normal world of the corner shop shelves crammed full of everyday items – nowhere feels normal now. It's like the doors have opened into another universe.

Then, I see Sharon. She hurries towards me looking at the purse she's sliding a bank card back into. She looks up, sees me and stops in front of me. In my way.

The sight of her solidifies me as effectively as the stare of Medusa.

'Hello.' She looks over my shoulder, her gaze lifting to André, her eyebrows lifting too, expressing a, *who is that,* thought.

'Sharon, this is Eli's and Jordan's father, André. André, this is Sharon.' A hot blush beads in sweat on my brow as I glance at him. 'She owns the ice-cream parlour. Her daughter, Maddie, is in Eli's classes.'

'Hello.' Sharon acknowledges André, a sly looking half-smile twisting her lips as she studies my ex.

André merely nods, a frown furrowing his brow in response to the excessive level of observation. I remember his mannerisms well enough to know he's taken an instant dislike to her.

'How is Maddie?' I ask, searching for something to shift past my embarrassment.

'Shocked. Like everyone. She isn't eating. It's brought back everything that happened in America.'

'What happened there?' André jumps in, his hands sliding into his coat pockets.

I don't know what happened in America either.

Sharon's head shakes. 'We normally don't talk about it. She was involved in a mass shooting in a school.'

I find myself stepping back, as though I've been struck. That is not what I expected to hear. 'Oh. I'm sorry. I didn't know.' My answer has the pitch of a robot. I have no energy for empathy today. I can't contemplate anyone else's suffering when I am drowning in my own.

'It was three years ago, it's nothing to concern you now. Let me know when you're free to meet up for a coffee. Eve can look after the parlour for an hour. Or I could come to you one evening when Jordan is in bed.'

'I'm not really up to it.'

'Okay. I'll see you soon anyway. Look after yourselves.'

André steps aside and she walks between us.

I remember the newspaper in my hand.

Peter is behind the tills. I lift my hand. 'My paper didn't come this morning. Can I take this one?'

'I didn't think you would want to read what the papers are saying today.' His grey-flecked eyebrows rise, punctuating the remark. He thinks I'm torturing myself too.

'I'll make that decision, thank you.'

I leave the shop, angry with him and the people who produce the papers.

'André, did you see the headline,' I turn the paper over to show him, walking on, my strides swift and long.

MOTHER DRINKS IN THE LOCAL PUB WHILE SON DIES.

I want to charge at the reporters like a raging bull.

André's fingers close around my arm. 'Stop.' As much as I remember how to read his unspoken thoughts, he can read mine too. 'Shouting at the press will not change this. We know that isn't how it went.'

New emotions sweep over my head, knocking me down from anger to grief. A two-metre-high storm wave drowning me in an instant. Then I'm in André's arms, my chest pressed against his, my cheek held to his. The muscular embrace so different from the softer embrace of a woman.

The body holding mine jolts repeatedly. He's crying too. His arms wrap right around me, holding me for his sake as well as mine.

We're standing in full view of The Greyhound's windows and the tourists eating breakfast at the outside tables of one of the cafés. I notice someone lifting their phone.

I break free, stepping back and wiping my eyes with the cuff of my coat sleeve.

'Do you want to buy a coffee before we go back and face the police?'

He coughs, clearing the tense grip of emotions from his throat, as his hand rubs his cheek. 'That sounds like a plan.'

My hand reaches for his.

I hoped André and I could return to being friends if he and Eli patched things up, but for it to happen like this… It is too late.

Wendy, Arla and Jack open the doors of an unmarked police car as we walk along the road towards the cottage, our hoods up even though it's no longer raining.

Click. Click. Click. The chorus follows us along the street.

'Miss Easton!'

'Jennifer! A word please?'

'Mr Pelle! Do you have anything to say?'

'How do you feel?'

'We are outside the house of…' A woman talks, not to us, but towards a large camera. The fluffy head of a microphone reaching out near her.

I break into a run for the last few paces, key in hand.

Jack's hand opens the iron gate for me to rush past and unlock the front door.

André ducks beneath the door's lintel behind me. Wendy, Arla and Jack follow.

'André wants to see Eli. Can you arrange that?' I ask as Jack closes the door.

'I'll do that for you. What time?'

'As soon as you're finished with us.'

'Can we sit at the table?' Wendy asks. The laptop is tucked under her arm.

'Yes.' I don't offer drinks. I don't feel hospitable.

'What did you find on Eli's phone?' I ask as I sit, dropping the newspaper on the table.

Wendy sits opposite me. The third chair, the chair Eli always used, is occupied by André.

Arla withdraws her notepad and pen from her trouser pocket and sits on the coffee table.

'That call made to you, Jennifer, Jen, at three thirty-two…'

Jack is standing behind Wendy holding his notebook too.

I look from one intent expression to another. Do they really think I did something?

'You said you didn't speak to him…' she continues. Her intonation implies I lied.

'I didn't talk to him. I didn't answer the call.'

'Why?'

'I was busy at the time.'

'Might he have been ringing to tell you he was walking to

Bowick? You didn't attempt to call him back? Didn't you care to know the whereabouts of your son?'

The newspaper headline screams from the table, shouting accusations at me. *Drunk mother! Dreadful mother! Guilty mother!*

I reach out and turn the paper over. 'Of course, I care. But do you have your phone to hand every second of the day? The battery ran out of charge. I missed the call. When I came home, I assumed he was in bed. And I assumed if the call was about anything important, he would have messaged me or called again. He didn't like me ringing him when he was with friends.'

'Is there anything you haven't told us?' Jack prods, pulling my gaze to him.

I deny the kick of guilt. *I turned the phone off. I was having sex.* 'Why? What else is on his phone?'

'The last message he sent was to a girl called Maddie Cox. It was sent just after he rang you.'

I breathe in. *What's coming?*

Wendy opens the laptop, clicks to bring up the screen, and navigates to something using the touchpad. Then the laptop is turned to face me. André leans across to look.

The image is the screen of a phone.

> My fucking mother does my head in. I can't stand her! It's embarrassing!

I look at Wendy, swallowing back a lump of emotions that gather in my throat then breathe deeply, fighting the desire to cry. 'I told you we argued that morning.'

Since they said he saw me, I've wondered what he thought. Now I know.

I bite the flesh inside my lower lip, swallowing hard again, continuing to battle the rush of emotions.

'You did.' She nods, poker-faced. Her expression waiting for me to say more.

Tears overflow, tracking down my cheeks. I wipe them off.

André's hand rests over mine. The action is unexpected but I welcome it.

'What are you doing?' his strong voice accuses Wendy. 'Jen didn't kill him. You should be out there looking for the bastard who did.'

My tear-dampened fingers close around André's hand.

Jack leans down, picks up the box of tissues from the coffee table and puts them beside me.

André releases my hand so I can pull out a tissue and blow my nose.

'I'm just trying to do my job and find the truth, André. Was he close friends with Maddie Cox, Jen?'

'I... I don't think so. He hasn't spoken about her at home. But they talk at school sometimes, they are in the same classes. Her mother said something to me earlier that seemed odd actually. She said Maddie is very upset. It surprised me because I didn't think they were particularly close.'

I have a vision, a memory of Maddie, of her raising her hand to share her homework in the class on Monday. Did she know I was the mother he'd messaged her about then? Her expression that morning did not say she knew about me and her mother. Did he tell her?

'We have some more CCTV footage to show you too.'

What now?

CHAPTER NINE

Wendy's fingertip slides over the touchpad and enlarges an image. It's a colour video.

'Eli and the boys he was with were drinking alcohol that night.' She clicks play.

'A man came forward yesterday evening,' she speaks as we watch the screen. 'Saying he bought them cans of cider in the supermarket. They gave him ten pounds extra for buying it. This footage is from the supermarket's cameras.'

Eli, and the same group of boys I saw on the footage yesterday, walk across a relatively empty car park. A heavy-looking white plastic carrier bag dangles from one of the boys' hands.

My fingertips rub my temple, as it pulses with a renewed surge of pain. I am a bad mother. I didn't know he had a girlfriend or that he'd started drinking. I was losing control before he died.

'Did his friends tell you they were drinking alcohol?' André asks, looking at Wendy for the answer. 'Was he drunk when they left him by the lake? How bad was he? Did they walk away from him when he was drunk and unable to look after himself? Did he drown because he was drunk?' His questions become an emotional flood. 'Or maybe some pervert attacked him and he couldn't fight back.'

Wendy raises a hand, palm outward, silencing him.

'How can you be sure it was not a drunken accident?' I throw in. 'Could he have hurt himself while he was in the water or fallen into the water after he hit his head. He'd undressed, he must have been swimming.'

Her hand lifts higher, like a referee calling for calm on a football pitch, silencing arguments over a foul. 'The autopsy identified alcohol in Eli's blood and stomach but it was not an excessive amount. The boys did say it was the first time they'd bought alcohol and they drank two cans each. The coroner said Eli was probably a little light-headed but it did not cause his death. He would not have been unsteady on his feet. Did he drink alcohol often at home?'

'Of course not.'

'Then he may have felt drunker than you and I would after two cans, but even so, he would have been fully conscious and physically able. The brand was not high in alcohol. He would have been tipsy, not falling over.

'Also, the level of force which caused at least two of the injuries on his head, and the angle of those injuries, means it is determinable as deliberate. We still have not found the item that hit him, though.'

'And if he was swimming with someone and an accident happened, why didn't they ring an ambulance, Jen?' André looks at me. 'I don't think these kids are telling the truth. It wasn't an accident.' His focus returns to Wendy. 'Can I see him now?'

She snaps the laptop shut. 'Yes. Jack will organise it. I have one more question to ask you both. The school have a memorial assembly tomorrow, will you attend with us?'

'I… At Bowick Academy?' I look at André. 'I teach there.'

'We want to watch the children's reaction,' Arla says. 'They're only together for a few more days before the end of term. We hope your presence will unearth some new truths.'

I'd forgotten, next week is the end of the summer term. 'Yes, I suppose so. Do I need to ring the school to tell them?'

'No, we'll let them know.'

'Would you like me to drive you to the morgue?' Jack offers.

'No,' André answers, rising from the chair. 'Your time would be better spent interviewing his friends. You can stand the officer outside the cottage down too. He doesn't need to sit there all day. I'll message when we're heading back.'

André takes it upon himself to hasten Wendy, Arla and Jack's departure, herding them out the door like a collie dog skilfully manoeuvring a flock of the local grey-and-white Herdwick sheep.

Only a few minutes after they've gone, while I pull the seatbelt across me and slot it into the holder for the passenger seat of his BMW, André says, 'You know Jack is playing the nice cop, don't you? Family liaison officers are there to find out what's going on behind the closed door as much as anything else. Family are always the first suspects. Don't treat him like a friend, he's not your friend. Be careful what you say. I reckon they are still holding some things back, which means they don't trust you yet. They aren't convinced you weren't involved.'

I remember when André drove a cheap fifth-hand Volvo. He bought that car when I was three-months pregnant with Eli to fit the car seat in. It scraped its way through the MOT. The road tax was worth as much as that car.

I reach down to my handbag and dig out some paracetamol, to treat the pounding in my head. I swallow them dry and rest my head back.

'Are you feeling ill?' he asks.

'Not really. It's stress and lack of sleep.'

We don't say any more to each other. The satellite navigation system's voice is the only thing that breaks through the classical music he plays *en route*.

When the car slows a good while later, I know he's turned into the hospital car park.

I open my eyes as he parks. He turns off the engine.

'He's not Eli. It's his body, but it doesn't look like he did in life,' I warn.

'You don't have to come in with me if you don't want to. But I… I need to go in and say goodbye.'

'I understand. I'll come for your sake.'

'Thank you.'

We wait for half an hour in a rectangular, colourless, emotionless room, with one window glazed with obscured glass. Then we are led into a room where Eli waits for us.

His body is on the medical gurney, covered with a white sheet. The member of staff peels the sheet back to reveal Eli's face.

Eli's blood-matted hair has been shaved, making the wound obvious today.

André's hand lifts and his fingertips touch Eli's cheek. 'He was shaving.'

'You shouldn't touch the body, sir.'

André's hand drops. 'He's not the boy I knew.'

I don't answer.

His shoulders jerk up and drop, a pained sound erupting from his throat. 'I'm sorry, buddy. I let you down. You should have always come first.'

We stand beside Eli's body for half an hour. As though our presence might make a difference to him. Tears run down our cheeks when we finally acknowledge we aren't changing anything, and leave. We won't come back. The human shell we leave behind is not Eli.

I pull a small pack of travel tissues out of my handbag,

withdraw one and hand it to André, then use one to wipe away my tears.

'I want to see where he died,' André says after blowing his nose. 'Have you been there?'

'Not since it happened.'

'Let's go there then.'

The car's Bluetooth system picks up a call on his phone as he drives towards Bowick. Camille's name appears on the screen in the dashboard.

His thumb touches the answer symbol on the steering wheel. 'Hi, honey. Are you okay?'

'Hi, babe,' she answers. 'I'm okay. How are you?'

Babe. I catch a laugh on my breath. Eli would have laughed with me later, if he'd heard the pet name. It doesn't suit André.

'I've seen him. It's so bad. Did you see what the papers said about Jen this morning? She's in the car with me by the way.'

'Oh, hi, Jen.'

'Hi, Camille.' I would rather have stayed silent.

'I'm so sorry. You must feel awful.'

To lose the son that you said was a nightmare, that you said, '*I can't stand kicking around my house, full of attitude and ego, talking back to me.*' André had lost his temper that day because she'd complained. For weeks, she'd been telling him he wasn't being tough enough, then he exploded.

'Yes,' is all I say aloud.

Raindrops suddenly tumble down on the clear glass of the windscreen. The wipers jump into life, swiping back and forth.

'Do you know when you're coming home?'

And that's selfish-Camille, putting herself above Jordan even in this situation.

André is happy with her, though.

'I don't know. It's good seeing Jordan and I want to know what's happening with the police. I need to be here right now.

We're on our way to look at the flowers people have put at the lakeshore. Then I promised Jordy I'd watch his football match, and there's a memorial service at Eli's school tomorrow.'

'So, will you be back for the weekend?'

There's no offer to come and stay here with him.

'No. I'll stay here with Jordan.'

I stare through the side window, watching the raindrops chase each other. The hours André is spending here is time borrowed from their life. He'll go back, and Jordan and I will be on our own with an Eli-sized hole in the middle of us.

We pass the Bowick town sign.

'I need to say goodbye, honey. I'll call you later. I need to concentrate on directions.'

'Okay. Goodbye, babe. Love you.'

'Love you too.'

'At the next roundabout take the second exit,' the satellite navigation says.

'That means straight over. Just stay on the main road through the town,' I direct as he ends the call. 'The turning is off the A road on the other side. There's a small parking area near the south end of the lake.'

The windscreen wipers swipe back and forth, the rubber screeching because the rain has slowed.

André turns the wipers and the satellite navigation off.

On the other side of Bowick, I lift a hand pointing out the turning. 'It's here.'

'How did Eli get out here?' The indicator ticks as he waits for a car to pass.

'He would have walked around the lakeshore from the town.'

The road to the car park is single track. Drystone walls and hedgerows embrace the car on either side.

'Did he often walk here?'

My shoulders shrug. The weight of guilt pressing down,

because… 'I don't know. Most of our conversations ended in rows these days. I avoided volatile subjects like where are you going, or where have you been. He thought I should trust him.'

'He was a teenage boy.' He glances my way for a second. 'You should have insisted.'

'There was no insisting, he was a teenage boy. He chose what he wanted to do, and I could never have stopped him unless he chose to stop himself.' Every word has a sharp edge, because he has no right to take the high ground – but also because I know what I should have done.

'Did anyone bully him at school?'

'I don't think so. He wanted to go in the morning. He always smiled when he walked into classes. I saw him talking and laughing with people in the playground.'

'And this girl, Maddie, what is she to him?'

I wish I didn't blush so easily. My mind churns over it all again, wondering what Eli saw that day. 'I don't know. How many fifteen-year-old boys talk to their mums about girls?'

'I wish we'd been talking.'

'I wish I'd answered the phone that day. Maybe he would have come home.' A sigh rolls out from my throat. A hundred wishes gather on my tongue. 'I wish I hadn't moved here; he'd never have been near the lake.' *I wish I hadn't left you*; he'd still have been talking to us both if I hadn't.

'Hindsight is always twenty-twenty vision,' he says as he turns into the car park.

I say car park, it's a lay-by. It's about one hundred metres long and it only fits a few cars parked in a row. It's not tarmacked either. It's a park-up spot for people who have come here to spend a day walking on Keln Rigg Mountain, not a place for tourists to arrive in droves to experience the view of the lake.

The rain has stopped entirely. There are clouds, but they're pale, and the air is warm. I look at my phone. No rain is due for a while. We leave our coats in the car.

His hands press into the pockets of his jeans as we walk. 'How far is it to the lakeshore?'

'Fifteen minutes ish.'

'And from Bowick? If he walked here?'

'Half an hour to forty minutes. Something like that. I've never walked it.'

The path to the lake hugs the contours of the foot of Keln Rigg Mountain. Emerald-green leaves clothe the branches above our heads, masking the sky, and on either side of the path, green carpets of ferns cover the ground beneath the trees.

Our shoes grind on the damp gravel, the rhythmic sound of our quick steps competing with the birds' songs.

'It is beautiful here. It's an impressive place,' André comments.

'That is the only thing Eli really liked about living here.'

'Is Jordan happy here?'

'Yes. They both miss their Oxford friends, but Jordan settled in quickly. You know I had to leave after the incident at the school.' A brief mention of those troubled months is enough to silence any conversation.

We walk a few paces without talking.

'He would have become used to you making the move here,' he says in the end.

'No. I think the press are right. I'm a rubbish mother and now everyone knows it.'

His arm wraps around my shoulders and pulls me close, just for a moment, then lets go. 'Not everyone thinks that, not me and not Jordan, and his perspective is the only one that matters.'

The path curves away from the rockface, into an area where the woodland often floods. Tall trees lie flat in areas, their roots ripped out of the ground in a storm, leaving craters in the earth, making it a mythical setting.

'This area is used for film sets sometimes.' I change the subject deliberately.

'You didn't kill him, Jen. If that's what you're thinking? You didn't. Whatever happened here, neither of us did that. And they will find the person who is responsible.'

Another surge of emotions tightens in my throat, preventing any reply.

As we walk on, the number of trees thin out, revealing glimpses of the sunlight shimmering on the lake.

'What's that?' André points through the tree trunks. 'Do boats moor here?'

He can see a part of the wooden jetty.

'The jetty is for a ferry. It stops in four places on the lake. Near Lowerdale, Bowick, here, and slightly further up on the other side.'

'Does the ferry run in the evenings?'

'No. The last run is at six, four on a Sunday.'

The path opens out as we reach the shingle bay. Like Lowerdale, the bay here is a small crescent beach. But here, people have rolled pieces of fallen tree trunks into the middle, creating a circle of seating, and within that is a ring of stones full of ash, where people have lit fires.

Today, there's no sign of the search that took place here. No tape. No white-clothed people.

'Do you think Eli and his friends set up that firepit?' André looks towards the ash-stained stones. 'He used to love building dens. Do you remember? I thought he'd become an engineer.'

'I remember. But that firepit is old. Lots of people use it.'

'Do you remember when we went to Exmoor, he was building a bridge for hedgehogs, and he slipped in the river and landed on his bum. He was soaked. You hung his shorts out of the car window to dry them on the way home.'

The memory lifts my lips in a shallow smile. Eli must have been four. 'He cried initially. But you and I could not stop laughing and in the end he laughed too.'

After the first tragic couple of years of Eli's life, moments of laughter were intensely precious.

'I remember when you decided you were going sea fishing on holiday. He climbed off the boat with an expression like a thunderstorm because the *"slimy"* fish you caught slapped his face when you pulled it out of the water. We couldn't make him laugh that day.'

A choked sound of amusement breaks from André's throat, before he sucks in a deep breath. It's sighed out as we walk the last few metres to the lakeshore, our eyes focusing on the pile of flowers lying around the edge of the lapping water. There are single roses, small and large bouquets, and some plush toys.

When I stand in front of the flowers, the warmth of Eli's spirit joins me, a slight breeze catching at strands of my hair and dancing around me.

'All these flowers would make anyone think he'd lived in Lowerdale from birth.' André squats on his haunches to read the cards among the flowers.

Eli didn't know this many people. The words in the cards must be impersonal statements of regret and sadness. But at least some strangers do not believe the papers and see Eli as an innocent boy whose life was cruelly stolen, and care enough to show it.

I walk towards the jetty. The water plays with the pebbles at the edge. Rolling forward and back. Breathing.

'Eli?' I whisper because I'm not sure André will understand why I am speaking to Eli. 'I love you.' My gaze sweeps across the water looking for him. I don't know where he drowned. 'What happened?'

The breeze trembles through the leaves on the branches that reach over the edge of the bay.

The same breeze raises goosebumps on my forearms.

My arms fold over my chest, my hands hugging myself.

The reflections on the surface of the water blur in the breeze.

On the far side of the lake, almost directly opposite, is a ricketier looking wooden jetty. The tall, silvered posts sink into the water at odd angles, and the line of the boards isn't quite even. It's a private jetty. Beyond it stands Nick's cabin. A wooden chalet-style house tucked into the edge of the wood.

If I can see his cabin easily he must have the perfect view of this bay.

What time did he leave the pub on Sunday? It was a clear night, with a super-sized moon. When I walked back from Sharon's everything looked as clear as it did in daylight. It had been a beautiful night.

Did Nick see Eli here?

If the boys are lying and they did come here with Eli, if they lit a fire that night, Nick must have seen it? And even if they didn't they must have been visible.

'People have said some nice things,' André says.

I turn, my arms releasing and falling to my sides.

His fingers move a small card. 'People liked him.'

'I doubt most of them knew him.'

'Then they're sympathetic. People are thinking of their own sons and daughters and how they'd feel if it was them.'

Sounds. Voices. Laughing.

Every muscle in my body tightens as I spin around.

The ferry slides into view, at the north side of the bay. The voices belong to passengers.

'I guess that's the ferry.' André's risen from his squat. He walks towards me.

My eyes follow the ferry's progress. Nick sees us, me, and lifts a hand to acknowledge my presence.

I raise a hand.

'You know the ferryman?'

'Yes, I use the ferry to travel to work.'

'I'm sure you're not hungry. I'm not. But we should eat something. Shall we go? What time does Jordan's match start?'

'Okay. The match starts at four, we have plenty of time.' I take one last look at the water. I don't see Eli but I feel him.

His energy walks with me as far as the path, then it's drawn away, in the way that water rolls back from the shore, unable to leave the lake.

It's three forty-five when we reach the school. Most parents and carers have collected their children and headed home, but a few are here, like us, to watch the football match. We are waved forward with others, directed to the gate into the sports field. The young, recently qualified, teacher looks away, avoiding eye contact, clearly unsure what to say to us.

Jordan will want this to be about the football and nothing else anyway.

The teams, a mix of boys and girls, wear red or yellow tabards, identifying their position and their school. Parents string themselves out along the sides of the pitch. Like others, we cheer and clap every goal, save, great kick or good try.

André's hands pound together vigorously when Jordan scores a goal.

I'd forgotten how loud André's clap is, his large hands make a booming sound. 'Come on, Jordy-boy!'

Jordan looks over and grins. He looks as though he's forgotten Eli has gone for the moment.

'Way to go, Jordan!' I yell.

André claps just as hard a few moments later when Jordan tries again and loses the ball, for the effort made. 'Go, Jordan!'

Eli used to swell with pride when his father was pleased with him. That's why it hurt so much when André turned on him. André played a big part in why Eli was such a sensible...

The thought dies. I'd always thought he never got into trouble. I was wrong. I gave him too much trust. But trust should not have been a bad thing.

When Jordan scores another goal, he runs to André to celebrate. They high-ten and perform a clapping routine André, Eli and Jordan created years ago.

I'm going to have to remind Jordan his father can't stay for long. André's life isn't here. We aren't that family anymore.

Jordan walks between us on the way home, holding our hands as though he's younger, as we carry the coats and bags. It is only when we reach the ice-cream parlour that I remember the crowd of news crews who will be waiting for us.

When we cross the brow of the slight incline in the road I expect to see them, but they aren't there. They must have become bored of waiting for us to return, or maybe thought we wouldn't return as the police car outside the house had left. We haven't rung Jack to ask for our police protection to return.

While I make a chicken salad, André helps Jordan with his mathematics homework. We eat seated around the table, in silence, because here Eli's absence is so obvious. They play on the Xbox until Jordan's bedtime, when André lies beside Jordan and reads to him again. He tucks the duvet in around Jordan and kisses his head before he leaves the room. I lean down and kiss Jordan's forehead too. Then turn out the light.

'I better head back to The Greyhound,' André says as we descend the narrow staircase. 'Camille is waiting for me to call and I need to check my work emails.'

'Okay. Thank you for coming. It's been easier having you here.'

He stops at the foot of the stairs, in front of the door, looking over his shoulder at me. 'You don't need to thank me, they're my sons too.'

I nod. Tired. Heart-broken. Empty. Now Jordan is in bed, I'm not sure what reason I have to breathe.

He turns, reaching out, opens the door and ducks under the lintel.

The sun is setting outside. The sky is a watercolour of sweeping blues, reds and golds.

'Red sky at night, shepherds' delight.' It will be good weather tomorrow.

He lifts a hand saying, 'Goodnight,' as he opens the front gate.

I shut the door, sadness soaking through my soul, drenching me as thoroughly as a monsoon. It was my fault. That's all I can think.

CHAPTER TEN

Knowing the press and police aren't outside makes me bold. I leave the living room curtains open and watch the sun set. The colours painting the wispy clouds slowly change from a vivid spectrum of warm tones to twilight hues.

My phone pings and vibrates. Jack. The start of his message shows. *A patrol car is going to drive past your house at least once an hour through the night...*

I open it.

We haven't deserted you. It'll just make sure the press don't become too bold.

Thanks. I text back. *But they aren't here this evening.*

I know. That's why the car isn't staying there. There was a flash flood in Yorkshire. They all charged off to cover it. But they'll be back when there's nothing else that is more newsworthy.

Or your car will return when you want to watch who visits me again.'

I've seen many true crime documentaries with the victim's families describing reporters tricking their way into the family's home, climbing walls and checking rubbish bins for the breakthrough story or a new enticing angle to spin. I've seen family members trying to get into their car surrounded by twenty people who won't move out of their way as they accuse the family of neglecting the victim. I've heard people saying they fled their homes because the press wouldn't stop hounding their children. I've also seen the detectives describe how they checked bins and examined suspects' social media to build a case of evidence. One father, on a BBC documentary, said he moved to France with his son after his wife's murder, solely to escape the press interest. I know André is right about Jack.

There are a lot of mistakes in my past they could find out and use to spin cruel stories about me.

At least tonight, though, I can stand at my window and not worry about being watched.

When stars glow through the twilight, and the blue becomes more midnight, I walk into the kitchen, lift the last bottle of wine out of the small wire rack, unscrew the cap and take a glass from the cupboard. The wine glugs as I pour a large measure.

The living room is silent and the curtains are still open wide. The stem of the glass dangles between my fingers as I sit on the sofa, staring at the sky.

When Eli was young, when he was at primary school and I had Jordan in the pram, sometimes he'd argue with me on the way to school and stomp off into school with a thunderstorm-face, as though he'd be angry for a lifetime. I'd leave, feel anxious and sick all day. At the end of the school day Eli would rush out, smiling, his eyes shining with the energy of a happy day and his father's smile on his lips, his ill-temper forgotten.

I long to see that smile. The need for it aches through the core of me.

Instead, I have his text. *'My fucking mother does my head in. I can't stand her! It's embarrassing!'*

He didn't mean it. I know he didn't. But—

Clunk.

A hard, determined, strike of the heavy iron door knocker has every muscle in my body jumping.

Clunk. Clunk.

My head was in memories, I hadn't seen who approached. To see now, I'd have to lean on the windowsill, and they will see me.

A reporter?

I rise, leaving the glass of wine on the coffee table.

There's no chain on the door to address unwanted callers, no one knocks unexpectedly. I lean against the door and open it a couple of centimetres. If it's pushed open, they'll have to climb over me.

'Bell? What are you doing here?'

'Jen.'

Belinda. The golden-autumn-blonde bombshell – that's what I've called her from the day we were introduced. Her hand lifts in a familiar self-conscious gesture, brushing her long hair over her shoulder. Her hair colour is natural and it changes in the sunshine, it ripens like the heads of wheat through the summers. In the dark, her colours become exotically silver.

I reach out and turn on the light, blinking for a second. Unsure about everything suddenly.

'How are you?' Her arms lift to embrace me.

I step back, denying it. A step that allows her to step into my home. I would have left her on the outside.

'I saw the news about Eli. I'm so sorry. It's awful.'

I am mute. Of all the people I thought might be at my door, it was never her.

'Where is your toilet. I've driven all the way up here without stopping and I'm bursting.'

'At the top of the stairs.' I tell her, stepping back again, and then she is wholly in my house and closing the door behind her. 'Be quiet, Jordan is asleep.'

She kicks off her heeled shoes shrinking to a couple of inches shorter than me. Her feet are size four, tiny and perfectly formed.

When we were together, she used to tease me that I had a foot fetish, but I only had a fetish for her feet.

She climbs the steep stairs soundlessly on those small feet.

I was attracted to Bell from the moment I saw her. It was not only her looks, it was the energy and infectiousness in her high-pitched laughter, and the light of life in her enchanting hazel eyes. I've stared into those eyes across pillows many times trying to work out each individual colour and why together they form the purest gold.

No words were spoken to acknowledge what was happening for weeks, but I knew she felt the same from the beginning. We surreptitiously watched each other in the staff room and laughed flirtatiously while we paced the playground on monitoring duty. In the end neither of us spoke first. One of the male teachers was getting married and invited all the teaching staff to his stag night. A few of us ended the night in a club, and in the obscurity of the busy dance floor we held hands through a slow song, and then we both leaned closer and shared our first kiss. It was my first kiss with a woman.

André knew I like women. It was a game between us when we were out, spotting attractive women and telling each other who we fancied most. A couple of times he suggested a threesome, but my sexual leaning was not something to fulfil his fantasies. I never took a step to explore my interest until I met Bell. It was a journey of blissful discovery, learning about another woman's body and another woman's way of loving.

I loved André but I became obsessed with Bell, and it split apart my family.

I told a million lies to André, Eli and Jordan, about why I was late and where I was. At work we would sneak off at lunchtimes and return flushed and grinning.

'Great workout!' she used to shout along the corridor to me, laughing.

After a year of disloyalty and lies we planned to set up a life together, to stop pretending to the men we were with. For her it was only pillow talk. I thought it was real. I rang estate agents and found a rental property. She walked around empty rooms with me while I listed the furniture we'd need. It was weeks later I realised it was only me talking.

'If you like it, go for it,' she'd said when she approved my choice of house near the school where we worked.

Then I told André. I broke his heart. It kicked him more than it would if I'd left him for a man, because I not only turned my back on him, I'd turned my back on his sexuality. He was hurt and disappointed, so was Eli, but André did try to understand and be kind.

I talked with Eli and Jordan about people having two mums and it being a normal thing.

'I know. But I don't want another mum, I want my dad.'

For Eli it was okay for other people to be gay or bisexual or anything else, it just wasn't okay for his mum – in his definition – *'to change your mind'*. It was awful timing for an excessively self-aware thirteen-year-old. It was too much to face a mother coming out of the closet. If he'd been older maybe he would have understood that people just love, and you can't limit love.

He'd tried talking to his friends about his feelings, but they teased him. They weren't really cruel but to a boy who was awkward enough in his changing body, being the centre of taunting was too much. Especially when André accepted a contract to work abroad for three months. Eli and Jordan's only option was to live in the house I planned to share with Bell.

That never happened.

On moving day, Eli, Jordan and I moved in, and Bell arrived with no boxes, clothes or furniture. She hadn't told her husband she was leaving. She never intended to leave him. We argued. Or rather I shouted and cried while she stood there, and the boys watched.

Then she left and whatever we had was over.

I took sick leave, I couldn't face teaching, and late one night I did something stupid while drunk – I took the boys in the back of a taxi with me, Eli sulking in one corner, and went to her marital home, to have it out with her. She didn't open the door. I shouted from the street, *'You're a liar!'*

Her husband came out. *'She doesn't want anything to do with you! Go away, or I'll call the police!'*

Gary is not like André. He doesn't accept Bell's sexuality.

I don't know what she really said or thought, but from that day on he made sure I knew what he thought. It was fuelled by jealousy, I knew that, and his jealousy had a violent streak.

He knew she had affairs with women, but he didn't like it if those women meant something to her, in case the women ended up meaning more than him.

He returned my night-time visit on many occasions. Knocking and kicking my front door at all hours. Shouting abuse. He even came into school once, a surprise visit to his wife, but while he was there, his glare threw threats at me across her shoulder.

Then he made a complaint to the police. He said I'd assaulted a girl in the showers at school. Of course there was no girl, but the rumour spread among the children and even though Eli was in a different school, thanks to social media, the rumours spread to his friends. That's why we left Oxford. That's why Eli was still angry, because he suffered for my actions. Jordan didn't understand it, he's young enough to take his mother's love for what it is, no matter what it brings.

The toilet flushes, and the bathroom door creaks as it opens.

She creeps down the stairs. Her toenails are painted with sparkly pink varnish. 'This house is cute,' she whispers.

This is how she is, she never acknowledges problems, never faces issues, instead she smiles and makes jokes. Until I realised this, it made life fun. But life isn't always fun, sometimes it's ugly, sad and cruel, and you can't hide from that forever.

'I didn't realise you moved so far out into the sticks. Where are you working?'

'There's a town half an hour away.'

'Could I have one of those?' she points at the glass of wine I left on the coffee table.

'Don't you need to drive home?'

Her lips, the blossom-pink lipstick only faintly showing after a day of wear, straighten into a confused line as thin furrows cut across the freckled skin of her forehead.

I tried to count her freckles once. She was an addiction of mine for years of my life. I've been clean for months now. 'Why are you here?'

'I thought you would want to see me. I know you must be hurting. It's dreadful. Poor you. Poor Jordan.'

She can't say that to me. She did this to me. Made us enemies not lovers. She is why Eli was here. *Oh,* it feels good to know there is someone I can pass the blame on to, until the music stops and the parcel ends up in my hands again. For now, though, she's here, the music plays and I will throw the guilt in her lap.

'André is here. We're supporting each other.' I reach for my wine and nurse the glass, using the glass as armour to prevent her stepping closer.

'I read the paper this morning. As soon as the school closed, I got in the car and just drove. I couldn't bear it.'

'This isn't about you.' My voice is a hostile whisper, conscious of Jordan upstairs. 'You've already played your part.'

'So you won't offer me a drink.' Her fingers tuck a strand of loose hair behind her ear.

Memories of my fingers stroking through her silky hair flood my mind. I was so happy at that point in my life.

'I don't know why you came. How can you think I'd be grateful you're here?'

'Maybe I didn't think.'

'Nothing you can do or say is going to help me. Eli died still angry with me because of us.'

'He wasn't angry with you. He was angry because of what happened, that's a different thing. He loved you.'

It's what I know. It's what I keep telling myself.

I shake my head, trying to shake away guilt. It won't leave me. 'You should have messaged beforehand. I'd have told you not to come.'

'I don't have your number, remember? You changed it.'

'How did you find me anyway?'

'The man in the Co-op told me when I said I was a friend.'

The man in the Co-op is going to get a talking to tomorrow. She could have been a reporter, or a random stranger who just read about us in the news.

I drink down the rest of the wine as though it's grape juice and put the empty glass down.

On her third introduction to the children, before we made the move to the rental house, I remember Eli running upstairs feet deliberately stamping hard, and slamming his bedroom door.

'Why can't you like her? I love her and I need you to get on with her.'

He'd been motionless under the duvet, but after I spoke, he spun round, throwing the duvet off. *'Because she's sly. She's taking you away from Dad and she rubs it in his face coming around here.'*

He'd seen through her long before I had. Beautiful, blonde bombshell, BITCH Bell. He was right. All she wanted was for me to leave André so I would put her first. She never intended to put me first. For her, the rental house was going to be a love nest.

'You need to go. I don't want your sympathy. Go home.' If she won't go easily, I'll push her out.

'I thought you'd let me stay here.'

'And what would Gary say to that? Just go. I don't want Gary following you up here.'

Her gold eyes shine bright with their magical quality in the electric light, and she doesn't move. She doesn't believe I'm serious. She still thinks she can manipulate me.

'I mean it, Bell. There's no place for you in my life.'

Her hand lifts, reaching out to me, trying to convince me with touch.

I lift an arm, as though I'm defending myself from a slap, and knock her hand away. 'Bell, I left to get away from the mess you made of my life. I don't need this now. Go.'

Her hand falls. 'Okay then, I'll go somewhere else to get a bite to eat and go home.' The tone in her words expects me to renege.

I won't change my mind. In the end I've put Eli and Jordan first.

She turns to slide her perfect feet into her high-heel shoes. 'I am really sorry for you.'

I don't reply.

She turns to the door. 'I doubt I'll see you again then,' she says across her shoulder.

'We said our goodbyes in Oxford.' I reach to hold the edge of the door, surrounding her, to force her departure.

'I'm sorry it ended.' She steps out.

'I'm not.' I close the door and immediately close the curtains too, with a sharp swish. Then I top up my glass.

Clunk. The knocker strikes.

The muscles in my arm jump, spilling wine from the glass.

I put the wine glass down again.

This time I lean up against the wooden door and ask. 'Who is it?'

'Nick. Are you okay? It looked like you were having problems with that woman, I saw you through the window. Was she a reporter?'

I pull the door open. PJ is sitting beside Nick's right boot.

'I'm fine. It's sorted. Would you like to come in?' Just for a short while. I need someone to stop me overthinking and brewing on Bell's visit.

'Yes.' PJ follows a pace behind him, looking up at me, in the way he has of asking for an ear scratch.

I lean down and stroke PJ's ear as I shut the door.

'Apparently, when someone dies,' I say, 'it takes forty-eight hours for people to turn from pity to pointing fingers and just about the same amount of time for people you've happily left behind to crawl out of the woodwork.' I turn and face him. 'Would you like a glass of wine? I want to ask you something, if you don't mind?'

'I will have a glass of wine, thank you. And you can ask me anything.' His colour is high, his tanned heavily freckled skin a vulgar salmon pink. Probably from the glow of alcohol if he's come from the pub.

'Sit down.' I point at the sofa. 'I'll fetch another glass from the kitchen.'

The thin plum-coloured jumper he's wearing matches my cushions. PJ lies down on the carpet, resting his head on the toes of Nick's scuffed black boots.

'Who was she?' he asks as the wine glugs into the glass.

'A piece of my past, that has no right to show up here and express any misery over Eli's death,' I say as I hand him the glass.

'Thanks. How are you?'

A heavy breath expresses my emotion as I sit at the opposite end of the sofa. 'Surviving. Barely.' I pick up my glass and turn side on to face him, my bare foot brushing the stonewashed denim hugging his thigh.

'It's shit,' he says.

'There is no suitable word for what this is.' I sip the wine. 'There is no single word to describe the pain, and I might say I'm coping, but I am not. I'm merely breathing again and again and my heart beats one more time and then another time. For Jordan's sake.'

He drinks a good mouthful and swallows it quickly, his skin

ripening like a strawberry. 'Have the police got any idea who did it yet?'

I shake my head.

'Sorry, Jen. I'm not the best at making conversation. I have no idea what to say to you really. I just… I wanted to make sure you know you're not alone here. If you need someone to talk to, or any help, you can call me.'

'Thanks. I don't know what to say either. Or do. I'm unravelling at the seams but trying to pin myself together for Jordan.'

He leans over and his warm palm rests on my calf. 'I'm sure you're doing a good job.' His hand lifts after only a second. 'What about the boys' father? He's been in the pub. Do you two get on?'

'André is a good father, and he's been supportive, but he won't be here for long. He has a partner and a job to get back to. I want to ask you about the night Eli died, though. Did you see anyone in Southend Bay? Your cabin is opposite—'

'No. I didn't see him. If I had I'd have told the police. Has Sharon been here? You two left the pub together that day.'

'We drank too much. Are you sure you didn't see anything? What time did you leave The Greyhound?'

'I don't remember. I didn't look at a clock.' His foot shifts a little, disturbing PJ. The dog rises in a sudden surprised movement, a moment later his chin rests on the cushion of the sofa, bronze eyes looking up at Nick. *Can I sit up there?*

'No,' Nick says.

I tap the sofa. 'Come on, come on up.'

PJ leaps up and sprawls out between us.

'They were drinking cider, Eli and his friends. They might have all been at the south end of the lake and lit a fire. If they were there they must have been visible from your cabin.'

His head shakes. 'There was a full moon. I remember that. And it was warm. They wouldn't have needed a fire, and I didn't see anyone there when I got home and unlocked the cabin, but I don't spend the night looking out the windows.'

'If they were jumping into the water, you'd have heard them shouting.'

'Not if I had music playing.'

'Didn't you notice anything in the morning?'

'The police were there then.'

He drinks a mouthful of wine. So do I.

When the glass leaves my lips. I change the subject to something else I want to know. 'Do you know what happened to Maddie Cox in America?' If she was Eli's girlfriend, would whatever happened there impact them here?

'I've heard the rumour.'

'What's the rumour?' I tuck both legs up on the sofa, bracing them with a hand as I sip more wine.

'She was in a school when there was a mass shooting. A teenager stole his daddy's gun and killed some of her classmates. She hid under a desk.'

My mouth hangs open.

'Sharon returned to the village with the girls afterwards. Sharon grew up here.'

'The shooting must have been awful.'

'I think so. I don't speak to Sharon. She's not a fan of me.'

'She's been kind to me.' Even if it's made me feel uncomfortable.

'You know, the next stage of this is that after about a week people start saying time helps you get over things.' His pale eyebrows lift. 'Of course, you never get over losing someone. But time means you learn to cope a bit better.' The low pitch of his voice tells me he's lost someone.

'Who did you lose?'

'My best friend. He died when we were eighteen.'

'Was it an accident?'

'Yes.'

'Were you there?'

His head lifts and lowers in a slow nod, his mouth shifting into a grim line. 'I was too drunk to save him. I didn't even realise he was dying. It was my fault.'

'I'm sorry.'

'You don't need to be sorry for me.'

'I can't believe Eli's gone. It still feels like…' A monologue flows out and continues until he leans over and pours the last drop of red wine from the bottle into my glass. I've told him everything. About Bell and how it made Eli feel. About the arguments between Eli and me. The only thing I haven't mentioned is what happened between André and Eli, that is for André to tell. But everything else about my past has poured out as liberally as the Merlot.

'You're a good listener,' I say, nursing my wine glass in two hands and looking over at the clock. It's five to eleven.

'My life has taught me patience.' There's a self-mocking tone in his voice.

'I should go to bed,' I drink the small amount of wine in the glass and put it down. 'I'm going into the school in the morning. There's an assembly for Eli.'

'Are you catching the ferry?'

'No, André will drive us there.'

He drinks the last of his wine, puts the glass down, and the muscles bunch in his thighs and backside beneath the denim as he rises.

PJ stirs, rising and jumps to the floor.

I stand too.

'I would say goodnight, but there's nothing good about it,' he says. 'And I would say sleep well, but I doubt you will.'

'No. I spend my nights wishing I'd done different things and wondering if Eli suffered.'

'I still have nights like that when I think about my friend. I'll give you my phone number.' He leans down, picks my phone up off the coffee table, turns it to face me so it opens without my consent, keys his number into the contacts and then opens the messaging app. His phone chimes in his pocket. He's sent a message to himself, so he has my number too.

'There.' The phone is held out for me to take.

Of course, it will be my choice to ring him or not. 'Thank you.'

'Mum.' A sleepy voice creeps down the stairs. Jordan's feet appear on the steps, the elasticated lime green cuffs of his pyjama bottoms at his ankles. 'I had a bad dream. A man was chasing Eli.'

'Sweetheart.' In a second, we're together at the bottom of the stairs. My arms surrounding him. He rubs sleep from his eye as he peers around me, looking at Nick.

'Hi, Jordan,' Nick says. 'I'm just leaving. I dropped by to check you're both okay.'

Jordan's gaze falls to PJ and he pulls free from my hug, wide awake now. PJ rolls to his back and bares his tummy for a rub.

The atmosphere becomes awkward.

Should I step forward and open the door.

'We have to go, PJ,' Nick speaks. 'I need to go to bed. It's late.' He opens the door. PJ scrabbles onto his paws. 'Bye.' Nick's gaze passes from Jordan to me.

'Bye.' I close the door behind them, switch off the downstairs light and follow Jordan upstairs.

We lie together in Eli's bed. Jordan sleeping, while I stare at the ceiling.

CHAPTER ELEVEN

A ghost of myself walks through the gates of Bowick Academy. It doesn't feel real at all. If André was not here, I might turn and run. But perhaps Wendy and Jack would catch me and turn me back. They flank us, dressed in black suits. In a way that makes them look like our bodyguards. But they might be watching me as much as the children.

The playground is quiet. The children are already inside the school. The teachers will be calling names and checking them off on their laptops.

Eli's name must have been removed.

André's hand wraps around mine as we approach the staff door.

I'm used to being Miss Easton here. With a son who disowns her in the classroom. I have no idea who the person walking through the door is today.

Today's picture on the front page of the paper is not the floods in Yorkshire, but one of André squatting down, looking at the bouquets of flowers at the lakeshore and me looking out at the water. I hadn't seen anyone near us. Like the day before, the picture was taken secretly from a distance. It's made me think we're being watched all the time. I've looked over my shoulder a thousand times this morning.

Sympathetic greetings cards arrived in the post this morning. One was from André's mother, Fay. She enclosed a letter I haven't had the courage to read yet. I told André. He nodded, in a way that implied he knew the contents of the letter. I told him about Nick's and Bell's visits. When I told him I sent Bell away, a firm, *'Good,'* was his response.

Paula waits for us in the reception area, at the front of a receiving line. The head teachers for each year have lined up as though this is a Royal visit.

'This is Eli's father, André,' I introduce. 'André, Paula is the headmistress.'

'Hello,' she shakes his hand. 'I am glad you could make it.'

'And this is Detective Inspector Wend—'

'We have met,' Wendy interrupts.

Of course, the police interviewed pupils in the school.

Geography-Geoff steps forward. 'I'm so sorry.'

He begins a pattern. 'I'm sorry.'

'I'm sorry.'

'I'm sorry.'

Everyone says the same words as they shake our hands.

'Come through to the hall.' Paula's hand encourages me to lead the way.

I would normally be leading a crocodile of children.

The teachers' chairs are spread out along the sides of the hall, as normal, facing the stage at an angle to monitor the rows of children sitting on the floor and see those presenting. Usually, I spot Eli amongst his class. Often, during assemblies, my gaze strays to him. My thoughts sifting through ways to break down the wall he built between us.

'Please, sit at the back, here.' Paula points at four chairs standing against the back wall. 'Then you won't feel on show but those who are speaking on stage will know they are speaking to Eli's parents.'

'Thank you,' André acknowledges.

We sit side by side, flanked, again, by Jack and Wendy. Paula walks to the front of the hall, as the children file in.

The youngest sit nearest the stage, the oldest, the taller, at the back. Eli would have moved up to his final year in September and taken a position in the back row.

A man, who I recognise as the chair of the governing board, enters and walks over to us.

'Miss Easton.' His hand rises, reaching towards me. 'I'm so sorry,' he says as I accept his handshake.

I am growing sick of the sorrys, but I imagine there are a lot more to come.

The children whisper to each other as they sit down cross-legged, glancing over shoulders at us and raising hands to hide mouths.

Eli's class walk into the hall. Maddie leading. Aiden behind her. Jason Parker and John Wood are behind him. The three boys who left Eli to die, I think.

What was Maddie to him?

They fold tall bodies into seated positions on the parquet floor.

'That's his best friend, Aiden,' I whisper, pointing him out to André. 'Maddie is next to him, and the two other boys this side of Aiden, I think were in the video footage too.'

His gaze remains on them as Paula takes centre stage.

'Children.' The hall's acoustics carry her voice easily. 'Good morning.'

'Good morning, Mrs Heart,' the children respond.

'Today, we are celebrating the life of a student, Eli Pelle. He did not attend our school for long but those who knew him knew him as a kind, studious boy and a good friend.'

Maddie looks over her shoulder at me and raises a hand to

say hello.

I lift my hand instinctively. It's better than sorry.

'Miss Easton and Mr Pelle, Eli's parents, have joined us to share in our remembrance. Those of you who knew him far better than I did, have things you want to say and read, so I will stop talking and let Maddie Cox come forward.'

Maddie? I must have missed something between them. They must have been dating.

Her strides are confident as she walks to the front. She climbs the steps to the stage, with her head held high, and yet her hand is pressed to her chest, at the base of her neck. She's an anomaly. There's that show of confidence but I know there's a painful experience hidden beneath. That is probably what that protective gesture manages.

My hand seeks André's.

When she stands behind the podium, she reminds me of her mother as her back straightens and her shoulders relax. Her hand lowers from her throat. She moves a piece of paper on the plinth and starts to read. 'By the Victorian Poet, Christina Rossetti…'

Was this poem chosen for her English teacher? Me? Or Eli? Maybe both of us.

Her clear voice becomes compelling.

The poem calls for the people grieving to let the spirit of the lost go.

I don't want to let Eli go. Not ever.

'Thank you, Maddie,' Paula says as Maddie leaves the stage. 'That is a lovely sentiment. Aiden Whitehead will speak next.'

Maddie's eyes settle on me as she walks back towards her vacant space on the floor. She smiles a little, but there's sadness in her eyes. Her gaze turns to Aiden as they pass.

My focus turns to him too.

His nerves show in his flushed skin. His shaking hands curl into fists as he crosses to the podium.

'My friend,' he begins. 'I didn't know you long, but we got to know each other quick.' He's written this. 'I thought we'd be friends for a long time... A lifetime...' He doesn't look up from the words he's reading.

I glance sideways at Wendy. She's watching the children sitting on the floor.

I look to see what she's looking at.

Maddie is leaning over to John and saying something behind a hand.

If she really cared about Eli, wouldn't she be listening?

'I don't know why you died. It isn't fair...' Aiden continues.

If Wendy suspects the children are lying, we need to increase the pressure on them, there's only a week left of this term. I need to teach next week, I need to watch them in the class. If they are lying, that will put the most pressure on them.

After the assembly, the teachers return to classrooms with the children. André and I are invited to the staff room for coffee and lemon drizzle cake with Paula and the office staff. Wendy and Jack don't accompany us.

There are more sorrys, and we're told 'his year' are creating an artwork for the school hall, made from pictures of things that remind them of Eli. A plaque is going to be made to ensure Eli is remembered. If I keep working here, I will see it every day.

'Paula,' I draw her attention in a gap in the conversation. 'I've decided to return to work on Monday.'

'Isn't that too soon?'

'There's only a week left of the term, and it will give me something to occupy my mind. Jordan has already gone back to school.'

'I suppose that's fine. If you're sure?'

'I am.'

She thinks I shouldn't, but she doesn't have the courage to tell me not to come in.

Exhaustion sucks at me when we walk out of the school. I've been putting a face on for other people. Hiding behind a mask. It will be worse on Monday. But I can come up with a task that means the children will work from their books and not talk if it becomes too much.

André's hand wraps around mine. 'What shall we do now?' He lifts my hand to his lips and kisses the back of it. A gesture of reassurance and care. A gesture that speaks of the years we loved each other.

I turn our hands to glance at my watch. 'Could we just drive? Just get away from here. Not from Eli, just this place.'

'Yes, we can drive. I need some time to digest all of this too.'

While I strap myself into the passenger seat of the BMW, my phone chimes. I pick up my handbag and dig it out. In case the message is from Jordan's school.

Nick. *How was the assembly?*

It was okay, I type back.

There's no reply. Which is also okay. I don't want a text conversation.

André presses a button. The roof of the BMW slides back.

'Put some music on.' He hands me his phone as he glances in the side mirror.

He drives off as I look.

The last message from Camille is amongst the notifications on the screen. *'I miss you. Don't be away for too long.'* It was received at 09.06, he hasn't replied or even opened the message, otherwise it would no longer be on the front screen.

I open his music and touch shuffle. Billy Ocean's 'When the Going Gets Tough' rolls out from the car's speakers.

We drive without a destination, weaving our way around narrow scenic routes, and take a chance on a remote pub to eat lunch. It's okay. The tables are full, so we sit at the bar and order sandwiches.

'What did you make of his friends?' I ask.

'The blond-haired blushing boy couldn't look at us.' He drinks from a glass of cola.

'Aiden. I know.'

'He looked upset. But whether that was because he was involved or in shock I couldn't tell.'

'I don't know either.'

'Brie and cranberry sauce on brown bread and tuna salad on white?'

André lifts a hand, telling the waitress where we are. We move our glasses. The waitress puts the plates down in front of us.

'Thank you,' I say, although I'm not at all hungry.

'Thank you.'

'That's why I'm returning to work,' I say as she walks away. 'I want to talk to them myself.'

His eyebrows lift and fall. 'You want to interrogate the kids.'

'I want to judge if they are telling the truth myself. It's Maddie I want to talk to most. It's her mum we met in the Co-op. She said Maddie was particularly upset. I don't know why she would be.'

'She was probably using it as an excuse to take time off school.'

'I don't know. I don't think so. I want to know how much Eli confided in her. Maybe she knows something.'

Our gazes catch. There are so many questions we don't have answers for.

I bite into the sandwich. It tastes like cardboard. My stomach drops inside me. I can't eat. I push the plate an inch or two away from me.

'Everything feels too strange,' I say.

'I can't accept it. At least you didn't waste the time you had. I haven't seen him for so long.'

'He still loved you. He never forgave me for leaving you.'

'He loved you too, no matter what he said in that message to the girl. Do you want any more?' he asks, looking at the plates.

'No.'

He slides his plate away, his sandwich half-eaten. 'Let's go.'

He drives to Keswick, and we walk down to where the boats launch on Derwent Water. It's a holiday-makers destination. We buy coffee in takeaway cups and walk along the path above the wall beside where the boats dock, watching the launches leave.

'If you're going to work,' he says. 'I might as well go home on Sunday evening. I can keep in touch by phone. But I want Jordan to stay with me the following week, when the summer holiday starts.'

My heart sinks to the soles of my feet. 'I can't let him go.'

'You should do what's best for him. He needs to be away from the press and the police.'

'Will Camille want him there? He'll worry.'

'He can stay with Mum, if he wants to, and you can come too then.'

'Fay won't—'

'Mum would be as happy as a pig in clover.' He uses her phrase. 'I'll see Jordan every day, and Camille will get to know him better.'

Before he becomes a troublesome-teenager who talks back to her.

But he is right, Jordan should spend time with him and Camille because Camille is a part of André now and Jordan can't have a good relationship with his father without knowing her.

'And after the holidays, I want him to stay with me every other weekend from now on.'

He'll be torn in half.

But that is my fault, I left Oxford. 'I'll talk to him about it tomorrow.'

'And this afternoon,' he says, 'I am going into that ice-cream shop.'

CHAPTER TWELVE

Jordan charges out from the school door, running across the playground straight into André's arms, his book bag and backpack swinging. André lifts him off his feet, spins him around once and sets him down.

Yes, Jordan needs his father in his future. Yet, even though I acknowledge it, secretly it kicks me in the stomach that he hugged André first.

'Do you fancy an ice cream?' André offers, taking charge of the book bag and offering a hand to Jordan.

'Yes. Please.'

Maddie is sitting outside the parlour at one of the picnic tables, looking at her phone.

When we approach, I glance at André and nod. *You go in, I'll talk to her.*

He nods back. *Message received.*

'Hello, Maddie.'

Her attention lifts from her phone. 'Hello, miss.'

'Thank you for reading that poem, it was lovely.'

A smile.

'Jordy, you and Dad go into the shop and choose your ice

cream. I'll sit out here with Maddie for a moment.'

'What do you want, Mum?'

'One scoop of mint will do me.'

They walk on.

I climb over the bench and sit beside her. 'Your mum said you're upset. I didn't realise you and Eli were close.'

'I liked him.'

Her answer says nothing. She could like him from a distance.

'Did you meet outside school?'

Her head moves slightly, her long hair brushing over her shoulders. It's neither a nod nor a shake, and if she blushes I can't tell beneath her thick layer of make-up. 'Miss, why didn't he tell people you were his mother?'

Is that an attacking move, to fend off my questions?

'What teenager would want their friends to know the teacher was their mother. Did he tell you who I was?'

'No. But I saw him with you and Jordan in the shop and the village sometimes and I wondered.'

I want to ask her about what happened in America. Say that I heard and I know she's endured something awful too. I can't. I shouldn't know about it. But what would an experience like that do to a child. How did that affect her? Could one encounter with violence lead to violence? Had post-traumatic stress left her prone to irrational anger? To hitting out violently, so blind with anger she'd pick up an implement and strike someone from behind more than once. I understand how sane and sensible minds can suddenly and irrationally break.

'What happened is awful. I'm sorry,' she says.

What did happen? Do you know? I close my lips and swallow the questions.

'I am sorrier than anyone,' I say. 'I'll be in school on Monday. I'll see you then if not before.' I smile over gritted teeth, extracting myself, rising and stepping back over the bench.

Her attention returns to her phone.

Something isn't right, but I can't work out what.

When I join them in the parlour, Jordan and André have only just reached the front of the queue. Jordan's gaze is running over the rows of tubs containing colourful ice-cream tubs.

'Bubble-gum and sugar plum sundae and the watermelon and strawberry sorbet?' Jordan decides.

Sharon looks at me, smiling, as she reaches into the chiller, scoop in hand.

'Can I help?' Her assistant, a cobalt-blue haired young woman, offers to serve the next customer.

'I talked to Maddie outside,' I begin. As André hasn't had a chance to grill Sharon yet, I will. 'She seems fine.'

Sharon's smile and her gaze drop away. 'Not everyone wears their emotions on their sleeve.' The metal scoop sinks into the blood-red sorbet. 'She is talking to the school counsellor. Maybe, you should speak with someone too.' Her gaze meets mine again as she presses the sorbet into the waffle cone.

'Maddie read a poem today,' André says, as she cleans the scoop. 'It looked as though she knew Eli better than Jen thought. Did she tell you they were dating?' The scoop hovers over the tub of blue and pink Bubble-gum and sugar plum sundae for a second, before cutting into it.

Sharon hands Jordan the cone, not answering.

'Are you having any ice cream?' she asks André. Making it clear she won't answer.

'I'll have a scoop of the rhubarb and custard please. I'm trying to get to know Eli's life here. If Maddie is very upset, I guess they were something.'

No answer.

'Did Maddie see him that night?'

Her gaze shoots to me as she passes André the full cone. 'No. She didn't see him that night, and there was nothing between them.'

Have the police spoken to Sharon? If he saw us together, she might have seen him that day.

'Do you want an ice cream, Jen?' Her tone is as cold as the ice-cream chiller.

'No, thank you. Not today.' I change my mind, I won't eat it if I have one.

Jordan looks at me, asking why. Across his shoulder, the blue-haired assistant looks at me too as she dips an ice cream in chocolate sprinkles. We are something to be stared at – the family whose son died suspiciously.

Maddie isn't outside when we leave the parlour. We sit at the picnic table where she had sat.

'Do you think the girl knows something?' André asks quietly, as Jordan's tongue scoops up the drips of red sorbet running down his cone and over his hand.

'Yes. I think Maddie saw him that night, and I think she knows more than she's said.'

I carry clean pyjamas, fresh from the airing-cupboard, in to Jordan. 'We need to change the bedding tomorrow, if you are going to carry on sleeping in Eli's bed.'

'Can I still use his covers?'

He's not bothered about preserving Eli's smell. I have his T-shirt under my pillow.

'Yes.'

He's tired. We went to the playground and spun the roundabout as hard as we could with none of us on it, just to make it spin as fast as possible. Then all squeezed into small child swings and swung as high as we could. We ended the evening with a burger dinner in Bowick.

When he's changed into his nightclothes, I lift the duvet for him to slide underneath.

'Dad!' he shouts. 'I'm ready!'

The creaky wooden boards beneath the carpet announce André's arrival.

While André reads, I sit at the end of the bed, thinking, not listening.

It must feel as though André is a part of our family again for Jordan. I need to manage his expectations tomorrow and tell him about André's desire for him to move between us in the future.

André closes the book and kisses Jordan's forehead.

I lean forward and Jordan rises so I can kiss his cheek. 'Sleep tight, darling.'

André turns out the light and closes the door behind us.

'Do you want a drink before you leave?' I offer André as we walk downstairs.

'Depends on what the drink is.'

'Tea or coffee. Nick and I polished off my small stock of wine.'

'I could buy some wine or beer from the Co-op, if you want to share a proper drink?'

'I'll pay.' He's been paying for everything since he's been here. He doesn't need to. The direct debit for children's maintenance never fails to appear in my account on the 2nd of every month.

'No. I'm okay with it. We can sit in your garden. I'd love to talk and get some of the bullshit circulating in my head off my mind.' He smiles, but the expression is heartless.

He slips his feet into trainers and opens the door. 'I'll see you in a bit.'

The door knocker raps gently when he returns, a quarter of an hour later.

He walks across the room to the kitchen and puts a full white plastic carrier bag on the work surface. 'I think I was caught on camera. At least tomorrow's headline will take the pressure off you – *Grieving father turns to drink.*'

A bark of laughter erupts from my throat as I reach for glasses.

'I bought three bottles. They were on a three for two offer.'

We take a bottle of wine outside and leave the back door open so Jordan will know where to look for us if he wakes. I sit closest to the door. André, opposite me.

'How are you and Camille? Is everything good between you?'

'Why?'

'I'm just asking, I'm not hitting on you.' One leg lifts, rests over the other and my foot begins to swing nervously.

'I'd hardly think you were, Jen. You left me for a woman. I didn't think you'd care, that's all. Eli made it clear you guys don't like her.'

'We have a reason not to. But you're still together so obviously you two have something.'

'We're getting married. We're engaged, and we're planning to have a child.'

Oh, that's something I wasn't ready for. I don't care from my perspective but the boys—

I close my eyes for a second. Collecting my thoughts. Boy. Eli isn't here to care. 'Jordan will find that strange.'

'I hope he'll get to know the baby from day one and they'll be close.'

I nod. Then my expression screws up. 'Is this why you're pouring alcohol into me, because you thought I'd be upset by your announcement.'

'No. I wasn't going to tell you now, but you asked.'

I lift my glass and toast him. 'Congratulations. I'm glad you're happy.'

'I was happy until Eli died. I wouldn't call myself happy now. And you? Where is your life at?'

'Not in the same place as yours. But Eli didn't like me forming relationships. He felt threatened every time I met someone.' I should probably say every time I slept with someone, which would be more accurate, nothing progressed as far as a relationship. 'In his point of view other people broke up our family. Bell and then Camille.'

'Who might have killed him? Don't you have any idea? He wasn't a bad lad, he worked hard to get along with people. Even Camille admits that in hindsight.'

My head shakes as I hear him. He's admitting Eli was not remotely at fault for his falling out with Camille, let alone André's overzealous reaction. 'I don't know.' I shrug. 'I'm sure the kids know something and Maddie's behaviour makes me think she's holding something back.'

'I agree that girl is hiding something,' he says. 'Her mother was looking at you weirdly. But I can't imagine a kid like that having a reason to kill Eli. It must have been an accident, but then why not call 999 for help and why hit him again? Maybe someone attacked them and they've threatened them. Told them to keep quiet. Maybe they've been scared into silence.' A bitter sound leaves his throat. 'I could shout at that nice copper – Jack. Stop asking us questions and find the bastard who did it.'

'The kids are probably so deep in lies they think they will be in serious trouble if they admit anything. But Maddie's mother was with me that night, she wasn't there.' The warmth of a blush crawls up my neck. I swallow a mouthful of wine, plucking up the courage to speak. 'We had sex the day he died. That is why she was looking at me.

'That's why I didn't answer his call that day. She and I met in the pub. He must have seen us kissing in the street. I think that is what his text to Maddie was about.'

The base of his glass strikes the table heavily as he puts it down. 'You should have told the police.'

'I feel guilty. Jordan was at a friend's house, Eli was out. I went to the pub. It was only the third time I've been out on my own since I moved. We were talking and she was flirting. One thing led to another. Eli said he wasn't coming home, so I did something for myself. Maddie doesn't seem to know, though.'

'He wasn't comfortable with your sexuality, was he?'

'That's an understatement.'

'If you're beating yourself up about meeting someone, it's life. Relationships must start somewhere. But he was upset because he cared. He loved you. If he hadn't cared, it wouldn't have bothered him. I bet he was just upset because he felt awkward. He would have been just as upset if he saw you kissing a friend's father. When I was his age, I admit I would have felt awkward if my mother picked up someone in the pub and was kissing them in the street. But are parents meant to never have relationships?'

A sigh breaks my lips apart. 'If I hadn't been with Sharon, I would have known he didn't come home.' I look into André's eyes. 'I'd have taken that call.'

'And if and if and if… He chose to buy the cider. He chose to go to the lake. You didn't make him do any of that. I'm sure he wouldn't blame you. He would want to come home to you.'

'My role was to protect him. I embarrassed him.'

'By being your honest self? No. He would have grown up to respect you more for it. I was hoping he'd come to my wedding. I thought it would be the moment to push the past aside. Love resides on a deeper plane than any other emotions, like anger, jealousy or dislike.'

'I want to know him as an adult.' I say. 'To see what he'd become.' I never will know now.

We reach out for each other's hand in the same moment, tears catching in our eyelashes.

His hand lets go of mine and rubs the tears off his cheek. 'At least we have Jordan.' His voice is rusty.

He lifts the glass and drinks more wine leaning back in the chair. 'You should tell the police you were with that woman.'

'Why? What difference does it make?'

'I don't know. But they should know everything about that day, if they are going to solve this.'

CHAPTER THIRTEEN

I'm awake when the darkness in the bedroom lightens to indigo as the sun rises on the other side of the house. A blackbird joins the dawn chorus from the telecoms wire outside the cottage.

I throw the duvet aside and get up. My head is heavy and my brain thick from the red wine I drank last night, but I can't sleep, there is no point in lying in bed any longer. The day has to progress, no matter that my heart has a crack through the middle.

The door of Eli's room is ajar. I push it wider, looking at Jordan curled over on his side under the duvet. Should I let Jordan stay with Fay? That is the question that has been circling my mind for hours. If I remain here alone, I might stay in bed and never dress or eat, I am living for Jordan. But I don't think I can go with him, I can't leave Lowerdale, and leave Eli at the lake.

I try to avoid every creaky board under the carpet on the way downstairs. Settling on the sofa, I pick up the laptop with time to waste. There must be something on the internet about the shooting in Maddie's school in America. I type *'school shootings in the USA'* and guess the year it might have happened based on her age.

Information appears for twenty-four different shooting events in schools in America in that one year.

I don't know which state she lived in.

The news articles share statements from victims.

'I did the thing you aren't supposed to do, I ran to the back of the class and I was trapped there…'

'I looked at my classmate, and I knew she'd died, her head hung down.'

'Someone was praying, so I prayed.'

'I thought my son was injured when he was carried out of the school, but it was other-people's blood.'

'He looked me straight in the eyes, saw me crying and fired anyway.'

'He didn't hit me, he didn't aim the gun at me. I don't understand why he left me and killed my friends.'

'Two boys said to me, let's run, let's get out now. He'd left our room and I didn't know where he was, but we ran out of the school. As I was running blood dripped on my shirt, and I said to another boy, whose blood is this? He told me it was mine, I had a bullet wound on my head.'

One fifteen-year-old boy said he sat up against a door to prevent the shooter coming into a room where twenty other children were hiding with him. He'd been shot twice through the door and survived.

'It's not the gun that kills people it's the person,' the news website quotes a politician in an argument about changing gun laws. But it's the politics that give a child or a mentally ill person access to a gun.

'As a teacher I know when I face the empty desks I must be strong for the kids. But at times I leave the room, lock myself into a closet and cry for a few minutes. Then I have to pull myself together, go back into the room and teach.'

'My son won't talk about it, and we don't talk about it because we don't know what to say.'

Poor Maddie. Whatever her involvement with Eli, she has experienced her own trauma, and if the people working for the press in America are like they are here, they would never have let her forget it. That's probably why Sharon came home.

The hands on the clock on the wall point to five thirty-eight. I close the laptop, leave it on the arm of the sofa and make a cup of tea. I sit in the garden until the screen on my phone says 06.01. Then I open contacts, scroll to Nick's mobile number and touch call.

'Hello, Jen. Are you all right?' His voice is deeper than normal, with a just woken frog in his throat.

'You said I could ring any time. Is now okay?'

'Yes. What's the matter?' I imagine his knuckles rubbing the sleep from an eye.

'I have another question.'

'What?' He's awake now, but less certain.

'Where did Maddie go to school in America? Do you know?'

'Texas, I think. It's not something I've heard Sharon talk about. Why?'

'You don't know the actual school?'

'No. Why?'

'I was looking for it, that's all. Maddie was friends with Eli.'

'What difference does that make?'

'I want to find out more about the people he knew.'

'I wouldn't worry about Maddie or Sharon. Focus on looking after yourself and Jordan.'

'I am, Nick. But I need to help Eli be able to rest in peace too.'

A sigh slips through the phone's speaker. 'As long as you're okay.'

'I'm far from okay. But I'm going back to work on Monday. I'll see you for the commute.'

'Sorry. Okay was the wrong word. But you know what I mean. Are you sure you're up to working?'

'Jordan is already back at school. I need something to do.'

PJ barks in the background, a single sharp bark that's a request for something. 'I need to let PJ outside. Do you want to stay on the phone?'

I bet the dog sleeps at his feet on the bed. 'No. Thank you. Go.'

'Well… Call me anytime you like, but I'll say goodbye for now then.' His breathing changes, he's moving, to open a door for the dog.

'Bye'

He ends the call.

Texas is a big place.

I pick up the laptop and sit at the table.

The list of results for the search question I'd left open in the internet browser includes two schools in Texas with shooting incidents in my calculated year. In one incident, a twelve-year-old shot three children. The news headline on the second incident at Robert J Jones High School tells the story of a fifteen-year-old boy entering a school with a semi-automatic rifle and opening-fire. Thirteen children died, twenty-four were injured. Students describe it in the article as target shooting, but there was no clear reasoning behind those he chose to shoot.

I change the search question, looking for more information on Robert J Jones High School.

On the fifth link among the pictures of victims being led away from the school I see bloodied blonde hair and a familiar face. I expand the picture. It is Maddie. Younger but the same. Blood stains her hair, neck and T-shirt. The horror of what she's seen lingers in her eyes.

The text beneath the image doesn't mention her name.

'I was hiding under the table,' a victim says. 'My friend was in front of me. He shot him in the head and the chest. It's his blood on me. I don't think he saw me hiding.'

I should be more sympathetic towards Maddie. Whatever she knows or doesn't know about Eli, this was tough.

'Mum.' Jordan walks downstairs.

I shut the laptop and stand up. 'Morning, darling.'

We eat toast. He smears chocolate sauce over his. Then the two of us watch TV until André knocks on the door.

I glance at the clock. It's just after nine. We're still dressed in pyjamas. I open the door. The press photographers are back this morning, a smaller group than before. Beyond André their lenses point at the doorway.

Click. Click. Click.

His hand pushes me backwards. 'Bastards,' he says as he steps in and shuts the door. 'Clearly the aftermath of the flood was less sales-worthy.'

'Dad,' Jordan jumps to his feet, the TV left on a still frame. I meant to tell him this morning that André must go home, that in the future it will be me and him, or him, his dad and Camille.

His arms wrap around André's torso.

'Hi, Jordy-boy.' André's hand rubs over Jordan's hair. 'What do you fancy doing today? It's glorious weather.'

'I want to see Eli's flowers by the lake. I saw them in the paper, and a girl at school said she put some there yesterday. Can we swim in the lake there too?'

'Sure, if that's what you want to do. I don't have any swim shorts to go in with you, though.'

'You could buy some in the village,' I say. 'There's a clothes shop to accommodate the tourists, or use a pair of Eli's. They would fit you.'

'I'll buy some while you two dress.'

The sun's warmth beats down on my bare shoulders from a cerulean-blue sky. Canoeists and paddleboarders are out on the lake, but no one else is in the bay.

I feel Eli's presence as I walk closer to the water. The sensation of his long arms wrapping around me stops me walking. I embrace the feeling – embracing him mentally.

André's hand rests on top of the baseball cap on Jordan's head. Jordan's head tilts back and they smile at each other.

I glance around, looking for the sunlight to catch on a long lens somewhere along the bank of the lake. No one appears to be watching us but they might be well hidden. I can't let that influence what we do, though. Today is for Jordan's benefit. It has nothing to do with the voyeurs watching our lives.

'I'll take a picture of you together.' I say to Jordan and André. 'Stand there, so the lake is behind you.' Jordan will need something to help him hold on to his father's love when André leaves. I step back a few paces, lifting my phone, and look at their images on the screen waiting until the picture will be perfect.

Jordan grins with pride as I tap the screen and take the shot.

'Will you send the picture to me, please?' André asks.

I open the image to share it. My finger hovers. There's a bright orb of light shining behind Jordan, at the height of André's shoulder. Eli. It must be his spirit. What I see is Eli showing us he's forgiven André.

I forward the image to him.

Jordan's gaze turns to the flowers. He thought they'd look beautiful. They look a bit gloomy now they're wilting. Neglected and rotting in the heat.

'The council will have to take the flowers away soon. Shall we collect the cards?' André suggests. 'We can keep them then.'

'Yeah, okay,' Jordan agrees, half-heartedly.

'The sentiments of the words will remain as beautiful as the day they were written,' I say, to draw his smile back.

While they set to work, I lay out the picnic rug near the circle of logs and sit down. In my mind's eye Eli's long legs and large feet stretch out on the rug beside me.

As André and Jordan move the bouquets, the plastic and paper wrappers rustle. They read some of the words aloud to each other.

My mind slips into the past, to the day we buried Eli's legs under the sand and made a car bonnet on top of him. Eli had giggled uncontrollably. I lie down and close my eyes, feeling the sun tan my skin, and immerse myself in wonderful memories.

'Jen!' André calls.

'Yes?' I rise up onto an elbow as my other hand screens my eyes.

They've reached the bottom of the pile. André holds a single card in either hand, Jordan has a stack in his hand.

'These are Maddie's and Aiden's,' André says as he walks over. 'They were side by side right at the bottom. Maybe they came together.'

'What do the cards say?'

He drops down on the blanket next to me.

I sense Eli leaning in between us as André reads, 'I am going to miss you. You were good fun. I wish I knew you longer. I won't forget you.'

'Is that Aiden's?'

'Yes.'

'Read Maddie's.'

'You were special. I'm sorry. I will always remember you. Kiss. Kiss. Maddie.'

'Do you think they were dating?' I ask him as if he could know.

His shoulders lift and fall in a shrug.

'It would have given him a really good reason to be upset with me, if he saw me with her mother and they were together.'

'Mum.' Jordan joins us, holding out the stack of large and

small cards. I take them and put them safely in a pocket of the beach bag.

'Are you coming into the water, Dad?'

'Yes.'

'I'll join you,' I say.

André and I strip off our clothes revealing swimming clothes underneath. Jordan is already wearing his swim shorts. The shorts he'll wear home are wrapped in the towel in the beach bag. They strip off their T-shirts, father and son in unison.

We walk into the lake, exclaiming and laughing about the cold temperature of the water as we wade just to our knees.

Eli whispers emotions through my soul as I wade deeper, while the boys begin a splashing war.

The water is entirely clear. I see my bare feet balancing on the stony bed of the lake.

'Mum!'

Jordan has retrieved the Frisbee from the beach bag. He spins it towards me.

We play in the water for nearly an hour, eat our picnic on the blanket and then I smother Jordan with sun cream again as André puts down stones to mark out a goal. They play with a small ball I'd brought as I lie down and watch the leaves on the branches hanging over the bay shivering in a slight breeze.

'Mum, look at me!'

I sit up with a start. Jordan is standing halfway along the jetty, preparing to jump in.

'No! Don't! It's too shallow!'

I'm on my feet. Running.

But he's heard me. He sits on the edge of the boards, a sulky expression twisting his lips.

'If you hit the bottom, you'll hurt yourself,' I explain as I walk the last few paces to join him.

I hear André talking and glance over my shoulder. He's speaking on his phone with his back to the bay.

Jordan's toes kick impatiently at the water and his hands rest on the weathered boards.

Jordan stops kicking his legs and turns to look at his left hand, as his fingertips delve into a crevice between the wooden planks.

'There's something gold here, Mum.'

He turns, trying to pick it out with the short fingernail of his forefinger. 'It's gold, have you got anything to dig it out with?'

'I have tweezers in my bag. I'll fetch them.'

I return with a pair of stainless-steel eyebrow tweezers and kneel beside him to look at whatever it is he's found. He's right, there's something small and gold trapped between the boards. It's stuck in there quite firmly, probably trodden into place and buried deeper by the ferry's waiting passengers.

After a few moments of picking at it with the tips of the tweezers, the golden object comes loose and flicks onto the walkway.

Jordan picks it up between his thumb and forefinger, his mouth opening as though he's in awe of what he's found. 'It looks like yours, Mum.'

'Mine…' I hold out my palm, and he drops it in the centre.

It's a small gold heart pendant, with a tiny blood-red ruby set in the top right-hand side.

It is not like mine. It is mine.

This is a one-off handmade piece. It hung around my neck for all the years I was married to André. He bought it for me from a jeweller who only made one-off pieces.

There can only be one reason why it's here – Eli brought it here.

CHAPTER FOURTEEN

'Dad!' Jordan shouts. 'We found Mum's heart!'

How did those people crawling along the floor in their white coveralls miss this?

They'd scoured the bay with their fingertips, surely, they checked the jetty. But perhaps they wouldn't have recognised the connection. Thousands of people have stood on this jetty. Maybe Eli hid it from them and showed it to us because we would tell the police it is important…

'André!' I shout. His phone is still held to his ear.

He looks over.

I beckon him with an urgent hand signal.

While he extricates himself from his conversation. I look into the water. What else might they have missed. Where is the gold chain that belonged with the pendant?

'Look in the water, Jordan. Can you see the chain?'

Eli must have brought the chain with him, and this slipped off.

My hand closes around the tiny heart, holding it in a fist.

A splash announces Jordan's drop into the water. He'd slid off the side of the jetty. The water comes up to his chest.

'What is it?' André asks.

'We found the pendant you gave me when I fell pregnant with Eli.' I open my palm and show him. I don't think Eli knew it was connected to his journey into my life. I don't think I ever told him because of everything that happened afterwards. Depression stole the emotions, the good sentiments, passed across in the gift of this pendant. But I had worn it, and held it, with hope, for hours of my life when there had been so little hope to hold on to.

He looks down at the piece of jewellery. 'You should have left it there. It might provide evidence. There might be DNA on it or something.' He lifts his phone, zooms in and takes a picture of it. 'I'll send a picture to Wendy and tell her she missed this.'

'Not yet. Wait. Don't let this spoil the day. What if they missed it for a reason? I think Eli wanted us to find this not them. A couple of hours more won't make a difference.'

'If he wanted it found, then he knows it will prove something. Be careful, Jordan, that's deep enough!' he shouts past me.

Jordan has waded in up to his neck, looking down at the bottom of the lake for a glint of gold.

I look back at André. He may have a different perspective, but he did not reject the idea that Eli wanted Jordan to find the heart. 'Do you feel Eli's presence here? I do.'

His gaze lifts from Jordan to me. His polished mahogany eyes looking into my eyes. 'Yes.'

It's a simple acknowledgement, but it means so much. Because, if we both feel his spirit here, I'm not imagining it.

'I'll send them the picture of the heart this evening. We'll have to put something down to mark where Jordan found it. I'll find a pebble and scratch the wood.'

The pendant safely placed in a pocket of the beach bag, we all search the water for the chain that carried the heart.

We give up at four o'clock, change out of our swim clothes beneath towels and head home. As we leave the bay, I hope Eli's spirit will walk with us, but I feel him slip away.

No one from the press or the police force are waiting outside the cottage. The press probably already have their picture for the Sunday papers. They are most likely chasing another story now.

As the cottage door shuts, the warmth of the sunshine is shut outside.

'Do you want a glass of water?' André asks Jordan, walking towards the kitchen.

I kick off my sandals and run upstairs, to look in my jewellery box. My necklace, with the heart pendant, was in the first small drawer. It isn't there, there's no thin rope of gold, and no small gold heart with a tiny scarlet ruby.

'It is my heart!' I shout as I run back down the stairs. Not that I'd really had any doubt.

André puts an empty glass in the kitchen sink. 'I'll send the picture to the police.'

'No. Wait. They can't do anything about it this evening. Send it in the morning.'

'Okay. I'll wait until the morning.'

We agree on a barbeque dinner, and so André is sent to the Co-op to buy sweetcorn cobs, sausages, buns and onions.

As we sit outside, in the last of the day's warmth, cold cans of cola in our hands and our stomachs full of hot dogs, André drops the bombshell, 'I'm leaving tomorrow, after dinner.'

Jordan sits upright, the cola-can abandoned on the table. 'What? Why?'

André reaches out and touches Jordan's shoulder. 'You'll be at school, Jordy-boy. I need to work. It'll be the holidays the week after. You can come and stay with me or Nan. I said to your mum, from now on I want us to see each other every other weekend at least. It's not going to be like it was before.'

He nods, his throat too full of emotion to reply.

'We can speak every day on the phone.'

His head bobs again.

Half an hour later, when I close the door behind André, I look at Jordan. He's been quiet ever since André mentioned leaving.

'You know Dad can't stay, don't you? He has to go home to Camille, and he needs to work.'

Jordan's expression sours. 'I don't want him to go. She always has him.'

He turns away from me and stomps upstairs, his footfalls deliberately heavy.

André hadn't stayed to tuck him in, he said he needed to look through work emails before Monday. It was not a good day to leave earlier.

I stand at the foot of the stairs, my hand on the newel post. Nothing I can say will make this easier. The angry footsteps progress to Eli's room.

There's a crash. Something has hit a wall up there. I'm running up before I even think about moving. There are thuds and thumps. He's doing what I've felt like doing at times – throwing and breaking things.

I rush into the room as he pulls out a drawer and tips it upside down on the floor. Empty crisp packets and Eli's unwashed, smelly, socks, that he'll have shoved in there to hide them from me, spill out across the floor.

'Jordan! Jordan! Stop!'

'I hate him!' He yells towards me. 'I hate him for leaving us!' His voice breaks. The raging tantrum fracturing like a heavy water-laden cloud in a thunderstorm. When the violence of the lightning shakes out the pouring rain.

I open my arms to him. 'It's okay to feel like that. It's okay.'

He clings to me as though I'm a tree floating on the surface in a tsunami.

'It's okay.'

It really isn't okay. It will forever not be okay.

Clunk.

A sharp knock strikes the front door. I sit upright, the duvet sliding to my tummy. My mind was a mile away. I was swimming in the lake beside Eli.

Clunk.

The firm knock strikes the door again. Someone is determined to obtain my attention.

'Mum, someone's at the door!' Jordan's shout rises from the living room downstairs.

The TV is on, he's playing a digital game or watching a programme.

The clock reads 8.52am The last time I looked it was 4.17.

The heart...

I reach out, looking for it.

It's still on top of the chest beside the bed.

Clunk.

The door knocker strikes again.

'I'm coming, Jordan! Don't open the door!' The gravel in my voice gives away the depth of my tiredness. They'll have to wait a few minutes longer. I change out of pyjamas, slide into denim shorts and pull on a fuchsia-pink T-shirt.

Clunk.

Another knock strikes as I walk downstairs. 'I'm coming!' I yell in a voice that has more clarity and no patience.

Jordan looks up from his game and smiles. I make a face, lifting my eyebrows and sticking out my tongue at the person on the other side of the door. His smile broadens.

Latch turned and knob twisted, I open the door with caution. Jack, Wendy and Arla are gathered outside. A marked police car has also returned in the street behind them.

'André contacted me,' Wendy says. 'Apparently you found something at Southend Bay yesterday.'

I step back a couple of paces, opening the door wide, accepting the invasion.

'Your paper was hanging out from the letter box in the door,' Jack holds it out for me to take. He's in uniform today. My eyes are drawn to the small camera lens that stares at me from the chest of his Kevlar vest.

'Thanks.' I accept the paper.

Arla closes the door in her wake.

The image on the front page today, is a lovely picture of André kissing my hand. The words are some nonsense about Eli's parents patching things up in the wake of their son's death. I throw the paper on the sofa, upside down so Jordan won't see the headline.

The police fill up the room.

Jordan is so used to them now, he ignores them, sitting in his green-and-blue pyjamas his thumbs working hard on the controls of the video game.

'Can we have the pendant?' Wendy cuts to the chase, the tone of her voice accusing, making it sound as though I stole the gold heart.

'Wait here.' My feet feel as heavy on the stairs as Jordan's had sounded yesterday evening.

When I give them the pendant it will become evidence and I'll never see it again. I swallow against the lump in my throat a dozen times as I pick it up and carry it downstairs in my fist.

Arla is waiting with a ziplock plastic bag, held open for me to drop the pendant in.

My hand hesitates. The gold heart is a part of the story of my life.

'Thank you, Jen,' Arla encourages me to take the final step. The heart rolls from my palm and drops into the bag. Now it's contributed to Eli's story and it holds secrets they need to unlock.

Wendy leans in to study it, as though the little pendant might break the case wide open and explain everything. 'André said it belongs to you.'

'It does.'

'Do you know how it came to be at the bay?'

'Eli must have taken it there.'

'Did you know Eli had it?'

'No.'

'Do you have any idea how it might have arrived at the bay between the time of Eli's death when the jetty was searched and now.'

'It was stuck between the boards, it must have been missed. Will you return it to me?' I ask, with little hope, but because I must at least ask. 'It has sentimental value.'

'No. The evidence will be kept in a secure facility once we've finished with it,' Arla explains. 'Whether we achieve a conviction or not. Even if someone goes to prison, they might appeal and then the evidence will need to be revisited.'

'Although, potentially, any forensic evidence is destroyed as it's been in your hand like that,' Wendy adds.

'We marked the spot where we found it. We can take you there,' Jordan declares from his position on the floor.

The knocker strikes on the front door again, more gently.

'Jordan, that will be Dad. Let him in and then go upstairs and change your clothes. I'll put the kettle on.'

I walk between the officers.

Jordan races to the door, and as soon as André steps in wraps his arms around him.

'You didn't waste any time coming,' André says, closing the door.

I look back, to say hello. His gaze reaches to me, his expression changing as he notices my dishevelled hair and lack of make-up. He knows it's unlike me.

Jordan lets go and charges up the steep stairs, using hands as well as feet, like a character in one of his Xbox games.

'Do you want some help?' André speaks to me across the heads of the detectives.

'Yes please. Who wants tea or coffee?'

They all ask for tea.

I lift the mugs out from the cupboard as André joins me and opens the fridge.

'Did you see the picture on the front page of the newspaper today?' He asks as he sets the milk carton down on the worksurface. His voice is quiet, but the detectives are only a few feet away.

'Yes. How has Camille taken that?'

André reaches for the teabags, so settled in the cottage it's as though it's his home too. 'She's a little pissed off.'

I touch his arm in a gesture of support as the kettle boils, spewing out steam.

He reaches past me to pick up the kettle. 'She'll get over it. Did you see the story on page two?' The pitch of his voice has dropped even lower.

'No.'

'The ferryman is a murderer,' he tells me as he pours the hot water.

'The ferryman... Nick?' I spin around to face him, glad the vessel of boiling water is in his hand not mine. The shock would have loosened my grip and scalded both of us. 'What happened?'

'It was years ago. He's served a prison sentence. He was a teenager. The boy he killed was his friend.'

'He told me his friend died. He said it was an accident. He didn't tell me he was involved.' No – he had said it was his fault. He hadn't explained that.

'Was he involved with Eli somehow?'

'No. He wasn't.'

'When are we going to get that tea,' Jack interrupts us.

'In a minute, mate.' André responds.

I turn again and pick up the milk, concealing my reaction. I top the teas up with milk. I don't know what this news means.

My son was murdered within a stone's throw of Nick's cabin and Nick is already known to be a murderer...

Fifteen minutes later, Jordan is dressed and he's planted himself back on the floor in front of the television. His thumbs working the Xbox controls with determination.

'Are you sure you'll be okay in here on your own?' I ask him as I pick up my mug. André is already in the garden with the detectives and Jack.

'Yes, Mum.' His concentration doesn't stray from the TV screen even for one second.

Maybe André is right, he would be better off with Fay. Not ignored and isolated here. It isn't good for him to spend so much time staring at the screen.

André and Wendy occupy the chairs around the garden table, Jack and Arla are on the wall of the raised flowerbed, sitting amongst the lavender, risking the attention of the numerous bees that are gathering the nectar from the small purple flowers.

I take the third seat at the table and embrace the warm mug of tea in both hands.

'We received further information from forensics yesterday,' Wendy announces.

I slide forward on the chair, my whole body keen to hear whatever she has to say.

'We have some DNA results. Skin cells were found on the swab used under one of Eli's fingernails and traces of body fluid.'

'He scratched his killer?'

'No, Jen. It's vaginal fluid and cells.'

'He was with a girl that night?' André's surprised voice clarifies.

'He spent time with a female, yes, André. Although we don't know if the female was with him at Southend Bay.'

'Maddie Cox.' I say her name as though it must be her. 'Was it her?'

'We don't know. However, we will. Maddie consented to a DNA test this morning.'

'When will you know?'

'Probably tomorrow.'

'I didn't know he was experimenting with girls.' I knew so little about what he was doing.

'Did it go further than that?' André asks.

'It would appear not. No semen was found on his body, but as I've said, he was in the water for hours.'

My eyes shut for a second. Was this sexual engagement the reason why he died? My son – drinking alcohol and having sexual encounters.

I drink some of the tea.

André's hand touches my shoulder, speaking without using words. *He was just being a boy.*

'Is that everything you need to say?' I ask Wendy, wishing we hadn't made them tea, so they would go.

'No,' Jack answers. 'We need another statement for the media. If you're going back to school tomorrow, we should put something else out. We need to keep using the press to find people who have seen or heard anything relevant.'

'Do you really think people will come forward because they publish a few of my words in the papers or recite them on the radio and TV.'

'Yes. People come forward for many reasons, and hearing you speak will prompt emotional responses whether it's empathy or guilt.'

'In this case, we hope the killer may come forward,' Arla adds. 'At the moment, this does not look like the action of someone who set out to kill Eli in a premeditated manner, because there is no clear motive. It is more likely whoever hit him did so on the spur of the moment, and they will be feeling guilty.'

'What do you want me to say, then? Let's get it over with.

André is going home tonight, and I want Jordan to have as much time with him as possible.'

'We are just doing our jobs, Jen.' Wendy speaks to the impatience in my voice.

'I know. I'm sorry. I want you to find who did it. I want you to do your job. But I'm just…'

'Emotional,' Jack fills in a word for me. 'We do understand, Jen. I promise.'

Drained or broken are the words I would have used.

'You didn't have to come so heavy-handed today, though, did you?' André answers. 'One of you could have handled this. And is your camera running? Is that why you're back in uniform?'

'No. I would have told you if it was. I'm wearing uniform because as Jen is getting on okay without me, I'm wearing two hats as they say.' It's a cryptic answer which I don't understand.

Wendy smiles.

They are watching me. Maybe it is with the camera off, but they have all come so while one talks the others can observe my responses and scribble the details in their little black books.

Arla's gaze lifts to look at me as she finishes her latest notation.

Wendy stands up, Jack and Arla stand too. 'We'll get out of your hair. Jack will help you write that statement.'

'Thank you.' I stand.

André stands too. 'I'll show you out. You crack on and get that statement sorted, Jen. Then we'll drive somewhere away from the village for the day.'

The mugs of tea are left on the table, none of them empty.

Jack helps André and me put together some words about us knowing Eli would want us to carry on. I say it doesn't mean we aren't heartbroken. We miss him every hour of every day. If anyone knows anything, if they saw him at any time the day he died, they should come forward. We want to know who he was with.

When I walk inside, the newspaper is unfolded on the floor, the front page visible. The picture of André and me. It looks falsely intimate.

Jordan switches off his game and gets up off the floor. 'That says you and Dad are getting back together.'

'I'll let myself out,' Jack says.

'Don't believe everything you read in a paper,' I say to Jordan. 'A lot of it is fiction. They have to fill the pages, whether there is any news or not.'

'We aren't getting back together,' André says.

'It says Nick killed someone too. Is that story true?'

'Yes,' André confirms it.

Though, we don't know the truth.

CHAPTER FIFTEEN

I am shattered before the day has even begun. The woman in the mirror faces me with dark sacks beneath her eyes. I try to hide the look with foundation. Jordan joins me in the bathroom, and we clean our teeth side by side. Neither of us mention Eli, but I know we both think about his face in the mirror beside ours.

We'd cried together, holding on to each other in Eli's bed last night. We'd spent the day playing a game of being normal people on a visit to Carlisle Castle. Then André left and the cottage seemed so empty. A gaping Eli-sized hole echoing in the middle of us.

When I open the curtains, the pack of reporters and photographers has grown again. They are clustered near the postbox a few metres away from the house. Jack sent out my statement at eleven o'clock yesterday, telling them I am returning to work. It means they know roughly when we will leave the house this morning. We have no choice but to run the gauntlet.

Sammy accompanies Jordan and I on our walk along the side of the road where there is no path, because the press are on the path on the other side.

I pull the peak of Jordan's baseball cap lower, making it hard for them to get a good shot of his face and I defend him with my body, walking on his outside. Sammy walks on the outside of me.

I would have defended Eli's life with my life, if I had the chance.

'Miss Easton! How are you feeling?' A woman rushes forward with a microphone held out. There's a large camera on the shoulder of a woman behind her. Others follow her, surging forward.

I raise Jordan's book bag, hiding behind it, and hurry on, holding Jordan's hand tighter and pulling him with me.

'Miss Easton made a statement yesterday. She has nothing more to say,' Sammy tells them.

They follow us persistently along the road.

Surely, we will become old news soon.

But then we will lose the influence Jack said the media may have on witnesses or the murderer.

Fortunately, a teacher is standing at the school gate. He lets me through with Jordan, and takes us into the school, so I can say my goodbye indoors.

I kiss Jordan's cheek, hang his baseball cap on the peg and wait until he walks into the classroom.

A deep breath steadies my mind, and then I leave via the back door. Running the gauntlet again. Perhaps I should have used the car today.

I half walk half jog the longer route around the back of the church, through the churchyard, and come down into the close on the far side of my house, where I make a dash across the road. No one notices me.

My pace slows as I walk to the lake. I don't think the press will guess I am travelling on the ferry.

As soon as I see the water the pulling sensation returns – Eli reaching for me. Reaching through me. My spirit reaches out to him too. I visualise him walking towards me as I approach the jetty. He falls into step beside me as I climb the steps and stands with me as I wait for Nick.

The ferry peeks its bow about the edge of the bay, on perfect time as always. As it progresses into full view, Nick lifts his hand, acknowledging me. I raise a hand acknowledging him.

FERRYMAN'S TEENAGE MANSLAUGHTER CONVICTION. The paper's headline flashes up in my mind's eye.

An anxious tremble tumbles through my stomach.

Nick's eyes seem to avoid me as he steers the boat alongside the jetty.

Water slaps against the stones.

A faded sky-blue cotton T-shirt hugs his chest and midriff, clinging to the contours of his body as he leans to release the rope from the cleat and the denim pulls tight over his buttocks and thighs as he ties it around the bollard in the stone.

When his amethyst eyes do look at me, his skin flushes to a ripening-raspberry-red that burns brightly beneath his tan as he stands tall and offers me a hand. He has kind eyes. They do not look like the eyes of a killer.

'How are you?' He smiles.

I can't smile back.

The muscles in his hand tremble almost as much as mine as I navigate the steps.

My hand is released. I sit on a bench.

'You don't need to put on a face for me,' he says. 'I thought we were friends. Did you see the article in the paper about me? Are you afraid of me now?'

'No. But you didn't tell me you killed the friend you were speaking about.'

He sits on the bench opposite me. It's something he's never done before. But today is a very different day. 'I didn't lie. I said it was my fault. And how do I open a subject like that?'

'You just say it. It would have been better to hear it from you than a newspaper. If you are calling yourself my friend, friends tell each other important things.'

'I did kill him. David. My best friend.' His eyes focus on mine, and his voice holds a determined clarity. 'We became friends when we were eight, we were friends for ten years. One punch. That's all it took. We argued over a girl in a club. The stupid thing was, she didn't like either of us. We were both drunk. He threw the first punch. I threw the second. He went down and never got up. Sometimes people die and there's no reason to it.' His hands lift palm upwards, expressing a lack of ability to control things. 'I've watched the CCTV film of us several hundred times, it's never made him get back up.'

I breathe in. I've not spoken to anyone who has killed someone before – and now I know what it feels like to be on the other side… 'You served a prison sentence.'

'Eight years, for manslaughter. I pleaded guilty. I did hit him. He did die. I didn't want him to die but he did.'

I don't know what to say. I don't know if this makes Nick any different today than he was two days ago.

'You're quiet. Have I shocked you?'

'Yes.'

'I've been thinking about what happened a lot since Eli died. Maybe tempers flared and that was an accident too.' His voice is not simply being sympathetic of my situation, it is as though he's making excuses and apologising on behalf of whoever struck Eli.

'Someone hit him more than once with a hard object. Probably a rock. That is not an accidental act in a fight.' I break the eye contact, looking down and searching for paracetamol in my handbag.

'Do you need something?'

'Headache pills. Do you have a bottle of water to wash them down with?'

'Sure.' He rises and turns to the cabin.

A moment later, after I've swallowed the tablets, he hands me a small open bottle of mineral water.

'Thanks. Don't you need to get going?'

'When I'm sure you're okay.'

'I'm never going to be okay. You might as well head off.'

His hands settle on his lean waist as he looks at me. 'People sometimes find it hard to be themselves around me when they know.'

I shake my head. I don't need this conversation this morning. 'Can we just set off. I want to get to the school before I lose my nerve.'

A smile briefly pulls at his lips. 'When you're with me, Jen, please, promise me, you'll just be who you are. Don't speak if you're not up to it, or shout or cry, whatever. Don't change how you treat me. Agreed?'

'Agreed.'

When he turns to release the rope, PJ comes to join me.

'I think you're brave, by the way,' he says as he climbs across the boat. 'It's really early to be heading back to work.'

'I'm going back because I want to see what his friends do. I hope they will feel guilty and admit what really happened. I'm sure one of them knows something they haven't said. That's why I asked about Maddie.'

'What's she done?'

'Eli sent her a text. I didn't know they were connected outside school, and I think she may have seen him that day but she hasn't told anyone.'

'Life and soul of the party that girl is. Loud. Like her mother. Not like her sister.' He winds the rope around the cleat on the boat.

'I don't think I've met Maddie's sister…' I didn't know she had a sister.

'Eve. She works in the parlour with Sharon. You must have seen her. Blue hair.'

'Oh. Yes. I have.'

'They're half-sisters, I think. Or Maddie may be adopted. They look quite different. Eve is eighteen.'

He walks into the cabin, his back to me.

'You said Sharon doesn't like you, but you know the family pretty well.'

'No more than most.' The engine whirs into life.

Sunlight glints on the waves the ferry creates as we cross the lake.

My fingernails comb through PJ's hair for a while, but then I lean out towards the water, trying to touch it. The very tips of my fingers reach the surface. There's a sense of touching Eli.

I used to draw patterns on Eli's back with a fingertip. Even recently, when he was lying in just his pyjama bottoms on the sofa, I'd mess around and draw a picture and ask him to guess what I'd drawn.

When I look up, my hand lifts out of the water, drips falling from my fingertips, I catch Nick looking at me.

'Be careful,' he says.

The sense of unfairness is a violent emotion. I've always taught the boys to be careful around water.

'Why do you think Maddie hasn't spoken if she saw him that day?' Nick asks.

'I don't know. She behaves strangely sometimes.'

'I think everyone feels strange at the moment. We're all sad for you.'

Sad… What a weak word to describe this emotion.

The ferry nears the Bowick jetty.

There are nine people waiting.

PJ stays with me as Nick secures the rope. My heartbeat thumps through every cell in my body.

'Ready?' Nick asks in a quiet voice, holding out his hand to help me up.

I swallow against a dry throat.

His hand is steadier now. Mine still trembles. 'You'll be fine. Call me if you want someone to talk to. I will stop taking passengers on and call you back.'

'Thank you.' I climb the steps.

'See you later,' he says as I step ashore.

'Yes.'

My feet are heavy, and my insides hollow as I walk from the lakeshore to the school. I'm a robot following a route. My heart and head are left at the lake, with Eli.

For a moment, I picture Eli travelling on the bus as I walk into the school. As though he'll arrive soon.

I breathe out a shaky breath as I push the staff room door open. I could easily run to the bathroom and relieve my stomach of the dry toast I ate earlier.

'Jen.'

Paula rushes to greet me. 'How are you? I was waiting for you. I didn't see you slip past. I want to speak to you. Are you sure you're up to this? I've arranged short-notice cover if you need it.'

'No. I can manage.'

'The children have been told you're teaching today.'

She walks into the staff room beside me. Every conversation stops, and every eye turns to look at me.

'Jen is here.' Paula states the obvious.

'Hello, everyone,' I force a bright voice, meeting a few gazes. 'Just to clarify, speak to me as you normally would. I am grieving but it doesn't make me inhuman, just be yourselves. Thank you.'

People smile kindly, and then conversations recommence, but in quieter voices.

I look at Paula. 'Thank you. I appreciate your kindness. I need to focus on preparing for the lessons now, though.'

'Okay.' Her hand touches my upper arm. 'If you need me, you know where to find me.'

That seems to be the next step after sorry – people expressing that they're available if I want to tell them how awful I feel.

I turn to my locker, turning my back to the room and the people in it.

The first lesson is with Eli's class. But the first tasks of my day are taking the register with my form group and leading them into the assembly.

'Five minutes to the bell and roll call!' Geography-Geoff shouts across the room. 'Let the fun and games begin!'

Conversations end and staff file out of the room. I hold back to be the last, bracing books and my laptop in front of my chest, shielding myself from conversation.

In the classroom my autopilot engages. I smile at the Year 7 children as they enter, chirpy and charged up for the school holidays that are just around the corner.

'Good morning, all.'

'Good morning, Miss Easton,' they deliver in return, with the commitment of the younger years.

And so the day begins as it does on every other school day. The rhythm of the school playing its melody. It makes it easier than I expected to live each minute through.

In the large hall as I sit and watch the assembly, I don't hear what's said. My mind skims through memories, drifting miles away, until suddenly my thoughts are drawn back into the room. Something, a sixth sense, urges me to look around. When I do my gaze immediately clashes with Maddie's. She was watching me. On some level my mind had felt it. She looks away.

When my eyes return to the stage, I sense her watching again. I don't look back. She will be in the classroom with me immediately after the assembly. I'll have my chance to study her then.

As Eli's class walk through the door for the first lesson, I observe the expression on every face, my heart pulsing so hard I feel light-headed – faint. They don't look at me. They look ahead or at each other, clearly unsure what to do. The silence is chilling as they take their seats.

Aiden comes through the door, the handles of a sports bag held in a hand that rests on his shoulder.

His gaze connects with me. There's a second where his lips rise, then the smile that was going to form falls away. He flushes to a watermelon-flesh scarlet. It's a sudden change of colour. 'Hi, miss,' he says as he passes me. It is not a guilty or dismissive tone. It is not a guilty look in his eyes either. His eyes glimmer as he takes his seat. Obviously crying, he wipes a tear from his cheek and focuses his attention on unloading what he needs from his bag.

Maddie is the last to walk into the classroom, back straight and head high. She looks me in the eyes. 'Miss.' The single word seems to say everything at once, I'm glad you're here. I'm sorry. I want to help. Are any of those sentiments real or has she learned how to master emotions after her experience in America.

'Can you close the door, please, Maddie?'

I can't look at the desk Eli always sat in, my gaze skims over it as I engage with the children.

'Good morning, everyone.'

As they reply, in a disorganised clutter of greetings, Maddie walks in front of my desk, past her usual seat and drops her bag down on the desk beside Aiden. On Eli's desk.

A breath is trapped in my lungs as she sits down.

She looks at Aiden, something unspoken and easily known passing between them.

She moves her bag to the floor and looks at me.

I hate her. I have a clear, definite knowledge of the emotion. I breathe it away. I can't hate a pupil. I look to those at the back of the room.

'Tell me what you've done since I was last in class?'

I know what they've done. I have the notes from the teacher who replaced me. I just want to check it's sunk in. They'll be facing mock exams early in the next school year.

'Open your books,' I tell them after the recap. Which Maddie had taken over, even though I did not ask her to participate. If she feels at all guilty, she hides it very well. But she has had a very significant opportunity to learn how to obscure emotions. 'We'll look more deeply at Shakespeare's imagery today. I want to talk about how he uses blood in the play.'

Every head lifts. Every child looking wide-eyed towards me.

It's usually comical when you stand at the front of a class and see the same reaction on every face. Not today.

Their reaction is horror. They did not expect me to discuss the murderous element of *Macbeth's* plotline.

I lift my lips into a smile, discovering I can act well too. 'Someone, give me a quote that mentions blood from the play.'

Book covers flip back, and some hands rise into the air.

Maddie's doesn't. She glances at Aiden, who looks at her for a second before looking back at me. Another moment of unspoken dialogue.

I point to Strictly-Emma with the long fringe like Claudia Winkleman. 'Emma.'

'Out damned spot,' she says it with passion, acting Lady Macbeth's mad sleep-deprived state.

I point at Arthur-the-king-of-children. 'Arthur, do you have one?'

He grins. *'Here's yet a spot. Here's the small of blood still.'* He rubs his fingers as if he is trying to rid himself of King Duncan's blood.

'Do any of you know how many times words about blood appear in the play?'

Heads shake. 'No, miss.'

'No.'

'Lots I guess.'

'How many, miss?'

'One hundred and nine times.' I tell them.

Maddie and Aiden watch me intently, apparently mesmerised

by my choice of subject. They are curious about where I'm leading them.

'Immediately after Macbeth murdered Duncan, he shows Lady Macbeth his hands.'

I hold out my hands, acting the part. 'Imagine his hands dripping with blood as he tells her, *'This is a sorry sight.'* Imagine how it would feel to have undertaken such a task. We see from this moment on, from the very beginning, that Shakespeare expresses a connection with blood and guilt.'

Guilt is the real theme of this lesson.

'From the day Lady Macbeth saw the blood dripping from his hands, Shakespeare describes her guilt growing through that same image. Look at page…'

I lead them through passages of text. Following the connection with blood and guilt throughout the play.

Maddie and Aiden glance at each other often. I've not seen it before. I'm not sure if they shared looks before and it didn't stand out to me because I'd have had no interest. I wish I could be a fly-sized drone and listen into their conversation after the class.

'So, when Shakespeare writes, *'they say, blood will have blood,'* Macbeth is telling his audience the blood of the murder victim will seek out the blood of his killer. Obviously today, this means even more to us with the developments of DN—' The school bell rings, calling out the end of the lesson. '—A.' I finish when the ringing stops. 'Thank you, everyone, good work.' I close the book in my hand.

The children shove their books into their bags.

'Maddie,' I say, before she can move from behind the desk. 'May I have a quick word before you go to break?'

'Miss.' She throws her head in a way that makes her ponytail swing.

Aiden stops beside her, his bag hanging from a hand.

'Do you need to speak to me?' I ask him.

There's a slight hesitation, a glance at Maddie, and then a decision to walk on. 'No, miss.'

He's the last to leave. I follow him to the door, close it behind him, and then turn, smiling for Maddie.

'How are you?' I ask.

She's standing, leaning back against the desk she was sitting at. Her bag hanging from her shoulder. Her arms folded over her chest. Her eyes trying to read me. She doesn't trust the question and she doesn't answer it.

'Why do you want to talk to me, miss?'

'Your mother said you've been struggling.' I can't bring myself to add, since Eli died. 'She told me what happened at the school in America. Remember, we have the school counsellor if you need to talk to someone. Don't suffer alone.' I don't think Sharon will have told Maddie that she's already told me Maddie is speaking to the counsellor.

'I…'

I've flummoxed her. Kicked the feet out from under miss confident. Her skin colour lifts to a peachy pink.

'Thank you for being a friend to Eli, Maddie. I saw the message he sent you. I know you spoke to each other outside school.'

'I've spoken to the counsellor. I… Eli was nice. I'm sorry.'

That feeble phrase.

'I'm sorry too. Go on, you can go. That was all I wanted to say.'

She walks past me without a parting word, leaves the room and leaves the door open.

An idea leaps in my thoughts. The school counsellor doesn't come in on Mondays. She's quite an eccentric woman. She has a filing cabinet, and I've seen her putting folders into it when I collected a younger child from her room. I think she keeps handwritten notes.

The filing cabinet must be locked, though. Her office will be locked too.

But there are labelled duplicate keys for all the cupboards in the administration office.

I leave the classroom. I have twenty-five minutes before the next lesson.

My passage through the school is not notable. I mingle with the children making their way to the playground and common rooms.

When I walk into the administration office, there is that moment again, when everyone looks at me with the same expression. I see their minds searching for the right things to say.

Their awkwardness is my advantage.

'I need something from my handbag in my locker, and I've stupidly lost the key. I have a brain like a sieve at the moment. Can I fetch the duplicate?'

'Oh.'

'Yes.'

'Go on.'

'The storage room is open.'

Officially, they should not let me look myself. But their concern and confusion about how to respond to me means none of them challenge me.

I walk through the office to the small room at the back, where keys are bundled together in boxes on the shelving. For the first time in days I feel alive, I have something to do to help.

The keys are labelled. I sort through the boxes. Staff Lockers. Stationery cabinets. Classroom doors. Counselling office. The counselling office key is in a box on its own. Two keys dangle from one key ring. The door and the filing cabinet key. I need to find my locker key too, to be able to show it if I'm asked.

I slip the counselling office keys into my pocket and open the box with the bundle of keys for the staff lockers. It takes a few minutes to find the one for my locker.

When I walk out, I raise a hand, showing them the purple plastic key ring and key dangling from a finger. 'Thank you,' I say. 'I'll get another cut.'

The counsellor's office is at the end of a quiet corridor. The door at the end is a fire exit. The office was deliberately selected because it's away from a thoroughfare. No one is here. I walk quickly, but casually, swapping the locker key for the keys in my pocket.

At the door of the office, I fit the key in the lock, glancing back along the hallway, and hurry inside. The filing cabinet is in the far corner. I stop and lock the door from the inside, making sure I won't be interrupted, walk over and pull the cord for the blind, so the slats cover the window, and no one can see me. The room is in shade, but not dark, daylight filters through the cracks in the blind.

The smaller key fits snuggly in the filing cabinet's lock. I slide open the top drawer. Old-style manila cardboard files are stored in alphabetical slots. The names of the pupils are written in pencil on the top edge of the files.

My fingers skim through the slots, sliding them forward as I read the surnames.

Cox, Madeline. I lift out a thin file.

Thank you for being one of those people who hates modern ways, Patricia!

The bell will ring soon, calling the children back to classes.

I fold back the manila cover. There are only a few pages of handwritten notes. I fold the sheets of paper in half, lift the hem of my blouse out from the waistband of my trousers, press the folded paper against my stomach and tuck my blouse back over the top.

I put the empty file back in position, lock the cabinet, open the blind, leave the room and lock the door. I walk briskly along the halls with arms swinging, trying to look casual, as adrenaline pulses.

'You won't believe it,' I say looking at the silent admin staff, as I walk through their office, waving the locker key on my finger again. 'I found mine. Sorry, I'm not thinking clearly. I'll put this back.'

All keys returned. I head to the staff room.

The brassy-notes of the school bell ring as I reach the door.

Everyone else has already left.

I lift my blouse even as the door shuts behind me, taking out the sheets of paper with shaking hands. I stuff them inside my handbag in the locker and hurry off, late for the class.

CHAPTER SIXTEEN

The ringing bell calls time on the second lesson of the day.

'Pack up then. Off you go.'

I used an online quiz to fill time in the lesson. I can get away with it this last week of the school year. We are allowed to have purely fun lessons in the last week. I consumed my mental energy navigating the first lesson. I only came here to teach Eli's class. But now I am here I have two more lessons to cope with before the day is over.

'Bye, miss.'

'See you, miss.'

'Thanks, miss.'

The children call as they exit.

There were some awkward silences and odd looks early on, but within a few minutes, they'd become used to the presence of the mother of a murder victim and just saw me as Miss Easton again.

I walk over to the window, unsure what to do with myself for the lunch hour, arms folding over my chest and hands clutching my bare upper arms beneath the short sleeves of my blouse.

There's a police car in the school car park.

My arms unravel. I move quickly, close the laptop and books, pick everything up and follow the crush of children heading along the hall and downstairs.

The administration staff don't seem to be aware that the bell has called lunchtime. They are all speaking into phones or keying numbers in to make phone calls.

I walk through the room again and tap on the door of Paula's office, with a single knuckle.

'Come in.'

Wendy and Arla are standing in front of Paula's desk.

'Hello, Jen,' Arla acknowledges.

'Why are you here?'

'The police want to take some children out of classes to interview them,' Paula says. Which means the staff are busy ringing their parents.

'Do you need me to do anything?' I offer instinctively.

'No,' Wendy answers. 'Although, perhaps, go home. I am not sure you should be teaching.'

'Patricia is counselling some of the children tomorrow,' Paula says. 'Perhaps you should—'

'If I think a counsellor will help. I'll find someone outside the school.'

Tomorrow, Patricia will find Maddie's empty file. But I'm sure she won't think it's anything to do with me. She's such a muddle-head she'll think she put them into the wrong file.

The walls of the tiny office close in. I turn away from them all and walk out with no goodbye. I need fresh air. I'll lock my laptop and books away in the staff room, walk down to the lake and eat my lunch there, with Eli.

When I close the door of my locker, shutting everything safe inside, I take a deep breath, lining up the bones of my spine one on top of another, so I stand straighter, so I can stand at all. Before I walk away, I glance through the window. My gaze catches on Aiden and Maddie in the playground. They're standing by a wall near the tennis courts with a group of others from their school year.

I can't help myself, my plan to walk to the lake evaporates in a second. Instead, I am heading to the playground.

As I cross the expanse of tarmac, walking through the middle of groups of children, avoiding those who run across my path, Aiden's head turns. His eyes fix on me, looking through the gaps between the heads and shoulders of his friends.

I try to smile, but my lips are too stiff. My hands curl into fists.

The teenagers part, turning and looking where Aiden is looking – at me.

Maddie is in the middle of the group of boys.

My teeth clench tight as I walk the last couple of metres.

'Hello, miss.' Aiden's voice is as sweet as honey.

I swallow against a dry throat. 'Hello, would you mind if we talk alone for a moment?'

'Sure, miss.' One shoulder shrugs. He glances at Maddie before he steps out of the small crowd around him.

I lead him away from his friends, following the tennis courts' fencing, walking side by side, feeling numerous eyeballs targeted on our backs. His hands slip into the pockets of his black school trousers.

'Are you okay?' I open.

'Not really, miss. I miss Eli. I dream about him. He's alive in my dreams, then I wake up and remember he's gone. What do you want to talk about? Did I do something wrong?'

I don't know Aiden, you tell me. 'No. I want to talk about Eli. Do you mind?'

A two-shoulder shrug gives his agreement. 'The police spoke to me again today. Do you know?'

'Did they?' *Already?* They must have interviewed Aiden first. 'Did you tell them anything new?'

'I don't know anything I haven't said.'

'You didn't tell them about the drinking initially. Have you lied about being with him when he died.'

'Drinking is illegal that's why I didn't tell them. But we had a drink, so what. Lots of people drink. I don't know who hit him, though, miss. I wasn't with him then. He stayed on his own. I tried to persuade him to come with us. I don't know why he was at that end of the lake or who did it, I promise. I wish I did. I wish I was there to stop it.'

'Where did you leave him?' The police must know this, but they haven't told me.

'We walked down to the picnic tables at the lakeside here and drank the cider. When I left, he was still there.'

'Why did you leave him on his own?'

'We were all a bit drunk. I wanted to walk back, and he wanted to call a taxi. He wouldn't come with me.'

There is something he's not saying. His voice has a shaky edge, and I think his hands are in his pockets to hide a tremble. 'And you chose not to use the taxi? Why would you walk alone? Most people would stay and come home in a taxi with him. It's a long walk if you're a little drunk. I don't believe what you're saying. Tell me the whole truth. It will feel better than lying, Aiden. And it might help the police find who killed Eli.'

'It won't, miss. I don't know who did it.' He stops walking, turns and looks straight into my eyes. 'Did the police tell you to ask me? Because Dad was in the room, and you're not allow—'

'No. Eli is my son. I want to know how he died.'

There's a second of silence as we look intently into each others' eyes. Looking for truth.

'I went home with Maddie.'

'Maddie was there?'

'You can't tell anyone, miss. Her mother hates her being with boys. She met us, and that's why I left him. She and I walked back through the woods. He said he didn't want to watch us kissing.

But you can't tell anyone because Maddie would be grounded for a year. Her mum isn't very nice.'

This is the truth. It's written in the eyes that look directly back at me, hiding nothing.

Maddie and Aiden. It makes sense. The looks they share. Why Eli didn't speak about her but spoke to her. She's a friend of his friend.

'Thank you. Was Eli alone when you left? You didn't see anyone else around there?'

'No. I told the police what I know.'

'The police told me Eli was with a girl at some point. But not before you left him?'

'No. No one else was there. The others had already left. He never said he had a girl or even that he liked anyone. That's why they tested Maddie, isn't it? Because he texted her, so they thought she must be the girl. They were only friends. She's my girlfriend.'

I breathe in, about to turn away, unable to think of what else to ask.

'Miss, people keep saying there was something wrong because he didn't tell people you were his mum. He told me, and I asked him why he didn't tell others. I asked him if you were a shit mother or something. He said you made mistakes, but you were a great mum. I'm telling everyone that.'

Eli's words, in his friend's voice, stirs warmth through my frozen heart.

I touch his arm for a second. 'Ask Maddie if any of the girls confided in her. He didn't accidentally meet a girl. He planned to meet her. He took a necklace with him. It was a girl he's met more than once.'

His arm moves away and he turns and walks back to his friends.

I don't understand why Eli would keep the girl a secret from his best friend? It's one more thing that doesn't make sense.

For the rest of the day. I wait to be called out of the classroom and thrown out of the school because Aiden has told his dad I talked to him.

When the final bell of the day rings, every muscle in my body relaxes with relief.

On the journey home across the lake, on a busy ferry, the tips of my fingers stretch out, reaching into the gentle waves made by the bow of the boat. I touch Eli's caramel skin and look at his smile.

The boat travels towards the south end. Towards Eli's bay. I sense him waiting there. Standing on the wooden boards of the jetty, eyes on me. He told Aiden how he felt about me. I wish he'd told me in recent weeks. I need words like that to hold on to.

The flowers and tributes have gone. The shore is empty. Denying that anything terrible happened here.

I watch long waves created by the bow and the stern of the boat rolling up against the bank, catching at the wooden stilts of the jetty and washing up onto the gravel. One walker waits at the end of the jetty. Nick fulfils the rhythm of his job, he ties the rope, welcomes the passenger, accepts payment and unties the rope. Nothing is out of the ordinary, except that Eli is no longer in the world.

The boat turns towards the west side of the lake. Nick's cabin faces me. The two windows that face the lake stare blindly in the ferry's direction. *I didn't see anything.*

No one is standing at the next jetty. But four of the tourists disembark there.

My gaze bumps into Nick's as he unties the rope. He looks away.

As the ferry travels on towards the Lowerdale Jetty, sadness sweeps through me, a high bow wave I am immersed beneath as life and time push forwards, when I want them to stay still. I don't want to leave the water, to leave Eli. But Jordan is waiting.

My fingers only lift from the water as the ferry nears the jetty.

'Are you okay?' Nick asks quietly as he climbs past me to tie up. He hadn't had chance to ask when I boarded, and I hadn't called PJ over to me.

'Mm.' The sound in my throat is non-committal. *No.*

He offers his hand to help me climb the steps before others. I'd rather stay until last.

'Would you like to speak on the phone later?'

'No.' The only thing I want to do this evening is read what is written about Maddie on the pieces of paper hidden in my handbag. 'Thank you,' I'm barely polite as I let go of his hand. The only person I want to see this evening is Jordan. 'Bye!' I remember to call when I am half way along the jetty.

When I step off the end, I look back across the lake, reaching for Eli's spirit, urging him to stay with me. He doesn't. He slips away.

I don't walk my normal route. I take the detour via the tourist car park and walk through to the primary school from the other end of the village. The after-school club uses the primary school's premises. Most of the children are outside on the sports field today, in the middle of a game of rounders. I don't see Jordan amongst them.

I take out my phone and call the club's number.

'Hello, Fun and games 4U.'

'Hello, this is Jordan Pelle's mother. I'm outside at the gate.'

'Okay, Jordan will be with you in a minute.'

The call cuts off.

My fingers slip through the gate and curl around the links of metal as I wait for him. One of the young men who works in the club, Niall, walks out of the school door beside Jordan, carrying Jordan's backpack and his book bag.

My fingers leave the links and I wave vigorously, realising

how much I missed him today. He waves back, smiling, and breaks into a run to reach me quicker. He must feel the same. Niall needs to unlock the gate before Jordan can come through. He calls something to Jordan that I don't hear. Jordan slows to a walk.

As he walks closer a large dark purple bruise is visible on his forehead. A large lump too.

'Hi, Mum.' Our gazes meet through the wire. The wound on his head looks angry.

'Hello, darling. How did you hurt your head? Were you playing football?'

Niall is a few paces behind Jordan.

'Hi, Miss Easton.' He reaches to unlock the gate. 'He's had a little accident.'

'Mum.' Jordan rushes through and his arms wrap around me. I see a large white dressing on his elbow too.

'I missed you today,' I say.

'I missed you too.'

He releases me, steps back and shows me his knee. 'I tore my trousers, sorry.'

'What did you do to yourself?'

Niall holds out Jordan's belongings, and a manila envelope. I take everything.

'There was an argument in the playground. We patched him up, but he bumped his head, so I have a letter for a head injury here. You'll need to keep an eye on him for the next twenty-four hours. He hasn't been playing rounders he's been watching.'

'Thank you.' I slide the letter into my handbag and rest a hand on Jordan's shoulder.

'See you tomorrow, Jordan.'

'Bye, Niall.'

'Argument…' I prompt gently as we walk away from the gate.

'Michael said Eli deserved to die because he was stupid for

going to the lake on his own. I hit him and kicked him, but he was stronger.'

'Oh, Jordy, darling.' I pull him tight against my side as we turn away from the school. 'Don't tell anyone in school, but I'm glad you hit him.'

'I don't want to go to school tomorrow, Mum.'

'Neither do I. Let's call in sick in the morning and we'll spend the day together. Do you want an ice cream?'

'Yes. Please.'

'Come on, then. But if anyone aims a camera at you, keep your head down.'

The warm day has drawn a dozen tourists to the ice-cream parlour, the picnic tables on the cobbles outside are all in use and the queue stretches out of the shop.

I wait behind Jordan.

His eyes fix on all the pretty colours in the freezer cabinet as we step inside the shop.

My gaze travels between Sharon and the blue-haired younger woman. Nick is right, Sharon's eldest daughter's facial features aren't at all like Maddie's. She's slight and slender too, and Maddie is curvier and taller. But the blue-haired daughter's nose and mouth are similar to Sharon's. Now I think about it, Maddie doesn't look anything like Sharon.

'Hi, Jordan. What do you want?' The daughter calls across Sharon. I hadn't realised she knew Jordan's name, but I suppose everyone knows our names now.

'Can I have a scoop of chocolate brownie and black cherry mashup gateaux, please?' Jordan asks. The flavours are Eli's favourites.

The girl's gaze drops away from us as she picks up a waffle cone. I wonder if she realises.

'Are you having one, Mum?'

I don't really want one, my stomach is in a tangled knot. I'm standing here with Maddie's stolen information in my handbag.

'Just one scoop of vanilla in a pot.' That was what I'd ordered the day Eli died, before Jordan knew. 'No. I take it back. I'll have a scoop of the chocolate brownie and the black cherry mashup gateaux in a tub.'

We sit on our favourite bench in the churchyard, eating Eli's favourite ice creams and talk about the things he did that made us laugh, and love him more. We will love him forever.

I should ask the National Trust if we can pay for a bench to be set up in Eli's bay, with his name on it for everyone to see, then our love for him will be remembered beyond our lifetimes.

When we reach our street, it's clear of reporters and photographers, but even so we run from the corner to the cottage. I open the door quickly and close it behind us with relief.

'Shall we sit in the garden and have a drink of lemonade?' I hang up my handbag on the coat hooks. Maddie's information will have to wait until Jordan is in bed.

'Have you got homework to do tonight?' he asks me.

'No. No marking or planning tonight. We can be as lazy as we like. Our summer holiday starts today.'

It's exhausting trying to smile and find words to help Jordan smile all evening. We eat pizza, play card games and watch a couple of episodes of the Marvel series he's into. But no matter how much I try to make it feel different, the small cottage is cold and heartless. I send him up to change into his pyjamas and clean his teeth at nine, and we lie side by side on top of the duvet to read more chapters of the Harry Potter book André started. With Eli's favourite R & B music band looking down on us from the poster Blu-Tacked to the wardrobe door.

When I tuck Jordan in, I kiss his poorly forehead as gently as possible. 'Sleep tight.' I turn off the bedside light and leave him to sleep.

It's still light. The line of sky visible through the living room window is the gleaming pinks and reds of a beautiful sunset.

I open my handbag and take out the folded pages – the secrets

I've stolen today. My heartbeat races with adrenaline as it had earlier. With a purpose. I put the pages down on the dining table, but before I sit down to read them, I collect a bottle of wine that André had left here, and a glass. To wash the information down.

The full glass ready beside me, I settle on the dining chair and slide the paperwork in front of me. Patricia hasn't written very much. She must use these notes as a reminder of what she's discussed, rather than a record.

My mouth opens as the first point penetrates.

A witness of a mass shooting in the USA.

These notes must have been recorded during the first weeks Maddie arrived at Bowick Academy.

From her hiding place, Maddie watched her best friend and other friends shot. She regrets hiding. Maybe if she came out, he would have stopped shooting. She thinks she should be the only one who died.

No wonder she'd looked at Aiden a dozen times while I'd led a lesson all about blood and guilt. If she tells her mother, I'll probably be dismissed tomorrow.

Maddie thinks he walked through the school searching for her and merely killed the others who were in the way. She feels responsible for the murders. The perpetrator was her boyfriend.

. . .

Her boyfriend? Aiden said Sharon didn't like her seeing boys, and she was a lot younger then. I can't imagine how awful it would feel discovering you'd dated a murderer even as an adult.

Maddie's mum found out that, at the age of twelve Maddie was dating a fifteen-year-old boy and her mother intervened. Maddie admits she had sex with this boy prior to this.

'This is why Sharon feels uncomfortable about her seeing boys. I would have intervened too.' I talk to an empty room, before drinking a large mouthful of wine.

Her mother confronted the boy at his home and forbid Maddie from speaking to him further. What her mother was unaware of, was that the boy came from an abusive family.

Maddie saw television reports after the event. After her mother's visit, the boy was beaten badly by his father. His response was to take his father's gun, shoot his parents, and take the gun into school. She doesn't know whether he intended to shoot her or if she let him find her, whether he would have stopped shooting.

'Oh my gosh.'

Another sip of wine and I turn the page.

There is no new information after this, but from the notes and dates of attendance, she spoke with Patricia regularly when she began attending the school. The dates stop after five months.

Then, the sixth page, the last page, is dated the Thursday after Eli's death.

. . .

The death of Eli Pelle has brought back feelings and memories from the past. Maddie is struggling to sleep. She has spoken to her GP about medication for anxiety. She has had nightmares and feelings of guilt.

Guilt? Guilt recalled from those who died in America, or new guilt?

I lean back in the chair, sliding the pieces of paper away, and drink more wine. The notes don't tell me any more than I know.

I haven't spoken to my GP! But she needed to!

Medication will never bring Eli back, though, and maybe I am self-medicating. I lift the glass in a toast to the misery, anger and frustration biting at my heels. I'm desperate to do something but there is nothing I can do.

Another sip of wine helps the emotions pass.

I can't stay here. Not in the cottage or the village. I can't do anything here. My fingers release the glass and reach for my phone that's laying on the table. André's right. Jordan needs to get away from the house and so do I.

Contacts.

Fay Pelle.

My thumb touches her number. It rings once. Twice.

'Jen, love,' she answers. 'Hello. How are you? It's so awful. I've done nothing but cry for days.' Her voice welcomes me without judgement before I say a word.

'Hello, Fay.' I should have called her before. But I've hidden from her for a long time. Leaving the connection to the boys. Leaving her for André to keep custody of in our divorce. But when we were married, she was my mum too, because I didn't have my own mother. 'I'm sorry, I haven't called you before.'

'Oh, honey, you have no need to apologise.'

'Can Jordan and I come and stay with you?'

'Of course you can. I have the room. You should be here with people who care about you. That is what Eli would want, for us all to be together and supporting each other.'

Eli... My eyes shut. How can I leave him alone at the lake, waiting for me to come back.

I can't run away. 'I'm not working tomorrow. We'll drive down. I'll stay until the weekend but then I should come back. I don't want Jordan to think I don't want him with me, though.'

'He won't think that, love.'

'I think he should stay with you all summer. It's not the wrong decision, is it? He won't hold this against me? He won't think I'm deserting him?'

'He knows you love him. We'll buy him his own phone so he can call you anytime. You won't be a million miles away. We aren't going to let him feel alone.'

'I...' Tears capture my voice. 'Eli never...' I try again.

'If you are feeling at all to blame you stop that right now. Neither you nor André killed him.' Her voice rings with anger.

I sniff back the tears dripping through my nose and reach for a tissue from the box on the table.

'The boys love you. Nothing you do will ever stop that. They think far too much of you to blame you for anything.'

'You'd be surprised. Eli said some terrible things at times. He wasn't sure at the point he died if he did love me.'

'Don't be silly. That boy loved the bones of you. Why do you think he left his friends and moved up there with you? He could have stayed with me. But he wouldn't let you go without him because he said you were useless at looking after yourself. He thought you needed him.'

'Don't set me off again.' I dab at my eyes. She's said what I needed to hear most, that he loved me underneath every argument and every other emotion.

We sniff in unison. Amusement cracks from my throat.

'I'll look forward to seeing you tomorrow as much as I will to seeing Jordan, and I'll give you a great big Nanna Fay hug.'

'Thank you.'

'You're welcome, dear. Tomorrow.'

'Yes. Tomorrow.'

She ends the call.

I'm left staring at the phone in the quiet.

CHAPTER SEVENTEEN

The sound of the wild birds' choir singing their dawn chorus fills the room, pulling me from a dream. *Glorious,* one of Eli's favourite words, describes the sound perfectly.

I am with Eli in a park, he's running to catch a frisbee. Jordan and André are here too, urging him to catch it.

Memory hits me. He's gone. When I get up, he won't be in his bed, or the house, or the world.

I don't want to leave the dream. I keep my eyes closed, savouring the images and sounds. The birds' medley makes it difficult to capture a note from a single bird, it also prevents my mind from finding the dream again.

I would feel guilty for sleeping, but the dream was wonderful. I want to spend a million more hours in dreams with Eli.

It's cooler in the room than it was last night. I reach out, pull the duvet over me and curl up on my side, focusing my mind on the last of the images from the dream.

Sleep doesn't return.

The birdsong winds down and becomes sporadic, like a music box's clockwork song slowing down.

Daylight infiltrates my eyelids.

I open my eyes.

6.15am, the numbers on the electric clock read.

I get up, make raisin pancake batter and sit on the sofa waiting until Jordan's footsteps make the boards creak upstairs.

I take the batter out of the fridge, turn on the hob and heat the frying pan.

When he walks downstairs, still in his pyjamas, the smell of freshly cooked pancakes fills the cottage.

'Yum,' he says, joining me in the kitchen. He greets me with a hug, his arms around my middle, his head resting against my shoulder, his chin against my breast. The bruise on his forehead is a darker purple.

We sit down and eat together, and I probably eat the most I've eaten since Eli died. It doesn't mean we've forgotten him. Raisin pancakes are his favourite. I think about opening the windows and imagine the smell of pancakes drifting all the way to the lake, so he'll know we haven't forgotten him.

The ringtone of my mobile phone shatters the introspective mood of our breakfast. The phone is in the kitchen, wriggling around on the work surface as it vibrates with the rhythm of the rings.

I leave the table and pick it up.

Jack.

'Hello.'

'Hello. Is that you, Jen?'

'Yes. Of course. What do you want?'

'We have the DNA results back for Maddie Cox.'

I don't breathe. I can't. Time stops.

'It's not a match.'

'It's not. Oh.' It's only confirmed what Aiden told me. But if not Maddie, then who? 'What will happen now?'

'We spoke to his friends again yesterday, but nothing new was said. We are still searching through CCTV. There are different routes Eli could have taken from Bowick to the Southend Bay, we will find some evidence of how he got there and who he was with.'

'But if he walked along the lakeshore there are no cameras there.'

'Whoever he met up with may not have walked that way, or if they did, they must have joined him at Bowick.'

My lips part. I can't answer. After all these days they're no further forward. I sniff away tears.

'Jen… Are you okay?'

'No.'

'Are you going into work today?'

'No. Yesterday was too much for Jordan and me.'

'Well, in my opinion you shouldn't have tried for even one day.'

I don't answer, I cut him off and put the phone down on the kitchen work surface. I feel like throwing it away so he can never call me again.

'Who was that, Mum?' Jordan asks.

'No one important. Finish off those pancakes. We are going to Nanna Fay's this afternoon, and this morning we'll buy something for a picnic to take over to Southend Bay. We'll eat lunch there before we leave.' With Eli.

The Co-op is busy with tourists buying morning papers, and eggs and bacon for English breakfasts. Jordan carries our metal basket as we walk along the aisles, picking out treats to eat.

'Hello.'

Sharon's voice has me spinning around.

Her eldest daughter stands behind her, looking at me with an expression that assesses and tries to learn something from me, as though she is keen to know something I know. The colour of the eyes I look back at are incredibly unusual. A blue that is slightly violet. A cornflower blue. Or perhaps they are more like the petals of forget-me-not flowers. Her hand lifts and strokes back her cobalt-blue fringe in a gesture that expresses unease as a hot radish-red blush even more strongly emphasises the shades of blue in her irises.

Eli stands beside me laughing at my terrible colourful descriptions. Not laughing with me anymore but laughing at me. *'Mum, don't be stupid.'*

I miss him with every cell of my body.

'How are you?' Sharon asks, her voice loaded with what sounds like disingenuous concern and she doesn't wait for me to reply. 'I had to go into school yesterday. They interviewed Maddie again. She had nothing to do with Eli's death you know.' Her voice drives that statement at me.

If I didn't know about Maddie's circumstances, I'd walk away, insulted, but I do know. The situation must be distressing for Maddie and Sharon.

'We should talk. Are you free for a coffee?' I say. I should clear the air. I haven't spoken to her properly since we had sex. I need to tell her I don't even want to be friends. It would be too awkward and I don't need awkward at the moment. 'Could you come to the cottage in…' I glance at my watch, 'twenty minutes?'

She looks at her daughter. 'Will you open the parlour?'

She nods.

'I'll come to the cottage,' Sharon confirms, and then she returns to the task of shopping, dismissing my presence with no words of parting.

'Can we have strawberries, Mum. And dip them in a pot of clotted cream.'

'I think we should. We deserve a little luxury.' My hand rests on Jordan's shoulder, casually, while in my chest my heartbeat races at a billion miles an hour.

Clunk.

The door knocker strikes down hard exactly twenty minutes later.

My hands still – Jordan's T-shirt, mid-fold, falls on top of the pile of clothes in the open suitcase.

I must be courageous and face this conversation.

'Carry on packing,' I tell Jordan, whose head is buried in the airing cupboard, looking for his favourite clothes. 'Find what games you want, too. I'll speak to Sharon in the garden. We won't be long.'

My footsteps are light on the stairs as I race down. 'I'm coming!'

I release the catch, turn the handle and— 'Sharon. Hi.' I step back so she can come in. 'Do you want coffee or tea?' She walks past me and I shut the door behind her.

'Tea. Please.'

I lead the way to the kitchen, leading her away from Jordan who is bumping about in his bedroom upstairs.

'How are you?' she asks as I pick up the kettle.

She'd asked in the Co-op and hadn't given me the chance to answer. I am not sure what the answer is though.

'Surviving.' I keep my back turned to her.

She doesn't say anything else and neither do I.

The silence becomes solid, too hard to break, as I gather together mugs, teabags and milk. It's that – *what do I say to the mother of a murdered son* – moment. I'm too frustrated and impatient today to be kind and break the silence.

'The sunset was gorgeous last night. Did you see it?' Sharon's palm rests on the work surface, near the sink, beside the mugs. The gesture feels threatening even though her words are entirely the opposite.

'It was pretty.' I pour the boiling water into the mugs, my heartbeat tumbling over itself.

'Maddie said you spoke to one of the boys in the playground at the school yesterday?'

Does she know about Aiden now? Should she know? I don't want to be the one that gives them away.

I feel a hot flush form blotches on my chest. I face her as I sense the blush creeping up my neck. I leave the tea to stew for a minute. She's standing inches away, uncomfortably close. But it's a narrow kitchen.

'The boy is Eli's best friend.'

Her hand slides from the work surface, hovering near my arm for a moment as though she's thinking about touching me.

She has a small kitchen too. The night Eli died we'd kissed in there, my back pressing into the work surface. My head shakes the thought away quickly and I turn back to the mugs.

'Do you take milk and sugar?'

I've never been a good liar. Eli and Jordan always mercilessly broke me down whenever I tried to keep secrets. During my affair with Bell, I'd felt constantly sick with anxiety. Every day I'd struggled to look André in the eyes.

'Yes, to milk. No, to sugar. Thank you.'

The conversation dries up again as I finish off the tea.

'We'll sit in the garden.' The back door is open. I turn and offer her a mug.

She leads the way out.

My mouth is dry as I follow, practicing the difficult words I have to say in my mind. I sip the scalding tea and burn my tongue. I have to say this carefully. I don't want to feel uncomfortable in her shop, Jordan loves the ice creams.

'I've been thinking about you a lot,' she says as she walks to the far side of the table. The feet of the chair's legs scrape on the concrete as she sits down.

I sit in the chair on this side of the table, taking a deep breath to say what I have to say before she can utter another word. 'What happened between us was a moment in time. I need to tell you it was only sex for me. If you thought it might be more, I'm sorry. Nothing else will happen.'

Her eyes widen, her eyebrows lifting. It is not what she expected me to say.

Surely she can't have expected me to say I feel anything. 'We've hardly spoken since and—'

'And Nick…' she interjects.

My mouth opens and closes like a fish's. Her expression waits for me to answer a question I don't understand.

'What about Nick?'

'The way you talked that day,' she says. 'You said the best relationship you had was with a woman. I didn't expect you to develop something with a man. I thought you are a lesbian.'

I don't like the labels people give to sexuality. I like who I like and if I chose to do anything with Nick it would be my business and not hers.

'I don't remember what I said that day, I was quite drunk and a lot has happened since.'

Her eyebrows lift again and fall quickly, displaying a silent expletive through the expression. 'Thanks for the orgasms and goodbye, is that it?'

'Shh.' I press my finger to my lips. 'Jordan is upstairs and the window is open.'

'Ha.' The sharp sound of amusement calls me ridiculous. 'You weren't silent that day. You're very noisy in bed.'

Why had I wanted to have sex with her? Sharon can be nasty. Her own daughter is afraid to tell her things. I want her to leave now.

There are full mugs of hot tea on the table.

'You should be careful. Men are liars.' The accusation is firm.

How had she behaved with the boy in America?

I have no idea how to respond. I drink tea, thinking of ways to get her out of the cottage as quickly as possible. This woman is poison.

'He punched his friend in the side of the head.' The statement is thrown at me like a slap.

'Who?'

'Nick.' She sips her tea, her posture proud and confident. Believing she's now thrown a punch that is going to hurt.

'Oh. The drunken fight. Those headlines are fish and chip wrappings already. I don't care what happened in Nick Mason's past. I have enough to deal with in my present.'

The eyes I'd let myself get lost in in the pub that day look at me with a cutting stare as sharp as the head of a diamond. She wants me to feel afraid, betrayed or hurt, anyone who wants me to feel like that is someone I do not want as a friend.

I set my mug down. I have handled far worse than the spite of this jealous, bitter woman. 'Are you going to spit on my ice cream cones from now on?'

Her expression changes in a millisecond, she leans back and raises her hands. 'Maybe. If you see Nick again.'

'Will you go.' I rise from the chair. She doesn't stand. 'Jordan and I are packing. We're going away for a few days. I want to carry on packing.' Enough with subtleties. 'Just go.'

'I'd still like to be friends,' she says, with a smile that looks dangerous.

I don't reply. Let me juggle that issue another day. I lift a hand, saying the door is that way.

Memories of the sex we'd shared return. She attacks sex. Looking back, it was aggressive. At times she had hurt me – bitten me.

She stands up, leaving the half-full mug on the table. 'Perhaps you should watch the video of Nick that is circulating around the youngsters. Maddie will show you it. You might see a different side to him then.'

She is still convinced the only reason I might say no to her is because there's someone else.

'I'll show you out.'

We walk through the cottage to the front door, she opens the door herself. Of course, there are people from the press there now. What will be in the papers tomorrow? I hope she is not stupid enough to speak to them.

'Thanks for the sex,' she says too loudly. 'See you soon.'

Not if I can help it.

I close the door.

Today is a very good day to get away from the village.

'I've packed everything, Mum?' Jordan calls.

He's standing on the top stair. He will have heard Sharon's parting shot, and that is probably what she wanted. Fortunately, I think his understanding of sex is still too minimal to really comprehend it. He won't pay attention to her words.

'Good work. Shall we head over to the bay now? We can paddle in the water and play football before we eat.'

The car comes to a standstill on the gravel of the Southend car park. I slide the gearstick into neutral and set the hand brake.

Jordan has graduated to riding shotgun beside me. My little car is used to Eli's long legs, squeezed into the footwell of the passenger seat.

Jordan and I release our seatbelts at the same time, eager to reach Eli's bay. He opens the door as I do.

I collect the picnic and beach bag from the back seat. Jordan's bent over. The car door is still open.

'What are you doing? Come on, Jordy.'

'Mum,' he straightens up, 'I found a necklace.'

I can see him through the open doors, through the gap between the back and front seats. A dusty gold thread, long and thin, trails from the grip between his forefinger and thumb.

'Put it down.' I drop the things on the car seat.

The thread of fine gold falls from his fingers to the ground.

I learned my lesson with the heart pendant. I'm already reaching for my phone, looking for Jack's number.

Call.

'That might be mine,' I tell Jordan as the phone begins to ring. 'It could be the chain the heart was on. Eli may have lost it here. I have to tell the police.'

'Hello. This is Jack George.'

'It's Jen. I think we've found the necklace the pendant was on. It's in the car park near Southend Bay.'

'Have you touched it?'

'Jordan picked it up but I told him to drop it where he found it.'

'Okay, someone will be out there soon. Stay there and don't touch anything else.'

'Okay.'

The call ends. With no farewell frills or formalities.

This might mean Eli hadn't walked to the Southend Bay, and if he hadn't, he had arrived with someone because he's never driven a car. It feels too convenient for the necklace to be here, though. What if he'd dropped it here in the hope of leaving a Hansel and Gretel trail for us to follow. Had he always wanted us to find this? Is it some sort of clue? Does where it is mean as much as what it is?

Was he with a stranger?

What if he hitch-hiked to get home and was picked up by the murderer?

Thoughts crush me, I can't think about how his last hours might have been lived.

'Come on, Jordan, let's shut the car up and stand out of the way.'

CHAPTER EIGHTEEN

The rhythm of rolling tyres, cracking and popping, disturbing the loose stones on the single-track road, announces the arrival of a car fifteen minutes after I called Jack. A marked police car appears around the bend.

The car stops, blocking off the road.

Jordan and I watch from our position at the rear of my car. My sweaty hand is held in Jordan's. I feel as though this is the final piece of the puzzle that will somehow put everything else into place, and yet again the police managed to miss it and Eli led us to it.

'You're so clever.' I tell Jordan as the doors of the police car open. 'How you managed to see that necklace, when no one else has, I don't know.'

'It was just lying there in the dirt.'

'It was a great find, Jordan.'

The officers smile as they walk towards us, hats being slipped onto their heads. Two women – Lucy and Marie.

'Hello, Jen. We've been asked to secure the area until forensics arrive. Can you reverse your car off the parking area carefully. We'll direct you.'

'If you move your car over, we'll leave and get out of your way,' I offer.

'We need to ask you some questions first, to record what happened. Where is the necklace?'

'There.' Jordan's hand releases mine and he points.

'I think it's my necklace. The one that was with the little heart we found on the jetty in the bay.'

'That's fine, Jen. If you move the car, we can make some notes.'

'Come and stand with me?' Marie beckons to Jordan.

'Go on, Jordy. I won't be a moment.'

I tiptoe over the gravel, as though I'm sneaking up to the car door, and climb in just as carefully, trying not to disturb anything in the gravel. Although it's probably far too late. I reverse at about one-mile-per-hour, conscious of avoiding the place where the necklace is.

Every muscle in my body is trembling when I reset the hand brake and slide the gear stick into neutral. I must get a grip on myself. I need to drive all the way to Oxford in a few minutes. There's no point in staying here. They'll seal off the bay again.

Jordan is already telling the officers the story of his new find, and Marie is scribbling notes into one of those little black books. I stand beside them and simply agree with Jordan.

Afterwards, Marie reads her notes back to me. 'Anything to add, Jen?'

'No that's all we can tell you. Will you move your car over? So we can get out before the lane is full of police cars.'

'Yes. You can head off. We have your number if anyone needs to contact you.'

When we're back in the car, Jordan looks at me. 'I wanted to see Eli.'

There's a tone in his voice, that makes me ask, 'Do you feel him in the bay?' He'd spoken as though he was going to sit down and speak with Eli.

'I've seen him.'

The police car reverses, tucking in against the hedgerow at the side of the road. 'Put your seatbelt on,' I tell him. Then add, 'Me too. I mean I feel him. I haven't seen him. I think he helped you find that necklace, so the police will find out what happened to him. I think for some reason he wanted us to find these things, not them.'

My phone rings while I'm indicating to move from the outside lane to the middle lane on the M6. The vibrations resonate through the cup holder between the front seats.

Jordan looks at the screen. 'It's Nick. Shall I answer it?'

'No. Leave it.'

An hour and a half later, I steer the car onto Fay's drive and park in front of the bright marigold-orange garage door.

It's a strange moment. It's a long time since I visited, yet it might have been yesterday, everything is the same. Except Eli isn't in the car. Isn't on the Earth.

The front door opens before I've released my seatbelt. Fay and André step out.

It's as though they've stepped out from a doorway in time. From two years ago. When Eli was here.

'Dad's here!'

I let Jordan climb out alone. Letting him enjoy this. Keeping my misery in the car and searching for tissues in the glove box.

'Jordy-boy.' André hugs him first, then Nanna Fay has a hug too.

I get out of the car with a tissue in hand.

'Jen, love.' Fay's arms open for me, as if I was one of the boys. My heart crumbles when I walk into those arms. I sob on her shoulder. Her hand strokes my back.

'I know dear. I know.'

André takes Jordan into the house. 'Nanna made you one of her chocolate cakes.'

I break away from Fay. I shouldn't cry like this in front of Jordan. The heel of my hand swipes the tears off my cheeks.

'Is Camille here?'

'No.'

Fay leads the way inside.

André eats dinner with us and tucks Jordan into bed.

It's agreed that tomorrow he'll take Jordan to a theme park with Camille.

As he reaches to open the door to leave, while we stand alone in the hall, he looks at me. 'Are you coming tomorrow?'

'Am I invited?'

'Of course.'

'I didn't think Camille would want me there.'

'She understands, Jen. We lost Eli. We lost *our* son. She knows how devastating this is for you.'

'It's fine, though. You three go. She should get to know Jordan without me there.'

'I don't want you to be alone here either.'

'I'll have Fay for company.'

His hand drops away from the lock, not opening the door, leaving it closed as he faces me. The intensity in his eyes admits he's thought a lot about what he's going to say next. He'd decided not to say it, but now he's changed his mind.

'I saw that video.'

'What video?' I have no idea what he's talking about.

'The one of the ferryman you know. It's doing the rounds on social media. It's had more than a million views. Have you seen it? It's the CCTV footage of the moment he killed that kid.'

'I know he hit him.'

'It's violent, Jen. He's violent. Jordan said the guy visited your house. Don't make any more mistakes.'

Any more... 'Who else are you calling a mistake? Bell?'

'I didn't mean it like that.' He steps forward, as though he'll reach out to touch or hold me, but his arms don't lift. 'I still care about you. I want you to be okay, that's all.'

'As you said, this is devastating. I'll never be okay.'

'I'd better go home.' He turns and opens the door.

He's devastated too. I know he is. I'd made it sound as though it was just me who felt like that.

'Goodnight, Mum!' he shouts without looking back.

'Goodnight, honey!' she calls back just before he closes the door.

I've seen how much he's hurting through his mother's eyes today too. I watched him cling onto her in the kitchen, when she made the dinner, the muscle working in his jaw as he'd fought his tears. I'd turned Jordan away and taken him into the garden to give them some privacy.

The chimes of my ringtone rise from the pocket of my skirt as the door closes behind him.

The screen says, Nick.

Talk about timing.

If I didn't need something to occupy my hands and mind I wouldn't answer, but I do. I carry the phone through the lounge, raising a hand to Fay, who is busying her mind and hands with knitting. I point at the open patio doors, telling her I'll take the call outside.

I touch answer as I step onto the garden's wooden deck. 'Hi, Nick.'

The sky is still a clear azure blue, there's not a single cloud, but the lowering sun throws long shadows across the small square garden.

'Hi. I hope you don't mind me ringing? But you didn't use the ferry today, and I just want to check things are all right. The police are over at the bay again. Has something happened?'

'We're okay, thank you. We've come away for a few days.' The hot planks of the deck hurt the soles of my bare feet. 'I need a break from Lowerdale. That's all.' I walk further away from the house, and step down onto the soft, cooler grass.

'Where are you?'

'With family.'

'That's good. You don't sound okay, though. You sound a bit… off.'

'Off? Really? My son was murdered.' I breathe in, fighting emotions. The breath releases as a strange sound as I fold, falling into a cross-legged pile on the grass. Folding in on myself. The blooming roses, penstemons and salvias in Fay's pretty flower border become a curdled blur of colours.

'Breathe slowly,' his voice is deep and insistent. 'Count in slowly for three and out for three. You can trust me, you know. Breathe in. One. Two. Three. Now breathe out. One. Two. Three…'

Another couple of counts and my breathing is under control.

'Has it been a bad day?'

'Every day is.'

'I'm not putting pressure on you, Jen. I genuinely called to check on you. I'm trying to be your friend. I know these emotions. It's like being in the sea, sometimes you crawl out onto the beach but then the tide rises, the waves hit you and suck all the sand from around you, then pull you back.'

'I know. You've been nothing but kind.' The perfumes from the flowers are heady in the heavier, cooling evening air. 'Do you know people are sharing a video of you on social media?'

'Of what? I avoid social media.'

PJ barks in the background.

'What's he barking at?'

'The ducks have probably come close. He's fine with them. I only have to worry when it's the swan. Those things look beautiful, but they hurt like hell when they attack. Go on, tell me what's in the video?'

'It's the footage of you hitting your friend.'

He's silent.

'Are you okay?'

'Have you seen it?' he asks.

'No.'

'That video shows the moment he died. I deserve to never escape it, but his family... Don't people think about them?'

My fingertips rub my temple. I'm tired and the pressure headache is thumping in my skull again.

'I told you the truth,' he says, as though he thinks I've thought something I have not.

'Sharon said you're a liar,' I say.

'Sharon? I told you she doesn't like me, or any man for that matter.' The pitch of his voice has risen. 'She's—'

'Don't get angry, I don't want an argument.'

'I'm not arguing with you about her. But allow me to be annoyed when someone calls me a liar over something so serious. Anyway, it doesn't matter now. That won't help you.'

I don't answer.

'Sorry. It's not your problem. We're adults. I can have it out with Sharon if I want to. You're focusing on yourself and Jordan. How is he?'

'Glad to see his nanna.'

'Good.'

'Do you want a drink?' Fay calls from the patio door, making a drinking motion with a hand.

'May I have iced tea, please?'

'I'm going, Nick. But thank you for calling. I have a shortage of friends these days.'

'Me too,' a deep self-mocking laugh punctuates his words. 'But that's my fault. I did what I did, I'll forever regret it and I won't ever pay enough for it.'

'My issue is my fault too. The bad relationship choice I told you about. Night.'

'Take care of yourselves.'

'I am.'

'Night, Jen.' He's the one that ends the call.

There are daisies around me, their white heads and yellow hearts breaking through the short grass. I let the phone rest in my lap for a moment, reach out, pick a flower and spin it between a finger and thumb.

'Jen.'

I tuck the daisy into my hair above my right ear, in the way I used to tuck them into Eli's hair when he was young, pick up the phone and unravel from my folded position.

Fay is walking onto the decking, holding out a mug. 'We can sit outside, if you like? If you've finished your call.'

'It would be a shame to waste this warm evening indoors.'

'You used to sit on the floor like that after Eli was born.' She nods towards my legs. 'Do you remember? You would dissolve into this pile of limbs and sit in the corner of the nursery, even after the two of you came out of hospital.'

CHAPTER NINETEEN

I embrace the white porcelain mug of sugared black tea with ice, cooling my sweaty palms. No one talks about the time after Eli's birth. It's a taboo subject. It's been avoided as though talking about it might curse me and make it happen again. It hasn't happened again.

'It reminded me,' Fay says. 'You sitting there like that, and at the time you feared you'd never love Eli.'

'But I did. I do love him.' The denial rushes to my lips.

She's prodded a sleeping dragon, it stretches inside me and spreads its sinuous, scaly wings to full length.

'I know.' Her hand touches my forearm, which rests on the teak table.

I haven't thought about this for years. I don't let myself. 'I love him. It was my illness that took those feelings away.' My voice has sharpened, every aspect of the guilt I feel now is rooted in my very first, dreadful, failure. I feel as though I have always failed Eli.

'I know,' she says again.

For two years after he was born, I wasn't me.

'You won't remember...' she says.

In my head, the dragon breathes warmth with the threat of a blazing fire.

'...how afraid you were when you recovered that your illness had damaged your relationship with Eli forever. But you loved each other so much. Postpartum Psychosis is a terrible thing. At least you had the years you've had together since. Treasure them, don't look back and regret anything, Jen.'

Those early years are not memories I want to face tonight. I am facing enough recent guilt. I do not need to be weighed down with past guilt too. But now she has said it the dragon roars out fire. Secretly, I am always afraid I love Jordan more. Because I loved Jordan from the moment he was placed into my arms, all warm and slippery. Eli was like a wriggling alien that had broken out of my stomach, who I didn't understand.

I sip the cold tea.

'Do you remember the strange things you did?'

I don't want to.

I know Fay well enough, though, to know she is thinking, and talking, about my illness for a reason. She's leading somewhere.

'It was quite frightening towards the end, before Social Services took you into care. You really believed some of the things you thought you saw.' There's a pause. I look at the glowing brown eyes that André, Eli and Jordan inherited. Eli used to describe her eyes as like star anise. Her pencil-thin eyebrows lift a little. 'Jordan told me he sees Eli, and you said you're talking to him too. He said you think Eli is showing you evidence. You know there are no such things as ghosts. Do you think under the stress of all this the psychosis is returning? Have you spoken to someone?'

I shake the whole idea away. 'No, Fay. I am not going mad. Feeling Eli's spirit at the lake makes Jordan and me feel better. Don't take that away from us.' I don't care if anyone else thinks we're crazy. He is there. André feels his presence too.

'I just wondered if—'

'Please don't. I've spent years afraid of the mania. I don't need that added to the pressure I'm under now. Unless you can tell me Eli's death is a figment of my imagination.'

The ringtone of my phone chimes somewhere nearby. My hand reaches out and feels around on the nightstand. I pick up the phone, pulling it free from the charger cable and hold it to my ear.

'Hello.'

I don't know what time I fell asleep, but for hours I'd stared into the dark with moments from Eli's early life playing through my thoughts.

'Jen, have you left Lowerdale?' It's Jack.

'Yes. What's happened?' I sit up, holding the duvet to my chest with my other hand.

'You shouldn't have gone away without speaking to me.'

'Why?'

'Because we are investigating the potential murder of your son. Wendy told you we needed to know your whereabouts when she spoke to you the first day.'

'I was numb the first day, I didn't hear most of what she said. I'm not a suspect. I don't—' Hang on a minute. 'Do you really think I might have killed Eli?' Wendy had said everyone was a suspect, I remember that. But they can't really believe I would—

'We need to talk to you. There's new evidence. Where are you?'

'In Oxford.'

'How long will it take you to come back to Bowick?'

'Four or five hours.'

'You must come back. Come to the police station in Bowick before 5 PM. Wendy will speak to you here.'

'Okay.'

'Bye.' He ends the call with a cut in his voice. He's actually angry.

I didn't think to tell the police I was leaving. I have my phone. I didn't think they would care.

The clock on the screen of the mobile phone reads 09.05. Jordan must be awake.

I slide my feet into slippers, and the phone into the pocket of my pyjama shorts.

The bedroom door is slightly ajar. Someone had opened the door, seen I was asleep and left me in bed.

'Jordan! Fay!' I call as I descend the stairs. I can't hear them. Hopefully André hasn't picked Jordan up already.

'Mum.' He appears at the bottom of the stairs in a second. 'Nanna told me not to wake you.'

I smile, thinking he's come for a morning hug, but he steps away when I try to enfold him.

'There was a fire beside Lowerdale Lake.'

'How do you know that?' Only one person lives beside the lake.

'My friend Charlie texted.' His best friend who lives in the farmhouse halfway up a mountain.

I accept the phone that's being waved at me. André had given him this old phone yesterday, so he could keep in contact with his friends. It's locked so he can't access the internet, but he can share texts.

The message showing on the screen reads, *There was a fire last night!! By the lake. We could see it all the way up here. There were fire engines and police sirens. Dad says it's the house the man who runs the ferry lives in. I could smell the smoke in my bedroom.*

'Here.' I hand his phone back, reaching for my own.

There's an email notification on the screen.

Due to an unforeseen incident, the Lowerdale Lake Ferry will not be…

My thumb quickly navigates menus to reach the full email.

> *...running today. Please keep an eye on the website for updates.*

Is this why Jack wants me in Bowick? Is it something to do with Eli's death? Or maybe it's something to do with the video that's circulating? An internet troll turned arsonist.

'Mum's awake!' Jordan shouts through to Fay, walking into the lounge.

I don't follow, I call the most recent number on my call list.

It rings to the point I think it will go to answer phone. Come on, Nick.

'Hello.'

He's all right. 'I heard there was a fire. What happened? Are you okay?'

'Morning,' there's a touch of ironic humour in his voice. I had not begun the call with hello.

'Are you okay? Is PJ okay?'

'I'm a bit shocked and PJ's a bit scorched, but we're alive and kicking. He spent the night in the vets.'

'Were you hurt?'

'Only in my wallet. There's a lot of damage. I'm not working the ferry as I'm trying to sort things out.'

'I received the alert email. What happened?'

'Someone threw a good old-fashioned petrol bomb onto the front veranda. The cabin's all wood and it caught. I was trying to put it out with buckets of sand until the fire brigade arrived. The place is a wreck.'

'I'm sorry.' The stupid phrase that's been annoying me slips out. 'Do you know who did it?'

'No. But the newspaper headlines probably spurred it. They were incendiary. Excuse the pun. I have to laugh though, or else...'

You'll cry. 'What were the headlines yesterday? I didn't look.'

'David, the boy I killed, his mum spoke to the press. I won't tell you what she said. But I've heard it all before. I've regretted that punch every day of my life since. I think about him before I go to sleep and he's the first thing I remember when I wake. It doesn't change what happened. I can't change it.' His voice breaks in a crack of sound that tries to hide his emotion. 'I've been hiding from my past here. It found me in the end.'

He may have served his legal sentence, but he's still serving a life sentence. I hope whoever killed Eli feels like this. I can't commiserate with Nick; I want their life to be ruined.

'The police called me,' I tell him. 'I'm coming back today. You can sleep at my house for a few nights if you need to. Jordan is staying here.'

'Thanks, Jen. But the insurance company have already reserved me a room in The Greyhound. Anyway, you might change your mind when you read yesterday's article. Everyone here is looking at me a bit strangely.'

I'm silent for a moment, unsure what to say next. Is there anything else to say? I'm more focused on what's happening now. 'I'm so tired. Jordan needs me here but the police insisted I return.'

'I'll come over this evening, and at least keep you company for an hour or two.'

'Thank you.'

'Mum! Nanna wants to know if you want bacon!' Jordan shouts from the open kitchen door.

I lean round and stick a thumb up in Jordan's direction. 'I'll speak to you later, then. I'm glad you're okay.'

'Thanks for calling. See you later.'

I end the call.

One of Nanna Fay's special iced teas waits for me on the breakfast bar in the kitchen diner. A newspaper lays beside it, folded in half and turned upside down.

'Good morning, dear.' She leaves Jordan to watch the bacon, and walks over. I think she's going to hug me. Instead, she reaches out and turns the newspaper over. 'Jordy says you know this man.'

The date on the top corner is yesterday's date.

The pictures on the front page include a woman of colour who I don't know, but beside her is an image of a young Nick. His arrest picture. A fair, freckled-skinned teenager with sad, hollow eyes. The last image is black and white and in terrible focus. It captures the same teenager, Nick, mid-punch as he throws his fist towards his friend.

I turn the paper over. Nick has told me everything this article implies. 'Yes. I know Nick,' I confirm to Fay, looking up. 'I was just talking to him.' I look over at Jordan. 'The fire didn't harm Nick or PJ badly. They're okay.'

Okay is another weak phrase like *I'm sorry*.

I smile towards Jordan, before turning towards the patio doors. They are open already, capturing some of the cooler morning air before the day heats up again, and releasing the smell of the cooking bacon. I walk outside, looking down at my phone, and open my social media to search for the video.

Nick Mason, I enter his name in the search box. That won't find it. *Murder.* I add.

The search finds it immediately.

He'd said he felt sorry for the family, but the face staring out from the account that shared the video first is the face of the woman in the paper. David Smith's mother.

Two young men stagger into the view of a camera that must be looking down from the top of a roof. One blond head, Nick, and the other dark. Neither of them looks sober. Their feet take random steps off a straight line. The other boy says something. Nick straightens up, pulls back his arm and throws a punch in a round swing. It looks unprovoked. The blow catches the other boy on the side of the head, hitting his ear, and he falls forward onto his knees, then his side, then his back. I wait for him to get up as young Nick waits too. The boy doesn't. Nick squats down and shakes the boy. The boy doesn't move. The footage stops.

The long thread of comments beneath the video are as violent as that punch. Condemning.

'Mum! The bacon rolls are ready!'

I look over my shoulder, pulled back into my own life. But I haven't forgotten what the video didn't show – Nick's friend hadn't thrown a punch. Nick said he'd hit him first.

I switch off the phone's screen and walk into the house. What should I think about this? It doesn't impact anything to do with Eli and it was a long time ago. He killed his friend, but I do understand that when he threw the punch, he never imagined it might kill his friend.

It's not the same as what happened to Eli, someone hit him with an intent to really hurt him, if not kill him. It only proves there was a deliberate action involved when Eli died.

When André lets himself in and walks through to the kitchen, we are sitting at the breakfast bar in our nightclothes, with glasses of iced orange juice, sharing our favourite Eli stories with Fay, making her laugh at some of the strange and funny things we remember. I haven't yet told Jordan or Fay I have to leave.

'Hello,' André acknowledges us all in the same greeting, with a shallow smile, his eyebrows lifting a little, expressing surprise over our apparent happiness. I feel comfortable here. At home. Safe.

'Jordan, clean your teeth and dress, Camille is waiting at home for us to pick her up on the way.'

André glances at yesterday's paper at the far end of the breakfast bar as Jordan slides off the stool.

I follow Jordan to the kitchen door, close it behind him and face André and Fay. Their expressions turn from smiles to mute concern as they wonder why I sought privacy.

'The police called me this morning,' I say quietly. 'I have to go back.'

'Why?' André asks first.

'Apparently I shouldn't have left during the investigation, and there is new evidence.'

'The investigation might last years,' Fay responds.

'Jack told me to go back, he didn't ask. He wants to see me at the police station by five.'

'I'll come with you,' André declares.

'No. Jordan needs you here. You stay with him.'

'He'll want you.'

'As you said, he's better off here and he has you and Fay.'

André's hand rubs over his face and strokes across his hair. 'I don't know…' I see what he feels. That sensation of drowning.

'I don't know what the right or the wrong thing to do is. But I need to go back. I better get dressed. I'll tell Jordan upstairs.'

CHAPTER TWENTY

Memories haunt me as I drive – of the first day I travelled this journey with Eli and Jordan. Our lives, everything we owned, were in cases and black bags piled up in the boot, and on top of the car. Overlaying those mental images is Eli's motionless off-colour body, empty of life.

The number plate of the car ahead of me, in the M6's outer lane, reads BOB 38.

I try to stave off the memories by thinking of famous Bobs the car might belong to. Bob Mortimer. The person who created *Bob the Builder*. The actor who voices Bob the Builder. The writer...

Jordan screams at me. *'Don't go!'*

He was angry when I told him I was leaving – so unlike my younger son.

If only we hadn't moved.

If only we hadn't moved.

The statement chants through my thoughts.

I want to turn the car and go back.

Then again, I don't. I'm returning to Eli, and the police have something new to say. It must be something important.

The signpost for the Burton-on-Kendal Services says 1 mile. I push the indicator on. It ticks through the seconds it takes to reach the slip road. I've stopped for coffee three times already, fuelling my mind with caffeine and feeding the panic-dragon in my chest.

When I open the car door, coffee in hand, the tremble in my muscles means I nearly hurl the coffee over the passenger seat. I save it from falling and drop it into the central cupholder. It's not far to Bowick now. I'll be there in half an hour.

Tall hills which become mountains rise up on the horizon, welcoming me into the rugged beauty of the Lake District. The motorway is busier at the weekends, when the tourists arrive and leave. Today, the gaps between vehicles expands, the traffic thinning out, but the narrow roads inside the national park will be flooded with tourists. The Scottish school holidays have already begun, there are plenty of people already filling up the tourist accommodations.

Impatience scrambles through my mind, fighting with concentration.

At last, the turning approaches. Twisty roads, winding their way around the lakes and over the mountains form the last part of my route, requiring all my attention until I drive into Bowick. The police station is on this road, on the outskirts of the town.

Here.

There's a small car park.

The white-lined spaces are tight. I park, open my car door and squeeze out, careful not to scratch the car beside mine. A shaking hand pulls my handbag out behind me and hooks the straps over my shoulder. The desire to be sick rolls in my stomach. I haven't eaten since breakfast, just drunk numerous lattes.

I press the button to lock the car. The sidelights flash and the locks click home.

'Jen!'

The shout comes from behind me.

Nick is standing beside a black Vauxhall Astra that's parked on the side of the road outside the car park's waist-height red-brick wall, waving vigorously at me.

My hand lifts, acknowledging him.

He breaks into a jog, running into the car park, and stops still in front of me. 'All okay? Have you spoken to them yet?' His physicality is a little threatening when the taut muscles underneath the thin cotton fabric of his grey T-shirt radiate heat.

'Not yet. And I'm probably the least okay I can be. I left Jordan upset.'

One blond eyebrow lifts. 'You look exhausted.'

'Thanks.' My gratitude is ironically spoken.

A grunt of an awkward laugh breaks from his throat. 'You're very welcome. No. Seriously. You don't look well. Do you need anything?' His fingers comb through his loose curls.

There's a large plum-red bruise on the back of his forearm, and scratches on his neck.

'No. I don't need anything other than to go in there and get this over with. Did that happen last night.' I point at the scratches.

'PJ didn't take to being rescued.'

'That placid dog.'

'He's not so placid when he's being roasted alive. Would you like a companion? I've just been in there to sort out some information for the insurance company. I could come in and sit with you?'

'No. Don't worry. I'll manage.'

'Okay. Well maybe I'll see you later. Give me a call when you're back at the cottage.'

I nod. Not sure I will, regretting my earlier offer. I hadn't thought about how tired the drive would make me.

'See you then.' His hands slide into the front pockets of his jeans.

'See you.'

We walk our separate ways.

A concrete ramp with a steel handrail leads up to the Police Station's reception. No one else is in the small wasp-nest-beige reception area. Eli saw a wasps' nest in a tree once. *'That's it, that's that dirty beige you see on the classroom walls at school, Mum.'* The wasps' nest became his favourite reference for a beige colour from then on.

Jordan used to moan at us. *'Why do you use silly comparisons for colours all the time?'* He never joined in.

'Can I help?' A grey-haired officer calls from his position behind a glass window.

'That breed of Russian Blue cat's fur, that's what that guy's grey hair looks like.' Eli had searched the internet for a match.

'I'm here to see Jack George, Wendy Carter or Arla Saye-Stevens. Jack rang me this morning and asked me to come in. I'm Jennifer Easton.'

'Ah. Okay. Take a seat and one of them will be out in a moment.'

There's a phone beside him but he doesn't use it, he rises from the chair and walks away, opening and closing a door at the back of his glass office.

The Holly Blue Butterfly – that was another blue colour Eli found via a search on the web.

A few minutes later, Jack opens the secure door into the reception. He's followed by a uniformed female officer. Lucy.

'Hi,' I stand up, caffeine fed energy pulsing into my limbs.

Lucy smiles.

'Jen, I'm not arresting you,' Jack says.

Not arresting me? 'Pardon?'

'But we do need to interview you under caution, because of the questions we want to ask, so I must read you your rights, and listen carefully this time Jen.'

My lips part, my jaw dropping and my thoughts scattering.

'You do not have to say anything, and anything you do say

might be used as evidence…' He reels off similar words to those I've heard on TV dramas.

'I don't understand.'

'Let me finish reading you your rights and then we can take you through to the interview room and explain.'

Interview room?

'I want a solicitor. That's one of my rights, isn't it? I'm tired. I haven't slept properly for nights. I'm in no state for an interview. Why am I here?'

'Because we have evidence that we want to speak to you about. But we will have that conversation in the interview room.'

'When you have a solicitor,' Lucy adds.

I sigh and rub my temple, the pain in my skull complaining with a violent aggression.

Jack reaches out and catches hold of my elbow, as though he thinks I'm about to faint.

I look at my hand, my skin is paler, as white as it can possibly be, ghost like – mashed potatoes.

'We'll find you somewhere you can lie down for a bit.'

'This is ridiculous,' I tell Jack as I walk through the secure door a step in front of him. His hand still holds my arm.

Apparently, the most comfortable place to wait is on the bed in a cell, although the door is open. He thinks I'll be better off here where I'm able to lie down.

I lie there, staring at bleached white walls. Unable to close my eyes.

A youngish woman with Asian colouring walks into the cell, dressed in a pale grey business suit that is contrasted with a vivid sunflower-yellow blouse. The blouse declares, I have a life outside this world. While the patent black shoes with wide, solid, high heels say don't mess with me.

The denim dungarees and vest top I'd thrown on this morning are creased and sweaty from the hours I spent in the car. I feel like a lawyer's client.

'Hello, Miss Easton. I'm the duty solicitor, Meera Joshua.'

She looks so young she can have only recently qualified.

Her hand with beautiful manicured yellow nails that match her blouse stretches out, reaching to shake my hand.

I accept, with a hand with uneven and broken nails. I haven't painted my nails or even used an emery board since Eli died.

She glances over her shoulder. Lucy stands behind her. 'Can you escort us to a nicer room. One with a window to open preferably.'

Do I smell? Did I use antiperspirant when I dressed?

'This way.'

We are led up two flights of stairs to a room with a wide window in a metal frame. Meera slides off her jacket and hangs it over the back of one chair as I sit on the other side of a small table in another chair. She leans across to open the window, persuading it to slide up a couple of inches with some effort. Once it's open, a breeze sweeps in. The fresh air is warm but welcome.

'Do you know what's going on?' I ask.

'Let's sort out the paperwork first. May I call you Jennifer?'

'Jen.'

'Call me Meera —'

'How much will this cost, I—'

She raises a hand and stops my words. 'My support here is paid by the legal aid service at no cost to you. If you need my help after today, then we can talk about that at a later date, but I think legal aid will cover that too. However, you want to be certain of my legal obligation to manage your case confidentially. I should make you aware, though, I am always bound to the justice system first, so I won't ever lie or present false information on your behalf.'

'I have no false information to present.'

'Here.' She withdraws a document and lays it on the table

between us. Then holds out a pen. 'Read it through and sign on the dotted line.'

I don't read it. I sign my name in black ink and push it back at her. I'd sign away my life to the devil in my current mental state, if he'd help me walk out of here and rush back to Jordan.

'Do you know what's happening? Why am I here?' I ask again.

'The police have evidence showing you travelling to Southend Bay around the time Eli died.'

'I was in Lowerdale.'

'You may have been, but your car wasn't.'

'It was. I was drinking. I didn't drive.'

'Save the answers for the interview. You haven't been arrested. They are just exploring what this means. So, what do you want from me, Jen? Why did you ask for a solicitor? Are you afraid of something? It is much better to be honest with me from the start. Then I can give you the best advice.'

'No. I'm not afraid. Jack, the family liaison officer, told me I can't leave the area. He said I had to come back. I was staying with family in Oxford. My son is there. I wanted to escape the scrutiny of the press. And… here… for all I know, Eli's killer might be watching me or even speaking to me. I… I'm struggling to cope on my own. I just want to be allowed to return to Oxford, and they've told me I can't leave.'

'The police have no right to tell you where to go if you haven't been arrested. They certainly don't have a court order to be able to present any restrictions. I'll tell them that.' Her surprisingly cool hand touches my wrist. 'Don't worry, you have someone on your side now.

'Okay. Shall we press on then? The sooner the interview is over the sooner we can send you on your way to your son.' She makes it sound as though all of this, this interview, will be over in minutes.

Lucy returns to lead us along the hall to another room. This room has no window. Wendy and Arla are waiting for us, sitting on one side of a table, the sleeves of their blouses rolled up to their elbows and their top buttons loose. A fan that stands in the corner near the door stirs the air in sweeping movements.

'Hello, Jen.' Wendy rises, holding out a hand. Which is odd, as we already know each other.

I accept the hand anyway.

Her palm is damp – sweaty.

'Jen.' Arla holds out a hand too. I shake another warm hand, then wipe my palm on the denim on the backside of my dungarees.

Meera and I sit, facing them across the table.

'Let's kick this off.' Wendy reaches over to a recording machine and pushes a button.

A red light flashes.

Wendy runs through the legal points of the interview again. I stare at her as the words travel through my ears, into my mind and take flight like butterflies.

'On the night Eli died,' Arla's expression and tone of voice are different than normal, sterner, clipped. I look at her face. Her rust-red hair is pinned up in a bun today. I look directly into her hazel eyes. 'Where were you?' she asks.

I haven't ever told them. They haven't asked me outright like this. 'With someone.'

'With who, Jen?'

I know my skin is flushing with blotches of red, like Sharon's raspberry ripple ice cream. I feel the embarrassment crawling up to my ears then across my scalp.

Wendy slides across a box of open tissues. I pull one out, realising a tear is rolling down one cheek.

'With who, Jen?' Arla repeats.

'A woman.' They will ask for more. 'Maddie's mother. Sharon Cox.'

Arla glances at Wendy for a second.

'We had sex,' I continue. 'We met in the pub in the afternoon and went to her house. Jordan was staying with a friend overnight and Eli was out. Eli messaged and said he wasn't coming home for dinner so I went to The Greyhound. I talked to Sharon. We had a few drinks and she invited me to her house. We had sex and I slept for a while. I walked home around midnight.'

'Did you drive that evening?'

'No. I walked home from her house to my cottage. I'd had quite a bit to drink.'

'Take a look at this.' Wendy opens a laptop that is on the table between us. She touches keys, then scrolls using the touchpad and turns it around. On the screen is a still colour image from CCTV footage.

'Is the car on the screen your car?'

The number plate is very clear, she can see it is my car. 'Yes.'

'Look at the date and time in the corner of the picture. The coroner's report identifies this is as being around the time of Eli's death.'

'Eli's murder,' I correct. 'Yes, it's my car. But the date and time must be wrong. I wasn't driving at that time that day. I was at Sharon's house.'

'The date and time aren't wrong, and tyre tracks in the car park where the necklace was found match the make and model of tyres on your car.'

'I was parked there when we found the necklace. When I phoned Jack.' Are they going mad? Or am I?

'These tyre marks were beneath the necklace.'

'This is stupid. Jordan picked up the necklace and dropped it again. We told the officers. It was not in exactly the same place. They wrote it down. This is wasting time.'

'Isn't that rather convenient. The two of you finding evidence in previously searched locations, and very obvious places, with good excuses for the presence of your DNA.' Wendy looks expectantly at me, as though her words will solicit an admission.

I don't answer. I have no idea what to say.

'Did you and Eli have a fight?'

I hold my silence.

'We have a statement from a witness who told us you did drive your car that night…' Arla pauses, as though waiting again for me to admit it was me.

I'm stunned. They might as well have fired a taser at me. I reel back in the chair, my mouth open and bile rising in my throat as my hands lift palms outwards, fending off this nonsense. 'Why would I hurt my son?'

'Perhaps it was an accident… A burst of anger,' Wendy prods.

'No.'

'A moment of insanity that you couldn't control.'

'No.'

'We have checked your records. When Eli was a baby, you threw him into a cot and left him with a bruise on his forehead, and that was not the only time you lost your temper with him.'

'You checked… It was over thirteen years ago! I was seriously ill! I didn't know what I was doing! I had psychosis!'

Meera's cool hand touches mine, implying I should calm down.

'I didn't throw him, anyway. I put him down. But I was agitated, and he accidentally hit his head. The full details must be on record. Social Services were involved and my mother-in-law at the time was in the room. She told me it was accidental.'

I don't remember, but Fay said she'd walked into the room and I dropped Eli into the cot because I hadn't recognised her. I thought she was an intruder. I thought she'd come into the house to kidnap him. I was hearing voices and seeing people at the time. It was then André told Fay I'd been behaving strangely for weeks. Apparently, I left Eli in the car at a country park. I'd forgotten he was there a couple of days before that too. Social Services arranged for me to be sectioned. I was taken into care for my own good. I remember very little, months and months were wiped out by illness and medication.

'Could the same thing be said again – that you accidentally hurt him? The text message he sent to Maddie implied you had a volatile relationship.'

'Isn't arguing with a teenager normal? When he was a baby I had psychosis because of the birth, it was postpartum hormones, a chemical imbalance. Now we have…' I close my eyes for a second, recognising I need to correct the tense from present to past. 'We had a normal relationship after that. He was testing boundaries and embarrassed by his mother's sexual relationships. I think he sent that text to Maddie because he saw me kissing Sharon.'

'You haven't mentioned that before.'

'It was private.'

'In a potential murder case, Jen, nothing is private.'

A breath sucks into my lungs. It annoys me that they say potential murder, implying that someone could get away with claiming it was not planned or intended and say it was manslaughter. 'I don't understand why my car would be there, that is all that matters. How was my car there?'

'Ms Cox says you drove it. She says she saw you get into your car that evening. She thought you were going to collect Eli.'

'Sharon?' Had Sharon already told them we were together? Did they know without asking me? Why would she lie about the car? To spite me for not wanting to progress our relationship?

The officers don't say any more. They wait for me to reply.

'It's a lie. Don't you think it's a bit strange Sharon has mentioned this over a week after it happened, and also on the same day I told her I wouldn't sleep with her again. It stinks of a malicious act.' *And I am used to them.*

'Perhaps she's been keeping this secret for you until you broke the relationship off.'

A muscle ticks beneath my eye. 'There was no relationship. It was one-off sex.'

'There was a complaint made against you at your last school, wasn't there? An accusation of sexual abuse.'

'And it was proven to be entirely unfounded!' I'm sure my expression displays the horror I feel at the mention of Bell's husband. I'm no poker player. 'The man who made the accusation was the husband of a teacher I had an affair with. He was jealous and he wanted me out of the way. He succeeded, because despite being cleared of any suspicion, mud sticks. I came here to escape the impacts of that rumour. It's that rumour and our move here which upset my relationship with Eli.'

'Is it normal for you to have a string of jilted exes who are out for revenge?' Wendy asks.

'Pardon?' How much laundry are they dragging out of my basket to be aired in this room?

'Miss Easton's previous relationships have no connection to this case,' Meera says. 'And if Miss Easton were a man, you wouldn't have made that comment, broken relationships would not have been pointed out. Be careful what you're saying, detective.'

I glance at Meera, and I know in that moment she fancies women too. She experiences institutional, cultural sexism, heterosexism, too. I now notice she has a small rainbow flag pin secured to the collar point of her blouse. Because she's undone the top couple of buttons the collar point is hanging in a way the little pride badge isn't obvious. She wears it to be obvious, so everyone knows she is not straight and says the right things to her, avoiding the embarrassment of having to correct them.

I prefer to watch people awkwardly tumble over their erroneous assumptions. What is considered *'straight'* in male and female culture is an excuse to point a finger at anything that deviates from what others see as the norm. Because anyone either side of the norm is not considered normal. A norm is an average, it is not what's right. And what is normal anyway? We're all a little bit different. A spectrum. We are all at different points on a human spectrum from looks to capabilities, from personalities to preferences. There is no normal, just a norm. It's like calling people black or white based on the colour of their skin, two ends of a spectrum that is huge. We are all our own shade. When Eli was at primary school, when he heard the word 'white' used to describe skin, he said, *'You're a light brown, not white.'* When I was tanned once, after we'd begun our colour game, he'd seen a pale piece of amber in a gemstone shop and held it near my skin. *'This is the colour of your skin.'*

'Were Jen a man, I'd say exactly the same,' Wendy responds.

'Nevertheless, it's irrelevant,' Meera throws back.

'The two items of additional evidence you and your son found in areas that were previously searched, did you put them there?'

'I…' I have no words. I stare across the table.

'Did you plant them there after the event, to make it appear that Eli was with someone else?'

'No.'

'We think,' Wendy says, 'you drove out to find Eli. You found him with a girl. Naked. Perhaps even about to have sex underage. You were both a little drunk. There was an argument. You lost your temper. You experienced a moment of uncontrollable anger and struck him. I doubt you intended to kill him, but you lost control and did not even realise what you were doing…'

'You are under no obligation to respond to that,' Meera says to me. 'It's pure supposition and you have the right to walk out of this interview at any point.'

My eyes turn from Meera to Wendy and back again. 'I'd like to leave please, and I will return to Oxford tomorrow to join Jordan there.' Their stupid theory doesn't deserve a response.

Meera looks at the detectives. 'Do you have any information beyond the sighting of the car? It sounds like Ms Cox's evidence is dubious and the tyre tracks are explainable. I doubt either will hold any weight with the Crown Prosecution Service.'

I stand up, expressing my desire to leave immediately with physical action.

Wendy stands too. 'We have a warrant to search your car. We will be taking it for forensic examination. Please give me the key.'

'Good. Then you might find out who was driving it.' My voice does not express just how much the thought of someone using my car turns my stomach. Why is my car in that picture? It was parked in the street when I walked home.

I search around in my handbag for the keys, they've worked their way to the bottom of the bag. My shaking hands struggle to release the key from the key ring.

'Shall, I?' Arla offers, holding out a hand.

'No. I'll manage.' When it's free, I slap the key down on Arla's waiting palm. 'There.'

Meera leads the way out of the room and Lucy takes us back through the police station, down to the reception, and opens the door for us.

Then, I am standing outside with Meera in the sunshine.

'Can you manage without your car?' Meera asks, juggling her jacket and briefcase.

'I can catch a train back to Oxford. I'll call a friend to help for now.' Nick. He isn't working today. He has a car. He's offered to help many times.

'Are you sure? I could give you a lift somewhere. I'm heading back to Penrith.'

'No honestly, it's okay. My friend lives in Lowerdale. He's not far away.'

'Call me if there are any problems.'

'I don't have your number.'

She clicks her tongue and rolls her eyes. 'That would help you. Sorry.' She reaches into a pocket in her briefcase and withdraws a business card. 'Send me your email address and I'll forward a copy of that agreement you signed.'

I take the card, drop it into my handbag and dig out my phone. 'Thank you.'

'Nice to meet you.' She lifts a hand and sort of waves as she walks away.

I ring Nick's number.

'Hi, Jen, are you all right?' His pitch is concern.

'Hello. I'm sorry to have to ask this. The police are seizing my car. Would you be able to collect me from the police station and take me home?'

'Yes.' There's no hesitation. 'I'm still in Bowick. I'll be there in a few minutes.'

Nick's car stops on the road, and the lock releases on the passenger door. I open the door and drop into the seat. 'Thank you.'

'Why have the police impounded your car?' he asks immediately.

'It was seen near Southend Bay the night Eli died. They were asking questions as though I killed him.' I secure the seat belt.

'No. They didn't…' His head shakes as he knocks on the indicator and steers the car away from the curb.

'They did.'

'The first thing I'm doing is taking you somewhere to eat. You've lost weight. Then I'm taking you home to get some sleep.'

'I'm not hungry and I won't sleep.'

'You need to eat and sleep; Jordan needs you to be healthy.'

'I'll eat some fries from a drive through.'

'You won't. You need some vitamins and minerals. I'll take you to a pub for a proper meal.'

'I don't want to be in a public place.'

'I'll go into Booth's and buy you something healthy then. I'll cook for you.'

'I'm not hungry. Honestly.'

'If I cook you a dinner, you'll have to humour me and at least eat a few mouthfuls. Call your doctor too, while I'm driving, and ask for something to help you sleep. You need that, Jen.'

I concede, too tired to deny his recommendation.

I'm hanging on the General Practitioners' phone line when he steers the car into Booth's supermarket car park.

'You're number two in the queue.'

'Do you mind if I wait in the car?' I ask.

'No. I won't be long.'

'Hello, Lowerdale Surgery, how can I help?' The call is answered as he walks away from the car.

'I'm Jennifer Easton, my son was murdered last week. I've not been sleeping. It's making me feel ill. I need something to help me sleep, for tonight.' There's a sudden memory, of the weight of drugs, of the strength of the medicine they gave me when I was sectioned. I've avoided antidepressants ever since.

'I'll ask a doctor to call you straight back.' Shock and awe carry in her response. The answer would normally be: there are no appointments, you'll have to wait. But the impact of murder must bump the mother up the queue. 'Is this the best number to reach you on?'

'Yes. Thank you.'

She ends the call.

Nick returns with a full carrier bag.

I feel sick, not hungry. I don't understand how my car was on the road that night. It was where I parked it.

Nick opens the boot of the hatchback. I twist round in the car seat, so he'll hear me. 'Will you take me to Southend Bay?'

He doesn't answer me. He slams the boot closed.

'No,' he answers when he opens the driver's door. 'The police still have it closed off. They're back on their knees out there checking nothing is missed.'

Checking nothing *else* was missed.

As he starts the car, I shut my eyes, looking into the darkness behind my eyelids, searching for memories of that night which I might have forgotten in some sort of drunken or psychotic haze. But I had not been confused. I was almost sober by the time I walked home.

Nick parallel parks into the place on the road where I usually leave my car. When he's set the hand brake, I open the door, digging the door key out of my handbag. Fortunately, I can't spot any members of the press in the street.

Nick collects the shopping from the boot.

Bottles – wine bottles – chink in the bag.

My phone rings as he opens the garden gate. 'It's the surgery,' I tell Nick, and hand over the door key.

'Hello,' I answer the call.

'Hello, Miss Easton?'

'Yes.'

'This is Dr Varma. How can I help?'

'Just a moment. I need to find somewhere quiet.'

I follow Nick into the cottage, leave him to shut the door behind us and walk through to the back door, pointing to let Nick know I'm going into the garden. I shut the door behind me.

'I...' I explain what's happened.

She asks a few questions, her tone empathetic. She has my records – she must know I'm an at-risk person for mental health. I've lived with that shadow for so many years.

I see Nick through the window, unpacking his shopping onto the kitchen work surface.

She prescribes Lorazepam and tells me the prescription will be sent electronically, so I can pick it up before the chemist closes. Then makes an appointment to check on me the following week.

'There's a prescription I need to collect from the chemist,' I tell Nick as I walk into the Kitchen.

He's studying the dials on the cooker. He turns the oven on to 180 degrees Celsius before looking at me.

'I'll come with you, while the oven heats.'

'Okay.' I don't fancy walking up the road alone in case any photographers or reporters appear.

He walks out of the house first, and on the outside of me along the road, looking all around us. My self-appointed bodyguard. Manic laughter echoes through my thoughts, although it doesn't reach my throat. I'm too tired. Too emotional. Too… lost.

We reach the ice-cream parlour. I touch Nick's arm and steer him to the opposite side of the square. For the first time I'm glad Jordan isn't here, he'd want to go in there and I couldn't today. Despite myself, I look through the shop window. The glazing is mirror-like with the sun on it, I don't see Sharon, but through the open door I glimpse her daughter with the cobalt blue hair.

I look at Nick. 'Sharon told the police she saw me get into my car and drive that night. She didn't.'

Nick's hand reaches out and holds mine. It's comforting, familiar, because we've held hands so many times when I've boarded and departed the ferry.

'We had sex,' I tell him. 'Sharon and I.'

'That day.' He holds my hand a little tighter, his fingers wrapping a little further around mine.

'Yes.'

I remember the look he'd given me when I talked about Bell – the moment you come out to people.

Some people say, what was it like when you came out? They don't realise *we* the not perceived as *straight* people, the not one of the 'norm' people, come out a thousand times in our lives.

'I fell asleep in her bed. When I woke, she wasn't in the house. I left then. I didn't go to my car.

'I told her the sex was a one-off yesterday. She didn't take it well. I think that's why she lied. She even accused me of having sex with you.'

Our gazes collide. Perhaps with the same thought.

'The fire, Nick? Would she do that?'

His pale eyebrows lift. 'Maybe I'll tell the police tomorrow.'

We stand in the chemist for ten minutes, waiting for the prescription to be dispensed, checked and signed off.

On the way back, Nick looks towards the ice-cream parlour at the same moment I do. Sharon still isn't visible. That place of treats sends a sense of terror through me, my skin tingling as the hairs on the back of my neck stand up.

Today, the A frame publicity board reads, *Many people would kill for our Strawberry and Watermelon Sorbet, they don't confess. They don't want anyone else to empty the tub.*

We approach the cottage, safe and sound, with no unwelcome encounters of the photographer kind. I unlock the front door.

'You should take one of those tablets, I'll pour you some water,' he says, crossing the living room as I shut the door.

'Thank you. The glasses are in the cupboard above the kettle.'

I collapse on the sofa in a pile of exhaustion, take the box out of the paper bag and withdraw a pack of foil wrapped tablets. I free one. It rests innocently on my palm as he walks in with a full glass tumbler.

'You lie down while I cook the dinner.'

'Thank you.' I need someone to take over today. Someone who can do all the thinking and decision-making. I can't think about anything anymore.

I swallow the pill and wash it down with water, slip off my shoes and lie down, sliding a cushion under my head.

Nick bumps and bangs around, opening and closing cupboard doors, finding saucepans and utensils as the oven hums its electric tune.

'It's ready.' Nick's voice pulls me from a dream.

Eli is… I lose it, I can't catch hold of the fading images or the story and moments my mind had conjured up.

I sit up, my body heavy. The movement sluggish.

The food and Nick are at the dining table. He has a bottle of white wine in one hand, and he's pouring the wine into a glass, a second glass stands on the table waiting to be filled.

'Will you be offended if I turn the television on?' I ask.

'Of course not, it's your home.'

I get up. I only want the TV on to make sure we don't eat in silence. I'm not sure my mind will be able to form words. The television provides the conversation for us.

He eats, while I chew on a single mouthful, so tired I can hardly persuade my jaw to work. He's cooked a pasta bake with fresh basil and tomatoes, sprinkled with parmesan cheese and pine nuts. The sauce is full of flavour.

He points at his plate of pasta with the prongs of his fork. 'I'm vegetarian, I don't think I've ever told you that. I hope this is okay.'

'It's fine.' I manage five mouthfuls and half a glass of wine before I give up. 'I'm sorry. I can't do your dinner justice. I need to lie down again.'

'You don't need to apologise, at least you've eaten something. Do whatever you need to. Do you mind if I stay and finish my dinner? Or do you want me to go.'

'Stay for a while. You have no home to go to anyway, and the room at The Greyhound won't be that pleasant. Finish your dinner and sit down with me.'

I lie on the sofa, the sounds of his knife and fork touching the plate absorbing my concentration, helping me think of nothing else.

'Can I sit with you? You can rest your head on my lap.'

I was asleep again. I lift onto my elbow and give him space to sit at the end of the sofa. He moves the cushion my head had rested on onto his lap and I lie back down.

His fingers touch my hair, stroking it behind my ear. In a similar way to the way I've petted PJ on the boat.

It feels nice. My mother used to stroke my hair like this.

'When Eli was a baby, I had a type of postnatal depression. I suffered with delusions,' I say. 'The way the police spoke to me today made it sound as though I'm psychotic again. I have been under pressure recently. The false accusations that were made at my old school put a lot of stress on me and Eli argued with me a lot. What if they're right and I did drive the car without knowing. What if I did do something and I don't remember?'

'You didn't.'

'They've made me think maybe I did.'

'You didn't, go back to sleep.'

Nick's stroking fingers and the conversation on the television reach through my thoughts, carrying me away to a quiet place where Eli waits for me.

CHAPTER TWENTY-ONE

A breath pulls into my lungs in a rush and I sit up. I was drowning in my dream. Water had filled my lungs and I couldn't breathe. Eli was there, his face close. The face of the cold body I saw in the morgue.

I'm in the living room, on the sofa, not in bed. Bright daylight seeps around the edges of the curtains. The television is lifeless; a black, silent screen.

'You frightened the life out of me.' Nick is sitting on the sofa beside me.

His arms stretch up, as he stretches his neck and back too.

My stomach somersaults. My mind is half in the dream.

The clock on the wall reads eight thirty-two. We've been on the sofa all night.

'Did you manage to sleep too?' I stand.

His lips and eyes smile at me. 'Some. I didn't want to move in case I woke you.' He stands and stretches his arms and back again, his T-shirt pulling up and revealing his sinuous waist.

'I need to ring Jordan. I should have called him last night.' My heartbeat races as the anxiety that is my reality returns. I reach for my handbag, for my phone. It won't turn on, the battery is dead. I take it into the kitchen. 'Can I borrow your phone, Nick?' I call over my shoulder. 'Has it got any charge?'

'Yes. Probably.'

I plug the cable into my phone and turn the socket on. When it comes to life, I'm sure I'll see a dozen unanswered calls from Jordan. I don't wait, I head back into the living room, to borrow Nick's phone. He takes it out of his pocket, and it flares into life, having recognised his face.

'Thank you.' I accept it, and quickly type in Jordan's number. Every other day I would tell him off for answering a number he doesn't know. Today I pray he does answer.

'Hello.' It's not Jordan's voice, it's André.

'Hi. I'm sorry. I asked the doctor for some medicine to help me sleep. I was so tired. I never even thought to ring before I fell asleep. How is he?'

'He's okay. Jordy, it's Mum! He was worried. I was too, but we distracted ourselves with FIFA and we didn't want to disturb you in case you were asleep. He's outside eating brown sugar, banana and cinnamon with Nanna. Here he is. Don't go when he's finished talking, I want to know what happened at the police station.'

'Do you want a cup of tea?' Nick offers.

I give him a thumbs up. *Yes, please.*

'Mum.'

'Jordan, how are you, darling?'

'Where were you? You didn't call, Mum?'

'I fell asleep. And my phone died. Did you enjoy the day with Camille and Dad?'

'It was okay, but I miss you.'

'I miss you too. I'm coming back today.'

'Are you? We're going into town. Dad said he'll buy me new football boots.'

'Did he? That's nice of him. Was Camille nice?'

'She's okay. Dad and I went on a really high rollercoaster

three times. She screamed the first time and she wouldn't go on it again. Dad teased her. I'm going to go. Nanna melted brown sugar and cinnamon over sliced bananas and she says it tastes nicer warm.'

'That sounds lovely. Ask her to make it for me tomorrow.'

'Yeah. See you later.'

'See you later, darling. Hand the phone to Dad.'

'What's happening?' André asks as soon as Jordan's gone.

'The police think I killed him. They impounded my car to look for forensic evidence.'

'What? That's ridiculous.'

He was there when I had the mental breakdown. He would know if there was any chance I might do something so terrible.

'I used a solicitor because they interviewed me under caution. The woman I had sex with told them I drove my car that night and the car is captured on CCTV near Southend Bay. I didn't drive, but it was my car.'

'Here you are.' Nick puts the cup of tea on the dining table beside me.

'Thanks.'

'Who's that?' André asks.

'Nick. He gave me a lift home yesterday, and he's stayed because his home was burned.'

Nick smiles towards me as he returns to the kitchen to collect his tea.

'You let him stay in the cottage. Are you mad? Be careful. The papers are running another story on him today. He said in court the boy punched him first, but not a single witness saw it.'

'It was years ago,' I whisper as I hear the back door open. Nick's taken his tea outside to give me privacy.

'Well sometimes a liar is always a liar.'

I don't answer that. 'I told the police I'm coming back to Oxford today. The solicitor said they can't make me stay.'

'How, without a car? Do you want me to drive up and collect you?'

'No stay with Jordan. I'll come back on the train.'

'Message me when you know what time you'll be at the station. I'll pick you up.'

'Okay. Thank you. I'm not on my phone, it's got no charge left so I better go.'

'Okay. But keep in touch. I worried about you yesterday.'

'I will do.' I end the call, carry the phone into the garden and hand it to Nick.

'Are you running the ferry today?' The first trip should have already left.

'No. I need to pick PJ up from the vets. Can I use the bathroom to freshen up quickly?'

'Of course. It's at the top of the stairs. In front of you.'

'I know, I found it while you were asleep yesterday.'

I slide open one then the other of the living room curtains as Nick climbs the stairs, the handle of the mug of tea in my other hand. There's one lone man with a professional camera in his hand standing behind a car on the opposite side of the street. If he captures a picture of Nick and me leaving the cottage, what a headline that will make.

I sip the tea, my thoughts turning back to how on earth my car was in Bowick.

It was my car in the image. Which means, if I did not have a psychotic episode, someone else drove it. The muscles in my jaw stiffen at the thought.

Only one person had access to my car key.

Sharon.

She wasn't in the house when I left. But the car was in the street.

If she took the car, she had brought it back by the time I left her house, because the key was on the key ring when I opened the cottage door.

I sip the tea, my heartbeat throbbing heavily through every artery, large and small, all the way to my fingertips.

Why would she do that?

Her phone. She would have had her phone with her. Maybe the police can identify the phone signal as being in the area of Southend Bay at the time the car was there. I wish I'd left my phone turned on, it would have proven I was here.

'Don't go near the front window,' I tell Nick as he walks downstairs. 'There's a photographer out there, and I don't think he's taking pictures of the scenery.'

'Okay.'

My bare feet brush quickly on the carpet as I run upstairs. Eli's and Jordan's open bedroom doors and their empty beds tangle fingers up in my heart strings. I use the toilet, and it's only then I realise my overnight case is still in the boot of my car, with my wash things and toothbrush. I use my finger to clean my teeth and move to the bedroom to change clothes.

At the time Sharon took my car, Aiden and Maddie must have been walking home through the woods. Maybe she was looking for Maddie? But why take my car and not hers? And why go to Southend Bay? Maddie was nowhere near there.

I don't remember if her car was in the street when I left her house.

Did she start the fire at Nick's cabin? What reason does she have to attack Nick? And Eli?

They only have one connection. Me.

Could it just be because she wants me? Why?

None of it makes sense.

I walk back downstairs in a short denim skirt and a pale mauve T-shirt. Cooler and refreshed.

'I need to ring the police,' I tell Nick. 'I think Sharon was driving my car. It can't be anyone else. They need to look at the information on her phone. Maybe Maddie messaged her.'

His gaze meets mine, a muscle ticking at the back of his jaw.

'No.' The answer is firm. 'Ring your solicitor. Let her manage your relationship with the police now. You never know when they'll twist things. They took your car. This is serious, Jen.'

He's right. 'I have her business card in my handbag.'

'What time will you leave for Oxford?' he asks as I pick up my bag to dig out the card.

'I don't know. I haven't looked at train times yet.'

'I could drive you. After we've collected PJ. I can drive there and back in a day.'

'It's okay. I'll be fine on the train.'

His skin tone warms to a rosy red. He turns away to look through the front window, standing a distance away from the glass. 'I want to go to The Greyhound and change. I have some clean clothes there. How long do you think it will take for the photographer to get bored?'

'Never. I'll make another cup of tea, put it in a takeaway cup and go for a walk to lead him away. It will be an incredibly boring unsellable shot of me alone in a street, and meanwhile you can sneak out.'

'That sounds like a plan.'

'Let me ring the solicitor first, though.' I pull the charging cable from my phone. The phone has about an hour of energy now.

'I'll make you that tea.'

The business card in my other hand taps out a nervous constant rhythm on the edge of the work surface as I speak into the phone, explaining my thinking to Meera. '... I don't know of any real motive for her to hurt Eli,' I tell her. 'But she is the only person who had access to my car key.'

'I'll call the Detective Inspector and arrange to meet a member of the team at your home. They can take a statement there.'

'Thank you.'

'I'll text you a time when I have one.' She ends the call.

I look at Nick as I pick up the reusable cup. 'It is definitely easier having someone who knows the law on my side.'

'The police know the law. The only problem is you're never sure which side of it they're on. Sometimes they blur the law's edges if they think you're guilty.' He smiles, as though he's brushing the last thought aside. 'Would you like to collect PJ from the vets with me?'

'Yes. If you could drop me at the station afterwards. But I don't know what time the police will be here. I'll message you when I know what's happening.'

'Okay. I'll fit my day around you.'

'Thank you. I appreciate your help.' I head for the door. 'I'll call.'

'Be careful.'

I open the door and slip out, as he raises a hand in a parting gesture.

As soon as I close the door, the ringtone begins on my phone.

Jack.

I juggle phone, tea and gate latch. This will make an even worse photograph – no headline here – I think as his camera lifts.

Cup in one hand and phone in the other, I take Jack with me as I walk away from the cottage, in the opposite direction from the village square and the ice-cream parlour. I'm not going near Sharon today.

'Hello.'

'Hello, Jen. Your solicitor contacted us. She said you have something to add to the statement you made yesterday. You could have contacted me directly, I'm your liais—'

'You tricked me yesterday, dragging me back here to accuse me of killing my son. Why would I call you directly?' I don't trust him now. He'd sold himself to me as someone to turn to for help and broken that promise.

He has no answer.

'Arla and I will meet you at the cottage in about thirty minutes.'

'Have you told my solicitor that? Is Meera coming too? I won't let you in until she's here.' Paranoia drips from my voice, it will fuel their belief that I'm mad. More calmly I complete, 'I will not speak until she's with me.'

'Jen—'

'You've lost the right to call me by my first name. Use Miss Easton when we speak, and I will only let you in my home when Meera arrives.'

I end the call, instinctively wanting to look over my shoulder and see where the photographer is, but if I look, he has the opportunity of a better picture. I leave the phone by my ear and walk on. Hopefully drawing him away from the cottage.

When the police car parks in the street, later, I'm standing at the living room window, watching. Nick wasn't here when I came back. I'd walked to the churchyard, sat on our bench for a while drinking the tea, the photographer watching, then came home.

The car's doors don't open. They are not getting out. Maybe they know Meera's not here yet, maybe they know her car, if she works at the police station frequently.

Ten minutes later a silver Mercedes-Benz cabriolet pulls up. The roof lowered. Meera. She's wearing a pale green blouse today. An emerald-green bra is visible through the flimsy fabric. Her long black hair looks a little tangled when she climbs out of the car, windswept. She combs fingers through it, looking more like a film star than a lawyer. She says something to Jack and Wendy as they open their car doors.

I turn away from the window.

Clunk.

The door knocker thumps down before I reach the door.

Jack leads the gathering in. I don't offer them a drink, Arla and Jack have lost the right to hospitality in my home. 'Shall we talk in the garden?' I prefer being in the garden. I don't feel crowded there. I walk that way, not waiting for agreement.

Meera sits at the table beside me. Jack leaves the other seat for Arla, occupying his usual spot on the low wall of the raised border amidst the lavender heads and nectar-gathering bees. I hope he is stung.

'Tell us why we're here, Jen?' Arla withdraws her notepad from a pocket in the same moment Jack does.

I talk through my suspicions about Sharon and say, 'Perhaps she was involved in the fire at Nick Mason's cabin too.'

No expressions share their perspective of what I say. They might still think I'm crazy.

When I stop speaking, Arla looks up from scribbling things on her notepad.

Jack looks at Arla and nods, telling her something without saying it aloud.

'Jen, can we have your phone,' Arla asks. 'We will pass it on to the digital and electronics forensics team. It may prove your innocence. We know your phone was turned off the night Eli died?'

'My phone. I told you to check Sharon's phone.'

'Yes. And, if you are telling the truth, perhaps your phone will provide evidence of what you've been saying.'

'I need to keep in contact with Jordan.'

'If your phone rules you out of the enquiry, isn't it worth living without it.' Arla holds out a palm. 'Jen, you must recognise you chose to withhold evidence regarding your whereabouts the day Eli died, and you say you weren't driving the car but without proof the evidence sits against you. You've also found items in searched areas that were not present at the time of the searches.'

'Not one of those statements are admissible as evidence of guilt,' Meera intervenes. 'It's speculation. Stop trying to scare my client into complicity. Miss Easton has not given her consent to you taking the phone. What I heard, is Miss Easton saying she needs her phone. Do you have a warrant?'

Arla looks at me, as though Meera isn't in here, her hand falling. 'We can obtain a warrant in an hour or so, if necessary. We will be taking your phone, it's only a matter of when.'

I glance at Meera. She nods, agreeing that is possible.

'Okay you can have it. But I need to text André first, so he knows what is happening.'

'Can you think of a reason Sharon might have become angry with Eli?' Jack asks.

'No. But I'm not a police officer who is meant to be finding out why someone killed him,' I snap.

Arla stands up. 'All right, if that's everything, we'll leave you to your day.'

I stand too. 'I'm going back to Oxford,' I remind them.

'Then please give Jack the address.'

Meera and Jack stand.

I type a message to André. *The police are taking my phone. I'll buy a cheap one before I leave and send you the new number. Please explain to Jordan.'* Send.

Then I message Nick. *The police are taking my phone. I'll meet you in the tourist car park in half an hour.'* Send.

Nick replies immediately. *Why are they taking your phone?*

I don't answer. It's not a conversation to have on the phone they are going to examine.

Jack takes a plastic bag out of his pocket and indicates I should drop the phone in there.

'What's the address in Oxford?'

I tell him.

'Is there a telephone number?'

'Use André's.'

My arms lift, instinctively crossing. With folded arms I cling on to myself, my hands holding my upper arms, offering myself comfort. I have no phone, or car – and no Eli! My heartbeat thumps hard. I want to give in. I'm ready to collapse. But I have one thing; Jordan.

Fay said I used to sit cross-legged on the floor. I want to sit like that again. In a little broken pile of me.

Jordan is the difference between then and now. I can't give up.

A fragile hollow shell of myself follows Meera, Arla and Jack to the front door.

'Goodbye.'

'Take care of yourself.'

'We'll be in contact, Jen.'

I don't reply to any of them. I close the door, pick up my handbag and leave the cottage a minute or so after them, ignoring their cars still in the street. I want to be at the lake with Eli. I walk along the street, taking the most direct, the fastest, route. I don't see the photographer, but I don't care anyway. I'm not hiding anymore.

As I turn the corner of the village High Street onto the main tourist road, I run. Running to Eli. The soles of my pumps racing across the tarmac and onto the gravel path. I only slow when I see the water. It's as though his arms are wide open, waiting for me to run into his hold, welcoming me back. I stop at the water's edge, close my eyes and just feel him.

'He said you made mistakes, but you were a great mum.' Aiden's words reel through my head. *'That boy loved the bones of you.'* I hear Fay.

'I love the bones of you too.'

I open my eyes. He walks across the surface of the lake, over the reflections of the hills and the woodland. Barefoot. In the ripped denim jeans he wore that day, and his favourite T-shirt. Perhaps I am manic, after days of poor sleep. Perhaps I am just imagining this. I don't care. I'd rather be manic and see him.

My hand reaches out as though he will be able to come and hold my hand.

'I miss you,' I say quietly.

There's a sound. A human sound. Behind me. A cough – the fake clearing of a throat to draw attention.

A reporter? I spin around, ready to shout. It isn't anyone from the press. Sharon's eldest daughter is here, sitting on the fallen tree trunk at the edge of the woodland, where Jack has waited in the past.

'Hello,' she pushes away from the tree and straightens up.

I don't want to talk. I want to be alone with Eli.

Long, tanned golden-topaz legs walk slowly towards me. She's wearing a buttercup-yellow miniskirt and a buttercream loose cotton vest top that reveals the clavicle bones pushing beneath the skin at the base of her neck. Her blue hair is tied up away from her face in a ponytail today. She is stunningly beautiful, but she looks as though, like me, she's lost some weight when she really didn't need to.

'Hello.' I answer. She must have come here to be on her own too, and she was here first.

She carries her shoulders a little forward when she walks. She isn't as confident as her mother or Maddie. Perhaps, despite her hair colour, she's shy, and perhaps her hair colour is to spite her shyness.

Large blue eyes, with the veined blue of forget-me-not-petals, the colours she has drawn out with the dye in her hair, study me. '*A Holly Blue Butterfly's wings*' – Eli whispers in my ear.

Moisture glistens in her eyes. She blinks and a single tear escapes. A hand wipes it off her cheek.

Why is she crying?

'Were you speaking to Eli?' she asks.

'Yes. I feel him here. I'm sorry I don't remember your name.'

She smiles. 'It's Eve.'

'Were you at home the night Eli died?' I can't help asking. She might know what Sharon did? 'Did you see your mum go out that night?' I force a conversational tone into my voice. 'I thought I saw her in a car. She might have seen something important?'

'No.' Her tanned skin reddens to a ripe peach. 'I... No. She would have said something if she has information. I better go, she'll be expecting help in the shop. All this good weather brings in a lot of customers.'

She turns away, but then turns back. 'I'm sorry.'

Most people say that before anything else – and there's something else in her tone. She hasn't said *'I'm sorry'* as an I don't know what else to say comment. She is genuinely sorry for something.

She turns, her hand lifting, as though she's covering her mouth as she walks away.

What could she be sorry for?

I watch her for a moment, and then walk, following.

Eli led us to the pendant, and the necklace. Had he led me here this morning to meet her? Have the police questioned the wrong sister? Was she with Eli? Did she lie? Does she know why Sharon drove my car? Nick said he didn't know whether Maddie had been adopted, if Sharon had adopted Maddie her DNA test and the DNA found under Eli's fingernails would not have led to this sister.

She is just the sort of girl Eli would like – because he may laugh at the colourful description game now, but it was his obsession once, he still loves arrays of colour. Her hair. Her eyes.

CHAPTER TWENTY-TWO

I follow Eve along the path back to Lowerdale, a few metres behind her.

When she reaches the end of the lake path she looks left and right for cars on the main road, but not behind her, towards me. She jogs across, hurrying over. Then, as I've been doing lately, instead of heading for the high street, to walk through the village past my cottage, she turns towards the tourist car park and disappears out of sight.

I run a few paces but stop still when I can see into the car park. I don't want to be seen.

Nick's car is there. The driver's door is open and I see his boots on the tarmac below it. He's sitting side-on in the driver's seat.

I see his face through the side window. He's watching Eve approach. He doesn't look beyond her. He doesn't see me still on the pavement, behind the hedge. She walks towards him.

He stands up. 'Eve! Hello, love!' he calls, raising a hand as his voice carries to her and me.

The distance between them closes. When they meet, he holds her shoulders, leans forward and presses a kiss on her cheek.

They speak, sharing words quickly for a couple of minutes, before she walks on.

Nick's attention follows her, watching her walk away as intently as he'd watched her approach.

I walk on, no longer trying to avoid being noticed. 'Nick!' I draw his attention when I enter the car park.

He's not Nick the ferryman. He's wearing beige chinos and a pristine navy shirt, with the sleeves rolled up to his elbows.

He smiles as I reach him. If he's concerned I may have seen him talking to Eve, it doesn't show in his expression.

When I near him, the scent of an expensive cologne rises from his skin. His hair is still a little damp from a shower, and his beard is recently clipped, groomed.

'Can I borrow your phone?' I ask, without even a hello.

He takes it out of a pocket and holds it out. 'Who do you need to call?'

'Jordan.' I type in the number with Nick watching. When I lift his phone to my ear, I turn my back on him, and walk a few paces away.

'Hello,' André answers. I'd hoped he would. Jordan's number is the only one I remember. I'd learned it by heart last night because I wanted to be able to speak to him all the time when I left him behind.

'Can you ring the police? Can you tell them they need to speak to Eve Cox. Maddie's sister knows something, and she might talk?'

'Okay. I'll call them. When will your train arrive?'

'I don't know yet. I haven't looked at times.'

'You're ringing from the same number. Are you still with the ferryman?'

'Yes. Go, so you can call the police quickly. I'll call later when I'm on the train.' I end the call and turn around.

Nick's looking at me, standing with his hands in his pockets, his eyes asking questions. I re-join him and pass over the phone.

'The veterinary surgery rang,' he says. 'I need to pick PJ up now. Is that okay?'

'I need to buy a phone and a train ticket.'

'If you don't mind collecting PJ with me first. I'll take you into Bowick afterwards. Or the offer of driving you to Oxford still stands.'

'I'll be okay on the train.'

His car smells of the cologne he's used.

He starts the engine, slips the stick into gear and pulls away.

What did you say to Eve? I want to ask. I don't ask. I'm afraid of the answer when the two of us are alone in his car. The more minutes that pass, the more certain I am that there's a reason behind Eve's regret – a personal reason for her to say, *'I'm sorry.'*

Nick kissed her. A woman, who he's talked about and shown scarce interest in when he's mentioned her.

'The police rang me. I'm meeting them at the cabin later. They want to ask me more questions,' he tells me as he steers the car out of the car park onto the main road.

'I told them Sharon might have started the fire.'

He looks over at me, then back at the road. 'There was a police car in the market square. Near the ice-cream parlour.'

If he dislikes Sharon so much, why was he so familiar with Eve? But now I think about it, he never said he dislikes Sharon, he said Sharon dislikes him.

Why not admit there was some connection between him and Eve when he told me the family's story? Because Sharon doesn't like the girls being connected to men? Was that why his cabin was targeted? And somehow Eli was caught up in their relationship.

I stare through the window. I can't look at him. I don't want to say anything. I'm not sure what is safe to do or say anymore. I can't call the police on his phone in the car.

When he parks at the vets', I wait in the car. Ten minutes later, Nick walks out with PJ on a lead, a large white paper bag of medicines in his free hand. PJ's tail waves happily despite the white plastic cone around his neck and shaved fur on his side where the skin is scarlet and scabbed. Burned.

Would Sharon do that? Why? Why target Nick?

Nick opens the driver's side and releases PJ from the lead. As he turns to the rear door PJ jumps up, catching the plastic collar on the driver's seat as he leaps across the gap between the front seats and jumps onto my lap, scraping my neck with the sharp edge of the plastic cone.

'Sorry. You're in his seat. PJ!' Nick calls, throwing the bag of medicines on the rear seat. 'PJ, here.'

'He's all right. He can stay with me.'

I twist my head to avoid the sharp edge of his plastic cone.

Nick slides into the driver's seat, glancing at the time on the dash. 'I'm going to have to head back to the cabin and meet the police before I take you phone shopping.'

'Okay.'

PJ and I reacquaint ourselves as Nick drives back through Lowerdale.

A mile from the other side of the village, he indicates and turns off the main road onto a rough dirt track. The car bounces slowly along, navigating deep potholes.

If I could fly, I would fly back to Jordan right now.

Nick parks behind the cabin, facing a large shed that has no door. It's full of tools, stored in an untidy disarray on a long workbench. Beyond the shed, a concrete ramp slopes down to the water near the wooden jetty where the ferry is tied up. I presume the ramp is to pull the ferry out of the water if he needs to.

When Nick opens the door, PJ leaps off my lap, jumping onto the driver's seat and following Nick out.

I get out of the car too.

'Are you a mechanic, Nick?' I ask, looking at the tools in the shed. They imply he knows his way around the ferry's engine.

'I know my way around a diesel engine. I wouldn't claim to be a mechanic.' He turns his back to me and looks at the cabin.

The back of the cabin looks fine.

I follow him around to the front, walking over soft leaf mulch, leaves that have fallen from the branches above our heads in previous years. Some of the leaves on the branches have scorch marks. The flames had reached to the trees.

Charred black marks scar the wood of the veranda and the front wall of the cabin. It's worse than I imagined. The window and front door have been boarded up. They must be broken.

'Was the bottle of petrol thrown at your window?'

'It hit the window. It didn't break the glass, it fell onto the floor of the veranda. The flames, the burning petrol, ran under the front door and it caught the rug alight, that's how the fire travelled inside.'

Whoever did this really wanted to harm him.

Why?

His hands hold his waist, bracing the muscle there, as he stands and stares at the mess. PJ sits beside him. Their expressions similar – confusion.

Cracking, popping sounds, loose stones stirring on the dry ground, announce the progress of the tyres of another car on the track. Dust rises as the police car stops behind us.

Two male uniformed officers are in the car. One I recognise. Sammy. The doors open and they climb out, sliding on caps.

'Hello, Jen,' Sammy greets me. 'Mr Mason. I was told you have more information for us.'

'I do. I…' Nick walks towards them, beginning his story about Sharon disliking him.

Other voices travel from the direction of the lake – laughter and shouts. I turn and face the other way. The happy voices drawing me towards the lakeshore. There are people in Eli's bay. PJ is drawn by the sounds too. He walks ahead of me.

I step up onto the boards of Nick's private jetty, to see them better. A group of twenty-somethings are swimming over there. One of the men on the shore has skin the colour of dark honey, so close to Eli's winter caramel tone. He's a similar build to Eli too. From this distance I could persuade myself he is Eli, for a moment. But only a moment, he doesn't move or sound like Eli.

Pain grips at my shattered heart.

They shout to one another, excited and laughing. Eli and the girl would have been quiet, hiding their presence. That is why Nick hadn't heard them.

The group of young people take it in turns to jump into the water from the end of the jetty, their knees tucked up, bombing the lake, sending up splashes. The ripples spread, the sunlight catching the peaks.

Nick would have noticed Eli's body in the water from this elevated position.

The police told me Eli was found by a dog walker. They were already there when Nick would have untied the ferry.

But Nick walks PJ along the lake path before he starts work. Does he walk in that direction?

'Sometimes a liar is always a liar.'

I half turn and look at Nick. He's talking with the police officers.

My interest draws Nick's gaze almost instantly. He smiles, then looks back at the officers.

Eli is standing beside me. I feel him.

There's something not right. He's trying to say something.

CHAPTER TWENTY-THREE

PJ's plastic cone scrapes on wood. His cone has hit one of the stilts. He isn't on the jetty with me, he's underneath the jetty. This jetty isn't as solidly built as the public ones. The water is visible through thin gaps between the planks.

His sharp bark rings out, amplified by the cone around his neck. His barks ring around the area repeatedly as he races out from beneath the jetty, the plastic rattling on his collar.

I see what he's seen, a large white swan, serenely sailing through the water towards the bank.

'Go away! Go away!' PJ yells with his bark, tension in his whole body.

The swan swims calmly closer, undaunted.

The last thing PJ needs is a battle with a swan.

The swan is absorbed amongst low hanging branches which dip their leafy fingertips into the water.

PJ runs along the bank and disappears on the woodland path, his high-pitched bark travelling through the trees.

I run too, following. He can't hurt himself. 'PJ! Come here! Here! Come! PJ!'

His bark becomes a stationary sound, not far ahead.

He's facing the lake, beside a pancake of naked tree roots. This tree was ripped from the ground in a long-ago storm. What is left of the rotting tree is on its side in the lake.

'Go away! Invader! Invader! Go away!' PJ accuses the swan that calmly observes him from a couple of metres away, black eyes deciding whether to respond or not.

'Stop, PJ.' I reach to grab his collar. My fingers hit the plastic cone as he lurches into the water.

'PJ! N—' The denial dies. My attention is caught by something colourful swaying with the ebb and flow of ripples that originate from the group's games in the bay.

Caught on a branch of the fallen tree, is a small piece of fabric. Peacock-blue and sunflower-yellow.

It's a sock.

I step forward, not thinking about the water, my white pumps sink in the silt. PJ follows me as I wade deeper, trying to swim beside me, but the water sweeps inside the cone, dragging him down. I lift him out and half throw him, feet first, onto the bank. 'Stay,' I command in a hard voice.

The swan hisses, warning me I've invaded his territory now.

I'm up to my thighs in the water, my skirt clinging to my legs.

PJ barks at the hissing swan but remains on the bank.

I catch hold of the yellow toe-end of the sock and pull it free from the branch. It's a boy's sock. I know the image woven into the fabric of the sole is a picture of the superhero Static. I know because I bought this sock. *Static – Virgil Hawkins.* A rare superhero with brown skin, from a comic book. Eli loved this character because black heroes were so rare in cartoons.

I bought him this sock as a Christmas-stocking present when he was thirteen. Too old for things like this. But he had a nostalgic love of the character, and he still wore the socks at fifteen, even though I kept telling him they were too small now. The yellow heel pulled right under the sole of his foot. He didn't care, no one could see inside his trainers.

I see his shoulders lift, shrugging off my complaint, when I told him to throw the socks away. I feel his arms enveloping my shoulders the morning he'd torn open the wrapping paper and seen the socks.

I told the police I didn't remember what he was wearing. I do now. I see his feet walking downstairs, and I see ill-fitting blue and yellow socks.

Why is his sock here? I saw them pressed into his trainer in the image Wendy had shown me. But, no, only one sock had been visible. André had said he thought they were still keeping some information to themselves. The police knew this sock was missing, and again their search had not found it but Eli's shown it to me.

With the wet sock crushed inside a fist. I look through the tree branches, into the water, and along the bank. I don't see anything else of his. Why is this here?

I wade out of the water, knowing the police are going to accuse me of planting evidence again. But I can't leave this here. Eli brought PJ to this point so I would find this. The swan hisses towards my back as I climb up onto the bank, water dripping from the hem of my skirt, running down my legs and squelching in my pumps.

PJ has given up barking, instead he stares at my strange behaviour then calmly follows me back along the path.

Could Eli's body have been pushed into the water on this side of the lake? Would he have floated to the other side? What if he was killed here? They've not found whatever he was struck with…

I break into a run, remembering the police officers are at the cabin. PJ sprints past me, spurred into motion by my urgent pace.

In the last few paces, I hear the sound of tyres on the dry ground. As I run out from the woodland path, dust rises in a small cloud behind the departing police car. I stop. My fist tight around the sock. PJ runs to Nick, drops and rolls onto his back for a tummy rub. *'Dad, I chased the swan away. Aren't I clever.'*

My heartbeat pounds against my ribs. I have no phone. I can't call for help.

Nick squats down and picks up PJ. 'You shouldn't be racing around, mate. What have you been up to? Have you been in the water, getting your wounds wet and muddy?'

The small hairs on the back of my neck rise as Nick looks at me.

I'm cold suddenly. Frozen. I don't walk towards him. I walk towards where the lake path continues towards Lowerdale on the other side of his property.

'We can head into Bowick now.' He rises from his squat. 'Buy you that phone and get you on a train. Have you been in the water too?' A frown wrinkles his sun-tanned forehead.

'No. Don't worry,' I say loudly, still walking, passing the jetty, no longer looking his way. 'I've taken too much of your day up already! I'm going to call for a taxi! I'll walk back to the cottage! I need to change my clothes, anyway! I pulled PJ out of the lake.'

'You'll need a phone!'

'I'll manage! I'll be fine!' I raise an acknowledging – goodbye – hand still not looking at him. 'Thank you for your help!' Those words taste rotten. *I think you killed my son.* The accusation presses at the back of my throat.

I'm alone with him in the middle of a wood, with no phone. No help. No witnesses.

When the trees have absorbed me, hiding me from his view, I run. Not a jog, a sprint.

'Jen!' he shouts after me. 'What's happened?'

I don't reply. I run for my life. When I was a child, I was a sprinter. I used to win races.

I don't hear him behind me, but that doesn't mean he isn't following.

Air pulls into my lungs. The muscles in my legs burn. I don't stop. I can't stop. It's a mile to the village. My feet strike the dry mud path.

A high-pitched cry screams in the air above. The toe of my pump catches on an exposed tree root. I fall, landing like a felled tree, unable to stop my fall with my hand that grips the sock. A stone cuts into the skin of my knee.

My ankle is painful when I stand, it takes several slow paces before it will easily take my weight, but it has to. I run again. The osprey calls above my head, sharp repeated cries. *Hurry. Run.* Eli, urging me on.

What if Nick isn't following because he's taken the car. He'll be waiting at the cottage.

Maybe the birds are trying to warn me.

Pain throbs in my ankle. Sweat trickles down my back.

Near the village, I leave the path, cutting a corner, running through the bracken carpeting the ground in the wood. If Nick is behind me, he'll hear my feet crushing the undergrowth.

I break cover, running out of the wood only when I must, running over the main road. A car honks its horn. I hadn't looked. I run the quickest route, up the main road and onto the High Street. If there are members of the press in the street, I'll ask them to call 999.

I slow, the muscles in my legs burning and shaking, laden with lactic acid, and my lungs heaving as I walk on.

There's only one person there. She has blue hair, and she's standing in front of my garden gate.

Can I trust her to help? She spoke to Nick.

I can knock on doors to rouse someone, but most of the street are holiday rentals, they're probably all out. I press the wet sock into the pocket of my skirt.

Have the police spoken to her?

Her palm drops down onto the wrought-iron gate, as though she's blocking my entrance.

'Hello.' A tremor of uncertainty ripples through her voice. The tone isn't confrontational, denying the threat in the movement of her hand.

'Hello.'

Her expression doesn't acknowledge my wet, muddy and out-of-breath state.

'Can I come inside with you?' she asks. 'I need to talk to you.'

I look beyond her, towards the centre of the village. No one. I glance over my shoulder. No one. I have no one else to trust. 'Do you have your phone?'

'Yes.'

'Can I borrow it?'

'Yes.' Dark eyebrows lower, in a brief frown, as her hand offers me her phone.

'Thank you.' I take it. 'Come in.' I'd rather make the call inside.

I reach around her as her hand lifts and release the latch of the gate. She steps out of the way so I can lead the way up the garden steps, pulling the key from my pocket. My handbag is in Nick's car. He'll come here. He'll be here soon.

I shut and lock the door behind us.

'Sit down,' I tell her, pointing at the sofa. 'I need to make a call. I'll be in the garden for a minute.'

'You'll need me to open the phone.'

No. I don't need that to call 999. I don't want to let go of the phone. 'I'm calling the police.'

'Oh.' Her skin tone is suddenly a deeper red than the peach it was before, more Victoria plum.

I turn away, lifting the phone to my ear as I leave the room.

'Hello, what's your emergency?'

'I need to speak to the police. I know who murdered Eli Pelle and he knows I know.' My heavy breathing adds to the pitch of urgency in the words.

'What is your name?'

'Jennifer Easton.'

'Where are you?'

'At home...' I tell her my address.

'Are you in danger? Is he with you?'

'I ran away. He's not here, but he might come.'

'Hold on just for a second and I'll put you through to the police.'

I look into the house through the window, watching Eve. If Nick comes here, she might let him in.

'Hello, Miss Easton, I've dispatched a unit, can you tell me what's happening?'

'My son is Eli Pelle. He was murdered. I found his sock in a different part of the lake. Only one person lives near that end of the lake.' I breathe and swallow back the overpowering panic. 'I've run from the lake. I thought he was chasing me.'

'Take a breath, Miss Easton, and tell me the name of the person you suspect?'

'Nick Mason.'

Eve looks at me, watching me through the window as I watch her. She stands and walks underneath the arch into the kitchen.

I think she heard.

I turn my back to the window. 'I need to go into the house, someone is here. Please don't end the call yet,' I whisper.

CHAPTER TWENTY-FOUR

Eve is standing in the kitchen when I open the back door. I let my hand fall to my side as I walk in, leaving the phone call live, hoping the call centre person can hear.

'Eli is pressuring me to tell you what happened.' Eve begins. 'He wants you to know. I want to tell you before I tell the police.'

'How is Eli pressuring you?'

'I hear him at the lake.'

She went to the lake to speak to him this morning. I don't know what to say.

'Shall we sit down?' she suggests, glancing at the dining table.

'No. Just tell me the truth.'

'We were seeing each other. We met a few times.' An unwavering gaze watches for my reaction.

'Were you with him that night?'

White teeth bite the skin of her lower lip as she nods.

I knew she knew something. 'You were.' I say for the benefit of the operator on the phone.

'He came into the parlour when I was working on my own the first week you moved here. Then he came in nearly every day. He asked me to meet him for a date two weeks later. Eli was gorgeous looking, funny too, and kind. I didn't know what age he was the first couple of times we met. When he told me, I didn't care he was younger. I liked him. We liked being together. We had fun.'

'Fun. Did you have sex that night? There is DNA on his hand. He's underage.'

'No. We played around, and swam, that was all. Eli always wanted to make memories. He said memories are like keepsakes you put on a mental mantelpiece. He wanted to swim naked in the lake.'

'His nanna says memories are keepsakes. How did you get to Southend Bay? The last sightings of Eli are in Bowick.'

'I drove to Bowick to pick Maddie up. She'd left already. I met him and we drove to the south end of the lake.'

'Did you take my car?'

'No. I used Mum's car. Mum doesn't know Maddie is dating Aiden, or that I was meeting Eli. She hates us having anything to do with boys. In America Maddie—'

'I know what happened in America.'

'Maddie didn't know about Eli and me, either. We kept it a secret because of the age gap. Maddie messaged me asking for a lift home. They were all a bit drunk. She wanted me to sneak her into the house. I didn't pick up the message straight away. They'd left to walk home by the time I got there. Eli was there on his own. He waited because he thought I'd come anyway. So, we drove on to Southend Bay.'

She breathes in a deeper breath.

'We were lying on the jetty, kissing and…' The words are cut off, strangled in her throat. She swallows and coughs.

'And…' I push, hurrying her to tell me everything. 'Did your mum find you? She stole my car. Did she hit him? Did she kill him?'

'No. But she came. She found us there. He was alive when we left him, though. Eli said he liked me a lot. He gave me a necklace that night. A small heart pendant with a ruby in it. He said it was special. Mum… It was accidentally pulled off my neck when we argued. He fell in the water. But he was alive. I pulled him out of the water.' Her eyelids fall, closing her eyes, as though she can't look at me anymore, then she blinks several times as she swallows and coughs.

Her eyes face me again with determination. 'I… I put the pendant and necklace back there a few days ago to stop the police thinking Maddie did it. I thought if I pushed the pendant in between the boards they'd think they missed it, and I left the necklace in the car park to make sure someone would find it. They wouldn't find her DNA, they'd find mine, but they weren't looking for me, and as we are not blood relations there is no connection. They would know Maddie wasn't even there. She didn't hurt him. I didn't…' Eve swallows again, in a way that suggests there's a lump in her throat.

'Didn't what, Eve?'

Eli liked her. I know that. Because the gift of the necklace meant a lot – and she'd gone back and pushed the pendant between the boards and left the necklace to be found in the dust.

'If you know about America, you'll know Mum is possessive.' Tears run down her cheeks and drip from her chin. She wipes them away. 'You'll understand.'

I'm unmoved. Unsympathetic.

'No. I don't understand. Are you admitting she killed Eli? Why? What reason did she have?'

'She didn't. I heard they'd found his body from a news bulletin the next day. I promise, when we left him there he was alive. He hit his head when he fell in the water, but he was breathing.'

'You left him there alone.' That's all I hear. 'Injured. Naked. At night. Drunk. He was fifteen!' I'm not sure who she is trying to convince me or herself. But this doesn't explain why the sock was closer to Nick's property.

She steps forward, reaching out, and touches my upper arm.

I lift my arm and throw the appeasing touch aside. Her phone still in my hand, still listening. 'I will never see him again!'

I watch this girl who liked my son for a few weeks cry.

'I love Eli!' I yell at her tears. 'He is everything to his family. You took him from us! Even if you're telling the truth, you left him alone and he died.'

The distant tunes of police sirens make her turn. 'Are they coming here?'

The sirens grow louder, rushing towards us.

'Yes. Now you can tell them the truth. If you really didn't kill him, then why didn't you tell them on the first day?'

'Because I didn't want our family involved. Maddie went through enough in America.'

I'm too angry to answer. I step forward, she moves out of the way, letting me pass.

As I pull open the door two cars dash along the Hight Street. Blue lights flashing. The sirens die as they see me.

Jack is driving the first car. He stops in the middle of the road, blocking it off, releases his belt in a rush, opens the door and leaves it open as he runs over to me.

'Are you okay?'

Sammy is in the car behind. He follows Jack to my door.

'I have something to say about the death of Eli Pelle.' Eve speaks from behind me.

'That isn't why I rang,' I tell Jack. 'I need to talk to you privately. Come in, quickly.'

'Miss Cox, PC Hills will give you a ride to the police station. Detective Inspector Carter will take your statement there.'

Eve leaves in the company of Sammy, as Jack steps inside the cottage.

'The call centre said someone was chasing you?' His gaze lowers to my wet skirt and muddy pumps as his hand pushes the door shut.

'Mr Pelle has called the station, complaining about us taking your phone. He said he didn't trust Nick Mason, and you were with him, unable to call for help. I was on my way out to his cabin to check on you and bring you this when we were told you phoned in.' He reaches into his pocket and takes out a cheap pay-as-you-go phone. 'For you.'

I don't take it.

'I bought it myself. It's not police issue. You can give it back to me when you have yours back.'

'You said, when. Am I cleared?'

'Or if. Anyway. Take it.'

'I'll swap you for that phone.'

I look at the one in my hand. The call has been closed.

'It belongs to Eve Cox. I have something else too…' I dig the wet sock out of my pocket. 'This sock is Eli's.'

He looks down at the wet ball of blue and yellow.

'I found it near Nick Mason's cabin. In the lake. Why would it be there, Jack? Eli must have been there that night and not at Southend Bay. I bought him this sock. It's his favourite cartoon character. It came from an American supplier. I've never seen them sold in the UK. The character isn't well known. Eli's never seen anyone else with these socks. They're special. That's why he wore them even though he'd outgrown them.'

Jack looks me in the eyes. 'And you didn't think you should have left it where you found it? That's the third time you or your son have touched evidence, Jen.'

My mouth falls open, is he still accusing me. I shake my head. 'I didn't drive my car that night. Eve saw her mother driving it. She had access to my key when I was in her house. I didn't kill my son. I picked this up because I didn't want it to disappear. You need to look along the lake path near Nick's cabin. Something happened there.'

He coughs, clearing his throat, and withdraws two clear plastic evidence bags from a pocket of his black vest. I drop Eve's phone into one and Eli's sock in another. Another important part of our family history lost. Memories – like keepsakes for the mantelpiece.

'They found a small piece of blue hair in a link of the necklace,' Jack says.

A breath sucks into my lungs. The blue hair is Eve's.

'There's a match with the DNA found on Eli's body.

'I'll drive out to Mr Mason's property now. You'll need to come with me, to show me where you found this.' He lifts the bag containing the wet sock.

CHAPTER TWENTY-FIVE

Pale, bloodless fingers tuck a loose strand of hair behind my ear as I climb out from the back seat of the police car. The hollowness inside my legs threatens to bring me to my knees.

Five cars stand stationary around the cabin. Three are marked police cars. Wendy stands on the cabin's charred veranda, talking to a uniformed officer.

I scan the people here. PJ is on a lead. The other end of the lead is held by an officer.

Nick is nowhere.

No. He is here. In the back of a car. Looking at me through the rear side window. A police officer stands beside the door. Nick's hands lift. Metal glints. Handcuffs. I expect to see anger in his expression. It's the same expression he displayed the day he stood on my doorstep with the bouquet of flowers. I see only concern for me.

Had he said he was sorry then? I don't remember. But everyone said it.

'Jen!' Arla calls. 'Show us where you found the sock.'

'It's this way.' I point and walk towards the path.

Quick footfalls hit the ground behind us. Jack catches up. 'Call

André, Jen. He's rung the office again. He's concerned and he's not going to believe you're okay unless you call.'

I take the old-fashioned phone Jack gave me out of my pocket, turn it on and press in Jordan's number. It rings.

'Hello,' André answers. Even in that single word I hear his fear.

'Hi.'

'Jen.' Relief ripples through his voice. 'What is going on?'

'I'm still in Cumbria. I'm okay.' I walk towards the path, leading the police while I talk.

'I'm on my way there. I'm as far as Birmingham. The police aren't—'

'I'm with them. Jack gave me this phone.'

'I'll be there in a couple of hours. Call that solicitor if you need help.'

'Okay. Thank you.' I end the call.

As I approach the fallen tree, I point at the branch. 'It was there.'

Arla looks around, scanning the area without moving a centimetre. 'Call in the forensic team, Jack, and let's do a fingertip search.' She looks at me. 'Thank you, Jen. Jack will take you home.'

I'm not sure I can go back to the cottage and simply wait. Not when I know Eli has brought us so close to the truth.

'Maddie! Maddie!'

Glimpses of blue hair catch the moonlight. She's running along the path to the lake. Her voice reaching to me as she calls for her sister. Her hair is ice-blue in the dark.

I'm the only one left here, sitting on top of the picnic table, with my feet on the seat, waiting for Eve. Maddie gave up waiting and left. I drink the last drop of cider from the can, crush the can in a fist, stand

and jump to the ground. I throw the empty can towards the public bin and score.

'Here, Eve!' I wave.

The moon is a full circle and larger than normal. It's so bright out here, it's like daylight, especially with the moon reflected on the water.

'Eve!' I call again as she reaches the open area of the bay.

'Eli.' Her voice changes as we walk to each other. 'Where's Maddie?'

'Gone.'

She looks over her shoulder, concern tensing her shoulders.

'She's fine. She's with Aiden. They're walking back. She thought you weren't coming.'

'Why didn't you walk with them?'

'I didn't want to watch them kissing when I could wait and kiss my own girl. I knew you'd come when you read her message.'

'My phone was turned off, I was at my friend's house.'

Her smile melts something in my stomach. I lift my arms, and she accepts the offer. Her hands catch hold of my T-shirt at my waist as our lips come together.

No one knows about this. About us. Not Maddie. Not Aiden. Not our mothers. No one. We are each other's secret. My older girl.

She breaks the kiss. 'Let's go to Southend Bay. We're less likely to see others there. It's warm and bright, we could swim there.'

'I've never been skinny dipping. That's one for the mental mantelpiece.'

I ride shotgun, with the window down, my arm resting on the sill. I feel older with a girlfriend who drives.

There's a gift for her in the pocket of my jeans. Mum's old necklace. I'd planned to ask Eve to meet me in Lowerdale but then I saw her mum with mine and I decided to walk to Bowick with Aiden and meet the others. I can't message or ring her because her mum looks at her phone. Mum won't miss the necklace. She hasn't worn it since she left Dad. It's a heart. I want to show Eve she has mine.

'I don't have to rush back. Mum was in bed when I took the car keys.'

In bed... The thought churns through my stomach. Is her mum still with mine? Maybe Eve doesn't know. I'm not telling her. Who wants to think about their mum having sex, and definitely not her mum with mine.

Eve parks up in the small parking area, and we walk the rest of the way along a shadowed path through the trees, her hand in mine.

We walk into the bay, laughing. I don't remember what about. We often laugh. I liked her the minute I saw her blue hair, then even more when she looked at me and smiled. 'Your eyes are lapis-blue.' I told her. She laughed. Her laugh has a musical rhythm. Three beats of sound. Ha ha ha. Ha ha ha.

I stumble on one of the tree roots that stretches into the bay. Her hand catches my arm. 'I may be a bit drunk.'

'You're fine. You're funny.'

I sit on one of the logs around the firepit and pick a music playlist on my phone.

She sits next to me, the hem of her short skirt riding up her thighs. The bare skin makes my mind turn to sex.

She's so beautiful.

Everything is beautiful here. The lake, the woods and the hills. I didn't want to move here, but now I am here, it's a good place to be. Because here is Eve. But I won't admit I like it here to Mum. Not yet. She deserves to feel guilty for a bit longer.

Eve leans – her shoulder toppling against mine. Her head settles into the crook of my neck. My head rests on top of hers.

She lies to Maddie and her Mum all the time so we can be alone. I think she likes me as much as I like her, although neither of us have spoken about our feelings. I'm going to today. It's too early to call it love, but I want to give her the heart because I feel submerged in her. She's in my head all day. I don't think love is far away.

I leave my phone on the log. My hand creeps up under the hem of her skirt and I press my lips against hers then open my mouth and slide my tongue into the warmth her mouth. Shivers tremble low in my stomach. I'm turned on by everything about her.

Her fingers touch my stomach, lifting my T-shirt, and releasing the button securing the waistband of my jeans.

She makes me feel like I'll explode. My fingers touch soft velvet, then slick pearl and slip inside, her thighs open a little wider to allow it.

Her hand reaches out as though she'll lean back on the log. But instead, it lifts.

There's a rock in her hand.

The kiss ends and I'm left looking up at dark-blue fingernails pressed on a rock as it comes down. Pain slams through the back of my head.

There's a loud scream. It ends as I sit up. It came from my throat. The duvet slithers off the edge of the bed onto the carpet. The beat of my heart pulses madly in my chest.

Footfalls race upstairs. 'Are you all right?' André's words reach through the bedroom door. He doesn't come in.

'Yes. Sorry. I had a dream.'

But did it happen like that?

No, it can't have. Why would Eve hit him like that, for no reason at all?

I sit at the edge of the bed. 'I'll get up. Would you put the kettle on?'

'Yes. See you in a minute.'

The streetlight on the other side of the curtain casts shadows across the room. It's still dark outside.

The alarm clock displays 02.03.

I dress, quickly, sliding my arms into a clean T-shirt, pulling it over my head and down, then stepping into loose jeans. I need a belt to keep them up. I've lost so much weight.

'I dreamt I was Eli,' I say as I walk downstairs. André's turned the lights on. 'He was with the Eve. She killed him.'

He's reaching to take mugs out of the cupboard, while the

kettle spews out steam. 'It was just a dream, though, Jen,' he answers without turning.

'It felt real. I was in Eli's body. The police think I'm crazy. I feel like I am at times.'

The mugs are put down, and he turns to the fridge not looking at me. 'I haven't slept for nights either and I feel crazy too. It is crazy.' He lifts the two-pint carton of milk.

I hold the back of a dining chair, bracing myself.

He pours the milk and returns it to the fridge.

We used to get through eight pints of milk a week because Eli drank it by the gallon.

André arrived just after seven last evening. Jack stayed until then, passing on information that was being drip fed through to him from the interviewing officers in the police station. Finally completely trusting me with everything they know, now they believe I am not involved.

Under caution, Sharon admitted driving my car to the lake, but like her daughter she said she left Eli alive.

She stole my car *'to stop her daughter from doing something she'd regret.'* That is what she'd said. *'Because Eli was legally too young for sex.'*

Jack didn't tell me those details – I heard Arla speaking angrily through his phone.

'She spoke as though she thought we'd accuse the girl of being a paedophile and grooming the boy into having sex. As though we did not have enough intelligence to understand the difference between young people falling for one another and people maliciously taking advantage of youth.

'Wendy had a quiet word with the daughter about it. She's highlighted the risks and impacts of young people making choices they may regret when they're older. Of course, it's of no consequence now anyway. And I think the mother was using it as an excuse to explain arguing with boy.'

So that was Sharon's motive – Eli was legally too young for sex and her daughter would risk a prison sentence.

The only thing Nick has admitted to is throwing stones into the trees late at night because he thought he heard someone in the wood.

Apparently, teenagers sometimes hang out in the wood at night. He'd thrown stones, he said, *'but they weren't big rocks.'*

Nick told me he hadn't heard anything that night and now suddenly there were teenagers in the wood. Everyone had been lying to me.

André thinks Nick is covering himself by saying he threw stones. Perhaps he's hoping the police won't find any other evidence and he'll continue claiming innocence. One sock near where he lives doesn't prove anything.

André and I wonder if Eli tried to walk home and something happened with someone on that path. But he was not dressed. Maybe I was wrong and he did not undress himself but someone stripped his body afterwards to make it look as though he was hurt in the water.

It's the whys I don't understand. And I was sure he'd undressed himself.

André brings in two full mugs and puts them on the table. I sit down as he does.

'They are still looking for evidence around the lake. I went for a walk hoping I'd feel more like sleeping afterwards. I saw the lights and I could hear the generators running, even from this end of the lake.'

'They are missing something,' I say. 'Eli is still trying to tell me things. That dream was too real. Why would Nick kill him?'

'Why would Eve? Throwing stones into trees to chase people away at least has some sense to it.'

'You think Nick accidentally hit him? The coroner said Eli has three head wounds, Nick would be an unlucky shot.'

'No, I don't really believe that. There can't be two fatal

accidents in one man's life. What are the odds of that? He looked violent in that video. But I admit I don't understand why he'd kill Eli. The police will be busy trying to find evidence to charge him with before the twenty-four hours are up. You know, he could have burned his own cabin to dispose of evidence.'

A dull ringtone plays and a vibration shivers through the ceiling. I look up. I left my borrowed phone on the cupboard beside the bed. I rise and run because it can only be one person, or rather one group of people. The police. I race to the bedside cupboard and catch the call just before it is rerouted to voicemail.

'Hello,' I pant breathlessly into the phone.

'Hi. Jen. It's Arla. I need you to send me photographs of the soles of the shoes you wore when you walked on the shore path yesterday, and don't wear them again, we'll need them.'

'Okay. I'll use André's phone.' My borrowed one doesn't have a camera.

'And what shoe size are you?'

'Seven.'

'Thank you. I'll wait for the images.'

I hurtle downstairs. My muddy, still-wet pumps are on the shoe rack beside the door.

'Can I borrow your phone?' I ask André, my free hand reaching out urgently.

He hands it over. I turn the shoes and photograph the soles.

'What are you doing?' André asks.

'They must have found suspicious footprints. Arla asked for pictures. I presume to rule out mine.'

I send the images in a text to the number she called me from.

Thank you. Returns a moment later.

'I'd have thought your trainers couldn't be confused with a man's footprint, unless he has unusually small feet,' André forces a smile as I sit down.

'Nick doesn't have small feet.' I pick up a hot mug. 'I'd rather sit in the garden.'

A ping announces a text on his phone. It's Camille. She was messaging him all evening. I hand his phone back.

'You didn't have to come. I don't want to harm your relationship,' I said when he arrived here.

'It's okay. You're on your own. You need someone, and she understands. She isn't like you and me. We used to hold on to the things that annoyed us for weeks. I think that's what broke us apart.'

'Have you stopped blaming Bell then?'

He'd laughed. *'A long time ago.'*

I head out into the garden, closing the back door behind me, leaving him to speak to her in private and sit at the garden table. I lean back against the cottage wall so I can look up at the night sky.

I wish I knew what was happening at the police station, and by the lake, but wishes are hopeless unachievable things. They do not come true.

The more I look at the stars the more stars I see. They look like a billion pinholes in the sky.

As if to spite me, a shooting star races through the dark then disappears. I dare a wish – to know what happened that night. Wishes may not come true, but hope is a seductive emotion.

'Hey! I know someone's out there! Hey!' Nick's voice calls in my mind, shouting towards a dark wood. *'You're not funny! Go away!'*

Only it wasn't dark that night. I re-imagine the scene, in bright moonlight.

Jack told me Nick called 101 and complained about teenagers around his cabin. He'd had windows broken before and threatening objects left outside. I can't picture Eli damaging property or intimidating anyone. I told Jack that. Eli wasn't brought up like that. He helps people. He has always genuinely cared about others. He was more likely to be a good Samaritan than an assailant.

I close my eyes. Listening for Eli to tell me more.

Something races past me, snapping branches. It lands with a thud not far away. A large stone. A second crashes its way through the trees.

'I know someone's out there!'. The ferryman is throwing rocks randomly. He's drunk.

I want to get home.

A dog barks.

I need to cross his property or go back. Will he recognise me if I call out?

Another missile races through the trees and falls into the bracken.

I turn and run. My foot catches in a tree root, tripping me up. My trainer slips off because the laces aren't tied and just tucked in and the trainer pulls off the ill-fitting short sock. I slide the trainer back on, leaving the sock, and run. Another heavy stone breaks the branches near me. A heavy thud, a lancing, sharp, pain, pierces the back of my head.

I open my eyes and look at the sky again. Is that how it happened? It doesn't fit with his injuries or how his body was found.

The back door opens then André walks outside, mug in one hand, phone in the other.

My head turns to look at him, still resting against the bricks. 'Eli is trying to tell me what happened. I know it. He's putting thoughts in my head.' I lift my legs, resting my heels on the edge of the chair, and hold my ankles.

The light from his phone's screen lights up his dark face as his gaze rises from the phone to me. He's going to say I'm being stupid. I'm imagining it.

'What do you feel?'

André said he felt him by the lake the other day.

'I feel his words. Not a clear voice. I think I'm forcing it now though. I imagined him trying to cross Nick's land, and Nick throwing things.'

'That doesn't fit with your dream, does it?'

'I know, that's why I think I'm forcing this. Eli is trying to help me work it out and maybe he can't see the detail to be able to share it.'

'I've begged Eli to speak to me,' André says, sitting side-on in the chair opposite me. He leans back against the cottage wall. 'I stood by the water when I went for a walk, and I pleaded with him to speak to me. I never used to believe in spirits, but I have felt his presence by the lake. I agree, he wants us to know who killed him. Jordy told me he saw Eli when he found that pendant.'

Somewhere in the distance a barn owl screeches, it's an unearthly scream.

André glances towards the sound.

'How is Camille?'

'She can't sleep. She's blaming herself for me not seeing Eli. I told her, I was the idiot who lost his temper.'

'She sounds as though she's changed since I last met her.' Or I misjudged her.

'She's grown up a bit, maybe.' He smiles, then takes a sip of coffee. A sigh erupts when the mug lowers. 'I want him back. I want to change everything.'

'Me too.'

'It isn't going to happen, no matter how much our hearts break.'

'Mm.'

When we've finished our tea, I spend the rest of the night trying to sleep on the sofa, while he attempts to sleep on cushions on the floor.

Every item, every piece of furniture, every ornament in this room holds a memory of Eli. The day we chose them, the day we carried them in here, the day he touched or moved them, or nearly broke them.

I close my eyes, reaching for his spirit. Clearing my mind. Just listening. Just waiting for whatever he has to say to fill my thoughts.

. . .

A golden-blonde-haired woman is at the edge of the woodland. On the lake path. I can't see her properly. 'Maddie?'

'Maddie?'

Her hand lifts and strokes her hair behind her ear, as she walks into the moonlight her nails are dark. Painted blue, maybe?

CHAPTER TWENTY-SIX

'Hey.'

Fingers touch the bare skin on my shoulder and shake my body gently.

André leans over me. 'Morning.'

His fingers slide from my shoulder as he straightens up. He's changed his T-shirt, his hair is damp, and he smells of soap and shampoo.

My arms stretch up and a yawn splits my jaw open. Then I remember, as I do every day. Eli is dead.

I sit up. Sadness sweeping across me in a wave, on a daily rising tide.

I reach for my phone, looking for messages or calls from the police, or Jordan. There are none. The clock reads 08.22.

'How do you feel?' André asks.

'Like I've been hit by a truck.'

'That'll be the drug. I let you sleep. I know you need it.'

'Did you sleep?'

'Some. There's a cup of tea on the side. I've spoken to Jordan, he's fine, and I also rang Jack. Nick is sticking to his throwing stones story. But did you know Eve is his daughter?'

'Pardon?'

'She's his daughter.'

'I saw them speaking. He kissed her cheek, but he didn't say… Sharon doesn't like men. She doesn't like him.'

'That may be true, but eighteen years ago he fathered a child with her.'

'Why didn't the police connect him with the DNA on Eli, if he is Eve's father?'

'Because he pleaded guilty they didn't take his DNA when he was charged.'

I stand up and stretch my back. 'That gives him a motive. What if he was trying to keep Eli away from Eve?'

'I asked Jack that. Nick told them Eve found out he was her father a few months ago through a public DNA testing website. He used the site hoping to reconnect with his family. He didn't know he had a daughter until she tested herself, looking for her father.

'He let her and Eli meet at his cabin. He wasn't against the connection. Eve's confirmed that. There's no evidence he did anything wrong. Apart from throwing rocks at sounds in the wood—'

'And withholding evidence,' I add.

'They did find a rock with blood on it there,' André continues. 'It's not been tested yet. They don't know if it's Eli's blood but Jack said it's highly likely.'

'Maybe they were both involved. I'm going to wash and change my clothes. I want to walk to the lake.'

There's an image in my head, as I climb the stairs, of a woman's hand. She has dark blue fingernails.

'I told Jordy-boy you were sleeping and that you're okay!' André's voice follows me upstairs. 'Mum is keeping him busy!'

'I'll call him later!' When I can manage to put a smile into my voice.

I shower quickly, to wake my brain up, slip on jeans and a

loose cotton blouse and apply make-up. As I walk downstairs a feeling pulls through me, an urge to hurry.

'I have to go to the ice-cream parlour,' I tell André as I step from the bottom stair.

'It's a bit early for ice cream.' André is looking through the front window, his hands on the windowsill. He straightens and turns. 'The press are here in force again and there are no officers. Maybe we shouldn't go out.'

'Eli wants me to be there. He's pulling me, in the way he used to tug on my hand as a child.'

'Here, Mum. Come on. Come on.'

'There's something the police are missing still. Eli is trying to tell me, but I can't work it out.'

'Maybe we should leave it to the police now.'

'No. I have to go.' My feet slide into sandals, and I pull the straps over my heels with a finger. 'I need to go there now.'

He's wearing shoes already.

'Come on.'

'No need to rush.'

'Tell Eli that. I'm serious. He's wants us there.'

I unlock and open the door. A chorus of clicks greets us.

'Mr Pelle!'

'Miss Easton!'

With no officers to deter them, the pride of reporters and photographers surge across the street and surround us, thrusting phones and microphones in front of us.

'Please tell us how you feel about the arrests?'

'What's happening?'

Urgency presses under my ribs. Eli wants me to run. We raise hands in front of our faces, pushing through them as quickly as we can. The parlour isn't far away, I just have to get through this swarm.

'Get out of the way!' André shouts. 'That's all we want to tell you!'

When we reach the brow in the road, before it drops down towards the village square and the parlour, three marked police cars can be seen. Three? The reporters stop and let us walk on as they take pictures of us amid the scene. This is why Eli wants me here.

'André, Eli is showing me someone holding the rock that hit him with a deep blue or maybe a dark indigo or navy nail varnish.'

'If you think you're seeing what he saw, he can't have seen that, Jen. The rock hit him on the back of the head.'

'Don't ask me to explain it. I'm only telling you what he's shown me. The blue fingernails were in my dream last night, and I saw them again this morning.'

I jog down the shallow slope in the street, the soles of my sandals slapping on the tarmac. André easily keeps pace with his longer strides.

It's a woman's hand on the stone in my head, it wasn't Nick.

I run onto the cobbles. Officers stand in the street, arms spread wide. 'Stay back please,' they tell strangers.

'Move along.'

The picnic tables are empty, and the front door into the living accommodation beside the ice-cream parlour is open. A man clothed in white coveralls walks out the door, holding a full clear bag of evidence.

'Excuse me.' I race around an officer.

'Jen!' André's voice tries to hold me back.

'Jen! You can't go in there!' It's Lucy who holds out a hand, telling me to stop.

'What's happening?'

'I can't tell you. I'm sorry.'

'I'm Eli's mother!' The plea is half a scream, expressing that this involves me.

'I'm sorry. I can't tell you anything.'

'Jen.' André is beside me again. His hand embraces my upper

arm, and tries to pull me backwards. 'There's nothing we can do here.'

'I'm telling you…' Sharon's voice comes from somewhere outside.

I free my arm from André's grip and spin around, full circle, looking for her among the officers and watchers.

More people are gathering, clustered near the Co-op. She's not among any of the groups of people I can see.

'I told you!' Sharon's voice snaps.

I pinpoint the direction her voice came from. She's around the corner, on the other side of the parlour, where the narrow path leads to the church. I run, leaving André behind, dodging out of Lucy's way as she reaches to stop me. I ignore her calls for me to come back.

All the crucial evidence has been found by Jordan or me. It's all come from Eli. He has one more thing to say.

My foot twists on the uneven cobbles, and I nearly lose my balance. André catches my elbow and holds me up, beside me again. I walk the last few steps around the corner.

Sharon's sarcastic, trill laugh greets us.

She's gesticulating at two police officers, her back turned to us. One of the officers is Marie. She sees us across Sharon's shoulder, but her attention doesn't stray from Sharon.

Maddie is leaning back against a wall near her mum, her arms folded defensively over her chest.

When she sees me, her arms unravel and she pulls away from the wall, standing straight. I think she's going to speak to me, but then she looks at her mother.

Sharon doesn't know I'm behind her.

'Mum,' Maddie warns. Nodding and looking towards me.

I walk towards Sharon. A predatory creature, a wild cat, stalking her down.

Her gesturing hands fall still, her arms dropping to her sides, her vocal complaints ceasing as she turns. Her eyes narrow, as a frown cuts deep lines into her forehead. 'This is all your fault,' she accuses.

My gaze falls, looking at her hands. Navy-blue nail varnish glistens on her fingernails. The same colour I've seen in my mind's eye. Whatever else Sharon says, I don't hear it.

'I remember,' I tell André, turning back and looking at him. 'She was wearing that nail varnish the afternoon we went to bed.' I see her hand lifting a glass of white wine in my memory. 'It was her.'

'Stop them! They're wrecking my home!' Sharon is shouting at the officers again, no longer caring about my presence. 'Eve didn't do anything!'

No. Eve didn't. I face Sharon again, but my eyes are drawn to Maddie standing behind her.

There's something in Maddie's expression. Doubt? Fear? She is looking at her mother and it's not with concern for her belongings.

'Do you know what happened the night Eli died?' I ask Maddie in a calmer voice, walking past Sharon, leaving her to rant on. 'Do you?'

Her skin floods with a blush as deep as the scarlet colour of the parlour's strawberry and watermelon sorbet.

She does. 'Tell them,' I urge.

'Jen, don't interfere here,' Marie warns.

Sharon has stopped protesting, everyone's attention focuses on Maddie.

'Maddie.' My hand lifts, reaching out, as my voice morphs into the tone of her teacher. 'Tell them.'

Sharon glares at her daughter. Her expression a warning.

Maddie looks away from her mum, looking only at me and her lips part. She's going to speak. 'Mum came home in your car. Eve was driving Mum's car. Mum thought I was in bed, but I was in the street. Over there.' A pointing finger indicates the corner near the Co-op just across the square. 'Eve unlocked the house and went in alone, she looked angry. I think she thought Mum followed her in. She didn't. She got into her car and went out again. She didn't come back for another hour. I was in bed then. I woke up because I heard her showering.'

I had woken up and crept out of their house during that hour. Sneaking out like a criminal. Afraid of being seen by Maddie.

Her eyes turn to the police officers.

'My body camera is filming, Miss Cox,' Marie tells her. 'Anything you say is being recorded and may be used as evidence in a court of law…' She talks through the legal obligations that need to be said if any of this will stand up as evidence in a court case.

I know Maddie's suddenly stubborn expression from the classroom. She's had enough of the lies, she's happy for anything she says to be used in a court.

'She behaved oddly the next morning too. Distracted. She didn't talk to Eve and me when we ate breakfast. She turned the radio on to hear the news. She doesn't do that normally and she wasn't shocked when they announced a body was found at the lake. I didn't think anything more about it at the time. Why would I? Who thinks their mother might kill someone.'

Until they do.

'Miss Cox, Ms Cox, you will need to come with us.' Marie lifts a hand. 'You'll need to make a statement at the station, Miss Cox. Please follow my colleague to the car.

'Ms Cox, I'll take you with me.' Marie looks at Sharon, releasing the handcuffs from her uniform. 'You are under arrest for the murder of Eli Pelle. Anything you…' Her words continue, running through the legal rights that were quoted to Maddie a few minutes ago, and me a few hours ago.

'Officer 2213,' Lucy speaks into the communication device on her body armour. 'We have a subject under arrest for the murder of Eli Pelle, can we have assistance from officers on site. We're at the side of the square, in the pathway leading to St John's Church.'

'Are you seriously saying that because I wasn't at home that night, that's enough evidence to arrest me. That's ridiculous,' Sharon throws, refusing to turn so the handcuffs can be secured.

André holds my arm, as though he senses my urge to become involved.

'Ms Cox. You can make your case at the station. Resisting arrest will not help you at all.'

Maddie is already ducking into the back of a police car parked across an exit from the square.

Running feet approach. Three officers round the corner. One of them is Jack. 'Is everything okay here?'

Sharon groans out her anger, but turns her back to Marie, complying as she holds her hands together behind her back, her lips purse as the handcuffs click into place on her wrists.

'I think we have things under control now,' Marie answers. 'We need to take Ms Cox and Miss Cox to the station separately. Miss Cox has provided new evidence which places Ms Cox at the scene at the time of Eli Pelle's murder. I'm arresting her.'

'You can let go of me,' I tell André, as Arla walks around the corner too.

'I found trainers that fit the footprint profile.' A low voice speaks on the far side of the house. The speaker probably not realising we're close enough to hear.

'Get them to the lab, get things confirmed. The clock's ticking,' Wendy's voice travels too.

'There's a diary,' another voice says. 'It may contain some evidence.'

I turn to do what? I don't even know…

André's hand touches my arm, stopping me again. 'No. Jen, let the police get on with it now. They have all the pieces of this jigsaw. Let them put it together.'

Twenty minutes later, we are sitting at a round table on

plastic chairs in the garden of a café, with a parasol above our heads, providing shade. Drinking tea from mismatched china mugs, in the company of Jack. He is in uniform today, and it means we stand out, of course we do, every news bulletin in the last hour will have spoken of the arrest. Everyone in the café glances or outright stares at us.

Jack has tried to persuade me to go back to the cottage and hide behind a locked door. I rejected that idea because today I would feel trapped there.

'You have to wait and trust us.' Jack's words are a broken record, he's repeated and repeated the word trust. But the police broke my trust.

'Patience was never my thing,' André responds.

'Nor mine. I want to be at the station, undertaking the interviews myself.'

André's hand covers mine in a gesture that says we're in this together.

'It takes time to gather evidence,' Jack asserts. 'Rushing at things risks a weak case, and if there's a weak case the Crown Prosecution Service won't even agree to a charge. It doesn't matter what the girl said. They won't waste taxpayers' money on a case they don't have any level of certainty will succeed.'

'I want to walk to the lake.' I stand, the plastic chair legs sliding awkwardly over the paving.

'I need to stay with you,' Jack says.

'Then come.' I want to be near Eli.

André rises.

Jack concedes and stands too.

Jack walks beside me as we leave the café. The lone photographer from yesterday stands outside. He's lost his exclusive, there are a dozen others around him.

Click. Click. Click.

'Miss Easton, have you got anything to say!'

'Mr Pelle, what are you feeling now!'

Jack moves to the other side, to walk beside André, placing himself in the way of their camera lenses.

I look over my shoulder towards The Greyhound and see myself that day – smiling, flirting. Eli would have seen Sharon laughing at one of my stupid jokes. Her eyes glinting with an obvious attraction to me. I leaned towards her and started a kiss in this street.

I fancied her, and I fancied the offer that was put on the table.

She touched me with the same hands that held the stone that killed my son that day.

Navy-blue nails!

'Jack.' I look across André. 'The laboratory needs to look for blue nail varnish on the rock that killed him. Sharon was wearing blue nail varnish that day, and she's wearing it today. I forgot to tell Wendy.'

'It doesn't work like that, Jen. We don't tell forensics to look for anything. The experts must be impartial. Otherwise, we skew their opinions and risk evidence being missed or questioned by the perpetrators legal defence. If the experts find something like nail varnish, they'll tell us to look for whatever they have found among the suspect's possessions for a match. The forensics team are good at what they do. Trust them.'

There's that damn word again. It's as useless as sorry.

A tight pain, an iron band wraps around my ribs, pulling tighter and tighter.

'Jen.' André's arm braces my waist, as anxiety steals my breath.

Breathe... One. Two. Three. I hear Nick. Is he innocent? Did I run from him without cause?

'I'm okay,' I tell André.

A phone rings in one of the pockets of Jack's body armour as we walk around the corner from the High Street and onto the footpath beside the main access road.

'Hello,' Jack answers and drops back a few paces.

André and I cross the road as I capture my breath back,

thinking about the lake, and Eli waiting there. The pace of my steps increases, the desire to reach Eli pulling me with a maternal magnetic tug.

I run the last few metres to the water. André runs beside me, a sound of amusement breaking from his throat. We stop at the water's edge. The silence is complete. There are no tourists, no walkers, no ferry. I don't even hear birds. The lake is as still as glass.

'Is he here?' André asks. 'I don't feel him. If he's told you everything he needs to, has he gone?'

'Hey! Miss Easton! Mr Pelle!' Jack shouts behind us.

We turn, looking back.

His phone is in his hand. Time ticks by unbearably slowly as he walks across the bay to join us.

'What is it?' André prods, when Jack is nearer. Neither of us want him here.

'They're releasing Nick Mason without charge, at the moment. There's no evidence to keep him in any longer.'

'He admitted throwing rocks.' André complains.

'There is no evidence that he threw the rock that was found. Or even that it was Eli he threw stones at. And the injuries the coroner recorded are not consistent with the accidental strike of a thrown stone either. We will know who held the rock soon enough. I doubt whoever used the rock would have successfully removed their DNA from the rough surface.'

'Nothing explains Eli's sock yet,' I say.

'No, and that alone doesn't prove he died there. Ms Cox will be released too eventually. Even if we find enough evidence for the Crown Prosecution Service to say we can charge her, she'll be bailed. She is innocent until proven guilty in a court of law, and there's no good reason to deny her bail and detain her. There's no evidence of any threat to anyone else. No judge would put her in prison before a trial.'

'Thank you for warning us,' André's voice dismisses Jack. 'Can we have some privacy now please?' As Jack walks away, André tells me quietly, 'I want to say goodbye to Eli.'

'Me too.' I whisper back. 'I can't stay in Lowerdale. I can't bring Jordan back here. I'll say goodbye then I'll pack what I need from the cottage and we can leave.'

When Sharon is released, she will be walking around the village and serving ice cream for months before a trial.

CHAPTER TWENTY-SEVEN

The black glossy hearse travels at walking pace along the crematorium's drive, through an avenue of neatly clipped maple trees.

I swallow three times, fighting against the lump in my throat. Jordan's hand tightens around mine. André reaches for Jordan's other hand. Beside him Camille wraps a hand around André's other arm.

The hearse draws to a standstill in front of us.

Fay stifles a sob with her handkerchief. Jordan sniffs back his tears.

The flower decorations beside the coffin are visible through the glass. The shapes are letters. They spell OUR BOY. Our precious son, brother, grandson.

There is a heart-shaped decoration too, on top of his coffin. I chose every flower in it. Eli would have laughed if I handed him a bouquet in real life. The heart shape is formed from numerous different yellow flowers, apart from one single ruby-red rose.

The crematorium is not far from Fay's home. He won't be buried here, though. We're taking his ashes to Lowerdale Lake.

The pallbearers open the doors of the hearse.

They are all in black suits, white shirts, black ties.

I should have told them not to wear black. No one else is wearing black today.

The blouse I am wearing is Chelsea FC blue and my skirt is white. André, Jordan and all Eli's friends waiting in the crematorium chapel are wearing Chelsea Football Club shirts, or at least the club's colours.

When André and I decided the funeral would be football themed, Jordan cheered. He is sad, but he's glad we're sharing the sport they love with Eli one last time.

André lets go of Jordan's hand and moves forward to help carry Eli's coffin. It is important to him to carry Eli on this last journey.

Jordan's sweaty palm shakes my hand a little. He's grown in the months it's taken the police to release Eli to us, but not quite enough to hold Eli's coffin evenly. He is ten centimetres taller, and his body is changing. I bought his first anti-perspirant a few days ago, the same brand Eli favoured. I know how it will go, how his moods will swing, and his voice will crack, and growing pains will wake him in the night. A desire to keep him young forever is constantly with me. Young and safe beside me. I make him tell me every time he goes out, where he's going to, with who and why.

André's lips stiffen, he's biting his lower lip, as he lifts the weight of the coffin onto his right shoulder, bracing it with his left palm.

Camille presses a quick kiss on her fingertips and blows it towards him. He smiles for an instant. A brief broken expression. In his chest I know his heart is in pieces, because my heart is shattered into a billion sharp shards too.

The coffin is too short, surely, too narrow to contain Eli.

Fay reaches for Jordan's other hand and offers Camille a hand, and we walk behind Eli, in a row of four, united in grief.

I swallow against the pain in my throat, fighting the urge to cry. The aisle in the chapel is too narrow for four. We separate. Jordan and I walk in front of Fay and Camille.

Elton John's 'Rocket Man' plays out, a song Eli loved from childhood. There are no hymns. We want people to simply sing the songs Eli loved.

Every seat is full, a sea of Chelsea-blue, and every eye that looks at us is red-veined or glistening.

My heartbeat flutters as though a bird is caught in my ribcage.

At the front of the chapel, there are pictures of Eli. Across various ages. All important memories, moments, in his short life. The day he was born. He is in my arms and André's arms are wrapped around both of us. I reject the emptiness I'd known that day, because today my broken heart is overflowing with love.

The first time we took him to the beach, he is sitting with a bucket and spade. He's two. It was taken not long after I'd been discharged from the hospital. It was one of our first adventures as a family when I'd started to recover.

The day he'd learned to ride a bike. He's grinning into the camera so proud of himself. I'd been proud of him too. My heart bursting with the precious feelings of love I'd learned for my son. Made even more precious because I hadn't known those emotions for the first couple of years of his life.

His first day of school, standing straight, chin up, in his uniform. That wide, proud, baby-toothed smile there again.

Him holding Jordan at their first introduction, less than an hour after Jordan was born. His attention is wholly on his little brother, mesmerised, his eyes shining with an expression of complete awe.

Then the boys together playing with a big truck Eli received from Father Christmas. The image has captured him mid-laugh. Jordan had chewed it. Eli was trying to teach him – *'You push. Push it, Jordan. It's not edible.'*

The first game of football together. Jordan is two and half, Eli nearly eight. He was so patient with Jordan's efforts to kick. Eli mid-motion, striking the ball to kick in a goal on his first day in the football team.

Eli tucked under André's arm standing in front of a tall snowman they'd taken two hours to create. That smile, older here, a little different, but it still overflows with pride. Proud of the snowman and proud of his father. He's ten.

The picture of Eli dancing with me on the floor at André's cousin's wedding. We were oblivious of the picture being taken. He is tall in this image. Forearms balanced on my shoulders, long arms stretched out, hands hanging limp, as my hands hold the waist of his shirt. We are looking at each other with love and respect. I don't remember what we were talking about, but I remember laughing. It was a moment not long before I left André for Bell.

The last image is Jordan, Eli, André and me on our last family holiday, an image taken by an automatic camera on a rollercoaster at Thorpe Park.

There's a particular tone to a sob and a sniff which draws my attention. A crown of blue hair among brown, blonde and black. Eve. She and Maddie are here, with Aiden. I knew Aiden was coming, he contacted me to ask about the funeral, I hadn't realised he was bringing Maddie and Eve.

Does Sharon know the girls are here?

She was charged and bailed six weeks ago. She's continued living and working in Lowerdale. Jack told us. Should her daughters be here?

Jordan and I stand in front of our seats in the front row, facing the female celebrant who will lead the remembrance. Fay and Camille move into spaces further along, leaving a chair for André to join us on the other side of Jordan.

There are no prayers, instead we take turns walking to the front and recalling our best memories, in faltering voices.

Jordan's voice is brave and strong as he tells everyone how much he loved Eli and how good Eli was at keepy-uppies.

I speak after him, tears in rivers on my cheeks. I wipe them away numerous times, probably smearing foundation everywhere.

When I finish speaking, the first notes of 'Wonderwall' by Oasis, play out. From my vantage point on the platform beside the coffin, I look across everyone who has come to say goodbye to Eli, watching everyone singing with breaking voices. A man stands right at the back, behind the last row of chairs, in the corner. He's not wearing the football club's colours. He's wearing a white shirt and black tie. A blond-haired man. Nick. It's Nick.

André's cousin Michael stands beside me. He is speaking next.

I look down and descend the steps. Jordan reaches for my hand. I think to comfort me.

André is the last to the speak. I watch the emotions in his expression, knowing Eli knows how much his father loved him. Afterwards we sing a more recent song that Eli had listened to on repeat for weeks after his argument with André – Avicii's, 'Without You'.

The celebrant reads a poem and Eli's coffin sinks into the floor.

The Greatest Showman, 'This is me', plays as the coffin lowers. This is our final goodbye.

Jordan and I clasp each other's hands so tightly it's painful.

The celebrant reminds everyone the wake will be in the hall here, and then the song that Jordan chose plays. Sam Smith's, 'Lay me down'. The chorus trails behind us as we walk along the aisle, to leave the chapel ahead of everyone else.

Jordan had typed in an internet search for funeral songs to choose this. I find the song too sad, but we let Jordan have the last word. Eli would have wanted that.

As we near the back of the room, I look for Nick in the corner. He's no longer there.

The flowers that were with the coffin are outside, in front of the chapel, displayed for everyone to see as they walk from the chapel to the reception hall.

The commemoration hall has a huge bar across one side, and circular tables, big enough to seat eight, are dotted through the space. They are covered with brilliant white tablecloths and sprinkled with shining blue confetti. The heavily-laden buffet table is at the far end.

'Jordy.'

Jordan turns to face André.

'Do you want a drink?'

I weave a path around the tables, heading for the bar ahead of them. I don't know if Jordan wants a drink, but I do want one, before others reach the room.

'What can I get you?' the barman asks.

'A large white wine.'

'Make that three white wines, a pint of bitter and a small cola. I'll get these.' André's hand touches my side. 'I'm buying for Mum and Camille anyway.'

'Thank you.'

'Hello, Miss Easton.'

Aiden's voice has me spinning around. André is busy paying.

Maddie and Eve stand with Aiden. Three sets of eyes staring at me.

Maddie's expression has none of the confidence I knew her for. 'We're sorry,' she says, taking it on herself to speak for them all. Her eyes and expression apologise for the actions of her mother not only my loss.

I look to Eve. 'How are you?' She's wearing a loose, blue, men's shirt as a short dress, with a thick belt cinching in the waist. The collar is open, two or three buttons undone showing off the pendant hanging from a thin gold necklace. A gold heart with a small ruby embedded in the top right of the heart. It isn't mine. That pendant is in an evidence bag in storage somewhere. This is a replica that André asked a jeweller to make and send to her. He said, if Eli wanted her to have the same necklace, he was going to make sure she had one. He received a thank-you card. That was all. I hadn't expected to see her wearing it.

I notice her beauty today as I had at the lake when she'd watched me. The blue shirt intensifies the colour of her eyes. *Lapis* – that was another word Eli liked to describe blue.

I swallow against the pain emotion ties into the taut muscles in my throat.

'I'm okay,' she answers.

It's not the truth, it's just an answer that avoids the longer conversation that would follow a negative response. I've said the same thing so many times. The truth is my life has fallen apart. But we stand on the polar ends of that. My life fell apart because her mother killed my son, because I've lost my son – her life has fallen apart because her mother killed my son.

Eve touches my forearm for a second, offering silent, impotent comfort.

'It's nice to see you.' This is now my well-used bland phrase. It's helped me escape several conversations. 'Thank you for coming.' I start to turn away.

'Miss,' Aiden stops me. 'Are you coming back to school?'

'No. Jordan and I are staying here for now.'

'Will Eli's ashes be buried here?' Eve asks.

I'm not sure whether I should tell her, but what harm can there be in telling her. His ashes will be spread, no one will have an opportunity to defile them. 'No. We're taking his ashes to the lakeshore.'

Her lips part then close on what I sense would have been a request to join us there.

No.

'Excuse me.' I turn away. I need that wine.

CHAPTER TWENTY-EIGHT

The rainfall is light, so light it's more like mist. Clouds hang over Keln Rigg, hiding the mountain's peak.

Jordan's hands are pushed firmly into the pockets of his Parka.

André's hands are captured in the pockets of the black Harrington he's wearing.

My hands embrace the urn which contains Eli's ashes.

We have permission to do this, and André and I have agreed to pay for a new bench in the bay. It will have Eli's name on a plaque.

'I'm glad it's raining,' I say to André. 'It's less likely anyone else will come here.'

'May I carry him to the water?' Jordan's hands lift out of his pockets.

'Yes. But let Dad open the urn.'

I pass it over. I trust his hands to shake less than mine. 'We'll take turns to sprinkle his ashes and say goodbye.'

My soul reaches out to feel Eli's as we walk to the water's edge

I don't think he'll come. I think he's gone. I haven't felt him here since the day they arrested Sharon.

A breath touches my heart and a gentle sense of knowing wraps around me, like an embrace. He is here.

'Hello, Eli. I miss you. We miss you.'

André and Jordan look towards me, then over the lake.

'Hello, son,' André says, as he squats and rests one knee on the ground for balance. The gravel is wet and dirty. He doesn't seem to care.

Jordan squats beside him.

My gaze is drawn further across the water. Nick's cabin is repaired. Patches of lighter, younger, *green*, oak stand out against the old silvered oak. The ferry is not moored at his jetty, it's running. He might pass us.

'Mum.' Jordan calls for my attention. The fine rain has settled on Jordan's and André's hair, like dew.

Jordan holds the urn steady as André releases the lid.

'Do you want to sprinkle some first, Jordy-boy?'

The care Jordan takes expresses the gravity of this.

We haven't even begun learning how to live without Eli. We're surviving. Me barely. I've lost pounds. While Jordan hides his emotions by thumping his thumbs on a controller to master video games or kicking a ball into a goal on a football field.

André takes his turn, sprinkling the ashes on the gravel among the pebbles near the water.

The water breathes, reaching up onto the gravel, lapping at the stones as though it's reaching for the ash. Some floats away.

'Jen.' André offers me the urn. I squat down and accept the vessel. 'You will forever be missed and always loved, Eli.' I sprinkle the rest of his ashes near the water. 'Whether we are standing here, or miles away, you are always with us.' The water laps up towards us again.

'He heard us,' Jordan says, standing up.

I pass the empty urn to André.

'He's there.' He points to the jetty, as though Eli is standing there.

I rest an arm around Jordan's shoulder.

'You're the best brother,' Jordan tells him.

André swallows hard, his Adam's apple shifting. He coughs. 'I'll fetch the flowers.'

'I'll come with you, Dad.'

I walk towards the jetty.

A distant sound of an engine throbs rhythmically. A moment later, the bow of the ferry peeps around the curve of the distant bank, PJ in his position at the fore. The ferry travels into full view.

Nick is at the steering wheel. He looks this way, looking for passengers on the jetty, and sees me.

I shake my head, briskly, clearly, so he won't think I want him to stop here.

His hand lifts, acknowledging me for an instant, in the way he used to every morning, then the boat turns away.

The police did not charge him with anything, but I'm still not sure if he was involved. He hasn't contacted me.

'Here!' Jordan shouts. I turn. He's running towards me with the flowers in the shape of a heart. The one ruby-red rose so prominent amongst the otherwise yellow flower arrangement.

He and I hold the heart together and lay it beside the water, near the jetty. The shallow waves from the wake of the ferry pick it up and take it onto the water. We don't try to catch it. We watch it sway and bounce, as the rain gently falls and slowly soaks through our coats.

'Shall we find somewhere to eat before we head back?' André suggests.

'Yes, but not near here.' I don't want to risk seeing Sharon. We are driving straight back to Oxford.

I take one last look across the water.

There's a glimpse of blue on the far shore. Eve. She is walking along Nick's private jetty, looking towards us. She knows it is us.

She's dressed in royal-Chelsea-blue leggings and a long white jumper, seemingly uncaring that it's raining. How has she heard that we're here today? I had told her we would come after the funeral, but that was three weeks ago and she can't have known what day we would come – and to be here at this exact moment in time…

Eli's embrace releases me. He's going.

I raise a hand.

Her hand lifts.

He's gone to her. Perhaps that is why she knew we would be here, because he told her we'd come.

I'm glad. If she hears him, it means he is not alone here.

Maybe they were in love.

CHAPTER TWENTY-NINE

When Eve makes her promise to speak the truth in the Carlisle courtroom, her eyes remain fixed on her sister, determinedly avoiding Sharon who sits in the dock, or the jury, or any of the other observers, including André and me.

The heart pendant is visible, hanging on a gold chain across the neckline of a dress with five bands of colour. The dress is sewn in tiers, rings, with a blush-red bodice fitted across her shoulders and bust, then from there pink, orange, yellow and blue bands of colour and frills. One hand holds a poppy-red jumper in front of her stomach, like a defending shield.

'Miss Cox, can you introduce yourself, and tell us your connection to the defendant?'

'I am Eve Cox, Sharon Cox's eldest daughter.'

'May I call you Eve?'

'Yes.' Eve's voice trembles. She is a witness for the prosecution, providing evidence against her mother.

Three weeks of detailed forensic evidence presented by experts in their fields have led to this point.

Tiny remains of blood splatters on Sharon's trainers, caught in the stitching she'd failed to clean, were identified as Eli's blood. The soles of those trainers match footprints on the lake path near Nick's cabin, and the soil caught in the treads of her trainers has traces of plant material that matches the spot where a bloodied stone was found. The stone that is coated with Eli's blood. The same stone has traces of a brand of nail varnish found on Sharon the day she was arrested.

'Will you tell the court who your father is?'

'Yes. His name is Nick Mason.'

A witness, a stranger, a tourist, confirmed they saw me entering my cottage, giving me an alibi and ensuring the jury knew someone else had driven my car. The footage of my car, cropped to close images that I could barely make out, showed Sharon's face. It wasn't clear, but the matches to Sharon's hair and profile were pointed out. They had also found images from earlier in the evening, showing Eve driving Sharon's car. In one image I could see Eli in the passenger seat. He'd wound down the window, and his arm rested on the side.

'When did you discover Nick Mason was your father?'

'About a year before Eli Pelle died.' Her voice grows in strength.

Excerpts of Sharon's diary were shown. She was a journal keeper, it recorded everything from details of new ice-cream recipes she created for the parlour, to what she had watched on TV. A handwriting expert confirmed that this diary also recorded Sharon's hatred of the possibility the girls were connecting with boys, her fears Nick had discovered who Eve was and her anger when the fear was realised.

I don't like Nick's intentions.

Nick is up to something, I know it.

Nick is sneaking around Eve. I think he knows she's his.

Nick was watching Eve when we were in the pub. He's trying to get to her. He knows, I'm sure of it.

Eve wouldn't tell me where she was going. Something is going on. I keep thinking she's meeting Nick.

Eve received a text with an x. A kiss. It was from him. Nick. They both know now. She's been meeting him secretly. He's made her keep a secret from me. I am going to make his life HELL.

'How did you discover Nick Mason is your father?' The barrister asks.

On the day Eli died there was only one statement in the journal.

Today, I killed two ~~birds~~ men with one stone. Well, one boy and one man. Now that is that...

For about a week after that, there were no comments written in the diary.

Eve swallows and breathes slowly for a second before continuing. 'Mum wouldn't talk about my father. I sent my DNA to an ancestors' discovery website. They have a database of DNA. I hoped he, or someone else in his family, might have done the same thing.'

'Was your father's DNA registered?'

'Yes. He was. He didn't know I existed. He hoped to reconnect with members of the family he was estranged from.'

The place where the police found the rock on the shore path was pointed out on a picture of the lake, on a large screen. The forensic expert had zoomed in on the overhead image taken by a drone, to show more clearly where it was found in relation to Southend Bay and Nick's cabin. It was found in the undergrowth in the same area I found the sock. The jagged lump of rock was displayed, and the forensic analyst showed various close-up images of the blood, and the nail varnish. Showing just how the stone must have been held and used.

He was alive when it was used, the blood was oxygenated. They theorised that he was hit as he already lay on the ground. Probably unconscious from a less significant injury. Then he was rolled into the water. He drowned while still unconscious.

'What did you do when you found out he lived in the same village as you?'

'Mum, Sharon Cox, didn't want me to know my father. She told me many times I shouldn't look for him. But I already knew Nick Mason, to a degree. A lot of things made sense then. It made sense my father was someone she knew when she conceived me. Maddie was adopted. Mum is my natural mother but I don't know how she conceived me because she didn't want a man, a father, involved in her life or mine. She said I should be happy with one parent. One was enough.'

'So, what did you do?'

'I messaged him, through the DNA website. He was shocked but excited. We arranged to meet away from the village.'

Evidence presented not only identified the traces of nail varnish as Sharon's, but also identified Sharon's DNA on the stone which killed Eli, in skin cells caught on the rough surface.

I don't understand why Nick said he threw rocks. Why lie about that? The police have never progressed his questioning. There is no evidence he was involved in Eli's murder. Or that he threw stones. Or that anyone other than Sharon was in the wood that night.

'Who knew about this meeting?'

'Only him – Nick – and my sister Maddie.' Eve smiles slightly at Maddie, her eyes remaining firmly on her sister.

Eve is living and working in Carlisle. When Maddie turned sixteen, she moved in with Aiden's parents. Aiden and his parents surround her on the seats of the viewing gallery. I know she is with him, and I know Eve is in Carlisle, because Aiden added Jordan on his social media. He calls Jordan, *'little brother'*.

'Do you and your sister keep many secrets?'

Eve swallows. 'Can I have some water?' She looks at the judge.

'Of course.' The judge looks at a clerk to fulfil the request.

I stare at Sharon in the dock as the water is fetched from a dispenser.

Sharon resolutely, but apparently blindly, watches her daughter.

How can she sit there and claim innocence?

The small cardboard cup is handed to Eve. She drinks the water quickly, one hand still clutching the jumper at her waist.

A psychologist described Sharon as a pathological narcissist. A woman who is so focused on herself she has no empathy, concern or even interest to the benefit or consideration of others.

'We have kept secrets,' Eve answers as she hands back the empty cup. 'All of them from our mother. We had to keep secrets from our mother.'

The defence barrister raises a hand. The judge nods, bestowing agreement for the barrister to speak. 'That question and statement are irrelevant, Your Honour.'

'The relevance will be made clear,' the prosecution barrister replies.

'Then save the question for when it has relevance, and I will decide then whether it should be admissible.' The judge looks to the jury. 'Disregard that comment from Miss Cox please.'

Eve is speaking with so much emotion I doubt it will be forgotten.

'Did meeting your father go well?'

That day must have been a big deal for Nick. The papers said his family disowned him when he'd killed his friend.

'Yes. We built up a relationship. We see each other often now.'

A coarse sound of disgust releases from Sharon's throat.

She is not helping her case. She's made mocking sounds and judging expressions like this during every aspect of the evidence provided. I did not expect her to treat Eve in the same way.

I reach for André's hand. His fingers thread through mine as they used to when we first dated, before Eli filled our hands. I feel the new wedding ring on his finger. Camille was going to come, but she has already fallen pregnant and her morning sickness '*is something terrible. You were lucky, Jen.*'

'When did you meet Eli Pelle?'

'Within a week of his move to Lowerdale. He came into the ice-cream parlour where I work. We became friends first. After a couple of times of meeting we became more than friends.'

'In what way did you become more than friends?'

'He was my boyfriend.'

'What did your mother, Sharon Cox, think of that?'

'She didn't know at first. I didn't tell her because I didn't trust what she would do. Maddie – my sister – will tell you what happened to her, and now...' She swallows and swallows again, but she can't hold back the tears that drip from her eyelashes.

The clerk walks across the room with a box of large-size tissues. Eve plucks one white tissue from the box and dabs away the tears, smudging her make-up.

'Did your mother, the accused, find out about your relationship with Eli?'

'Yes. But she found out about Nick first. She saw a text from him on my phone with an x at the end. She insisted I hand my phone to her. She could be violent. She would have slapped me if I didn't give it to her. She looked through the message stream and saw that I knew Nick was my father.'

'How is this connected to Eli? When did Ms Cox learn about your connection to Eli Pelle?'

'Mostly I met Dad, Nick Mason, at his cabin. I didn't tell her when I was going there, but she knew I saw him, and apart from locking me in the house forever, she couldn't stop me. She tried to stop him instead. She threatened to tell people he'd been to prison. Most people in the village knew. She left horrible things outside his cabin. Like dead bits of animals from the butchers and fish guts, because she knew he's vegetarian and it would upset him. Dad doesn't like animals being killed. Mum can be horrible. She can be crazy.'

The defence barrister raises a hand again and the Judge nods.

'I really don't see how any of this is relevant to the murder of Eli Pelle, Your Honour.'

The judge looks at the prosecution barrister. 'Is this story progressing to the details of what happened the night Eli Pelle died?'

'Yes. Please allow Eve to tell her story her way, Your Honour.'

'Progress then,' she looks towards Eve.

'One day, Mum broke into Nick's cabin and left a note on the table. It said, I'll kill you if you don't stop speaking to Eve.' Eve's voice wobbles, the hand that holds the tissue trembling.

'Your Honour,' the defence barrister raises a hand again. 'This is irrelevant.'

'Can we progress to how Miss Cox believes the defendant found out about her relationship with Eli Pelle.'

The prosecution barrister nods, and addresses Eve again, 'When did your mother find out about your relationship with Eli Pelle?'

'She saw us together, Eli and me, at Nick's cabin. Nick let me use the cabin to meet Eli so she wouldn't see us together. But she was leaving one of her nasty packages, when she knew Nick was in the pub, and she saw us through the window. We were lying on the sofa kissing. She banged a hand on the glass. I thought she'd break the glass if I didn't go out. When I went outside she dragged me into the car by the hair and when we got home she locked me in my room. She didn't let me eat until I swore I wouldn't see Eli or Nick again. I lied. As I said, I lied to my mum a lot. I would have moved out, but I didn't have any money. She didn't pay me for working in her shop. She didn't want me to be independent. Dad, Nick, said I could move in with him, but that would have left my sister, Maddie, alone with Mum. I didn't want to do that either.'

My mouth is open. I didn't know Sharon was so cruel to the girls. I rest my weight against André's shoulder, light-headed. I also hadn't known Sharon knew about Eli and Eve before she and I… Did Sharon flirt with me in the pub for a reason? Did I fall for an act? And – no wonder Eli was so upset when he saw us. Sharon manipulated me that day. Those smiles were false. The hand that rested on my thigh was a deliberate act to seduce me. Was she planning to kill Eli then?

'Did you see Eli Pelle again?'

'Yes.'

'Did you see him the night he died?'

'Yes.'

The barrister's questions lead Eve through her account of that night. The story I know.

Sharon left me in her bed, drove my car to break Eve and Eli up a second time. Eve drove Sharon's car back, and Sharon brought mine back before I woke up.

'Are you certain Eli was alive and well, if annoyed, when you left him?'

'Yes.' The answer is firm, although her blush deepens to the scarlet colour of the jumper she's holding.

'Did you see him or speak to him after that moment?'

'No.' She swallows, and a line of watery mascara trails down a cheek.

I turn my cheek into the shoulder of André's navy jumper, wiping my tears away.

When she left Eli there why didn't he call me and ask me to collect him? – because he knew I'd been drinking with Sharon or because Sharon had not left and killed him then.

Whatever the outcome of Sharon's trial, I have a life sentence of guilt to live with.

'Thank you, Eve, that is the end of my questions,' the prosecuting barrister sits down.

That is not the end for Eve. The defence barrister stands. He asks questions from another angle, trying to tie Eve's words in knots and persuade the jury that Sharon's actions were protective – an 'expression of love for her daughter'.

'She doesn't love me,' Eve snaps. 'Not in the way most people love. Loving someone means you want the best for that person. She doesn't know how to love like that. She only knows how to obsess and control.' Eve almost shouts in the end.

'I have no more questions, Miss Cox,' the defence barrister sits.

Eve steps down from the stand, the red jumper still braced across her stomach as though holding onto that is helping her remain on her feet. The colour has drained from her skin. She is too pale now. I watch her leave the room, hoping for her sake she doesn't faint.

'We will take a break. The court is adjourned,' the judge announces.

'All rise!' the clerk calls.

André and I stand, our sweaty hands releasing their hold on each other.

Eve disappears through a door in the back of the courtroom. The judge leaves through a different door, and the members of the jury through another. Then people in the viewing gallery begin to file out of the room.

'I need some air,' I say.

André stands beside me on the pavement quite a few metres away from the court building. Every time there is a break, we leave the building and walk away from the courts, avoiding the press, Eve, Maddie, Aiden and his family. We've kept to ourselves every day. Neither of us want to endure conversations with others. We've found a park to spend lunches in, but these shorter breaks don't give us time so we just hide around the corner of the courts' building discussing the things we'd heard. Today I feel too numb to talk. It had never occurred to me in all these months since Eli died that Sharon had deliberately seduced me.

We return to the courts with enough time to use the toilets before returning to the uncomfortable wooden seats in the gallery.

The jury and the judge return.

'The prosecution calls Miss Madeline Cox to the stand.'

I reach for André's hand as she climbs the steps.

Eve is sitting with Aiden's family. The girls, again, only look at one another as though they agreed they would do this before the trial.

Maddie swears to speak the truth.

'Tell the court about your time with Eli Pelle the day he died?'

It's a very open question.

'Where should I start?'

'Tell us why you met him that day, and where you met?'

Maddie draws in a deep breath and her shoulders roll back. She looks as though she's coating herself in armour. Steeling herself. I hadn't understood why she did this when she was in school. I saw her toughened exterior and attitude as arrogant. I can see now, it's a defence system. She toughened up to survive the destructive life she led outside school. Perhaps the school counsellor had even taught her how to do this.

'Eli is my boyfriend's, Aiden's, friend. I met Eli with my boyfriend the day Eli died. They were with others in Bowick's picnic area beside Lowerdale Lake. Near where the ferry docks.

It was early evening, and the ferry had stopped running. I caught the bus over to Bowick to see Aiden and joined them there.'

'The jury have been shown the message Eli sent to you on the afternoon, the day that Eli Pelle died. Why do you think he contacted you?'

'I saw him quite a lot, because he and Aiden often hung out together. Eli and I used to speak about our mums sometimes because our mums are attracted to women. That day, he said he saw his mum kissing mine. I didn't know his mum was my teacher, Miss Easton, at the time.'

The skin covering my neck warms.

'His mum is okay. But he knew my mum was crazy.'

'Crazy…' the barrister stops her. 'Can you explain what you mean by that word?'

'She's erratic. I never know what mood she'll be in. She's suspicious. She's always asking to look at my phone, and even my school bag and books. Checking if I am talking to boys. Because she doesn't want me near boys. She didn't know I have a boyfriend. Every boy I know is listed under a girl's name on my phone. I messaged Aiden in code words we agreed.'

Maddie's relationship sounds very Romeo and Juliet – and Eve and Eli?

'Was your mother, the defendant, ever violent towards you?'

Maddie sucks in a deep breath and swallows. For a moment she doesn't breathe at all. When she breathes again she rubs the palms of her hands along the front of her dress. 'Yes.' The breathless pitch suggests she's never admitted it before. 'She slapped me and Eve a lot. Hard. And pushed us. I often made her angry. She has what people call a short fuse. Lots of stupid little things make her angry.'

'Carry on telling us about the day Eli Pelle died,' the barrister requests.

'They were drinking alcohol when I arrived. I sat with them and drank some myself as we talked.' There's tension in her shoulder and neck muscles. 'When people decided to go home, I messaged Eve and asked her to pick me up. She didn't reply. In the end Aiden and I left to walk home. Eli said he was going to get a taxi.'

'What happened after you left Eli alone?'

'The CCTV sho—'

'No. Only tell the court what you know from your experience.'

'Mum texted me thirteen times while we walked back to Lowerdale. Asking where I was. I didn't answer. It was a really bright night. It was easy to be out late. She tracks our mobile phones, though, but she couldn't find me, because Aiden and I were in the woods and there was no road to get there. Eve used to turn her phone off, that's why she hadn't got my message. She turned her phone on and picked up my message late and she forgot to turn it off again afterwards. That's why—'

'Objection, Your Honour!' The defence barrister calls. 'Miss Cox is presenting hearsay. If the prosecution wishes to present that evidence, they must call Eve Cox back to the stand.'

'Upheld. Please Miss Cox, only tell us what you, yourself, experienced,' the judge declares.

'You heard Eve say in this courtroom,' the prosecuting barrister continues, 'Eli was still alive when she and the defendant left Southend Bay, did you see Eve, the defendant or Eli Pelle that night after Eve and the defendant say they left him?'

'I didn't see Eli after I left him at Bowick. But when I walked back through Lowerdale village, I saw Mum and Eve. Eve parked Mum's car and went into the house.'

'The house?'

'Our family home. Mum came back in a car I didn't recognise, just after Eve. I know it was Miss Easton's car now because I identified that for the police.'

'We have heard evidence which confirms that, Maddie. What happened next?'

'Mum got into her own car and drove off.'

'What time did the defendant drive off in her car?'

'I didn't look at my phone. But it was between half-past-eleven and midnight.'

'When I went into the house, Eve was in her room. She had a red mark on her cheek, and her lip had split open. Mum had slapped her.'

'Did you find out where your mother went?'

'No.'

'Did you see or hear your mother return?'

'No. But I heard her in the shower later. I had a clock in the bedroom, so I know it was one-thirteen.'

'Was there anything else abnormal about the defendant's behaviour the night Eli Pelle died, or the following day?'

'The kitchen bin was empty in the morning. It was only half full in the evening. She was wearing a turquoise blouse with a knee-length denim skirt that day. I've never seen her wear those clothes since, and she used to wear the skirt all the time.'

'For reference, no similar clothing was found in the police search of Sharon Cox's property,' the barrister advises the jury.

'I remember,' Maddie continues without a prompt, 'putting a bag of rubbish in the wheelie bin, a couple of days after Eli died. I could see through the cloudy white plastic of the previous bag, and it looked like there was denim in there.'

That evidence is in a rubbish tip somewhere, then.

Sharon had knocked on my door the second morning after Eli died, with flowers in her hand. *I'm sorry* – I hate those words. She doesn't look sorry now as she watches her daughter condemn her, and she had not been sorry then.

'Maddie, have you ever known your mother be violent towards anyone other than you and Eve?'

For a moment Maddie seems to choke on her own breath, coughing and covering her mouth with her hand.

'Do you need a break, Miss Cox? Can someone bring some water, please?' The Judge offers.

The court waits as Maddie catches her breath and drinks some water.

'We can take a break if you need some time, Miss Cox,' the Judge repeats.

'No. Thank you. I want to tell you what happened.' Maddie's voice is firm as she passes an empty cup to the clerk. 'No one knows outside our family. But yes, I have seen Mum be violent towards other people.

'When we lived in America, I dated a boy there. I was twelve and maybe it was too young. But he made me feel special and happy and… We talked about running away together. His dad used to beat him badly and I understood because Mum could be cruel. Not many people liked him.' She wipes her palms on her dress again. 'Can I have some more water please?'

Maddie waits as the clerk fills another cup from the water cooler and walks across with it.

Maddie takes the cup, sips and continues.

'He used to cut himself. He talked about killing his dad sometimes. I didn't think he would do it. I thought he was only imagining how good it would feel. I think things like that about Mum sometimes, but I wouldn't do it. Mum found out about us. She made me tell her where he lived and took me there. His dad was there. She screamed at the boy and his dad. The dad stepped forward and aimed a punch at her, but the boy stepped in front of him and pushed his arm out of the way. Instead of thanking him, she slapped the boy. She doesn't slap like you would slap a small kid. It's not a tap. She uses all her strength, and it hurts. Like I said, she split Eve's lip with a slap.'

Maddie's throat works, swallowing six or seven times, and then she drinks more water.

She looks up at the ceiling when she talks again. 'The next day he stole his dad's gun. He shot his dad and came into school, and he shot some of the teachers and people in my class. I think if he'd found me, he would have shot me. I don't know what happened to him that day after Mum hit him. We left. But we left him with his dad.'

Maddie's gaze falls, and for the first time she looks at me and André, but only for a second, before her eyes reach for the safety of Eve.

'Thank you, Maddie,' the prosecuting barrister says. 'I have no more questions.'

The defence barrister rises from his seat as the prosecuting barrister sits.

'Do you know for certain where your mother went when she drove off in her car late at night on the day Eli Pelle died?'

'No.'

'So, you might think she was involved in the death of Eli Pelle, but you don't know. All you know is she went out in her car.'

'Her car was see—'

'Yes or no, Miss Cox.'

'Yes.'

'And did you ever ask your mother about the clothes you said are missing. The clothes you *think* you saw in the bin?'

'No.'

'So, we only have your word regarding the clothing you say your mother disposed of.'

Maddie's shoulders lift and fall in a shrug.

'Yes or no.'

'Yes. But I saw it.'

'Thank you, Miss Cox. You can step down.'

My heartbeat thumps firmly against my ribs, and André's heartbeat pulses in the fingers holding mine.

We entered this courtroom on the first day of the trial convinced a jury will never let Sharon walk free, but the defence keep forcing cracks into what appears to be solid evidence.

Reasonable levels of doubt, that is all they must prove. They don't need to prove she didn't do it.

'The prosecution call Mr Mason.'

'Oh.' The sound on my out-breath echoes about the otherwise quiet courtroom. I didn't know Nick was being called as a witness. I didn't know he was here in the courts. I glance at André as though he'll explain. Of course, he knows no more than I do.

Nick walks to the stand, wearing a black suit and a white shirt. He was at Eli's funeral, I'm sure of it now – his tie is Chelsea Football Club blue. Perhaps he wished he'd worn blue that day.

As Nick steps up into the stand, his eyes search the public benches. They stop when they see me. He holds my gaze as he swears to speak the truth as though he's promising to tell the truth to me.

'Mr Mason, the court has already been told yourself and Sharon Cox had a child together. Eve Cox, who is now nineteen. Can you tell us under what circumstances you became parents?'

He coughs, pressing the side of a fisted hand to his mouth as he clears his throat. 'I spent some time in prison. When I was released, I moved to Lowerdale. It was a new start for me, but I was quite desolate at the time. My family didn't want to know me. I had no friends. I'd messed-up my life. Sharon Cox chatted me up in the local pub. Flirting. Touching me. I thought she genuinely wanted a relationship. She didn't tell me she is a lesbian.'

I can see it happening. I'd experienced it. She flirted with me for a reason, and she'd flirted with him for a reason too.

'She invited me to her house, and we had sex.'

'Do you want to come back to mine, there's an empty house and an empty bed?' she said to me.

'The next day, she didn't speak to me, or any other day for that matter. I thought, okay it was just a one-night stand. She moved to America about two months later. I didn't think anything of it. Why should I? It happens.

'When she came back from America years later, she had the girls with her. I was never suspicious. It was so long ago, and we only had sex the once. It never occurred to me she had sex with me to have a child. Then I found out.' He clears his throat with another cough. 'I used one of those DNA records, find your ancestors sites. In case anyone in my family was on there and wanted to reconnect. I guess Eve told you what happened next.'

'Eve Cox told us Sharon Cox found out you were speaking to each other.'

'Yes, she found out and she started tormenting me.'

'Eve mentioned some of Ms Cox's acts. Did you report these to the police?'

'No. Eve was living in her house. I didn't want to make things worse for Eve and her sister. I rang the police a few times, though, when I thought she was outside the cabin, to scare her off. But I didn't tell them I knew it was her. I said I thought it was teenagers.'

'And on the night Eli Pelle died, did you see Sharon Cox?'

'My dog barked to tell me someone was outside. When I went out there, I saw her car parked up the road. I thought I saw her run onto the path around the lake, but I can't say it definitely was her. I threw rocks into the trees and shouted to chase her off. I'd had enough of her nonsense. I didn't know Eli was—'

'Objection, Your Honour,' the defence barrister calls, standing. 'This is supposition.'

'Upheld,' the judge confirms. 'Mr Mason, please stick to the facts.'

'I didn't see her and I didn't see Eli. But her car was there, and I have a picture of it on my phone. I showed that to the police when I reported finding Eli Pelle's body. At the time, they didn't think the picture was relevant. After all, his body and blood were in the bay on the other side of the lake.'

He found Eli!

I travelled on his boat that morning! He'd known!

'Thank you, Mr Mason. I have no more questions.' The prosecuting barrister looks at the jury. 'You have already seen the picture Mr Mason took. It was shown as part of the evidence following the movements of Ms Cox that night.'

Wendy had taken the stand to provide the evidence showing Sharon's movements using CCTV and phone data, she showed that Sharon drove to Nick's after Maddie saw her leave Lowerdale in her own car, after bringing mine back.

The prosecuting barrister sits.

The defence barrister rises. 'Mr Mason, you say you shared that picture with the police straight away, but you did not mention anything to them about Eli and your daughter Eve meeting at your home. Was this to avoid putting Eve Cox under any suspicion? And were you, instead, deliberately pointing a finger at a woman you dislike?'

'No and no,' he answers firmly. But his denial is impotent. Suspicion has been raised in the jury's minds. He had protected Eve, even from me. Hiding his connection to Eli's death.

'Eve rang you twice the night Eli died. Once around the time of his death. Did she call you to say she'd kill—'

'I didn't answer. I was asleep.'

'She rang again, though, just before you reported finding the body. You answered her call on that occasion. What was said? Did you go out to look for the body?'

He swallows awkwardly, his eyelids blinking a couple of times. He coughs.

'Would you like some water, Mr Mason?'

'No, I'm fine. I just. I can still see the boy in the water. But, no. I went to check if he was okay, because Eve didn't know. He was not okay.'

Jack's voice whispers through my thoughts, on that morning these people had knocked on my door with their flowers and their sorrys – *'If Eli was killed, the killer is often someone the victim knows... Even if the killer didn't know the victim beforehand, sometimes they show up and offer to help...'* – I should have believed him.

'No more questions, you can step down, Mr Mason.' The defence barrister states.

Nick looks at me again as he steps down. His lips mouth the word, *sorry,* before he walks away.

'We will adjourn for today,' the judge declares.

Tomorrow the barristers will commence summing up, then the judge will send the jury out to decide Sharon's guilt or innocence. She hasn't spoken in her own defence.

André and I let the exodus of the courtroom progress without moving.

Eve glances over her shoulder, looking towards us, just for a second as she stands to leave the room with Maddie.

When the door closes on the last person, André and I stand.

Outside, rain pelts down, so hard the drops bounce up from the pavement. Puddles build on the paving beyond the courts' covered entrance. André holds my coat for me to slide my arms into the sleeves. I dig a tartan umbrella out of my handbag. He takes it from my hand to hold over us – he doesn't have a hood – and we are walking to the hotel. It's fifteen minutes away, in Carlisle's town centre. We've eaten most meals together in the hotel restaurant and sat in the bar together until late at night. We aren't leaving each other alone.

It's good to have him with me, and it's easier now Camille and I have become friends.

'Jen! Jen!'

I turn. Nick is running through the puddles, no coat on. The raindrops forming spots on his black suit jacket.

André stays beside me, the umbrella held over our heads.

'Hello,' Nick's voice is nervous. 'Sorry to stop you. I just… I wanted to say… You should speak to Eve. She's trying to survive this alone. She's blaming herself. I keep telling her to tell you, but she doesn't have the courage. She thinks you'll be upset, and you have enough on your plates.'

'I don't mind her contacting—'

'She won't. You need to make the first move. I've tried a hundred times to persuade her.'

'Okay. I'll speak to her tomorrow,' I agree, half-heartedly. The raw pain of my own emotions is too heavy, I'm not sure I can carry anyone else's.

'Thank you.'

'Are you coming to court tomorrow?' André asks him.

'No. The ferry won't run itself. Eve is keeping me informed. How's Jordan?' He looks from André to me.

'Grieving.' I'm not sure what else to say.

'Sad, but coping,' André finishes.

Nick's hand touches my arm for a moment. 'I'm sorry Eli got caught up in this. I didn't know she was capable of this.'

Words gather and tangle up in my throat.

'I'll leave you two to get off. I'm sure you're tired. I only wanted to tell you about Eve. I… If… Well… You still have my number, I hope, if you want to talk about anything. I'm sorry, mate,' he says the last words to André then turns away.

'The ferryman likes you, and not in a friendly way,' André tells me, an eyebrow lifting.

'The ferryman lied to me.'

CHAPTER THIRTY

My eyes look from Eve's blue hair to Maddie's honey-blonde head. They're sitting next to each other in the front row of the observation seats, watching the jury walk into the room and file along the two rows of seats.

For the two days of summing up, André and I have continued our dance around everyone else, keeping our distance. I haven't spoken to Eve. I have enough to cope with managing my own and Jordan's grief. I know things must be hard for the girls, but we lost our son and Jordan's brother. My mind has frayed to thin threads of sanity, any slight provocation and the threads will snap entirely, and I'm afraid of that happening because of the months I endured the postpartum madness. Aiden's parents are stepping in anyway.

The last words the defence barrister spoke yesterday have haunted me all night. *'All the information you have heard from the prosecution team does not prove without doubt that Sharon Cox killed Eli Pelle. Eve Cox clearly told you her mother left Eli alive. Whatever you may feel about Sharon Cox's capabilities as a mother that has nothing to do with this case. You must focus on the facts, and the fact is there's no evidence to indisputably confirm Sharon Cox was with Eli Pelle in the moment he died.'*

Except that her nail varnish, her DNA and his blood were on the rock that hit him! The water may have killed him, yes, he had drowned, but she'd made sure he died.

The last of the jurors sits.

The judge turns in her seat slightly, facing them. 'You have heard all the evidence in this case. No more evidence will be presented to you. You will now retire to consider your verdict. Remember your responsibility is to consider if beyond reasonable doubt the defendant is guilty of the charge of the murder of Eli Pelle. The bailiff will escort you to a private and convenient place. They will neither talk to you, nor allow anyone to speak to you, unless it is to ask if you have agreed upon a verdict. Please retire.' She nods towards the bailiff who stands to take some sort of oath.

A few minutes later, the bailiff leads the twelve very different looking individuals, a cross section cut from British society, out of the room.

'All rise.'

After the judge has left, the courtroom empties.

'What do you want to do?' André asks, shaking out the hand I've been strangling for days, and have recently let go. 'The jury could take hours, or days, to come to a decision.'

'Let's go for a walk and find somewhere to sit for a while. Maybe in the park. I want a coffee.'

'Okay. I need to call Mum and Camille.' He pulls his phone out of his pocket as we leave the courtroom. 'They'll want to know the jury have gone out.'

'I need the toilet. I'll meet you outside.'

'Okay.'

He walks on and I turn.

The inhalation of breath into my lungs is restrained by a tight band of anxiety as I navigate the busy hallways, avoiding eye contact with anyone, avoiding conversation.

No one is waiting outside the ladies' toilets, or inside, although two cubicles are in use.

I shut myself in a cubicle.

It's been nearly eight months since Eli died, it still feels like yesterday. How much would he have changed between then and now?

If Sharon is found guilty, Jordan and I will return to Lowerdale. We both want to be near the lake. Near Eli. We sneak up there every few weeks and sit in Eli's bay with a picnic. We even took a picnic there on Christmas Day. We sat with blankets over our legs, in coats and scarves.

The cubicle door beside mine opens, rubber soled flat shoes walk over the floor. Water runs from a tap. When the water stops, a blow-drier roars. I wait until I hear the main door open and close, then flush the toilet and open the cubicle door.

A pale image of me looks back from the wide mirror above the sinks. Dark shadows circle her eyes, and her blouse hangs on bony shoulders which have all the definition of a clothes hanger. At least the weight I've lost has given me devastating cheekbones.

I lift the handle of the tap to turn it on.

The lock slides back in the other occupied cubicle. In the mirror, I watch the door open. Eve. Our eyes collide in the reflection.

'Hello,' I speak first. I can't ignore her here.

Her skin flushes, to what Eli would have called a raspberry-jelly-red, to the roots of her blue hair as she walks across to the sinks. 'Hi.'

The movement of the tote bag hanging from her shoulder draws my gaze down. She's been carrying things in front of her throughout the trial, the tote bag, her jumper or coat. Wearing loose clothing. Because her stomach is significantly distended.

My hands stop moving under the water.

'You're pregnant.' I shake the water from my hands.

She washes her hands and answers me through the mirror with a nod.

'By how many months?'

The bump isn't that large. But the bump that contained Eli was surprisingly small.

'You should speak to Eve...' This is why Nick wanted us to speak to her.

'Is it Eli's? You said you didn't have sex.' Had she lied to hide her pregnancy? Did she know about it then?

'Yes. The baby is Eli's. I didn't lie. We didn't have sex that night. We had sex before that night, a few times.'

She turns to the hand drier. It roars into life.

I have a grandchild. 'It must be due in a matter of weeks.' A part of Eli.

Oh. Eli!

'Why haven't you told us? André sent you the necklace. You have his address, you could have asked him to ring you, or messaged me via Facebook.'

'I wanted to tell you, but I didn't know how to. It's not a normal situation, is it?'

'But you covered it up here.'

'Because I didn't want the baby to become a part of this case. People, the press and even the jury, would judge him and me because of the gap in our ages. The police know. The prosecution barrister said it's irrelevant. But the jury may be impacted by unconscious biases. Our daughter has nothing to do with Eli's death.'

'Daughter?' I wipe my damp hands on the front of my black trousers.

'Yes. I was going to tell you when she is born. I need to get back to Maddie.' She walks around me.

I feel like grabbing her arm and stopping her. 'Will you give me your telephone number?'

'I'll write my number down and give it to you later.'

'I heard you're living on your own.'

'For now. If Mum goes to prison, I'll take over the ice-cream parlour.'

'How will you manage with a baby?'

'I'll use a nursery or a nanny. I'll have to work.' She takes hold of the door handle, and glances back. 'Dad really liked you by the way. I mean as more than a friend.'

The door is opened, and she's gone.

My hands tremble as I compose myself, looking at my reflection before I leave the room. All of them have been lying to me.

André is a hundred metres away from the front the door, speaking into his phone, or pretending to speak to keep people away. His hand lifts when he spots me.

My face must express everything.

He says something final into his phone. His hand lowers as I join him.

'You're not going to believe this. Eve's pregnant with Eli's daughter,' I throw the words out without preamble, shocking him as much as Eve had shocked me.

A frown pulls his brow into rows of thin creases. 'Pregnant?'

My nod confirms it. André and Camille's child is going to have a niece. 'It's true. She's been concealing the bump. That's why Nick told us to talk to her.'

His head shakes. Too stunned.

A vice of anxiety tightens around my ribs, the pressure gradually increasing, as the judge sits down. André and I sit down as everyone around us takes their seats too. It's like a wave that flows across the courtroom each time we are required to stand or sit.

The door opens to let the jury enter.

Fifteen minutes ago, André and I were drinking lukewarm coffee from takeaway cups on a bench in Portland Square. The small park we've been using; a sanctuary of green grass and tall trees in the middle of the city. My phone had rung and I jumped and spilt the coffee I held; there's a stain on my blouse. It was the prosecution barrister, announcing bluntly, 'The jury are coming back. This could be a verdict.'

They've been out of court for two days discussing the case.

André leans forward, his elbows resting on his knees, as though he is physically urging the jury to come to the right decision.

I try to read the thoughts behind their passive expressions.

None of them are looking at Sharon. One person looks at me and André, a few glance at Eve and Maddie.

My gaze turns to Eve. The woman who has my fifteen-year-old son's child in her womb.

Eli knew how to avoid a pregnancy. I brought him up to be careful. To have morals. If he were alive, I would say I am disappointed in your behaviour. But I was not a great role model in the months before his death.

I expected Eli to grow up and make a better go of life than me. He always claimed the moral high ground in our arguments.

'Have you reached a verdict on which you are all agreed? Please answer yes or no.'

My gaze returns to the jury.

An older man with long grey hair secured in a ponytail is on his feet.

'Yes.'

'For the count of murder. What is your verdict?'

His gaze reaches across the room and stops on Eve and Maddie for a second, before returning to the bailiff.

'Guilty.'

André straightens up taking a sudden breath as though he hasn't breathed for months. Every person in the gallery seems to.

Adrenaline pulses through my arteries into shaking muscles. I clap three times before I realise it's inappropriate.

Reactions and sounds of joy and relief come from Aiden's family and Maddie and Eve too.

No one listens to what is said to Sharon. No one cares.

She is led away by two officers within moments of the verdict being spoken.

Her sentencing will follow at a later date, but she will be taken to prison now.

Jordan and I can move back home.

CHAPTER THIRTY-ONE

The key turns easily in the lock. I expected the lock to be stiff. It turns as easily as it had months ago when Jordan and I collected our essentials for the months we would not be here.

I look over my shoulder as I open the door. Jordan's smile is nervous, not happy.

'Come here.'

We squeeze through the door together, my arm around his shoulders.

'Shall we have a drink in the garden, before we start unpacking?'

'I need to fetch something from Eli's room, Mum. Then I'm going to the ice-cream parlour. I'll unpack later.'

'Why?'

'I want to do something.'

His adamant tone tells me he's been planning whatever '*something*' is for days.

'Okay. May I come with you?'

His head bobs in a nod for a second before he deserts me, racing up the stairs, as though it was yesterday we lived here.

I walk into the kitchen, run the cold water and reach for a glass. It was a long journey here.

When Jordan thunders back downstairs his T-shirt is distorted at the stomach by the '*something*' shoved under it. He'd tucked the T-shirt into his tracksuit bottoms to keep whatever it is a secret. I don't point out the telling lumps in the outline of it. If this makes him happy, I'm happy. That's my motto these days.

I've been told by a psychologist I shouldn't let Jordan get away with doing anything he wants, '*just because his brother was murdered*'.

But we are both drowning in grief and conflict hurts us, so we avoid it, there is just one rule, tell me where you go and tell me who you'll be with.

I fill the glass, drink a little, and tip the rest away. The glass left in the sink, I join him at the door.

As we walk along the street, I rest a hand on his shoulder. He won't hold my hand anymore. *'I'm too old to hold your hand all the time, Mum.'* Soon, he'll be too tall for me to reach an arm around his shoulders too.

The edge of the cobbled area where the picnic tables stand comes into view. Jordan steps away from my touch, breaks into a run and disappears around the corner.

When I turn the corner, he's inside the parlour. 'Where's Eve?' I hear him ask Maddie, who is serving.

I join him.

Maddie smiles. 'She's in the house. Knock on the door.' She presses a second mint-green ball of ice cream into a waffle cone for a customer.

I could have told him Eve wouldn't be working. It's too soon. The baby, Elly, my granddaughter, Jordan's niece, is two-and-a-bit weeks old.

He passes me, heading out of the shop. 'I'll show you the door,' I tell him.

At least once a day, when he turns in a certain way, it strikes me how much more he looks like Eli. He grows taller every single week and his body matures more with every inch he grows. He's not a boy now. Loosing Eli swept the childhood out of his life anyway. He's a young man.

His knuckles knock on scuffed pastel blue paint three times, in a firm rhythm. He hadn't needed me to show him the door, he found it.

After a moment, he looks over his shoulder. 'She's not in.'

'Give her a minute. She has the baby and she lives upstairs. The ground floor is taken up by the ice-cream parlour.'

'I'm coming!' Eve shouts from within.

I lay a hand on Jordan's shoulder. He leans away from it, so it slides off.

The door handle depresses, and the door opens.

'Oh. Hello, Jordan.' Her eyes lift to me. 'Jen.'

'Can I come in and meet Elly?' Jordan asks.

'Only if it's convenient,' I add.

'Yes, I'd love you to.' She turns and climbs the steep narrow staircase ahead of Jordan.

I close the door and follow, pushing away memories of the time I was tricked into climbing these stairs.

Eve leads us into the living room, 'Do you want to hold her?' she asks Jordan. 'She's just been fed. She's quite settled.' Elly is in a Moses basket on the sofa.

Eve bends down and lifts the small baby. She's wrapped in a flamingo-pink blanket. Put your hands here and here, she shows Jordan.

Elly weighed six pounds and eleven ounces the day she was born, she looks bigger already. Long legs unravel themselves from the blanket, kicking out as Jordan takes her from Eve's arms.

'Eli was long, tall, when he was born.' I remember staring at him with no motherly instincts, just looking at a small human that stared back at me. But now... Warm, all embracing emotions flow through my chest. I love her instantly. 'She's gorgeous.'

'Mum, you take her. I want to give her my present.' Jordan's arms lift to pass her on to me – and she is so welcome.

'I brought her this.' Jordan lifts his T-shirt and pulls out the Chelsea Football Club teddy bear. 'It's Eli's. He'd want her to have it.'

EVE

Eli leans over me. The bare skin of his chest brushes my naked nipple. The hard boards of the wooden jetty press into my back.

His breath smells of the cider he drank with his friends earlier.

'It's beautiful tonight, isn't it?' His words touch my lips before his kiss does. I smile as we kiss. His kisses move to the edge of my mouth and run down my neck.

The moon is a giant silver sphere spreading so much light tonight I see everything. We swam in the lake, it was like swimming in molten silver.

The drops of water on his dark skin still look like silver.

'I'm pregnant,' I whisper to the stars as his lips surround my nipple and suck. It hurts. My breasts have become more sensitive.

His head lifts, and the weight of him leaves me as he rests on a bent arm beside me. 'You're on the pill. That's not a good joke.'

'I never said I was on the pill.'

'I thought every older girl is.'

'I never said I was.'

'Then why didn't you tell me to use a condom.'

'We've only had sex a few times. I didn't think it would happen that easily.'

He turns over, turns away, and sits up, his knees bent and his head down.

'Eli?'

I'm happy. I want this baby. He or she will help me access some money and get me out of Mum's house. I want a baby. I genuinely hadn't sought to become pregnant but I also had not tried very hard to avoid it.

I sit up too. The gold heart pendant with a small red ruby, that Eli gave me earlier, drops down between my breasts.

He unravels from his folded over position, standing up quickly.

I wrap my arms around my knees, watching him. He's stunning naked. Especially in the moonlight. I really like him. He's younger, but he doesn't seem young. He's been through a lot with his parents' divorce.

He turns and looks at me. His eyes catching the light and shining. 'I'm fifteen, Eve. I can't have a kid. You can't keep it.' His expression screws up, in a sour look.

For a minute, I'm not sure if he is serious. But his expression doesn't change. My limbs unravel and I rise, standing up too. 'I'm having our baby. I'm keeping it.' I didn't expect him to be pleased. I knew he'd be shocked. But I didn't expect anger.

'You're mad. I'm fifteen! I can't be a dad!' The tempo of his voice rises as his anger becomes distress. Then fear.

'You're sixteen in September.'

'And I don't want a kid! I'm going to pass my exams and go to college and university! I'm going to be an engineer.' His hands travel around in the air, in gestures that express his unhappiness.

'You can do that. A child won't stop you. I won't stop you.'

'What are the police going to say?'

'I haven't groomed you. You asked me out. You chased me. They won't care. I'm not that much older. They don't put teenagers in prison for having consensual sex just because they are underage. Anyway, it's happened. It's too late to change anything.'

'I'll be in school. I can't help pay for it. Get rid of it, Eve.' His head

shakes. His brown eyes are all black in this light. 'We're too young. I don't want it.'

'Our baby isn't an it!' My hands lift, palms out, anger flaring. 'Fuck off!' I shove him.

He stumbles back a step, his heel on the edge of the jetty. His arms lift, struggling for balance, trying to grab thin air. I reach to catch him, but our hands don't collide. Instead, his finger catches on the thin necklace the pendant hangs from. Links snap and he falls backwards, hitting his head on the stilt of the jetty and dropping into the water.

Splash.

Ripples spread out like they do when you throw a stone, and the molten silver on the surface of the water swallows him whole. He disappears into the darkness beneath.

The water isn't very deep here but in the dark with the moonlight reflected I can't see beneath the surface.

The ripples dissipate. He doesn't break through the surface.

'Eli! Eli!'

I run along the jetty to the bay.

'Eli!'

I wade into the lake, the dark water absorbing me, my hands searching beneath the surface, my feet slipping on slimy stones on the lake's bed.

'Eli!'

'Eli! Eli!' People don't sink they float. 'Eli!' But he's been drinking. 'Eli!'

Water sways around my waist as my hands search.

'Eli!'

My fingers touch something, I grab it and pull on the foot, an ankle. He rises to the surface, deadly still.

'It'll be okay. It'll be okay. It'll be okay.' I pull him with me to the shore.

'Eli, come on! Don't do this,' I beg, holding him under the arms and dragging his limp body out of the water on to the gravel.

His chest isn't moving. He isn't breathing.

I drop down to kneel next to him, uncaring that the stones hurt as I lean over and press down on his chest, with two hands, one over the other, pushing, pushing, like people do on TV. Willing him to take a breath and open his eyes. Push. One. Two. Three. Water dribbles from his mouth. Push. I take a breath, lean down, hold his nose and blow it into his mouth. Then again. Push. Push. Push.

'Eli! Come on.'

I force another breath into his mouth, into his lungs.

'Come on!'

Push. Push. Push.

Nothing.

Nothing!

If I stop to call an ambulance he'll die anyway.

I breathe for him.

Push. Push. Push.

Nothing!

'Eli! Wake up! Breathe!'

I breathe for him, holding his nose and forcing my own breath into his lungs. Push. Push. Push.

'Eli!' I thump his chest, as hard as I can, and I slap his damp face.

He won't get up.

'Eli!'

Breathe. Push. Push. Push.

He won't wake up.

I've killed him!

'Eli!'

Breathe. Push. Push. Push. There are still no breaths and no heartbeat in the chest I push down on.

I can't do it anymore.

I sit back on my heels and stare at the boy who lies still looking at me, with eyes that don't see me.

He's dead.

Oh my God, he's dead.

I can't stay here.

I crawl across the stone to our piles of clothes and search my pockets for my phone. I should call the police, but in my head is the thing that happened to Nick. That was an accident. He hadn't meant to kill his friend and he spent years in prison.

I ring Nick. It rings eight times. 'Hello, sorry I'm busy. I'll call you back.' It's voicemail.

End.

I touch another contact.

'I'm busy, Eve, I—'

'Mum. There's been an accident. Someone is dead.'

'What?'

She doesn't believe me.

'Mum! He's not breathing! He's dead! I just pushed him. It was an accident. He drowned.'

'He, who?'

She still sounds disbelieving.

'Eli.'

A gasp draws in her breath. 'Are you sure he's dead? Have you rung for an ambulance?'

'No. He's dead. I killed him.'

'Where are you?'

'Southend Bay.'

'I'm coming. Stay there.'

'I have the car.'

'I'll borrow someone else's. Stay there.' The call just ends.

I tug my clothes on over wet skin, hands shaking, as I stare at Eli, willing him to cough and move. To reach for me.

'Eve?' Mum whispers through the trees.

'Here!'

'Be quiet, your voice will carry over the lake.'

'Nick wouldn't tell.'

'I wouldn't trust that.'

She squats down, pressing two fingers against Eli's neck, feeling for a pulse. Then she holds a car key under his nose.

'What are you doing?'

'Checking if he's breathing at all. It would mist on the metal.'

'Is he?'

'No.'

Violent emotions hit me in the stomach and throat. I want a miracle.

'We need to make it look as though someone else was here. Is there anything of yours left here?' She looks around the gravel.

'No.'

I should have called an ambulance.

'What's that in his hand?'

The thin gold chain trails from his fingers. She pulls it free and passes it to me, rises up from her haunches, and in the next moment launches a hand towards me. The sound of the slap echoes across the lake as the force of it leaves me stumbling into the shallow water. A stinging pain burns in my cheek and ear and the soft skin at the edge of my lip drips blood. The metallic taste of blood fills my mouth as I press my fingers against my lip, trying to stop the bleeding. Blood drips into the water. I lift the hem of my sweatshirt to my mouth and wipe the blood away.

'What did I tell you would come of being with boys. Who else knows you were here with him?'

'No one.'

She rolls Eli onto his stomach with her foot, rolling him to the water's edge. It laps at his arm and his side, as though it's reaching for him.

'What are you doing?'

'Making it look like someone else was here. It needs to look as though he was attacked.'

'Why?'

'To protect you.'

'Shouldn't I call the police? It was an accident. Maybe—'

'It doesn't matter if it was an accident. You know Nick's story. It's manslaughter. Do you want to go to jail? Is there anything else here that will give your presence away?'

'A pendant.'

'Find it and find a stone that is large enough to have killed him,' she orders.

Splashes rise as I run out of the shallow water. 'There's a lump of rock by that tree.' I point at the stone, and leap onto the jetty. The pendant had fallen onto the boards. I kneel, on all fours, searching where we were standing, my fingers sweeping across the surface, until I feel it. 'It's here! I've got the pendant!'

I slip it into my pocket, running back along the jetty, she's picked up the stone and put it beside Eli.

'Go back to the car, and drive home. Leave me to clear this up. You need to get away from here.'

I can't move. I can't leave him here.

'Go, Eve. Take my car home.'

My feet run, racing away. I should have called an ambulance, the police. My fingers struggle to hold the car keys as I open the car, sit in the seat and put the key in the ignition. The engine purrs to life. I pull on the seatbelt and drive. I feel sick.

SHARON

Like father; like daughter. The words repeat in my thoughts as I pull on the handbrake of the car. I took Jen's car back, in case she wakes up, and used my car to drive here.

I turned off the headlights when I left the main road and turned onto the track to Nick's cabin. I crawled the car along the track at five miles per hour. I'm used to sneaking my way up here, but not usually when Nick is at home. I open the car door cautiously and close it just as carefully, trying not to make a sound.

I should have selected the men who fathered my children more carefully. But I thought a child was a child. I thought I could mould them. Nurture verses nature. It turns out nature wins. They are more like their fathers than me.

Maddie is as lustful as her adulterous father who left a friend of mine pregnant with a child he and she didn't want because he never intended leaving his wife – and how could I imagine that Nick's daughter would nearly kill someone. But she has Nick's temper.

'Are we having another storm?' I'd say when she was younger. Then I'd shut her away in her room until it was over.

Two birds one stone, that's the phrase in my mind.

I'm not going to let Nick take Eve away from me, and she's provided the perfect tool to dispose of him.

This is his fault. He encouraged her to see that boy.

There's a faint light on in one room of his cabin. I walk to the shore path, His dog barks. I can't let Nick see me, it will ruin everything. There are splatters of the boy's blood on my clothes. The branches of the dark trees swallow me, blocking out most of the moonlight. If it wasn't so bright tonight, I wouldn't be able to see.

There's a point where the path touches the water's edge, where a tree has fallen. Where a man might push a body into the water. Where it might float across the lake. I could have tried to bring the body, but it would have been too difficult. Instead, I have the rock I hit the boy with, safe in a plastic bag, and one of the boy's socks that I'd used to pick up his phone so I could turn it off and throw it into the bracken and ferns on the ground beside the path in the wood. Let the police work out how the rest can be true.

I throw the rock into the undergrowth, and the sock into the water.

Like father; like daughter. And two birds with one stone. Two men will be gone from our lives. Eli was breathing, it was faint, but somehow Eve had managed to keep him alive until I arrived. Until I knelt on the gravel beside him and smashed the rock into the back of his head. Once. Twice.

The cracking and the fleshy sounds of his skull splitting open like a boiled egg will never leave my nightmares. But he's gone, and soon Nick will be back in prison.

NICK

Suddenly awake, I open my eyes.

'Howool, howool, howool,' PJ's melodious howl sings along to the ringtone of my phone.

I glance at the clock on the phone as I pick it up from the bedside table. 03.53.

Eve, the screen says.

There was a missed call before that.

I touch the answer icon.

'Hello, love. What is it?'

'Dad. I killed him. By accident. Eli. I pushed him.' Her voice rushes. Shaking.

I sit up. 'What?' Incredulity is my response.

'I killed him...' Tears are sniffed, as the words are wrung out by shock.

'How, Eve?' This is a mistake. A cruel joke.

'We were on the jetty at the south end. I pushed him. He fell backwards into the water and didn't swim. He sank and didn't come back up. I dragged him out, but he wasn't breathing. I just pushed him.'

'Is he still there? Have you called the police? Can I help?'

'Mum is sorting it out.'

Sorting it? What the hell is Sharon's version of sorting it? 'Have you rung the police?'

'No.'

'Okay. I'll ring them. You stay out of it. I'll tell them I saw him when I was walking PJ.' This can't happen in a second generation. I know how this story goes. 'Don't say anything to anyone. It's too late to say it was an accident now.'

JEN

I unwrap the paper parcels, releasing the delicious smell of the deep-fried fish and chips.

'Wash your hands before you eat, Jordan,' I command, reaching for plates.

After he's washed his hands in the kitchen sink, he opens the drawer to find forks.

'Here you are.' I trade a full plate for a fork.

We sit down at the table.

This afternoon, we sat beside the lake, after leaving the teddy bear with Elly, and talked to Eli. We bought dinner on the way home.

Clunk.

The front door knocker strikes down hard, shaking the door and rattling the letter box.

Jordan looks at the door.

I rise to answer it.

'Eat your dinner, don't let it get cold.'

I look through the front window. I can't see anything to suggest who is there.

When I open the door, Nick is standing on the doormat, PJ beside his heel.

'Hello.' He lifts a bunch of flowers that are wrapped in green tissue paper.

'I…' Had not expected him. 'Hello?'

'Thank you.' I accept the bouquet. I don't invite him in.

He looks beyond me, towards Jordan. 'Hello, mate. Glad to have you back in the village.' His gaze returns to me. 'I dropped by to say welcome back, that's all. Anyway, I can see you're eating your dinner. I'll leave you to it.' He turns.

'Nick. I…'

'It's okay, I don't expect forgiveness. I want you to feel comfortable if you travel on the ferry, that's all. I won't charge you for rides.'

A smile pulls at my lips as I think about that journey. I'll be with Eli every day, before and after work. 'Okay. I planned to use it.' I will not let his lies prevent me from spending those journeys with Eli.

'Goodbye, then. I'll see you Monday, if not before.'

I close the door, take the flowers to the kitchen, open the lid of the bin and drop the bouquet in.

'Mum, your dinner's getting cold.'

I look at my youngest son, and my heart is full, overflowing with love. When I join him at the table, before I sit, I lean over and kiss the top of his head. 'I love you.'

There is no room left in my life for anyone except the sons I love so much. The sons who love me with a depth that is unmatchable. They, and my granddaughter, are all I need.

My mind's eye envisions her, Eli's daughter, embraced in Barbie-pink. Then I notice, as if my mind is manoeuvring my memory like a camera closeup, zooming in on the hands which hold Elly, on the fingers, the fingernails dark against the vivid pink. Dark blue nail polish shines on Eve's fingernails. The same colour that Sharon wore.

EVE

I close the front door behind me as quietly as I can. The world is cavernous, a large black cave I've become lost in. My eyes are blind to everything but the image of Eli's body I left in the bay. I can't leave him there alone. I can't sleep knowing he's lying there. Naked. Deserted. I've lain in my bed for the last couple of hours, the pain in my lip throbbing a constant reminder that the accident had happened. I heard Mum come home, much later than me. She showered and then her bedroom door closed. She is asleep. Her snores rumbled through our adjoining bedroom wall.

All the car's sidelights flash when I press the button on the key fob to open the doors. The sound of the metal locks releasing bounces back from the corners of the otherwise quiet village square.

I look across my shoulder, checking the dark windows of the rooms above the ice-cream parlour, no lights appear. I carry on, opening the door and occupying the driver's seat.

I press the button to lock the doors around me, securing myself safely inside, and turn the key in the ignition. The radio bursts into life. I reach out and turn it off. Any sound of normality grates, a painful reminder life will be entirely different from tomorrow. I killed Eli today.

How long will it be before Mum learns about the child, and what then?

I'd begun imaging that Eli and I could have a house together – a life together.

It was stupid to ever believe my life could be normal.

I drive in a dreamlike state. Inside a nightmare of my making.

It's still easy to see my way along the path, walking through the wood down to the Southend Bay from the car park. The moon is close to the horizon, about to depart, but it's still bright. A few hours ago Eli and I had walked this way, laughing as he'd struggled to keep a straight line.

When I walk out across the gravel in the bay, my eyes on the still body at the edge of the water, I'm not sure why I am here. I can't change this.

A dark stain marks the ground on the side of his head that's turned to the water. Blood. It has formed a dark puddle and a short stream running into the lake. There was no cut. He hadn't bled. Why?

Horror brings me down on my knees beside his hip as my stomach heaves. Gagging. The bitter truth of what's happened choking me.

The back of his head is a sickening mess. His hair is matted with dry blood. The skin torn apart, revealing pale, ivory, bone that's cracked open. One piece of his skull juts out at an angle.

I touch his back. Despite the night being warm, his skin is cold.

Mum hit him with the rock. I thought she was just going to leave it beside him.

My hand slides to his shoulder... The gesture expressing the all-encompassing guilt and regret sucking me down with him. I lean close, my other hand on the gravel. I want to hold him. How did it end like this? I'm sorry.

The sharp pieces of gravel cut into the palm of my hand that's close to his mouth. Warmth brushes across the sensitive skin between my forefinger and thumb. It's the slightest of sensations, but in the silence and stillness of the night, that slight sensation screams.

I'm alive! He shouts, again, with another breath.

I touch his lips as the warmth comes from his nostrils again, breaths that are so weak they don't show in any movement of his body. Am I imaging this because I want it to be true? I hold the wrist of the hand laying near his hip, pressing it firmly, feeling for a pulse in the radial artery.

It's there! A slight beat, then a barely there beat. So slight I must have missed it when I was panicking.

A slight beat when he breaths in, a barely there beat when he breaths out – as his body struggles to find enough oxygen in the too little blood that is left in his arteries and veins.

I don't know what to do.

I thought it had been too late to call an ambulance before. Now... He's lain here for hours. They'll want to know why. They'll see that Mum deliberately hit him. They'll know I was involved. There is no good reason why we would have left him here in this state. Mum had hit him so hard his skull is split open. I can't say this was an accident. It isn't an accident anymore.

But if they can save him...

He's been unconscious for hours. He is not going to recover from this. Not as he was anyway. He'll have brain damage. Even with his head to the side and the blood congealed, I can see his brain through parts of the wounds. I imagine him in a bed, in a wheelchair, unable to talk, or walk, or move at all. He wouldn't want that. I know he wouldn't, he had not even wanted a child to hold him back...

I roll his body over, turning him onto his back, the water stirs caressing his side. There's no life in the eyes that blankly look at me. Without ever making a decision to do what I am doing, I turn his body over again. It just feels the right thing to do. The water reaches for him.

This is better for Eli, he won't have to live a limited life, locked inside his mind, and perhaps even in his mind he won't be the same.

This is better for me and our child, when they find his body, eventually the police will find the evidence that proves Mum hit Eli, and I and the child will be free. I turn his body again. The shallow water takes his weight. The movement makes a quiet, gentle, splash – because I am being gentle. Being kind. To both of us. This is the best ending for all of us. For him, me, our child, and Maddie. Mum will go to prison for life, and we can all live.

It is better for him if he dies quickly now. I roll him one more time, on to his stomach.

The water rises slightly, reaching up, in its silent rhythm of movement, captures his powerless body and draws him a few inches away. I push him further out.

His beautiful, motionless, body floats on the silver surface of the water, a couple of meters away from the shore, the water gently rocking him, as though comforting a child in a cradle. I expect him to choke, to wake, to panic and struggle for the next slight breath. There is no sign of any particular point when the water fatally steels his last breath...

I take out my phone and call Dad again.

I had not killed Eli before. I have killed him now. I should feel sad. I feel heartless. Empty. This is better for the baby and me too. It will free us from Mum.

LIKE MOTHER, LIKE DAUGHTER

THE END

ACKNOWLEDGEMENTS

Thank you

♥

As always the most important people to thank are you, the readers. Thank you to all my amazing readers who support my stories by buying, reading and borrowing books from libraries and sharing your love of them with others. Thank you so much for taking the time to follow my author page on bookseller sites, sharing your experiences of the books with book clubs, for posting reviews on bookseller websites, for sneakily turning them around on bookshelves so everyone can see the covers. I appreciate all you do to help others discover the stories I write, because without readers books have no value.

Thank you also to my new publishing team at Bloodhound Books, without whom this story would not have developed into what it is today. It's been a great journey, and I really appreciate your belief in and commitment to this story.

Also, thank you to my long-suffering husband, who has to endure being told, '*please be quiet, I'm writing.*' I cannot express how much I value his belief in my talent and his personal commitment to support my writing.

Lastly, thank you to the lovely people in the Lake District who welcome me every time I stay there to absorb the atmosphere and seek inspirations. With a particular thank you to Jill and Jim Robertson, of Savage Fishing at Esthwaite Water.

SUGGESTIONS FOR BOOK CLUB QUESTIONS

1. When the characters were introduced at the beginning of the story, did you have any hunches about what might follow?
2. How did you feel about Jen's character as you travelled with her through the story?
3. Did you connect with the characters' emotions as you read the story?
4. What did you think of Jen's relationships with her sons? Do you think the boys were treated in the same way?
5. How did you feel about André's character?
6. Did you believe Eli's spirit was showing his family where to find new evidence?
7. If you were in this situation, would you take it upon yourself to find evidence?
8. How would you have responded if the police believed you, the mother of Eli, had committed the murder?
9. Which aspects of the story surprised you?
10. Which scenes did you enjoy the most?

11. Did you like reading the story in the more personal perspective of present tense and the first-person narrative?
12. Which three words would you use to sum up the story?
13. What do you think might happen next if the story continued?
14. Are you likely to remember this story and tell others about this author's work?
15. Were there any sentiments in the story that stood out for you, or sentences that you highlighted if you read a Kindle edition? If yes, why did these capture your attention?

A NOTE FROM THE PUBLISHER

Thank you for reading this book. If you enjoyed it please do consider leaving a review on Amazon to help others find it too.

We hate typos. All of our books have been rigorously edited and proofread, but sometimes mistakes do slip through. If you have spotted a typo, please do let us know and we can get it amended within hours.

info@bloodhoundbooks.com